RUBY LAKE

By
Ron Howson

For the paranoid: this is a work of fiction. Names, characters, businesses, places, events and incidents are either the products of the author's imagination or used in a fictitious manner. Any resemblance to actual persons, living or dead, real or imagined, or actual events or locales is purely coincidental, but we know who you are.

Cover design and editing:
Thomas J. Mason
thomasjmason@att.net

ISBN: 978-0-9909371-1-1

What a great book! Enjoyed every bit of it. If you like Sci-fi and adventure, here is one for you! I'd recommend it to anyone. B.W.

Okay, now that was fun. Had many heart pounding moments. Interesting from beginning to end. Can't wait for the next book. J.M.

Every now and then you run across a book like this and a writer like this, and think, "What an imagination!" Really like the way it was written. P.W.

Read it twice now. Loved it! Where's the next? H.P.

Within the first three chapters, man, you are sucked in and it is action, adventure, and danger from the beginning right on to the end. I highly recommend this book. T.D.

Great story! There were parts that really scared the c**p out of me. Really liked the pace. Not a boring moment. I highly recommend reading it! D.A.

This book starts in one place and before you know it, it takes you to places you would never expect. The main character is realistic and likeable. The plot has twists and turns. There is mystery and danger all the way through. I would recommend this book without question. B.G.

This looks like it could be the start of a great series. Looking forward to the next book. It had a good pace and completely kept my interest. I would recommend this book to anyone. L.J.

RUBY LAKE

Chapter One

Sitting in a room full of people was never Jason Brand's idea of a good time, especially these people. The mini-bureaucrats, that's what he called them, among other things. They are the ones who actually run the Government, and they have been given all the authority they need to make lives miserable.

That is their job, and damn, they are good at it. They are the guts of it. They are the hall monitors of the world. They are the appointed or the hired, but not the elected. This is the yearly budget meeting, where everything you do and need is made unimportant by people who, he feels, are truly unimportant.

What would make it worse would be finding out that while he was sitting there, his partner and good friend was dying a horrible and terrifying death alone in a canyon about a day's drive, a three hour lake crossing, and half a day's hike from there, and nobody in the world knew it. That is where Jason was supposed to be, with his partner, if it weren't for this damn meeting.

This was the third time in three years he had to account to these people, and he hated it. Every nickel and dime he spent was scrutinized and questioned. He sat looking at the circus thinking that the cost of all the time and energy, the people, the lights, the paperwork, for this one day alone, is probably more than he will spend in the next year.

It was as if he walked into some strange alien zoo. He wished they would just fire him, or cut the budget, or just tell him to go away. He would be happy with any one of those choices, especially to just go away.

But, it seems, they didn't want him to go away. For some reason they continued this spectacle year after year. They poked him with knives and dragged him through coals, threw stones at him and then stuck his head in the guillotine, but they didn't pull the lever. They just wouldn't do it.

He sat and wondered why he shouldn't just walk out. Tell them all to take a hike. He'd already put in his notice. After what happened two weeks ago, who could blame him? But then, there is that paycheck.

Then it struck him, the same as it struck him last year, "Hey, it's about two or three hours a year that I have to put up with them. I'll walk out of here and not have to even think about them ever again. I'm done

1

with this. They have to spend every minute of every day with themselves." The thought of that almost made him smile.

So he sat watching the show while, he would later discover, where he was supposed to be, there was a savage and desperate fight going on for a last few minutes on Earth. His partner was alone, terrified, with no help.

Jason even wore a suit and tie today. The first time he wore one since last year when he was here. He has two suits. Fiddling with his tie, he recalled the reason he had two. It was because he'd forgotten he'd already had one when he bought the second. That's how often he wore them. It was either a wedding or a funeral when he bought the first. It was his partner's wedding when he bought the second.

He sat pulling at his collar and tugging at his tie, trying to loosen it and get some air and hoping not to use enough force to pop the button. He drank sips of water, not because he was thirsty, but to somehow have the sensation that the tie wasn't choking him to death.

"Bunch of paper pushers," Jason Brand finally let out, "How long we gonna be here d' you think?"

His boss, Terry Borden, was beside him, as always. Another pencil pusher, yes, but he had gained the respect of Jason years ago because he knew the system and played the game. He was Jason's protector from the mini-bureaucrats; the buffer. He ran defense. If it weren't for his boss, he knew he would have been eaten up years ago by the people at the front of the room. It would be death by a thousand cuts. Paper cuts. Nasty and stinging.

"We're almost done. Just a bit longer. It's almost lunch time. They gotta wrap it up," Terry looked at him, "You coulda shaved."

"I coulda been out doing my job. I coulda been out having a beer. I don't know why you need me for these things," Jason responded. He sat forward and looked at the other two people sitting with them. One he vaguely knew. Jim was possibly his name. The other was a woman he'd never seen before.

"Look. It's hard enough as it is," Terry pleaded. "You know it helps me for you to be here. What if they have questions and I don't have the answers? Just do me a favor and play nice. It'll save me a lot of trouble later."

Jason leaned back in his chair and nodded, "Alright, Terry. Of course."

He was going to have to explain how he lost his motor. Last year was easy. A bear ate it. There wasn't a person in the room who wasn't laughing as he described how it chased him down a trail and into his boat and began to tear it apart as he was beating it on the head with his oar while trying to get away.

First came the top; the cowling. Then the wiring and fuel lines, finally the whole motor got pulled off along with part of his stern, and it took the oar with him. Then he topped it all off with a description of how he rowed across the lake with one oar.

This year was a shootout with pot growers up on a mountainside. They were using a fertilizer that was poisoning a stream, and he was sent to check into it. There were six of them at first, and then after he put three down, it was sniper versus sniper, and he won. Two of them knew what they were doing, the other panicked, and panic can be your enemy or your best friend for a sniper.

It was when it was all over and he got back down the trail and motored back across the lake that it happened. As he was docking, the man who ran the local store started taking shots at him and hit his motor; killed it. A Mercury, nice motor too.

It was a perfect set-up. There were always store deliveries with trucks coming and going at all hours of the day, un-noticed. He could distribute anything they could grow. But the enterprise ended in the crosshairs of Jason's scope. It was a clean sweep; the growers, the distributor – gone.

It made him feel so unappreciated. That's what he decided he hated about this so much. It was better when he didn't have to come here, he could just go out and do his job, crawling through abandoned factories, taking samples and getting lab results. But over the years, people come and go. People die. People retire, and people quit. New people get hired to replace them. The guy that used to come to these meetings was gone, so now it was his turn.

But some people just love meetings. Makes them feel all important or something, he guessed. Makes them feel that they were being included. Then, one day, if they played their cards right and worked real hard, and kissed the required butt the required amount, they could be a hall monitor too. They could be a mini-bureaucrat. Oh, what joy!

Not him though. He'd had enough of meetings. Briefings, briefings, briefings. Lectures, lectures, lectures. Yes, he'd had enough of those in the Army. Meetings and films. Rape, rape, rape. Suicide, suicide, suicide. After a while, it became a joke. But what wasn't a joke was that it increased rape and suicide, not decreased it.

It was the old "Don't think of an elephant" trick they were pulling. "Psy Ops," he thought. You're told to sit there and don't think of an elephant, and every now and then get asked, "Are you thinking of an elephant?" until that's all you can think about, because it can't be done.

You have to think of the elephant to know what you're not thinking about. Impossible.

They'd play a film about suicide and suicide prevention and signs that someone might be contemplating suicide and how they commit suicide and it's all suicide, suicide, suicide – don't think about suicide. If you'd never thought about it before, you sure were now. Not that you would contemplate it. Not that you would do it.

But it was drummed into your brain until some people start to question themselves because now, they can't get it out of their mind. All the while, some little slime-ball would be sitting off on the sidelines with his shit-eating grin ready to offer "help" in the form of drugs.

Drugs. Mind altering psychiatric drugs. Psychotropic drugs, addictive and deadly drugs. But he knew, and so did most of the Military know, once you take that pill, you are theirs for life. It was Psy Ops; marketing, and they'd joke, "What do you want to do today?" and the other would say, "I was thinking of raping something and then committing suicide, how about you?"

He was jolted out of his thoughts when his boss was called onto the carpet. "Poor guy," he thought. He'd had some lab equipment replaced and they seemed really angry with him for it. Now they were grilling him.

After some time, the woman at the front addressed Jason. "How do you explain this entry for ammunition? Ammunition? You have guns? Why do you even carry guns? You shouldn't have the tax payers putting up their money for something like this. How do you protect the environment with guns? And this, this! A Mercury 75 horsepower outboard motor. Why are we paying for toys?" She looked down and shook her head glancing at several pieces of paper in disgust.

Johnson. Emily Johnson. Not a bad looking woman, just a horrible person in Jason's opinion. He wondered if she is this cutting and abrasive with the other people at her job. What about her personal life? Is she this confrontational with everyone? Is this a job requirement for her? To be a horrible person? She is sure good at it.

Terry stood up to reply, "Ma'am, the items…"

"I'm not talking to you, Mr. Borden. I was speaking to Mr. Brand." She looked up over her glasses at Jason Brand revealing a deep level of contempt. "Why do you think that we should be paying for toys? The tax payers? Why do you think we should be funding excursions for you and your pals? Hiking equipment. Camping gear. Boating," She called them out as she slapped each paper down on the table.

"I'm surprised there is no ice-cold beer among the bills. Look, a backpack for your dog. Your dog? You expect us to pay for you to take your dog camping with you?" She half yelled.

The room was full, but more full than usual today.

There were reporters, lots of them, and they were looking for scraps of information about what happened two weeks ago. There were rumors flying around. There were rumors of troop movement, explosions, people vanishing, and even the murmur of zombies.

On the other side of the room were the other people, but only six of them. They were the people who only see markings on a paper, numbers and accounting. They really had no idea of what he did except this: he spent money and it had to be accounted for.

Jason stood up, smoothing his tie, thinking he would give his boss a little going away present, a little education about what he actually did and maybe make it a bit easier for the next guy that took his job.

"Easy, Jason. Easy," his boss cautioned.

"Camping, eh? Well. I'll try to explain some of those expenditures." He hated this more than anything. Glancing around, he could see the room was now riveted on him, and that made him hate it even more. "What we do is go to places people like you don't want to go. Not only that, but they are places you probably couldn't go. But that is what we do and that is part of the job. It is what we got hired to do."

"The items we use are things we need. We sometimes have to get to inaccessible areas. We go upstream, up a mountain, or into some wasteland where chemicals or biohazards may have been dumped and are causing problems, leaching into the drinking water and such."

"I know what you do, Mr. Brand," she cut in, "and I don't need to be lectured or schooled by you. This is about your budget and your seemingly inexcusable expenses."

He was thinking how she was probably drinking daiquiris with her friends discussing ways to make this difficult while he was out putting himself at risk. With some effort, he let the impulse to react to the hostility pass and said, "I was on a trail last week that took three days of hiking to get up. Once we got there, we set up and began to take samples of filth that you wouldn't want yourself or your children to be near. It was the run-off of chemicals and wastes from an old mine.

"After wallowing around in dangerous chemicals in a HAZMAT suit for several hours, we set up camp about when the sun went down. Well, that night a bear came into that camp and tried to eat us. Went right through that camping gear you are complaining about buying. Damn near had to kill it.

"I shot three rounds over his head, and he still wanted at us. Jerry, my partner, had some pepper spray and an air horn and hit him with that. Just about when I was ready to put him down, he turned and ran off.

"You call these toys? You think we're playing? Camping? Fun times, right? Well, you know, you're welcome to try it."

"So," she cut in, "What you are saying is that you could have done without the gun and used a can of pepper spray and an air horn. So why are you bringing guns with you? By your own statement, these things were unnecessary."

"Not hardly did I say that nor mean that," he retorted. "That was a bear. You don't know what makes them do what they do, other than they want to eat. But you don't always know what makes them come into a camp, and you don't always know what makes them leave."

"You can assume it is a smell of food, but that isn't always it. Sometimes they could be curious, they could be hungry, other times they're just plain mean. Anyway, for whatever reason they come, they often end up wanting to make you their dinner."

Jason took a deep breath and continued, "Sometimes you hear old stories about guys yelling and banging on pots and pans and scaring them off. Things like that used to work as long as men backed it up with a gun. But since most people don't carry guns anymore, the bears see us as an easy meal.

"They might not eat you right away. They'll kill you, alright. They'll do that right away, but they might not eat you right away other than a little sampling. They let you sit for a day or two first. Let you get nice and ripe and tender before they come back and finish their meal.

"It's not camping that we do. It's not only bear that we have to worry about, either. A bear might come at you and a bear might get startled and attack you if you stumble on it. I knew a guy who stepped over a log onto a sleeping bear. It scared the hell out of both of them, as you can imagine. But the bear mauled the guy before running off. He managed to crawl out of the woods and he got picked up by someone and brought to the hospital where he died.

"But it's the lions that are the real problem around these parts. The mountain lions. A bear might come into your camp and get rowdy and take what he wants, but the cat will track you. They'll follow you and they'll stalk you and when the time is right, they jump on you and grab you by the back of the neck, right below the skull, and break your neck.

"If they can't do that, like if your backpack is in the way, they get you by the throat until you've suffocated. Seen it happen to a hiker once. Was too far away to help. Watched the whole thing through the binoculars. That's the last time I went anywhere without a gun.

"He was probably following him for a while. Stalking him. That's what they do. I only saw the last bit of it. The cat got down low on its belly creeping up through the grass behind him real quiet, and BAM," he slammed his hand down on the table and the whole room jumped, "He tore into him.

"First, he slashed the hell out of him, then, once the guy was bleeding out from below the groin and arms, and was in too much shock to fight back, he got him by the throat and choked off his air and he held him there and by the time I got up to him, he had already had his lunch and ran off when he saw me coming.

"No, Ma'am. No way am I going out there armed with a can of pepper spray and an air horn. No way." Pausing for a moment and considering his next words, he continued, "I have been bit by rattlesnakes twice. Stalked by cats and had bear attack my camp. I've killed some of each, but only when I had to.

"My dog can smell animals. I can't. She can sense an animal around. People usually can't. She can hear them when I can't. Nobody can. So, yes, I bring my dog, Bo. I have a backpack for her and she carries her weight and then some. She's alerted me more than a few times to danger.

"You might think about this the next time you are chatting with your manicurist or sitting under your hair dryer wondering how to cut more of our budget. It's not just animals either, not them kind. They are dangerous, without a doubt. But worse than that are the pot growers. You walk into one of their farms and you're as good as dead.

"They protect their crops with good weapons designed to kill people like me and top of the line surveillance for people who are just going along trying to get somewhere else, like hikers. If they're unlucky enough to wander into the wrong area, the growers just kill them.

"I would prefer you bought us a helicopter, but I don't think it is in this budget you keep talking about. We can't even use a helicopter sometimes. After this meeting, I'm going to a lake. About a mile or two across this lake is an inlet that I have to follow.

"There is an old mine up there and some things appear to have been dumped in it or around it or near it. Who knows? But fish and other wildlife are getting sick. We have to follow the stream and get to the source. It takes a boat to get across the lake.

"Once I'm there at the inlet, I take my gear, all that camping equipment you are taking issue with, and pack it in, along with safety equipment and suits so I don't get myself poisoned. I have to pack it all in, as well as my test kits and whatever else I might need.

"You can't even get near it with a helicopter, it's in a canyon. Deep. I get the idea that you think this is a pleasure tour. Get out and see some nature and do a little camping. Sounds like a good life, right?

"But I'll have to haul this stuff into a boat and cross the lake, pack it onto my back and drag it up that canyon. So, consider that the next time you are comfortably sitting having your latte in your climate controlled office discussing what else you can cut out of our budget. Hey, the next time you sit on the pot, think about it, we have to do our business..."

That was enough for Terry and he stood up and cut in. "Ms. Johnson. I think that we can all agree that in order to properly do a job, any job, you need the proper equipment." He'd seen Jason get on a roll before and could see it coming now. What was about to come out of his mouth would not be something you hear in offices, especially government offices.

Johnson showed good sense and let him speak this time. "We are all conscious of expenses and take the use of tax-payer money seriously. I think that this meeting will serve to heighten our awareness even more. Over the next year we will certainly try to limit expenses and continue our on-going efforts to eliminate waste."

"That was a good save," Jason thought. This is one of the reasons he had grown to respect his boss. He accepted the fact he was about to go where he shouldn't go and sat back down while his boss stepped in. Diplomatic, that's what he was, diplomatic. Damn good save.

"I expect that," Ms. Johnson retorted.

Jason was never quite sure what exactly her job was. She wasn't an accountant. He knew them and they were sitting there beside her at that long bench with their glasses and files and paperwork he hated so much. She was some kind of authority. A mini-bureaucrat, that's what she was. A mini-bureaucrat.

"We are going to review the receipts and expenses and your budget for the next year and will send you the results of the review with recommendations. That is the end of this meeting, unless you or anyone else in your office has something to add." She said this last part looking directly at Brand.

"No," Terry replied after glancing at Jason, more to let him know that it is clearly time to shut up than to see if he did actually have something else to add. "No. I think we are done."

So, that was the meeting. The yearly intimidation. "Not too bad," Jason thought. "Short and relatively painless." He knew, of course, that nothing of his would get cut. They needed that equipment and they needed him. They just loved to stick his head in the guillotine, but just can't pull that lever. Hall monitors. Mini-bureaucrats.

Back at the office, Jason was rushing to get out and meet up with his partner, Jerry Crozley. "Gizmo", they called him. But it was a meeting that would not happen. He was a good guy, a smart guy, and was always messing around with some new gadget or new equipment, which is why they called him "Gizmo". He was a scientist who took to the idea of testing for contaminants that people get exposed to all the time without ever knowing it and sometimes dying because of it, while the ones responsible grow rich.

Jerry took the job rather than being handsomely paid to use his talents in private industry. Jason liked that about him. He was a man with a purpose and liked what he did, and he did it well. They both did.

RUBY LAKE

Chapter Two

Terry was sitting at his desk with Jason going over the maps and likely locations for the leaching. "We have no idea what it is," Terry told him. "I have no idea what the hell it might be or where it came from or who even could have put it there."

Terry was looking at a satellite photo now. "I know there's an old mine up there," he continued. "But Jason, that thing was there before most chemicals around these days were even invented. Could be someone dumped something up there and didn't say anything. Who knows? Could be anything."

"Yup," Jason agreed. "Well, I'll let you know as soon as I'm up there." Jason grabbed the maps and a bag from the sporting goods store. "I better get going if I'm gonna do Gizmo any good. Don't want him to have everything done before I get there. Still no word?"

"No. Probably no signal in that canyon. There's a Ranger Station at the North end of the lake. I marked it on the map. Haven't heard from him since he left there. Didn't really expect to. They'll be waiting for you and help launch your boat and gear, if you need. Gizmo checked in with them before crossing the lake. I guess he left you something. Most likely the usual package.

"He's probably pretty well done with collecting samples by now, but you can check it all over and at least help him pack everything back out. Maybe take another sample or two. I want you to get me some water samples at the mouth too.

"Oh, hey. That reminds me. Don't forget to bring your own water. I don't think you want to drink what's running in that stream, even if you use your fancy filter. That'll add some weight for you, but it'll give you something to complain about at next year's budget meeting," he said, implying that Jason would be there again next year.

It was pretty usual now to leave a package for a late arrival. Like Jason, another guy was held up at a meeting a couple of years earlier. In his haste to catch up, he forgot his maps and ended up in a wrong canyon. It took two days to find him after he fell off a ledge. The coroner said the fall didn't kill him, and he was alive when the animals started eating at him.

Outside was the RV Jason had been using for a few years. It was pretty well set up with lots of storage on the roof for his equipment and a tow hitch for the boat. It wasn't big, but it was four-wheel drive for those hard-to-get-at places; nothing more than a place to sleep, a small kitchen and tiny bathroom, and a generator.

It was never his favorite place to stay and whenever he could, he would get a motel room. But when you are out away from civilization, it was nice to not to have to sleep on the ground. Having a dog with you can be particularly difficult. Some motels just don't like them, and for the most part, Bo seems to prefer the motor home, the big dog house, over a motel.

Bo was large. Jason was never quite sure what kind of dog she was, probably a mix of Saint Bernard and something else with a lot of hair. She was a rescue dog that he picked up from a shelter in Pahrump. She had these piercing grey eyes, so she probably had some kind of Husky or Malamute or some such in her. Not that it mattered.

The hair was an issue, but he liked the dog enough, and Bo was too good of a dog to make it a large issue. If he didn't vacuum every now and then, it would start building up and drift like snow under the furniture and in the corners. But a few minutes of vacuuming weren't a huge problem and, the simple fact is, if it weren't for that, he wasn't sure how often he would vacuum. At least now he had to do it and did it.

He started taking her with him on hikes and he trained her well. She grew to be a big dog, so he put a saddlebag on her so she could carry her own food and some water and a couple of other things. It worked out well and she never had an issue with it.

Getting her to come back when she ran off in some direction after a rabbit or chasing down the source of some smell was the first thing he worked on. He didn't want her to get into trouble running after a pack of coyotes, or worse, end up being a snack for some cat.

A coyote will eat a dog. A pack of them will outsmart a dog and kill it. A man he knew had Rottweilers on his place down in Southern California. He lived on the edge of the mountains and the coyotes would come down from the hills and get whatever animal or free food they could. Cats, dogs, trash, and even a kid would disappear now and then.

So, he got himself a pair of Rottweilers. Every now and then one of them would disappear. So he'd get another one. Drove him nuts. He did this several times, one of them would disappear and he would replace it. Couldn't figure it out.

He was a dog lover and would never intentionally hurt one or allow one of his pets to be harmed. He imagined the animal fighting for his life, and losing, while he was away at work or in the middle of the night. One day it struck him; it was never the female dog that would vanish, only the male.

Jason and he talked about it over beer and barbecue whenever he was in town, and came to the conclusion that it was never in the daytime that the dogs disappeared either. He recalled that they were always home when he got back from work. It was only at night and only the male would be missing.

He got himself some infra-red to watch at night. He would wait up, sitting on his balcony, waiting for a chance to see what was taking his dogs, anything - a mountain lion, coyotes, Bigfoot, or even aliens, he just wanted the mystery solved. So there he sat one night when his dogs started making a ruckus.

He looked through the infra-red and, sure enough, it was a pack of coyotes. He looked over the balcony and saw the female dog there on the patio, and the male dog running off accepting the challenge.

The man managed to call the male back and put them both inside the house that night. The next week, he had motion sensors and lights put in the backyard, thinking that the light would scare the coyotes away. When it was all done and tested, he put the dogs back out.

Again, he hears noise from outside, but only the female is barking. He looks out and the male is gone. Outside in the hills, just beyond the spill of the lights set off by the motion detectors, he could barely make out the silhouette of his dog, surrounded by about eight pair of eyes gleaming in the light. He grabbed a spotlight and shone it toward the animals and he saw the weapon being used against his dogs.

Coyotes are smart animals. They plan and coordinate. Coyotes are afraid of people, but dogs aren't as much. Not really. So they will sometimes adopt and raise a dog in their pack and use it to get what they need, like go into a yard and chase a cat out for the pack to catch, or rummage through the trash. They will use their pet dog to do things like that.

In this case, the dog they had was in heat. So they used that to entice the male dog to come out and mate with it. That is what he saw that night. In the dark, about fifty yards from his house, there was his dog surrounded by eight coyotes ready to pounce on him once he was in the act of having sex. That was the mystery of his disappearing dogs, and that was the last dog he ever lost. After that, he only got females and he never lost another dog.

So that was the first thing Jason did with Bo; get her to come any time, no matter what important adventures she was having. Being a female, he didn't have the problem with her that the guy with the Rottweilers had, but still, she had to come when he saw she was in danger or about to be.

So he played "Tag" with her whenever he could. He would call out; "TAG!" and she would try to catch him. It was one of her favorite games and every time she caught him, he would reward her with lots of rubs and petting and a little treat.

After a while, he never had to worry about her being too far off. He would say the magic word and she would come, tail wagging and happy, even if there were such important things like a rabbit or squirrel to chase or serious things to smell. Now he could let her be a dog and do all the important dog duties - running, chasing, sniffing, and he could do his things, things Jason is sure that Bo could not see as very important at all.

She sat on the floor between the driver's and passenger seat. Black hair and bright grey eyes. A stunning looking dog. He reached over and said, "You ready?"

She perked up her ears and he petted her down her neck and a hand full of hair came away. "I'm gonna have to brush you when we get back." She understood the word, "Brush" and she sat up and gave a little squeal and licked his arm. It is one of her favorite things. He started the RV and she looked around through the windows excitedly - and they were off.

Ruby Lake is in Northern Nevada and has become one of the most important sanctuaries in the United States for migrating birds. One time, in ancient days, it was huge. Back before there were people. But the poles shifted, and so did the Earths' crust, and it drained. No fault of Man. But it should be protected by Man. There aren't many places for migrating birds, like ducks, to stop and nest from the far South all the way into Canada. So it was an important trip as far as the agency goes.

Something was wrong and things were dying. Something had gotten into the water. Ruby lake is fed by run-off from the mountains as well as a series of springs coming from deep under the rocks. It could be that there is volcanic activity and the water is being poisoned by sulfur. But it is more likely that someone dumped some chemicals out in the middle of nowhere, thinking it just wouldn't matter and would save them the cost of disposing of it safely.

Whatever it was, it was his job to find it and fix it. Maybe not fix it himself, but at least let his boss know how to do it. Was it in containers and the containers leaked? Did they just go out and dump it out on the ground and try to cover it up with dirt, the worst thing to do? Or maybe it was solid or powder and the rain washed it down through the canyon into the lake. Maybe, maybe, maybe. But he would find it. But first he had to find Gizmo.

It rained the last two days, so the water could be running fairly fast and the tracks would be washed away. No matter. They already agreed on the route they would take and how they would get there, and all approaches lead to the same gorge.

Both he and Gizmo would launch at the lake and get in as far as they could through the various ponds to the mouth of the river. From there, they would follow one of the short contributories to the main gorge or canyon.

Hopefully he can get on a solid spot to unload his gear from the boat, or else he will have to wade a little bit and make a few trips back and forth before the gear is offloaded. Bo would just jump in any time she wanted, except when the motor was running. But the actual lake part of Ruby Lake is not that big, the rest is marsh and ponds.

The stream runs through an old dirt road about four miles from the mouth of the river. But not knowing where the problem started, north of the road or south of the road, they had decided to boat in and head south on foot. You can get almost daily rain in this area at this time of year, and the roads aren't kept up that well. They decided it was best to just hike it in.

"We're going to the Nevada Swiss Alps, Bo." That's what it's called; the Nevada Swiss Alps. Lakes, trees, streams, fishing, hiking, skiing, and the best thing about it, not many people know about it. Ruby Lake, Ruby Ridge, Echo Lake.

There are probably less than five hundred houses around Ruby Lake. Maybe one day he would retire somewhere in one of those mountains, he mused. Then, out loud he thought, "Yah right. When will I ever retire? When I'm dead?"

RUBY LAKE

Chapter Three

The going was uneventful, and near the end of the day he heard, "Turn right in one half mile," from the nice lady on the GPS. There was no other way around it. They would have to drive this bumpy dirt road up two miles past the launch area to the Visitor Center, check in, and pick up what Gizmo left for him; the usual copies of maps and papers that he knew he already had copies of, then bounce all the way back.

There wouldn't be enough time to cross the lake and get unloaded before it got dark, so he would get the gear into the boat and get it launched and tied up and ready to go first thing in the morning. That was the plan, anyway, and now, he was debating whether or not he should even take the time to get the package.

The motor home with the boat following behind made the turn easily enough and they went east about a mile and a half before the nice lady told him to turn left. There were some signs up ahead and a little pull off. He thought it would be a good time to give Bo a break. Leaving the engine running for the air conditioning, the side door flew open and out jumped Bo, running straight to the nearest bush, taking a good sniff before starting to do her business.

Jason stretched and cracked his back, letting out a good groan and took in the countryside. Off to the east was a range of mountains, Ruby Ridge, which still had a little snow on it, some brush and trees near the lake, and otherwise barren and dusty rolling desert hills in the lower parts.

Clouds were cascading over the mountains and he could see lightning strike as it came down the face. Later, the thunder would tell him it was about twenty miles away. The signs provided a little shelter from the wind, so that's where he stood and started to absentmindedly read some of the posts and notices.

"Warning: Flash floods after downpours." Along with safety tips.

"Warning: Rockslides in canyons and gorges." Along with safety tips.

"Warning: Rattlesnakes." Along with safety tips.

"Warning: Mountain Lions." Along with safety tips, and more.

Looking over the rest, there were the usual: pets on leashes, excessive alcohol, drunk boating, fishing areas, notice, notice, notice. You could be breaking a law just by standing here reading the laws. Same old things in any park these days.

Then, there was a missing person poster: a picture of a girl who looked to be about twelve with a number to call. Then another one, this time a hiker, male, about thirty years old.

Bo let out a bark and Jason turned to see that she was nose deep in some sage going after a lizard or something. Watching for a while, he turned and looked at the clouds moving in and figured he had about an hour before the rain would reach him.

"Tag!" he yelled out, and she came running. Dashing around the signs this way and that to keep her from touching him she barked and jumped, the waggo-meter showing the level of excitement. She finally caught up and touched him and got her reward, getting rubbed all over her neck and head and getting her treat.

As he was walking away, he glanced once more around the notice board and saw more missing person notices before heading back to the motor home, not drawing a conclusion, but having an odd feeling that there should be a conclusion drawn, just not yet registering what it was.

When Jason opened the door to the motor home, Bo leaped in first. In a minute they were rolling again, Bo happily panting, and Jason wondering if there really were that many landslides in the area, or if the animals were really that threatening, and wondering how so many people would go missing. But mostly, for the first time, wondering if Gizmo was alright.

The accelerator seemed to press itself as he found himself consumed with a sense of urgency now as they rattled down the washboard dirt road toward the visitor center, going sideways now and then from the tires bouncing so much they were barely making contact any longer.

Twice he could see the trailer with his boat trying to swing around and pass him. Up ahead was a park ranger truck heading in their direction. Slowing down to let him by, he saw the ranger slow to a stop. They met on the road with windows rolled down.

"You Jason Brand?" the ranger yelled out the window.

"Yah, that's me," he replied.

"Heard you were coming. We were expecting you. There is a package for you." The ranger glanced in the rear view mirror. "It's back at the center. Figured you were just running late. We closed up for the day so I taped it to the outside. Nobody's coming around here tonight. You can just go ahead and get it or come by in the morning."

"Alright. So I'll just go and... What, on the front door?" Jason asked. "I'll just go and get it off there?"

"Yah. Just grab it. If you're around in the morning, I'll come and see yah. It's late and I gotta get going. Relative problems, you know. If you're gone when I get in, well, stop by before you two leave," he said.

"Alright then. Thanks. See you later," and Jason continued bouncing down the road, but slower now.

The ranger didn't seem to be disturbed or troubled by anything, especially a swath of missing persons. Any idea he had that Gizmo was in trouble was probably nothing. Imagination.

They arrived and he grabbed the manila envelope off the door and got going straight away without even looking around. Back down the washboard road they went. Bo didn't like it. She didn't like the bumpy ride and the noise from every angle of the motor home.

They finally pulled off that road and onto the one leading to the boat launch, where bumpy took on a whole new meaning. The recent rain had left it scarred with deep ruts and pot holes. Jason was wondering if he were going to need to switch to four-wheel drive. They arrived at the launch area, just as the storm blew in.

He searched for the most level spot to park off to the south of the launch and sat there for a time, watching the storm coming down from the mountains and across the lake.

Rain like this is sometimes referred to as a monsoon in these parts and he thought back to a time he was stuck on Lake Mojave in one of these. The difference in temperatures colliding along with the wind and rain is a fierce combination, and like Lake Mojave, it blew hard and poured hard and, when it was full blown, hail started pelting the RV making a racket that set Bo off barking. The motor home pitched in the wind and the boat behind jumped up and down.

Jason could see how getting caught in it would be dangerous. The torrent of rain would topple trees and cause rockslides in those canyons he was about to head into, and if you were caught in it, you might not get back. You might never be found under the rock and mud.

Now he did worry about Gizmo. Every time the wind picked up and screamed around his RV making it pitch and rock, only added to his concern. He looked out the windscreen and up into the sky and considered what he would be doing right now if it were him out there.

Shelter. Of course shelter. But shelter is not enough. Safety and shelter. You don't want your site washed out by a flash flood, so you can't be down low. You don't want to get blown away, so you can't be up high.

You want protection from the force of the storm, so you want to be either behind some trees that won't get blown over or around the corner of a gorge so it blocks off the wind and rain. Then, if it is all gone to hell, you curl up and wrap something around yourself and just sit on your haunches until the storm is gone and you do the best you can.

"What am I thinking, Bo? He knows what he's doing as well as you and I do. Right?" True enough. Gizmo did know what he was doing and both of them had been in worse storms. Cold, snowing, blowing, on a lake, in mountains and hills and valleys. You name it. After years, you've gotten pretty good at reading where you are and reading the weather and preparing yourself. Neither of them were any Jeremiah Johnson, but they had become competent hikers and campers over the years.

He got up and walked over to the cabinets and pulled out a can of dog food. "Look," he said while rocking the can back and forth as if to animate it. "It's dog food, Bo. Ya want some?"

She wagged her tail and jumped up on the side of the counter for a moment. The lid was flipped off and he held it up to his nose and smelled, and looked down at her. "Yum. Kaka. Your favorite," and put it in a bowl for her. Then it was his turn and he grabbed a beer and a sandwich and sat down at the tiny table looking at the envelope.

In the envelope were maps in clear plastic and some local articles. "Yup. Same old stuff," was his first thought. They had already gone over the maps, so he knew he had maps. Those got put to the side and his beer bottle put on top as a paperweight. Next were some articles from the local papers.

He scanned the first few and saw that they were talking about something in the lake or up the stream or running down the stream into the lake. "Alright, Gizmo. That's why we're here and we already know about this." So he tossed those under the maps under the beer.

Next were articles of missing persons in the area. That was unusual. He looked them over and saw that two of them were the same ones he saw up at the notice board. But there were more here. He looked them over, thumbing through them. There must have been about twenty. He couldn't figure out over what period of time they had gone missing. Were these all in one year? Ten years? Was there a big landslide that buried a camp area upstream?

"If I were a younger person living around here," he thought," I bet I'd get pretty bored and get out the minute I could. Join the Army. The Peace Corps. It would be hard to keep me nailed down here. I'd be a missing person too, probably."

Wondering if he were just trying to convince himself not to worry, it struck him that Gizmo would not have put them in there for no reason. But why would he put them in there and then take off anyway? That didn't make sense.

Why didn't he just wait a day for him to show up if he thought there was danger? That settled it. He wouldn't, and that is the answer. He wouldn't go if there were a problem; therefore, there was no problem.

That being solved and his mind more at ease, he looked out the window at the storm again. Once the temperatures had mixed for a while and the overall temperature was lower, it didn't seem as violent. The rain was still coming and the wind was still blowing, but it calmed down a little.

He opened the tiny closet and grabbed a jacket and hat, snatched his beer off the table and out he and Bo went, down to the boat ramp. It blew hard enough at times to make him pause. Sheets of water would pour down and what would almost seem like something solid would catch the corner of his eye from time to time making him turn and look. But there was never anything there.

They walked down the ramp toward the edge of the water where Jason could see debris floating and being blown across the lake toward him. He started to slide on the wet slime that all ramps are famous for and grabbed Bo by the back to steady him saying, "Whoa."

Standing there now with his arms crossed in front of him looking out toward the center of the lake, he raised his beer and took a swallow, bringing his hand and head down after taking a gulp, he spotted a piece of flotsam that looked familiar.

"Shit, did he lose that?" It was Gizmo's plastic compass. At least it was one just like he had. He was crouching at the edge of the lake to try to reach out and grab it when he noticed the dead fish. About twenty of them were right there at the shore, blown tight against the concrete. He stood up and thought about Bo, looking around and seeing her standing in the reeds just as she was about to lap up a drink of water.

"BO!" he called. She stopped and looked up. "Bo. Come girl. Come on."

She trotted up to him without the magic word, "tag" even being spoken. "Good dog," he told her. There was something in the lake and it was killing things. How was he going to make sure she wouldn't drink? What about in the stream they'll be going up tomorrow? She's going to get thirsty.

He'd never had to do it, but he'll have to keep her right beside him the whole way. He'll have to keep her out of the water as much as he can. Of course, he trained her not to eat or drink things when he tells her, "No." On his job, he had to do it. But he's never had her cross a lake, and hike up a canyon and through a gorge with a stream running through it and not take a lap of some water.

He considered his options. Maybe he should leave her with the ranger? Not a bad idea. Maybe he should tie her to the motor home? No, that's too mean. She'd be vulnerable to attacks from animals too. The ranger, leave her with him, maybe he'll do that, a much better idea. Or, lock her inside the motor home? No. That would be horrible.

Pondering it as they made their way back to the motor home, his conclusion was arrived at. "You know what, girl?" he said as he got inside and Bo began shaking herself off and rolling over on the carpet and rubbing herself dry on anything she could, "Maybe what I'll do is just assume that you will do what we trained to do. Maybe I'll just tell you not to drink the water and trust that you won't do it, and instead, come and ask for it when you need it. Just like we have trained and done so many times."

Another problem solved, he opened another beer and started thinking about sleeping and a short time later, he was crawling up above the driver's seat into his bed. As he was drifting off, he thought about the compass and how he was so distracted by Bo almost drinking something she shouldn't, he forgot about grabbing it. Oh, well. He'll look for it in the morning.

Chapter Four

If there is a real danger, if there is a threat to life, you are supposed to have four people trained on how to deal with it, four to the team. Four. Not one, like sending Gizmo out by himself, and not two, like when he meets up with him. If there is a real danger, it takes four.

Once it is determined that there is a real danger, it takes two to go in with the full HAZMAT suit, air filters or air supply and full protective covering and the whole nine yards, and two to stand back and watch and be able to rush in drag them out if they collapse. Not one and not two, four.

Only twice had he been involved in catastrophes where they need the full four. It is the rules for HAZWOPER, Hazardous Waste Operations and Emergency Response, and he is a first responder. He'd always thought it was a stupid acronym, HAZWOPER, but he hardly ever has to use it and if someone ever did ask what he does, he would never say HAZWOPER. He would say he was a First Responder or something like that.

Telling people he works for the Environmental Protection Agency is another thing he never did any more. He drifted off to sleep, thinking about how the agency changed. How it used to be an agency that protected The People from disasters from toxins. A disaster didn't have to be huge and catastrophic. It can be slow and unknown, creeping and deadly.

No. Both he and Gizmo agreed on that. A disaster for a family would be drinking from a contaminated water supply and finding out too late that their entire family was dying from some cancer. Their whole family line would be exterminated. That is a disaster.

A disaster is living on a family farm for generation after generation and finding out that a dump site had been quietly poisoning you, your crops, or your animals for so long that your animals are sick and dying along with your family. Or that your crops have been soaking up the poisons without anyone knowing. That is a disaster.

Or that the entire year you have spent working, plowing, cultivating, planting and watering is now all for nothing. Your crop as well as your land is now worthless. In fact, it is less than worthless, it is dangerous and deadly.

All those loans they took out to finance them through the next year, all the tens of thousands of dollars in fuel that year, all the equipment they bought that can easily run in the millions of dollars - all gone. It'll all be auctioned off and the banks will take what money they can and pass the loss off to the next farmer and then they'll hit up the Government for whatever they can scam from them to keep it all going. That is a disaster as well.

There are all kinds of disasters. That's what he was there for, to take care of disasters and maybe even prevent one now and then. But the agency has changed, and that is another disaster. Now, you hear about armed raids on health food stores; armed raids on farms; armed raids on the Gibson Guitar factory.

Jason never understood the logic behind it. What danger are they? What disaster were they avoiding? The only disaster he saw was the disaster of turning what he did, what he liked to do, and what he was good at, into something shameful.

So he never told people who he worked for any longer, never mentioned it. Not unless he absolutely had to tell them. He fought fascists in Iraq. His cousins fought fascists in Vietnam. His father and uncles fought fascists in Germany and in Korea. His ancestors fought fascists in the Revolution. He'd be damned if he was going to be one. Hell no.

He made it plain and clear to everyone he could, he carries a gun to protect himself. He takes guns with him in the wilds. But he would never use his guns against Americans for wanting raw milk.

He thought about a meeting in which he was sitting where there was some person there to coordinate between branches of the Government. It was the EPA, SWAT, the local Sheriff, DEA, and a swath of other letters. They were there to coordinate a raid on a business, a local family-owned hardware store. It was how insane it was - this idea that a local family were being treated like they were some kind of criminals or terrorists and treated as though they were dangerous.

This was never the purpose of the EPA. It was never to go and strong-arm American businesses and farmers and families.

Somehow, it all changed. The mini-bureaucrats, they were taking over the country. How easy it was for them. Establish an agency to "protect" the people. That's what the EPA used to be. Then, once the agency is established and funding is there, begin changing the laws and objectives little by little, until the agency is no longer what the public thought it would ever be. Now it is armed and dangerous. Now it has morphed into a threat to The People. That is another disaster.

Sure, they carry guns. Of course they do. But only for protection against things that want to kill him or eat him. He never agreed to be an offensive arm of the Government against the people. Never. He made that clear at that meeting before he stood up and walked out.

"I will never be a part of this," he stated. "I will never bear arms against The People of America. I will never be a part of it," he stood and looked around the room at the people there wearing side arms including a couple with armored vests and M-16s.

Then he looked straight into the eyes of his boss, "If this agency or this Government ever gets to the point where they are nothing more than armed thugs going around bullying the population, I will turn my weapons on them before I use them on the people we are supposed to be protecting. Are you insane?

"These people had an accident and spilled a bucket of tar. They are not terrorists. But if you do this, YOU ARE! What you need to do is go there and ask them to clean it up. Educate them. Help them! Tell them how to clean it up! Did anyone go there and talk to them? Did anyone try that? Forget it! I'll do it!" he told the room. Then he walked out, followed by Gizmo and half the room.

He did, too. He went straight down and talked to the owner and told him what was going on. That an army of well-armed assholes were about to come in and close him down at gun point and kidnap him and hold him in chains and cage him like an animal without trial, and then, when he paid enough to his attorney and the Government and he did get out, they would drag him through the endless courts until he had not one dime left and his business would be gone along with everything he owned. He just didn't put it in those words, but that was what would happen.

They went out to the loading dock and he saw what was spilled. It was roofing tar. Sure, it was a mess, but not worth closing down an entire business for. They had a clumsy new guy there that let it fall off the forklift. The top row of buckets fell off and that was that.

They had already cleaned up what they could with a shovel. They scraped the rest as good as they could with a trowel. They tried what they could to get it up. In the end, they took a mop and some gasoline to get the rest. But they tried. They weren't criminals and they did not need to lose their livelihood over it, nor did they deserve to be on the receiving end of a Government assault. Jason told them to spread some cat litter on it, let it soak up, and pick it up several times a day.

The owner did that right away while Jason was standing there. "Look," the owner said. "We have an accident every now and then. A customer can spill a bucket of paint in the parking lot. We fix it. A container of pest control gets damaged. We fix it. We clean it up. But this is nuts, the government, wanting to shut us down over it.

"We are a family business. My dad owned this store, and before that, his dad," he went on, panting as he poured the kitty litter, "and before that and before that, back to when this was a trading post for settlers. We're not criminals. We help people. We give to charity. We are part of the community."

Then he stopped and stood up straight and looked Jason in the eye and lowered his voice. "You know…I'm afraid. This is not right. I know that the new hardware store down the street is in with the local politicians. I know it gives them money." He looked at his worker, the one who dumped the tar, and told him to spread the litter around, let it soak up, and then pick it up and keep doing it over and over until it was all cleaned.

Then, looking back at Jason, he said, "But I don't. I don't give them money. You know, I paddle my own boat. I don't ask for handouts. I don't do that. Never have. I'll help people that need help. It's not that I'm a tightwad; I give to charities, people that need it. But I don't give to politicians. They should paddle their own boat, just like me."

"But the new guys down the street, they're different. That new building supply store, they're not from around here. Their corporate headquarters is in Chicago. They got more money than any local business guy. So they give to the local politicians, the City Council, you know, they support the campaigns, Mayor, congress, and the local guys. I don't. I paddle my own boat and think they should too."

He stopped and looked out the back into the alley past the spill. "So now, all of a sudden, there is a problem with my business license. There is a problem with my payroll taxes. There is a problem with the IRS and the State. My insurance. The ingress and egress. The Fire Department. Now this?

"The writing is on the wall. It's the pay-to-play thing that that Chicago Politician was talking about. You know the one I'm talking about, the one with the hair. Who pays the most to the politicians, well, that's who gets to play and stay in business. It's like a protection racket, except now it is the official policy of government. They are the thugs now. The gangsters. The real gang-bangers, and they are the biggest gang in town."

Jason couldn't even think of a reply. The owner stood there for a moment and said, "There's a whole big government. It is huge. Then there is me. Just me. They have endless resources and money. I have what I can keep them from taking, and what's left, my family and I have to live on.

"But it's all of them, all the courts and the officers and the lawyers and the police. It is endless and it is huge. But there is only me here.

Maybe it's time to sell and move on. I always planned to hand this store over to one of my kids. But maybe it's time to move on."

"Well," Jason finally started talking, "I'll go and do the paperwork and let them know you are cooperating, whatever that means, and that you are taking care of the problem. At least you won't get yourself handcuffed and hauled off today, maybe." He held his hand out to shake and said, "Take care of yourself and good luck."

RUBY LAKE

Chapter Five

That was the first time he handed in his resignation. He went back to the office and did the mountain of paperwork for these buckets of tar, and brought it to Terry Borden with his resignation on top. "I'm not gonna be a part of this," was all he had to say to his boss.

Terry looked at it and put it aside without even reading the whole thing. He knew what it was. Then barely flipped through the report and paperwork for the Hardware store and put it all aside.

He stood up without paying any attention to any of it, like it never even happened, and said, "We have a problem. Catskill Chemicals is having a problem. There are reports of dead people and the area has been roped off. The roads are blocked about a half mile in all directions. I need you there right now. It's you and Gizmo, and the Fire Department is sending the two back-ups. You are lead."

Jason protested, "No. Wait. The Fire Department? We haven't worked with them. What about our guys? I mean, how bad is it? Can't we get our guys in there?" They have to have four to a team, two to go in and two to stand back and rescue the first two if they go down.

"Our guys are too far away. Won't make it back for at least a day. We have to coordinate with Fire. They know what they're doing. Did the same training as you," Borden told him.

"Sure, trained. But how do you know they know what they're doing? I mean, we know our own moves. We worked together," Jason argued.

"It'll be alright. They know what they're doing. They probably do more of this than you," Borden replied.

That shut Jason up. He's probably right. The Fire Department has to be ready for this all the time. They have to deal with it all the time, and they get the best toys; the best equipment.

The intercom came on, "The video link is all set in the conference room, Mr. Borden."

"Let's go," and he walked out with Jason trailing behind him.

The wide screen was giving an aerial shot of the factory and someone was talking over the satellite connection. "There are three bodies outside on the lawn. We don't know if they are alive or dead, but that is as far as they got. There is no movement we can see.

"An explosion was heard by a civilian who was approaching the factory; a salesman or something. He called it in. If he'd been a few minutes earlier, he'd be lying there with them. No idea what they were making just yet. We have a guy from the night shift with the fire Department now, so we should have an idea of what it is pretty soon.

"A helicopter should be at your location any minute. As we get information, we'll transmit it to you in flight. We thought we saw one of the civilians in front move, so Fire is gonna suit up and start rescue procedures on the folks outside there. There are birds outside lying on the ground, so it is being assumed that this is an airborne toxin of some sort. Terry, make sure your guys bring their Buzz Lightyear outfits."

They could hear the helicopter approaching and that ended the meeting in the conference room. Jason grabbed his gear and he and Gizmo dashed for the parking lot where it was putting down. They tossed their gear in, hopped up, and were gone.

It was about a five-minute flight, and in cases like this, every minute could mean lives. There was no new information of any value transmitted on the way. The night shift worker turned out to be the security guard. He had no information on what they were working on except that they had a new contract for pharmaceuticals.

They were pulling their suits on and checking their gear one more time as they came up to the plant. Gizmo yelled to the pilot into his mike, "Circle around the complex so we can take a good look down lower."

"Can't do it," the pilot called back. "I can get you a look from the West, and get some altitude for the rest. But the East side is downwind. We don't know what we'd be breathing. But I can give you a look if we get up high enough."

They came up from the West and then the pilot took them to look at the North end. There was smoke coming out a side vent. "Look. Must be on fire still. They had an old Halon system. Looks like it worked pretty well except for over there. But the smoke could be coming from anywhere. This thing goes six stories underground, so who knows. I heard you two are going in there."

Jason and gizmo looked at each other, "Yah. Hey. Take us around once," Jason yelled. The helicopter circled high up and they could see the hole blown out of the East side. There were no more bodies they could see and they wanted to get in there fast. Minutes mean lives. "Okay. Put us down."

The pilot put down close to the staging area where they had a command post set up with a convoy of ambulances. The Fire Department HAZWOPERS were there still in their suits without the helmets. They walked up to introduce themselves and shake hands.

"So. Did anyone get a good look inside?" Gizmo asked.

"No. The explosion must have taken the power out. There's no light at the entry except for the emergency exit light. It's too dark. Couldn't see hardly anything and we didn't want to go in without you guys here. I guess we're your backup. My name's John and this is Dan," he said.

"Good to meet you. I'm Jason Brand and this is Jerry Crozley. We're good to go if you are. All we need is radio and a video feed."

"We got it all in here," John pointed at the mobile Command Center. "Come on. We'll get you set up."

The radio checked and the cameras on their helmets relaying to screens in the center, they made their way down toward the entrance. Another feed next to the decontamination area would be monitored by John and Dan.

If anything went wrong, if Jason and Gizmo fell or went unconscious, John and Dan would rush in and drag them out. In the meanwhile Jason and Gizmo would go through the building, save whom they could, dragging them by the collar to safety as they came up on them, all the while working toward whatever it was that was leaking - and whatever it was leaking.

The last thing on was the oxygen tanks. "Shit. I forgot how heavy these things were. Alright, Gizmo. You all set?" Jason got the thumbs up from Gizmo and they moved toward the entrance. "I've got positive pressure. How about you?"

Positive pressure is important. Especially when you walk into a building like this. The pressure on the inside of the suit has to be more than the air pressure on the outside. That way, if you spring a leak, the pressure will keep the bad stuff outside the suit from getting in.

"Mine's fine, Jason. Everything is good. You're worse than my mother. Make sure your zipper is up. Comb your hair. Don't knock up your cousin, Lucy. Don't breathe any deadly chemicals. Nag, nag, nag," Gizmo said, drawing a chuckle from everyone listening.

"How's the video feed? You guys getting it okay?" Jason asked the two firemen. "Cuz you know what we're seeing: Jack shit through a peephole."

"We're good on the video, guys," Dan responded. "Everything is clear. We will be right here. You guys just say the word and we're there. Just take it easy and slow and be careful."

"Alright," he said as they walked up the walkway toward the door, "We're about to go in." He paused for a moment and did one last visual check on Gizmo. Gizmo did the same for him. The suits they were wearing would keep any chemical or biohazard off them, and the air supply would give them about an hour before they had to come back out.

The vision in the suit is like taking the end of a fat tube and looking out. You have to point the tube exactly where you are trying to look. Tunnel vision. You can't see side to side. You only see straight out. It's a little unnerving, especially in the dark. You could be standing two feet from a person. If you didn't turn and look directly at him, you wouldn't know it. It's like looking out the mouth of a cave.

Everything within your suit is amplified. You hear your own breathing, like Darth Vader. You can listen to your own heartbeat. You can hear your stomach growling. The sounds from outside the suit though, are muffled. You are in your own little world, completely contained.

Approaching the door, Gizmo, listening to his own breathing, started reciting, "Breath deep, the gathering gloom," he growled out in a lowered, dire-sounding voice.

Jason gave a little laugh and joined in and they said the next part together: "Watch lights fade from every room." It was a poem, the "Late Lament" from the Moody Blues.

Then John and Dan joined them. "Bedsitter people look back and lament,

"Another day's useless energy…"

"Alright you Knights in White Rubber Suits. Before you two embarrass yourselves and break into a dance, let's get serious." Terry had just arrived. His voice cracked through the comm.

"Doesn't matter what. It just never gets old." Dan said with a laugh.

"Yah, yah," Terry said as they all had a little chuckle. "What do you have? See anything?"

"Nothing yet, give us a minute. We are stepping inside now," Jason said, looking around the reception area. He could barely see up or down without bending his torso. The camera feed attached to their helmets had a wider angle, but could not see down or up or side to side without the body movement either. "The people that made it outside must have been working here. Nobody in here." He looked around at the desk and checked the phone system over. It was dead.

Gizmo looked at him and chuckled. "I know," he said," you were thinking you could just call everyone on the intercom and tell them to come out." They looked down the long hallway. The further in it went, the darker it got until it lost all light from the front entrance windows. "You check the doors on the left, I'll check the right?"

"Sounds good to me," said Jason, walking up to the first door and opening it. "Empty," he reported. He turned around to see Gizmo coming out of the door on his side. Deeper they went into the hallway and checked the next set of doors.

"Blood," Jason said.

Gizmo turned from the door he was checking and looked. They both walked inside. Light from the windows glistened off the blood on the desk and the floor. "Where's the guy, or girl - the person?" Jason wondered. "They couldn't have walked away. Maybe they did, but that's a lot of blood."

"Jason," Terry's voice came through their headsets. "Give me a good look around. Did you look under the desk?" Jason found the middle of the desk through his visor and stood back from it and bent down to get a look. Terry could see on his video feed there was nothing. Just blood. "Check the closet."

Gizmo turned around the room. He did an almost 360 degree scan. "I don't see a closet. No closet here," he reported, and then turned back to Jason. "Next?"

They walked out the door and deeper into the darkness. One more set of doors on either side of the hall before it made a turn. They both looked inside their rooms. Nothing. "Where the hell did everyone go? Is today a holiday or something?" Gizmo asked.

"Terry?" Jason called. "It's not some kind of holiday today, right?"

"Um, no. Is it? Wait." He checked with the others in the command center and came back. "No. No holiday. There were people on the front walkway and a salesman was on his way in. So they were in business. No holiday."

"So how about this? Maybe they had an evacuation plan. Maybe they were all going where they are supposed to go. Can you check with that security guy and ask him where they were supposed to go?" Jason asked.

The two responders continued down the hall until it made a turn toward the elevators. There was an exit sign for the stair well, still lit with a battery pack. There were three stories above ground and six below. They approached the stairwell and Jason said, "Well, I guess we go down. That's where I'd keep all the good stuff. Ready?"

"Ready," Gizmo answered.

Jason opened the door and started to step through. He thought he sensed some motion near the bottom of the stairs. "Hello! Anyone there?" he called, taking another step through. "Hey! Anyone down there?" he called out again with no response.

He bent over to get a good clear look at the stairway before going down. "Alright man," he told Gizmo. "We better get moving if we're gonna save anyone here." He started down, almost tripping on the first step. "Watch yourself. A little hard to judge in this suit." He saw Gizmo following him and didn't need a reply.

They got to the bottom and Jason opened the door into the hall. It was pitch black. The only thing lit was the exit sign. They turned on their helmet lights and went in, scanning the hall that went off in either direction. Jason said, "Let's not split up yet 'til we know a little more. Sound good to you? I vote we go right."

Gizmo shone his light in that direction. "Alright. We have to find some people soon. How many did they say worked here? We should at least see some bodies." He checked with Command, "Hey up there. So what's with that evac plan? Where did they go?"

Terry came on again, "They were supposed to come outside is what they were supposed to do. The security guy doesn't know anything. Look. There is supposed to be a chart right at the exits, like at the stairways. Look over on the walls and see if you can show me one."

They went over and looked around the door they just came through. There was the chart. "Here it is," Jason told him. "You getting this? It shows them, stick men, going up the stairs and going outside. Well, that's brilliant!" he exclaimed, then, lowering his voice a bit, "On the other hand, there's not much more to say, is there? Go upstairs and get out. It seems to me that with such simple explanations, maybe they couldn't."

"Maybe the stick men had the day off," Gizmo joked.

"Yah, or they were at a stickman convention," Jason replied. "We'll keep checking rooms."

Deeper and deeper into the darkness they went, aware of every breath, looking out through the mouth of their tiny cave. The first sets of doors were locked. They banged on them and yelled. Jason thought he caught some movement down the hall and swung around to shine some light. Nothing. "Did you see that? Did you see something? What was it?" he asked.

"I don't know," Gizmo said. "Maybe it was a cat. Whatever it was, it was moving pretty fast. Scared the crap out of me!"

They moved on to the next door, paused then opened it. Together this time, they peered in. There was nothing but blackness in all directions, except where the light spilled out from their helmets. They were blind in all directions except straight ahead.

Aware of nothing except their own breathing and the sound of their own hearts beating, aware of nothing that is, except this: something was wrong. "Shit. I don't mind saying, but this is scary stuff," Jason half whispered with a little chuckle. "Where the hell is everyone?"

They crept into the room, Gizmo stayed at the entrance holding the door open. Charts covered the wall on one side. There were four desks in the center. Jason scanned with his light by turning his body and Gizmos' light followed as he watched where it went.

They scanned the room this way through their tunnel vision until Jason's light fell on something; a person. "Hey!" he called. Quickly, Gizmo moved to focus his light on it. "There's someone there." He swung the beam back and forth, but found nothing. It was gone.

Jason moved his beam around the same area until it fell on something again. "There!"

Gizmo tried to move quick enough to find where he was focusing the beam, swinging his body to direct the light. It happened so fast. They both caught it in their beams. It reacted so fast it almost flew. It seemed to take one leap for the door and went right by Gizmo, knocking him down. The door slammed shut and Gizmo hit the floor.

"What the…what the hell!" He was down, and something was there. Something really fast was there. He was down and that meant he was vulnerable. Something could tear his suit. He was scrambling to get back up, but he kept sliding on his feet. "Jason! Blood, I can't get up!"

Jason ran over and grabbed his arm and steadied him. They both stood there with their backs against the wall, listening for any more movement, and frantically panning their lights for anything else in the room. Any noise was being drowned out by their own panicked breathing and hearts thumping. Nothing. No sounds except their own amplified panting and their own racing hearts. That's how they stayed, motionless, until they calmed down.

Once the heart rate came down and the breathing returned to something more normal they spoke. "Okay Gizmo. Now, I don't know about you, but that scared the piss out of me!" Jason blurted out. He looked at the blood covering Gizmo's suit and checked to make sure there were no tears in it.

"What…what…what in the HELL was that? I thought it was a person. Didn't it look like a person? Man, it was quick!" he exclaimed.

"Yah. Yah," Jason agreed. "But what the… Why? It didn't seem to want to be rescued very much, did it? Was it a person? It looked like a person. But man - fast."

He thought for a moment and said, "Look. Let's see if there's another one. You got the door, right? You guard the door. Don't let anything out. I'll go and see if there is something else in here. I'll go between the desks and I'll see… I'll flush 'em out. You hold the door shut."

"Okay. Fine. But what if there is another one? Maybe we should just get out of here," Gizmo said.

"What, and go back and tell everyone we came out because we got scared?" Jason asked.

"Yah. You're right," Gizmo said. "Don't want people saying how the big-strong Firemen had to come down instead. Never live that down."

"Well, let's get a damn good look and see if there's another one. Let's see what it is," pausing for thought, "Look. I'm going down the wall here on the left. You keep your light on me and on the wall all the way to the corner. I'll go down the wall turned sideways and put my light between the desks. If something is there, well, we should see it move again."

"Okay. But that last one was fast. What if it comes at you?" He asked.

"Uhm, yah. Good point." Thinking for a time, he turned back to Gizmo. "Look. It came right by you. It didn't hurt you. It was like it was scared. But we know at least one of them is out there in the hall, and I think that probably the other one, the thing we thought was a cat was another. So, maybe we should see what the hell they are before we go out of this… You know, before we go out. Out of the room again and into the hallway."

"I have a gun," Gizmo told him. "But it's in my pants. Under my suit. What do you think?"

"No way. Don't open your suit," Jason told him. "I'll go and see if there's another one; see what these things are. You ready?"

Jason stepped down sideways as tight as he could get against the wall, his air tank scraping all the way. His light went between the rows of desks as planned, all the way to the end. "Nothing," he said. Then he started coming forward again. "Shit. What if they're under the desk? I'm gonna go back and see, just check. I'm gonna get some light in there - under the desks."

Slowly he moved to the first row in the back. He took a few steps in and bent over to shine the light in under the first one. Nothing. There was some litter, that's all. He moved in more toward the center of the room to see under the next one. Empty. He realized that now, if something were under there that moved as fast as that other thing, he would not be able to get out of the aisle in time if it came at him.

One more time, just in case, he checked under the closest desks. Then, lifting himself higher on his toes, he shone the light over the desks into the next isle and right under the desk in the next row, and there it was. It made a scream and darted away out of the beam.

"There!" Jason yelled. "Right there! Did you see it? Where did it go?"

"Get back here, Jason. Get back here. Hurry up." Gizmo did see it, but just for a moment, the same as Jason. It darted out of the light. "Come on. Look. It doesn't like the light. I think that's it."

Jason scrambled back to the front of the room. "Okay. That weren't no damn cat. That's no danged cat. I don't know what it is, but it ain't a cat. Let's look at this door. Does it lock? Let's lock it in here. Let's get the hell out of here. Go back topside. Regroup."

"I'm with you - and bring some guns," Gizmo said.

Jason turned back toward the back of the room and said, "Okay. Get ready to open the door. I'll keep my light going back there, keep him back and away and hiding from the light, and we'll get the hell out of here."

Gizmo opened the door and started to creep out. Jason was so close behind, he was almost stepping on him all the way. He twisted the lock and stepped into the hall and let it shut. They both heard movement noise inside the room and then scratching on the door.

They turned towards the stairway and there, blocking their way, were about a dozen of them. Jason grabbed Gizmo by the arm and began walking backward down the hall, studying them as he went. "Are they people?" he asked.

"I don't know, and they aren't talking. They look like people from here. But why aren't they getting out?" Gizmo asked.

They backed toward the turn in the corridor. There was a sign with a stair and a "down" arrow. They slowly moved back and turned the corner, and there were even more of them. As soon as they saw the light, they turned away. "People,' Jason decided. "They really don't like light." They started backing up the way they came. "I wish now we didn't lock that door. Wasn't thinking. We locked ourselves out. There was probably only one in there."

"Yah, maybe," Gizmo said. "But we couldn't stay. We'll run out of air. We'd have to come out. Better now than later. Look. There has to be a stairway on the next floor down. Let's go down one flight and come back up the stairwell. We know the stairwell is clear. We were in it already. We'll get out and tell everyone there are some live things down there, maybe people."

Jason agreed. "Okay, let's go." They snuck into the stairway with the down only arrow and he paused. "Hey. What about it, Command?" he called on his radio. "Haven't heard from you in a while. What do you think of all this?"

Nothing. No answer. "You try, Gizmo," he urged his partner.

"Command?" Gizmo called. "Anyone there? Hello! Hello! Shit! Nothing!"

He turned to Jason. "Let me look at your... Oh man!" he exclaimed. "The wires are melting! The coating melted off! The circuits are getting fried! That's it, that's messed up! Whatever was in that explosion is so corrosive, it melted the electronics! The ceramic parts are alright, but the wiring – bad!"

"This is bad, Jason. This is bad," Gizmo whispered.

Jason checked over Gizmos equipment quickly and saw the same thing. "What if they aren't violent? What if we just go back down the hall way and go up the stairs and get our asses out of here and they just don't do anything? We haven't been attacked or anything. All we know is they're just really quick and they don't like light."

"And they're really creepy! Don't forget that. Oh, and did I mention scary? There's well over two dozen of them out there," Gizmo said.

Jason looked down at the bottom of the stairway. There was a fire hose and an axe. He went over and grabbed the axe and said, "Let's see if they are violent or not. So far, they are just scared off by light. I'll go first and shine light to the front. You stay right behind and shine yours to the rear. We'll get to the stairs, close the door, and I'll race you to the top. We'll get our asses out of here."

"Hey, we hit that stairway, better move fast, or I'm runnin' you over," Gizmo said.

Jason stepped out with the axe in hand. Gizmo followed and turned backwards. They were there. A lot of them. Front and back. All turning when the light hit them. They moved as planned toward the stairs and the mob kept their distance. Jason's light flickered and he paused. He started to move again and it flickered again.

"What?" Gizmo asked.

"My light. It's going out. I think the wiring is getting eaten. We better move," Jason told him, and at that very instant it did go out.

The question of whether they were violent or not was instantly answered. The throng turned and rushed toward them with screams like wild animals.

Gizmo turned around to counter an attack, and they stopped and turned away from his light, but the crowd Gizmo held at bay behind them came rushing. "Back to the stairs," he said turning front wards and backwards as fast as he could as they went. It was a deadly game of red light, green light. Only when they got to you and crossed that line, the game was truly over.

They squeezed through the door to the stairs just as the mob reached them. Jason was last in and pushed the door shut and held the latch so it couldn't be opened. There was gnashing and growling from the other side, but no attempt at opening the door. He put his foot at the base of the door and released the handle and gently stepped back. "You ever play Fallout?"

"Yah, but I had guns, dammit. We better get out of here right now. Let's do the plan. Down here, straight to the stairwell, up and out. Ready?" Gizmo asked.

"Let's go." Jason did what would pass for a run in the suit, Gizmo right behind. They didn't even wait to see what was on the other side of the door. They bolted out, Jason with axe in hand, Gizmo grabbing the fire extinguisher on the way through, and took a right turn and headed straight for the stairway.

They turned the corner and saw the fire. One of the people was screaming at it and ran straight into flames. They were blocked off. They spun around and ran to the other corner, toward a sign that read, "Clean Room", and turned. At the end of the corridor was another "Exit" sign and on the right about midway was the Clean Room. They could hear the mob approaching.

They started down the corridor toward the sign when Gizmo's light went out, and they froze. They were now in total darkness. The only thing they could focus on was the "Exit" sign. The only thing they could hear was their own breath and their racing heartbeats and the muffled sound of the crazed approaching mob.

Gizmo reached out and put his hand on Jason's shoulder so they wouldn't get separated. They crept toward the exit sign, Gizmo making sure not to lose contact, and Jason making sure he wouldn't. They moved as one, slowly and quietly toward it.

Feeling a little dizzy, Jason wondered if he might have sprung a leak in his suit and breathed in something. He was having trouble concentrating, almost spinning.

"Air," he said as he tried adjusting the flow. "I'm running out of air. We gotta get back up or we're in real trouble. Maybe if we run for it, we can get to the door before they know we're there."

There was no answer. "Gizmo, we might be able to sneak past...Hey. You hear me?"

Jason knew their electronics had been eaten. They were out of touch. He would just have to do what he thought was right and Gizmo would have to figure it out as they go. The other option was to yell, in which case they could be mobbed.

In near total darkness, he began to move toward the exit, Gizmo's hand on his shoulder. His every breath amplified in his suit. His heart racing. His foot hit something in the dark and he almost tripped. It might have been an arm, it might have been a leg, but whatever it was, the thing attached to it screamed, bringing the mad horde running toward them. He couldn't see them, he could only hear them.

"The Clean Room," Jason thought to himself. "Gotta get in there." He scrambled, feeling his way along the wall of the corridor, feeling his way to a door. With the mad horde almost upon them, he reached a handle and swung the door open. The Clean Room!

There was light, and for the first time they got to see what was chasing them. They both stood and looked for a second, taking in as much as they could in the brief time they dared before the things turned from the light, and the door was slammed. This time, they were inside the room when they locked it, and checked it twice. He could hear the muffled sound of Gizmo yelling something.

He was frozen, trying to digest what he had seen. The horde had no lips, showing teeth all the way to the gums. Big bulging eyes. Where there should be a nose, there were instead two cavities straight into the skull. The skin seemed to be almost liquid with boils and welts. They had little clothes, torn clothes, or no clothes. As soon as the light from inside the room registered to them, they turned from it. But it was enough time for Jason and Gizmo to see all they needed.

They were now in a room with a door that entered an area of pumped in clean air. Through that door, there would be another room with clean air; the actual Clean Room with the cleanest and purest in the place. It would have constant pumped clean air and its own power, provided the explosion didn't take it out. They had to get inside.

Jason ran to the first door and opened it and heard the swish of air pressure. "Good. It's still functioning," he thought.

They both stepped inside. Jason tore at his helmet to get at some air. Once it was off, he breathed in and out several times to get oxygen in his blood again. Hands on his knees and bent over, he looked at Gizmo who looked like he was having a fit.

He had his helmet off and his tank on the floor and was trying wiggle out of his suit. With arms flailing and exasperated noises, he finally succeeded in getting it down to his knees and he reached into his trousers and pulled out his gun.

Turning and looking wild eyed at Jason, gun waving in the air, he yelled, "Zombies! Zombies! They're zombies!" with his gun still waving. "Zombies aren't real! Those are zombies!"

Jason, still panting, just looked at him in shock. Then a voice came through, "Those weren't Zombies."

They spun and looked at the back of the room and saw a glass wall with four people behind it, staring at them. Real people. Normal people. They were there in the Clean Room. Jason and Gizmo were in the entrance to it. It was fed air and had positive pressure constantly so nothing could get in.

Jason and Gizmo were in the entrance where, after a time, with constant input of air, and provided they follow the right procedures, they can progress to the next room, the Clean Room itself, where the four were looking at them now in disbelief.

"What do you mean? Not zombies!" Gizmo yelled, still waving his pistol. "I saw them. Those were zombies. What the hell? Zombies!"

He pointed the gun tapping his chest with it and said, "I know zombies when I see one. I've seen them. I watched..." Realizing how ridiculous he was about to sound saying he knows because he saw them on TV, he cut himself off and said, "And who the...who the hell are you?"

"We work here. This is Research and Development. I'm Dr. Bradley, and these are my colleagues, Drs. Rosen and Murphy, and our lab assistant, Miss Peterson. We work here."

"What? Are you some freak scientists? You made zombies? You Frankenstein assholes. Zombies? Really?" Gizmo continued ranting.

"They're not zombies. They're people. Let me explain," Bradley said.

Gizmo was not listening to what the man was saying. Instead, he was looking inside the Clean Room. There were electronics; lots of electronics. Phones, faxes, mass spectrometers, and gadgets he had no idea of what they were. Electronics, that's all that mattered. Pointing at some of them with his gun, all he had to say was the word, "electronics", and Jason knew what he meant.

Gizmo was a genius, a fact that he'd proven many times over the years. He could make anything work with duct tape and Popsicle sticks. Once inside, he could restore communications to the Command Center. Inside that room would be his own private electronics shop.

Jason reached for the door and gave it a pull. It is possibly the most secure door inside the facility, sealed airtight, and it didn't even budge. "Let us in." He tried the door again.

"I can't open the door. It'll ruin our work. You aren't allowed..." Bradley was saying.

Without hesitation, Jason picked the axe up and smashed the key pad cover on the door laying the workings bare and took the axe and wedged it into the workings and yanked. The door came free and they rushed inside.

Bradley stepped back while the others stood and stared in shock. "You can't come in here. You're not allowed."

Gizmo, pointing his gun at him, replied, "Shut it, you zombie making freak," while Jason walked up to the fax, flipped it over, and smashed it with the axe. Gizmo looked at the workings, "Perfect. I'll have us out of here in ten or fifteen."

Jason grabbed his helmet from the outer room and came back in. He flipped it over and began disassembling the communications. He ran out and grabbed Gizmos' and did the same. Most of the parts exposed to the outside were destroyed. He grabbed the axe and broke one open to get at the inside wiring and electronics. The rubber grommet sealing the system had been eaten. Most of the parts were okay, but anything coated in plastic or rubber was destroyed.

He grabbed an air tank and turned it over. The plastic knobs were melted. He ripped them off to expose the valves and mumbled, "Well, that explains the air."

The helmets were brought over and laid out beside Gizmo. His hands were deep inside the fax now, like a surgeon doing a transplant or a doctor delivering a baby. He briefly leaned over without taking his hands out of his patient and looked at the helmet. "Batteries fried too. Get one of their cell phones, and that monitor, open that up, will ya."

Jason grabbed the monitor and yanked the plug. He turned it over and pried it open, cracking the plastic covering. He looked at the four stunned lab workers and held out his hand. Without a word, Murphy took out his cell phone, checked it to see if by some miracle there would be signal, and gave it to him.

Bradley watched him hand it over and looked at him and said, "You are not supposed to have a cell phone in the Clean Room."

And Murphy replied, "Shut the hell up, Bradley."

And Rosen chimed in, "Yah. Shut the hell up, Bradley."

And Peterson said, "Really."

Jason watched patiently while Gizmo dissected the equipment and, bit by bit, restored the electronics in the helmet. Parts were now hanging out in a maze of newly connected wiring and transistors. He turned and glanced at the four shut-ins and noticed that three of them had taken position in front of Bradley and were intently looking at him, blocking him in, cornering him. "What's going on?" he asked.

They didn't respond to him, but Murphy said to Bradley, "You move, I swear I'll kill you."

Bradley stood against the back of the room, pinned by his three co-workers, and glanced at one particular work station, Feeling the tension, Jason asked, "What's going on?"

"I think it's the fail safe. He wants to push it. Press the button. Kill us all." Murphy wouldn't take his eyes off Bradley and continued.

"There are things, not so much here, but down below that can't get released. Bad things. Research, things that, if they got out, would be…bad."

He walked over and dragged a lab chair back over to the corner and pointed to it. "Sit," he demanded, looking at Bradley.

"You can't do this. I'm the senior technician. You work for me," Bradley protested.

"I so don't give a shit. You are going to sit, or I'm gonna make you sit. But you just try to move one inch..," Murphy threatened.

The other two took a threatening step in his direction and Bradley decided to take his offer and sat in the chair. Murphy was wielding a microscope like he would hold a club, and Peterson held a sharp and pointed lab device. The seriousness of the situation was evident. They meant business. If Bradley moved, they would deal with him in a decisive and permanent manner. Just then the radio cracked.

"Command!" Gizmo yelled. "Command!"

"This is command. Holy shit, we thought you were dead." It was Terry.

Jason rushed over, "Terry. We're on the third level in the Clean Room. We have four survivors. We have clean air and some power. I don't know for how long, but we're good for the moment. We are going to need six new suits down here."

"And they have zombies!" Gizmo yelled.

"They're NOT ZOMBIES," Bradley cut in.

"We tried to get you help when we lost contact with you. The fire Department guys came after you. They said they got attacked by crazy people. It wasn't really clear. It was too dark and they lost their lights. They are back topside. What's the situation? Who attacked? What's down there?" He asked.

"Zombies! Bloody zombies!" Gizmo yelled.

Dr. Murphy stepped over to them and said, "Perhaps I could explain."

Gizmo motioned a welcome toward the mass of wires they were talking into and Jason stepped back.

"We do research for pharmaceutical companies. Experimental drugs. Experimental compounds. They contract us to do that." He paused and looked at Bradley. "Some things we have here are pretty dangerous in their raw form. Really caustic. Eat your skin right off.

"There was an explosion. Near as I can tell what happened was two things. First, the acidic material, the vapor, was drawn into the ventilation system. It feeds the entire building. The safeties we have for this, the sensors and filters and such, well, the acid ate them. So it went all throughout the facility. It didn't shut down. We have our own system inside here. Our own air, in the Clean Room here, we're sealed off, separate from the rest of the facility.

"At the same time, there is a mix of psychotropic drugs we were developing. Very powerful neural inhibitors. The raw form, undiluted along with materials for it, was near the explosion. In extremely small amounts, it is very effective. But this was an entire tank of a concentrated drug that was turned into a vapor and drawn into the ventilation with the acid."

"Zombies. I can't believe it," Gizmo was shaking his head. "Psycho, psychiatric drugged up zombies, Terry."

Again, Bradley spoke up. "They're not zombies. They're people."

Murphy glanced at Bradley and back to the mass of wires, "So, really, here is what happened, and we do have a video feed and short circuit here, so we watched the whole thing, that is, until the feed was melted."

"The neural inhibitor really does work. It inhibits. There are certain parts of the brain that control certain functions. Reason. Contemplation. Memory. Respiratory and the rest of the autonomic system, that's different. Then there is the base, animalistic part, deep inside.

"In tests, when this neural inhibitor is applied to subjects, things like reason and all higher-level functions of the brain are inhibited. That's what the drug does. In small amounts, it inhibits a little. In large amounts, it was found to inhibit these functions completely. When there is too much of the drug, it ends up destroying the receptors in the brain that stimulate any higher-level reasoning. A chemical lobotomy - and then some.

"When the people in the facility were exposed to the combination of the acidic vapor, the same caustic material that degraded your communications, it began rapid decomposition of their skin. This would be horribly painful, and most would have died quickly from the shock from the pain of it. There are a great number of nerves in the skin. It is the largest organ of the human body.

"But these nerves were quickly eaten. If it weren't for the inhibitor blocking any sense of pain, they would have died from shock. We were able to watch the development over our security system. We watched human beings degrade into a simple stimulus response mechanism, with absolutely no higher-level brain functions.

"We watched their faces and the skin on their bodies and protrusions like the nose, ears, eyelids, and gums melt away. All that was left was impulse. Eat. Attack. Kill. Those other levels, the higher ones, they will not return."

"What did I tell you?" Gizmo cut in. "Guess what. Mindless killing flesh eating crazy people that attack you, you know what that's called? Zombies! That's what. They made zombies. Psycho drugged up, lobotomized zombies. Unbelievable!"

"Actually," Murphy continued, "Mr. Gizmo's description is quite accurate. There is nothing of them other than internal organs that could be considered human. Those things that make us human no longer exist in them.

"But, sir. That may not be the biggest problem. There are three more levels of building built below us into the ground. I don't know how familiar you are with some of the construction of these types of facilities. They are quite secret, but I'll tell you what I know.

"The very bottom level is containment. There is nothing alive that ever comes back from that level. Person, test animal - doesn't matter. Any biohazards that can't be contained are there. Ebola strains. Earth changing catastrophes, if they escape. Nobody really knows exactly what is down there. At least none of us, except Dr. Bradley and people like him. Anything that goes down never comes back up."

"So. Now that this happened, the explosion, how secure is it?" Jason asked. "Bradley, you're gonna have to start talking about this."

"Well," Murphy continued, "As far as I know, if there were any danger, it is set to incinerate any biological organisms. Bodies, germs, bacteria. Incinerated. But I don't know how intact the system is now. I just can't say.

"The next level up contains things that are deemed to be needing quarantine, that is: watched and tested to determine if they go down to the bottom floor. I've never seen a thing or person or animal come back from there either. Never a slide, a test tube, or a living thing.

"That is where testing and developing occurs that nobody will ever know about except people like Bradley. I'm sure there are several Clean Rooms down there, and there may be survivors like us. I just don't know.

"The next level is for a new contamination. New strains. We don't know the threat level. But let's say I accidentally poke myself with a syringe that may have a strain of some virus. Or let's say we are developing or working on something that mutated into an airborne pathogen. We don't know anything about it yet, and can't determine how dangerous it is. It is sent there and is studied. It will be determined if it goes down deeper or not.

"There are some people that find these things fascinating. There are some that think that, if they can make it, the enemy can make it, and will try to weaponize it. They try to develop these things as well as find a cure. This is big money for pharmaceuticals and big money from the Defense Department."

Murphy sat down. He looked up at Jason and Gizmo and then at Bradley. "We had no idea what we were getting into here when we were recruited. No idea. But now, well, let's get the hell out of here. Being here was like being in prison. The rest of the details must come from Bradley. He's the guy that knows."

The other two were looking at Bradley with disgust now, still clutching their weapons.

"Over there, what Bradley wants to get at, I'm sure is the fail safe. It is for when or if something does get loose or evades security. He wants to push that button. It'll kill everyone here. It'll incinerate everyone. Then, it'll blow it all up. Blow us up.

"The problem is this: We don't know what's down there. He does, and let me tell you something: he's crazy," he looked down at the floor and back up at the two rescuers. "If he were to blow this place, we don't know what would be in the air. We don't know what would escape. We don't know what anyone downwind from this facility would be breathing. Would it kill them? Would it cause a mutation? Would it end life on Earth?

"We don't know these things," and he looked again at Bradley, "But he does, and he's insane. As mad as a hatter."

Terry's voice came over the radio, "Well. That explains the military showing up just now - a whole lot of them. Okay. So let's get you guys out of there. I get, from what I just heard, that light keeps them away. But the acid will eat the lights. So we'll bring extras, and, if they burn out, we can use the others. We'll wrap them in something. Lead foil, and guns, we'll bring guns just in case."

"We need six suits," Jason added. "We can't move without new suits. Ours are melting. Remember, third level. Clean Room."

"Okay. Just hang tight and we'll have you out in about twenty minutes," and Terry clicked off.

They sat and waited and listened for signs of intelligent life outside their room. Time passed as slowly as molasses. Every minute seemed like an hour, until they heard some shooting from the hall. They heard the outside door smash open, then voices, then the entry outside the Clean Room was opened.

Dan and John were there along with some military personnel carrying weapons. They stood outside the glass and looked at them like zoo animals.

"What?" Gizmo asked. "You brought our suits, right?"

"Yah, sure. They're right here." Dan opened the outside door again. "Bring those in," he instructed the men outside. Soon, six wrapped suits were piled outside the glass wall. "We'll step outside and let the air clear. You can come out when you think it's safe and suit up and then show these folks how to put 'em on." They all agreed on the sequence and procedure. "Okay then. See you out here in a few," and Dan disappeared through the door again.

Jason and Gizmo went first and suited up. Once they were done, they called for the rest to come out. Just as they began for the door, Bradley made an attempt at the fail safe.

Murphy was on him and cracked him on his head with the microscope he still held as a weapon, while Peterson dived at him, stabbing him in his arm and Rosen stood on his back. They then grabbed him and dragged him to the outside room to be forcibly suited up with a few punches to the head.

The route back topside was cleared. There were a few gunshots behind them when all were ordered to evacuate with no more shooting. They arrived at the top and approached the command center. Inside were Military brass looking through what appeared to be blue prints and schematics for the facility. A helicopter with a Catskill Pharmacies logo was landing. Jason watched the interaction as he peeled the suit away.

It was clear who was now running the show. It was not he, nor his team, nor was it the Military. It was Catskill calling the shots now. They were there to salvage. Not to protect the People, nor to destroy the threat. Jason and his team were sent off along with the Fire Department personnel. The military began taking instructions from Catskill.

Later that day, there would be an explosion. The wind would carry a cloud across a small town two miles away. The town was occupied beforehand with folks wearing gas masks and carrying guns. Why waste a perfectly good opportunity to test a new drug?

There was never another word about it other than that there was an explosion at a chemical factory with some injuries and loss of life, and life went on.

Chapter Six

Jason was jolted awake the next morning at 4:30 by Bo barking at something outside the motor home. He listened to hear footsteps outside on the gravel and reached for his handgun. There was a loud knocking on the side door and a voice, "Hello. You up in there?" the ranger called.

"Yah! I'll be right out." He hit the floor and pulled on his boots and splashed water on his face, looked out the window and saw the ranger walk down through the dark to the launch. Bo was ready to jump out. The door flew open and they both bounced out onto the ground.

The ranger looked around and said, "Gonna be a nice day today. Probably get some showers this afternoon. I hope it's nothing like yesterday. Your friend was probably pretty unhappy in that weather. That was nasty for a while. Got hail and everything."

"He can take care of himself," he said, holding out his hand to shake, "I'm Jason Brand."

"Jenkins," the ranger said, and shook hands. "Good to meet you." He took his Maglite off his belt and directed the beam to the edge of the water illuminating the dead fish. "Think you can figure out what that's all about?"

"Well. That's what we're out here to do. I'm hoping it's just an underground movement. Sulfur or something. But you never know. We'll take samples to a lab. Sometimes people do dumb things and dump stuff. They're usually just scared and don't know what to do with it. Don't want to get in trouble," Jason said.

"I hope so. Hope it's something simple. Need help with the boat?" Jenkins offered.

"Naw. I got it. I have to pack it anyway and get ready for a hike."

"You be careful up there. There'll be lots of rocks falling after a rain like last night. The gorge empties pretty fast, so the stream won't be too swollen by now. It's the rocks you have to worry about," the ranger told him.

Jason looked at him quizzically, "So, what do you think? Is that why the rash of missing persons?"

"You know what? I just don't know. We haven't found them to ask. But then, if we did, they wouldn't be missing, would they. Some people just take off. You know, tired of the small-town life. But some were hikers.

49

"Maybe they got in trouble. Rocks. Animals. Who knows? Maybe they'll show up. You know, that happens. Someone will scream and alert the whole world when someone is missing. But they forget to do that when they show up, so we still look."

"I guess so," Jason said as he patted Bo, "and I guess once people get the idea people are going missing, they can get desperate and react before they need, before the person is actually missing."

"For sure. Before you know it, there's a whole new urban legend. The Secret Monsters of Ruby Lake," Jenkins snickered. "It's okay with me. Fewer people messing it up the better as far as I'm concerned. Hey. Nice dog. Look at them eyes. Beautiful."

"Thanks. This is Bo. Hardest working dog ever," Jason boasted.

They stood and chatted about ranger things: weather, fires, and visitors to the park, all the while giving Bo all the attention she could ask for.

"Well," Jenkins eventually said, "Sun's coming up and I got ranger business to deal with. Do me a favor and just let us know when you guys leave."

"No problem," Jason told him, and the ranger walked to his truck. Bo and Jason stood for a while watching the sun lighten up the backside of the mountains and started back toward the boat. "Good guy, huh, Bo? Let's look at this boat."

The boat had a foot of water from the rain the night before. He checked to see if he'd forgotten to take the plug out, but no, there was just a pile of rubble that blew in and clogged it. He freed the drain and let it pour out while he went back inside and made breakfast, thinking, "I have to remember to look for that compass."

With the water drained and the gear stowed, he launched. The lake bottom dropped surprisingly fast and the boat was floating free of the trailer and he had it tied up in no time. His wheels spun on the slime covering the ramp and he had to use four-wheel drive to get back up.

With the RV parked and secured, he walked onto the dock and stepped into the boat with Bo jumping in after him. He let the outboard warm up a minute then cast off, and they were gone.

Crossing the lake, navigating through the series of ponds, dodging the sandbars that move and shift after a rain, took longer than he expected. He didn't want to walk in the water, but mostly, he didn't want Bo to get in it until he knew it was safe. So getting up close to the mouth or at least to the side of it was the goal.

They lucked out. There was a natural ramp of sand and smooth stone fairly close to the mouth where he beached his boat and tied it to a tree. Bo was out safe and dry, barking and running and sniffing and following her commands not to eat or drink anything. He let her explore for a while before he called her over to get her backpack secured and then hauled his gear out. He loaded her pack with water for both of them and food for her. Then he stuffed some 550lb cord in her side pouch.

The last thing to do, after putting his backpack on, was to pull his rifle out, which he slung around his neck, making it easy to get at without getting tangled in the rest of his gear. It was a Savage 111, a 30.06. Nuttin fancy. He kept the scope that came from the factory. He never had a problem with it and zeroed it in the first day he got it, and it stayed zeroed.

"A good gun with an angry round," he would say. Not much he could run into that he couldn't take care of with it. But that's not the reason he finally chose the Savage, although accuracy and dependability would turn out to be a big bonus. It was because this rifle only weighed four pounds.

That means a lot when you are hauling your entire trade and supplies up a hill. Every ounce of weight counts. If you did a lot of shooting with it, your shoulder is going hurt and be black and blue the next day because it is so light, but who shoots off a lot of rounds with a 30.06?

He pulled out his map and looked at it. Not because he didn't know where he was going. It was just habit. Up the hill, follow the stream through the gorge it carved out for the past many thousands of years. Not much more to think about. Enough people go up there that there should be a trail of sorts, maybe not a good one after the rain, but a trail.

RUBY LAKE

Chapter Seven

The first leg of the hike was the hardest, with a steep rise where the water picked up speed before it dropped into the lake. It took a good half-hour to get up, about five minutes for Bo. He was winded by the time he reached the top and glad he wouldn't need to drag a tent and sleeping gear up this stream. From there, looking forward, he could see rise after rise as the gorge turned this way and that.

Somewhere along the way on this rugged trail, he should run into Gizmo. He grabbed a water and turned to look back at the lake. He had a view from one end of the lake to the other, with the sun just starting to hit it and the mountains beyond. He took another pull on the water bottle and, as he turned up the trail again, and said, "Nice place, isn't it, Bo?"

She kept bouncing and hopping ahead of him, turning every now and then to make sure he was following and giving a little bark at times as if to let him know he was being too slow. The stream was still running hard with run-off from the rain and there were times there was no trail left at all. They would climb up the cliff and scale along the side of it when they could and catch the trail beyond where it washed out. That way, they kept out of the water.

If they couldn't do that, Jason would cross the water in his waders, drop his gear, and come back and carry Bo across. Bo would climb up on his shoulders and he would take the front legs in one hand and the back in the other and carry her across. It's the fireman hold, doggie style. Then they'd be on their way again.

They were coming to another rise when Bo started acting up. Smelling in the air and growling was her way of showing something was around that she didn't like. It was her danger warning. He looked around, especially behind where he had just come from to make sure they weren't being followed or stalked.

Noise from the rushing water could drown out any sound from an approaching animal. In the best of conditions, some of them were silent anyway. He saw nothing behind him. They were deep in the gorge with the mountain continuing up on one side and a plateau on the other. The plateau, having tall grass, was the most likely place for a hiding predator.

He studied both hills and saw nothing. Finally he pulled out his rifle and looked through the scope. Bo gave a growl and started looking toward the hill with grass, so that is where he pointed the scope. He'd long since quit hauling his heavy binoculars. The scope could do two jobs; aim and look; a much better use of weight.

Bo growling meant something is there. It didn't mean something might be there or she thinks something is there. If she says there is something there, there is something there. He just had to find it before it was here, where he was. That was the idea. Take a little time and find it. Avoid trouble. Chase it away. Scare it. Deal with it, before it deals with you.

Jason never considered it in any way other than this: these animals, they eat just like anything else. Just make sure it doesn't eat you. There is no emotional involvement in it for them. So don't add your emotions to it.

He studied the plateau through the scope. The wind was blowing, moving the grass back and forth in waves. He was looking for a movement, that's all; some movement out of the ordinary.

He caught sight of a bird taking off and studied the area to see if something made it move or if it just wanted to move. He studied the grass and adjusted his scope near where it left. He adjusted it until he could see individual blades of grass, then moved it out farther, then closer.

Time passed and he caught nothing through the scope. It was not "If" something is there, he reminded himself. He wasn't checking to see if something was there. There was something there. What it is and where it is, that's another thing.

Bo did her job. Now he had to do his. It could be a raccoon, a mountain lion, a bear or anything. She kept looking toward the field, so Jason did the same.

After a few minutes, he looked at Bo again to see if the direction she was focused on changed. Then he lifted the rifle and looked again through the scope, this time lower, scanning the cliff and then down to the stream. There it was; a badger. It is a fierce fighter.

"There it is, Bo. Mr. Badger, right there." He watched it bathe itself in the sun, rolling over on its back and letting his belly warm up. "Let's go, Pooch," he said, and she instantly turned and bounded up the next rise.

Jason caught up with her and decided to take a break and eat a bit. He found a flat rock fairly high up and easy to reach. He plopped his backpack down, and then himself. Bo came over and he pulled her pack off as well.

Lunch was simple; dried food for Jason, and for Bo, more dried food, of course. It reduces the weight to have dried food. But Jason always had a can of dog food for her as a reward for when they reached their destination.

They sat and rested. Bo had her head on his leg and Jason was petting her. Now and then, she would get up and lap up some water he had for her in a cup. It was time to move on when she lifted her head up abruptly and started growling again.

They were both high up enough now to get a better view of the field where she was looking. Jason lifted up his rifle and looked in that direction. He studied the field again; watched the grass waving in the breeze, looking for a sign.

Another bird flew off. He looked in the area around it to see if an approaching animal scared it. This time, there would be no badger. There was something in the field.

He was scanning slowly across the field when he saw it. Small. But he saw it. It was an ear. He wouldn't have noticed it if it weren't for a fly or mosquito buzzing it and making it flick. It was the flick that he saw. That was the movement he was looking for. He studied it.

He adjusted the scope to make it clear. The grass was almost at the same height as the ear, but the ear wasn't waving like the grass. As the grass waved, the view of what was below that ear came into focus. It was the head of a large cat. It was a mountain lion, and it had its sight on him and on Bo.

Jason continued to study the cat, amazed that it would sit so still and silent, watching and calculating its potential prey: them. He could almost feel the stare of the large animal piercing through the grass and across the gorge at him.

"Bad kitty. Right, Bo? Baaaad kitty!" He lowered his rifle and patted Bo on the head. "Good job, girl," and lifted the weapon again, wondering at the concentration of the animal.

He caught a look at its eyes when the grass moved. It stared right at him, and he stared right back through his scope. Finally, the cat slowly blinked one time from the sun, and then licked its chops showing its three-inch fangs and continued staring.

It was clear. It wanted them. But wanting and getting are two different things. He decided to give it a scare and let it know that it was going to have to work for its dinner. He focused his scope on a nearby clump of dirt, clicked the safety off and fired into it. The cat jumped up and ran. So did two others that Jason had not seen this whole time.

"Ho! Three of them!" he exclaimed. He watched through his scope as they ran into a clump of bushes. "Well. Let's see if that will change their minds about their dinner plans."

Chapter Eight

They got their gear back on and prepared themselves for the next leg. He should run into Gizmo any time now and would find comfort in numbers, even if it's only two plus Bo. "Let's go, Bo," he called.

The damage to the trail from the rain was beginning to slow them down more as they got higher. There had been rockslides up until now, but they were easy to get around. The water was deeper than normal, but they had managed to get through it.

Now, it was a large slide with the water backing up behind. He checked on each side to see about scaling the walls to get around it, but decided against it. The sides were too wet and too loose. He could end up burying the both of them.

So, climbing over it, was what he decided. The boulders were large, a couple of them as large as a small house, with water running in between them. They navigated their way to the top of the pile of rock and saw the water being dammed behind it.

There was a six-foot tree branch close by, left broken by the falling rock, and he tested the water to see how deep it was. The branch went all the way in and didn't touch the bottom. He couldn't wade, and he couldn't carry Bo through it.

The stream was pulled down like a giant drain or toilet bowl that never stopped flushing, spinning round and round endlessly. If you were unlucky enough to fall in, you would get dragged down by the current and pinned in the rocks below, and you'd have your name and picture up at the park with the rest of the missing persons.

The only way through was to scale along the side of the cliff; what he didn't want to do. He stood up and navigated the rocks to the edge. There was a ledge created by the slide about six feet up he could probably cross on. He called Bo over and lifted her up first. Then he got up himself.

It was much harder than he expected with the pack on and he considered leaving it and going on without it until he ran into Gizmo, which should be soon. But he made it up and followed his dog across, making it about half way to the end before he was stuck. Too much weight to leap and too slippery to get a good jump, he clutched the side of the cliff above the churning water.

Bo was on the other side now, barking. "Alright, alright. I'm coming," Jason told her.

Swinging off his pack, he took it and swung it back and forth until it had enough momentum, letting it go and sending it plummeting toward the edge of the water. It landed up against the cliff and bounced and rolled. He watched, hoping it wouldn't fall in. It rolled once more and stopped. Then it slid toward the rushing currents.

Bo was near, still barking. "Fetch" he called to her. Just then some dirt landed on him. He looked up, half expecting the side of the cliff to be heading down on him. He didn't. What he saw was a cat frantically clawing and gripping at the side of the loose cliff above him, sliding down on him.

He ducked his head and flung his free arm out and made contact with the cat. It was about 180-200 pounds of pure muscle descending on him. The cat, off balance in the slide, could not connect with its prey and went down into the churning bowl of water.

Jason found new agility for the rest of the climb, and reached the end of the ledge just as Bo hauled his gear back from the edge of the rushing current. He grabbed at his rifle and turned to the cat. He watched it being pulled into the circling whirlpool, round and round until its head vanished.

The stalk and ambush predator was gone. Almost in a panic, he quickly spun around for the other two to join the first in a planned and organized ambush, and terror struck as he realized how foolish he had been to just focus on the one while the other two pounced. He raised his weapon ready to fire, imagining a wall of claws and teeth jutting toward him. Then he swung his rifle back toward the cliff, but they were nowhere to be seen.

"Perhaps," he thought, "this one had just gotten too curious and too close to the edge of the cliff, never intending an attack. Yet."

Bo barked, and he looked back at the whirlpool. First, there was a claw coming up the jagged side of a rock out of the water. Then another. Then the head. Then, it pulled itself up, giant and deadly claws, sharp as knives, claws that could rip you apart, finding its way into the tiniest cracks in the rocks to the safety of the slide they had just walked over.

The cat shook itself off, looked at them, and let out a roar. His teeth were about three inches long, maybe more. His claws were about the same. They could rip any man and most animals apart with those weapons.

Jason lifted his rifle, acquired him in the scope, put the crosshairs right behind the ears as it turned from them to cross the ledge they had just climbed over and come toward them, and he pulled the trigger. The cat dropped with its brain stem severed. It was dead instantly.

Again, he spun to make sure the others weren't behind him. Then he scanned the cliff above, where the cat had been. Nothing. He looked at Bo, who was no longer reacting to danger, but prancing back and forth in excitement. He expected Gizmo was close by and may come down when he heard the shot. He expected him to call out. But then, he expected to have met up with him by now.

He looked at his watch. It was going to be dark in a few hours, and they had better get moving. He grabbed his pack and swung it onto his back once more and began the assent.

They moved faster now. It was more serious now. The cat was serious. The other two cats were serious. The dead fish was serious, and no Gizmo yet, that was serious.

Chapter Nine

At least he knew that the lake wasn't the source of whatever was in the water. The fish upstream were sick and dying and many more littered the banks. Whatever it was, it was up ahead.

He came to a stretch of trail that he could see a good thousand yards before it went into another climb. Something was up there. Maybe it was a part of a campsite. Maybe that's where Gizmo set up. He sped up, keeping his eye on the spot.

It appeared to be lying next to the trail. Maybe he set up right beside it, right off to the side of the trail. That is a good, clear marker, easy for him to find if he is off hiking or taking samples. He got closer. Bo leaped ahead to it and stopped and sniffed it. Jason was a couple of minutes behind.

It was mangled and dirty, whatever it was. It wasn't a campsite. It looked like it was clothing, maybe a jacket. It could have been washed down from a campsite up above in the rain. He dropped his backpack and took the barrel of the rifle and prodded it over.

He grabbed a stick and crouched closer and rolled a flap over. It looked like blood, but he wasn't sure because of the rain. He took the stick and lifted a little more and saw gashes in the material.

Some kind of animal shredded it. Rakes all across it. Claws slashing it apart. He crouched, examining it when he turned and looked up the trail and saw something else. A backpack?

He walked toward it. It was a backpack. Not too far from the backpack was a rifle, lying on the ground. He hurried past the backpack to the rifle. It was a .308, a Bushmaster. He ran toward it. Gizmo carried a Bushmaster.

He passed a box of ammo lying on the ground, but went past it to the weapon. He checked the chamber. Empty. He dropped the magazine. Empty. He ran over and picked up the box of ammo. Two rounds were left. He looked around for spent cartridges. None.

"Whatever happened, if this was Gizmos', he emptied and reloaded several times. But maybe not here. No, not here. There was no brass," he thought.

He walked again toward the backpack when he saw something reflecting the sun at the side of the trail. He passed the backpack for the second time to see what it was. It was a knife. A hunting knife. Lying there on the side of the trail.

He tried to piece it all together. He's coming down the trail, shooting, emptying his weapon, possibly reloading farther up the hill, dropping it when it was empty and having only two rounds left, he runs, down the hill. He dumps his backpack for more speed and pulls his knife.

Something is pursuing him. He's scared, maybe. But not so scared that he is unable to function or think, or he wouldn't have dumped his weight and pulled the knife. He loses the knife here. Perhaps it caught him here. But the knife is dropped. Then, there is shredded clothing near the bottom.

He looked for signs of being dragged. He looked for any signs of animals. Footprints. Anything. But the rain had erased any evidence like that. He looked back up the hill. "Maybe up there," he mumbled to Bo.

He called Bo and told her to heel. He didn't want her away and getting hurt. He thought about the sequence again as he walked back up toward the backpack lying on the side of the trail. "Let's see. Came down the hill. Pretty sure he didn't go up. Fired his gun. Emptied his mag, or mags, reloaded and emptied several times because there are only two rounds left."

It reminded him to load his rifle. He'd used two rounds now. His magazine only holds five. That leaves him with only three rounds, and this guy fired, who knows how many.

He dropped his magazine and put two more rounds in, then pulled his bolt back and fed one into the chamber and slammed the bolt forward. Then he snapped the magazine back in. Now he has six shots. Plus, he'll stick the remaining two into the bushmaster. Maybe there's another box in the guys' backpack.

He stopped and checked. No ammo. But he'll have to go through it more thoroughly. Continuing the replay of possible events, "So, he's emptied his magazine for the last time and sees he has two rounds left. If the first forty didn't do the job, the last two probably aren't going to help. But maybe he just doesn't have time to reload."

"So he dumps his gun here. Running down the hill, he peels off his backpack here. Grabs his knife. Loses it here. Torn up, possibly bloody clothing down there."

Jason looked at Bo and said, "So what was he running from, Bo? Let's go up the hill a bit."

Maybe the guy was drunk and couldn't hit anything. This Bushmaster firing a .308 will put down anything he could think of in these parts. Especially all those rounds.

They walked slowly up the trail, looking for spent brass along the way. He paid particular attention to Bo in case she gave him any warning. He came over the crest and into a flat area where the stream carved out a small lake. There was camping gear strewn about; a tent in shreds; an old campfire surrounded by rock someone had made.

Off to the north was a large boulder where he finally saw brass lying on the ground and walked over and looked. Two empty magazines were lying in the dirt. He tried to imagine how the rounds were ejected from the Bushmaster and where they would land.

"That would place the man...right about... here, probably." Looking down, he saw what could be where the toes of the man's boot dug in. He looked out in the most likely direction he would be shooting: off onto the flat grassy area where the cats were, where he saw them earlier today, where they had been stalking him. "But three magazines, that's not forty, that's a hundred and twenty rounds," he mumbled to himself.

He pulled his rifle up and looked through the scope onto the field to see if there were any dead animals, and searched again for something that makes it's living by hiding, stalking, and ambushing. It's what they have done for as long as they have existed, and they are good at it.

Was Gizmo up ahead further, Jason wondered, or was this his gun, his shells, his gear, and his blood? Maybe they got him and dragged him off and ate him. He went back to the destroyed campsite and kicked over a few items to see if he could identify anything.

Then he saw it. There, half buried in mud, were pieces of a torn-up bag with "Environmental Protection" on it, with the rest of the bag shredded and lying somewhere else. Under the words, was what was left of the logo, a circle with a blue field inside.

He stared at it, reading it over and over, refusing at first to believe his own eyes. But, there was no doubting it and there was no use denying it. The bag said what it said.

Bo growled. Jason looked up to see what direction she would point in. "No time to grieve now," he told himself, "You'll end up the same, and you have to think about Bo." She was looking down the trail now. He checked through the scope again. He couldn't see them, but he knew they were there. Bo told him, and Bo never lies.

Chapter Ten

He figured it took them a good eight or nine hours to get up here. Going back down would be much easier and faster. If he had to, he would dump his and Bo's packs and power through it. Get the ranger and a hunting party up here and track down these animals. Drag back what was left of Gizmo and his stuff. Poor bastard.

"No way are we spending the night here, Bo," he told her.

Should he take the Bushmaster? It only had two rounds. But that would give him eight shots before a reload with the six in his gun. No, he decided. He should get down quick. He didn't need the weight.

If he starts now, he'll be at his boat right around sundown, give or take an hour. If he left his backpack, he could make even better time. He'd leave the one on Bo for water.

He realized he was panicking. He has to think straight and not panic. He put that cat down with one shot. "Think straight. Don't panic," he told himself.

Crouching down beside his dog, he scanned the area ahead of him again. "Why would he fire so many rounds? Why didn't he leave any dead animals? Did they get dragged off and eaten as well?" he wondered.

He went through his pack and pulled out some snacks for the two of them, some for now, and some for the trip down. They munched on them for a few minutes, and he scanned the sides of the trail again. Seeing it was clear, he stood up, put his backpack and the Bushmaster close to the dead fire, he then emptied his own box of ammo and shoved them into his vest, and started at a quick pace down the trail.

Twenty rounds in a box, and that's all he had, minus the two rounds he already fired.

They went past the backpack again, past where the knife was found, down to the shredded clothing and stopped.

He checked behind him to make sure nothing was following. "Paranoid," he thought. Then he looked at the hills off to the left and watched the grass blow. Then he looked up the face of the cliff above where he stood, above where the remains of the clothing were.

"Keep your head, Pal. No panicking," he said to himself, and pulled his rifle around again and scanned all around, Bo, fully alert, faithfully waiting for him to get moving again.

Satisfied, he started. He let the momentum pull him down the hill into a slow jog. Bo was happy with that. She could run like this the whole time. She kept pace slightly behind him, the way she is trained to do on jogs. Not too close so that she could trip him. Not so far that another dog or person could get between them.

They rounded the spot where they first caught sight of the gear and were about to descend to where the mountain lion had met its end when Jason pulled up to an abrupt stop.

There is an old, tried and true maxim if you are following someone or stalking someone. DON'T LOOK AT THEM. That is it. They teach it to Intelligence people. They teach it to snipers. Don't focus on them until you are ready. You don't look directly at them. It works for people and it works for animals.

There is a sense that everyone has. They know when they are being looked at. It is natural radar. Especially with people. It's that feeling they get when you do that. Someone is watching. Something bad is going to happen. The feeling Jason was getting now that brought him to a sliding stop.

He crouched down and looked straight ahead. Bo came up beside him and nuzzled his ear. Then she looked straight ahead, ears up and nostrils filled with the surrounding scents. That's where they stayed, perfectly still with that feeling of being watched, that radar burning.

Was it from the front or was it from the rear? Was it from the sides? If there were an attack, from where would he come, if he were an animal? Do animals even think that way? Do they plan that way?

Sit perfectly still. It's a natural thing for animals. Don't move. It's the movement that'll get you killed. Bo knew it. She stood there without moving a muscle. Rabbits do it. They'll run out and stop. The predator is watching for motion; something they can track. Something they can stalk. It's the thrill of it. The reward - dinner.

He sat frozen. "Check behind you," he said to himself. He did. He had that feeling. The hair was standing up on the back of his neck. He could hear himself breathing and his heart pounding after the run. He wondered if they could hear it as well. He looked through his scope again.

"Am I the hunter now?" he pondered. "Do they have this same feeling? Are their "spidey" senses tingling too? If it's the same cats, I wonder if they know I killed one of their own? Would that make them cautious of me, or would I be a threat to be eliminated?" Another question to which he had no answer. Do they even think like that? But he is being the predator now. If one moves and he sees it, it's dead.

Bo was still, but hadn't sounded an alarm. Jason lost track of time. How long had they been in this frozen state? He glanced up at the sky and saw clouds moving in. He had to get to his boat and across the lake before it started to rain.

They began to creep forward, up and over the crest, down to the punch bowl where they left the cat. Crouching, quietly, rifle in hand, he rounded the corner and began the descent. There was a good clear view of the flat grassy area and he stopped again and trained his scope on it.

He sat, frozen, making certain nothing would pounce on him from above like the last time. He brought his rifle down to where they scaled the cliff and where the cat fell on him. He moved over to where the cat lay dead. Except it wasn't there.

He swung the rifle from left to right across the fallen rock to see if it moved. It wasn't there. It just wasn't there. He scanned the entire rockslide. It wasn't there.

"If the other cats came and dragged it off, that means they could be down in the gorge with me and Bo," he thought.

Then he wondered, "Would these cats eat another cat?" He wondered if maybe it wasn't really dead. Maybe he only knocked it out. Maybe it came to and ran off.

No. He knew his shot. Well placed. Just where he wanted it. A shot he has made before. No. It was dead. But that meant something was there. Something took it. He checked again through the scope to see exactly where it was when it dropped. The blood was there. No way it could have fallen back into the water. No way.

So something took it, and that means they are now on the same turf, in the same gorge, surrounded by the same cliff walls, with only one way out, and since he did not pass any wandering wildcats on the way down, they were between him and his escape route; between him and his boat; between him and safety.

Now, Jason allowed emotion to enter. He got determined. He got mean and he got mad. He wasn't about to end up being a mass of shredded clothing half buried in mud like what he saw up the trail.

There was no way around it. There was no other way.

He was going hunting.

Chapter Eleven

A crack came from above him that made him jump. Thunder, and the clouds were rolling in. He got up and started moving to where he left the dead cat. "Tracks. I need to see the tracks. See how many, and where they went. What direction. Were they even cats? Did they go up one of the cliffs, or down the trail towards his boat?"

There were three cats when he fired that shot. That's what he saw. Maybe he missed others. Maybe they didn't run off like the others.

A pride of mountain lions can have as many as five cats, the mother and four cubs that she would teach how to hunt until they were full grown. They were nearly full grown now, and she was teaching them well.

Did he miss something? That was the question. He's got to see the tracks before the rain washes them out. Maybe it wasn't cats that dragged it off, so he'd better move.

Down they went. This time, he had Bo running point. She set the pace. Down the hill to the punch bowl they went. If something was in front, she would tell him.

They got to the dammed up water and he waited and looked around before lifting Bo to the ledge again. If these were cats, they would be on you before you would know they are there. They are quiet. They are fast. They are deadly.

There would be no way to hear the movement of approaching danger over the rushing water, so he moved fast. They would be the most vulnerable on the cliff. He wouldn't be able to use his weapon.

He checked the knife clipped to his belt. Adjusted it to be the easiest to grab in a hurry and wondered if he should snap open the loop that held it in the sheath. He decided against it. It could drop out if he opened it. It would be his weapon of last defense, and he may need it. The other guy did.

Trying to picture what he would do if they were attacked, he imagined being pulled off the cliff into the spinning water, pulling his knife, and being dragged down and pinned to the rocks below. They scurried across the slippery ledge to the rockslide and leapt off, running to where the animal died. Bo sniffed at the blood. Jason stood back and looked the scene over. No drag marks. No carcass. No nothing.

He ran to one side of the river to look for tracks in the soft dirt, then the other. He checked the cliff face and saw what may have been

69

footprints of animals sliding down. There were two sets. "Good. Two of them. It's probably the same pride," he said to Bo. So now he knew where they had been. But they were sliding down. He needed to know where they went.

"What did they do with the animal?" he wondered. They had to drag it. It would be easy to see that. They didn't just eat it right here. There was nothing to show, other than a blood stain, that there was even anything here, and the rain would soon wash that away. He wasn't sure that they would eat their own kind. It was one of those things that he cursed himself now for not learning.

"Not a trace," he said out loud. They jumped down off the rockslide to the trail below to look for tracks when it began to sprinkle harder. He still had about a mile to go to the boat. He could do that in about forty-five minutes, given the rough terrain.

He walked across the entire width of the gorge looking for tracks and mumbling to himself, "Not a damn sign. Nothing. Maybe they came straight up the stream. But no, not a cat. They can swim and they will jump in after something, but that wouldn't be their choice if they had another."

Walking over to the river bed, he looked down anyway to see if the bottom was disturbed, then looked back up to the rockslide. He could find not one sign. Not one print. Perhaps they got up behind him further back on the trail. Maybe they did that. Got behind him.

That's gotta be it. Stalk. Ambush. Eat. They must have gotten behind them. They would be downwind from him too. Smart animals.

The hunter once again began to feel like the hunted.

Bo barked toward the trail they had just come down. Somewhere behind the rockslide, he heard the roar of a mountain lion. Bo went wild.

"They did it," he thought. "They got behind me." He didn't see it. He didn't know it. But they did it. They got behind him and it was now a matter of time before they make their move. The shot didn't scare them off. Killing one of them, one of their pride, didn't scare them off.

Jason contemplated what to do next. The rain will be pouring down soon. If it is going to be anything like yesterday, it would not be pleasant there in the canyon. In fact, it'll be downright dangerous.

Boating across the lake in a storm like that would be dangerous too. He could do it, but if anything happened, both he and Bo would be in some bad water at a bad time. That is, if he made it to the boat before the ambush.

The other option; go back up the river after them and put them down. He knows they circled behind him, so it is a pretty good guess they are stalking him now. He could go after them. Track them. Stalk them. Hunt them. Kill them. They asked for it.

There was another option though. One he began to feel more comfortable with the more he thought about it. Move quickly downstream, pick up his pace, get a little distance between them if he can, and set up an ambush. Get in a blind; a protected area. A place they can't get at. Wait for them.

That's what he'll do. It's safer. It will be on his terms. It'll happen where he chooses. He will go. He will set up his own ambush. He will wait for them. He will wait for them and he will kill them.

So they ran. He ran as fast as he could, leaping over rocks and taking turns and twists with the trail, Bo jumped along with him, having no trouble keeping up. The rain started coming down hard now. He could feel himself slip almost every time he took a jump and landed.

The clay was like slime that he would slide in as it built up in cakes on his soles. The pebbles that washed down from the sides onto rocks he jumped on were like marbles that he could roll on.

He didn't know how far back they were. He knew they were cats, and cats like catching things that moved, and they were moving. If he went down, if he fell, who knows if they would be on him or not.

He came around a bend and saw what he was looking for. Cliff faces on either side. About twenty-five feet up one side was a rock with a tree where the root found purchase and was now growing out the side of the cliff. It was just a little too high for the cats to jump and just a little too steep for them to climb, hopefully. But it was perfect for him and Bo. He would get up there and it would be his ambush spot; his sniper position.

They ran directly under the tree and Jason quickly looked back up the trail to see how far back they were. He heard them roar again. They were close, but he couldn't tell how close, and they were headed his way.

He called Bo over and rummaged through her saddle bag. Pulled out the 550lb. cord and looked around for a heavy stick and tied the cord to it. He threw the stick over the tree and let the cord slide through his hand until the stick was at eye level. Then he tied the other end of the cord to Bo's backpack.

He took one more look around and saw them. They were rounding the corner, coming up over some boulders left from a slide, and coming after them. If only he had a little more time, it would have been perfect.

He told Bo to stay, grabbed the cord and propelled himself up the cliff to the tree. Swinging his leg around it, he could see they were going for Bo. She was barking and growling. Her hair was up on her neck. She began to crouch and snarl. He looked again, they were coming. She wouldn't have a chance against two full-grown mountain lions. They were about to make a run for her.

He could swing his gun around and shoot. But what if he missed the moving targets? What if he only got one? His dog, and another friend, would be dead. He decided to stick to the plan, what was left of it. He reached down to the cord and started pulling, hand over hand, and Bo lifted off the ground.

The cord was slippery in the rain. "Shit, you're heavy!" he yelled. He could see the cats clearly now. They stopped for a brief second, confused, and watched the dog rise up in the air. It registered to them, they were about to miss out on a meal if they didn't hurry. So they darted toward Bo.

Jason saw them dash at her and yelled as loud as he could without slowing down. He knew they would get there before Bo was up high enough. So he yelled a blood curdling roar. It worked.

It made them pause and slowed them for just the seconds he needed to get her up a little higher. They were under her now, leaping and roaring and slashing at her, Bo, growling and nipping at each jump they made at her.

He got her up and onto the ledge, and clambered there himself, finally whipping his rifle off his back and ready to point it down at the animals when one of them got hold of the cord with the stick tied to it. It yanked and grabbed at it tooth and claw, pulling Bo into him toward the edge and into their waiting claws.

Jason had to decide to let the gun go or let Bo go. He grabbed Bo and held her. He could feel the weight of the cat pulling on her and knew he would not be able to hold for long, and if the second cat joined in, they would both go down.

Bo was yelping, trying to claw her way to the back of the ledge. He held onto her, put his foot against the tree and, pushing with every bit of strength he had, reached for his knife and brought his arm almost under his own throat and cut the cord.

It fell on the cats, draping over one of their heads and on the back of the other. One of them pounced on the stick that was tied to it, seeing that it was not alive and not food, looked back up at the two hostages on the side of the cliff and jumped at them. Jason watched over the edge, knife in hand, looking down as they leaped and scratched over and over to get at them.

Chapter Twelve

Once he had convinced himself that the cats couldn't get at them and they were safe for the time being, he sat back against the cliff wall and let out a long breath. "Bad, BAD kitties, huh Bo?" and he gave her a little pet on the neck and sat there catching his breath while Bo barked and whined and snarled down at the cats, taunting them and making them more and more furious.

He looked over the ledge again to see where his rifle had landed. It was stuck on a rock about four feet down. The plan would have been perfect except that they couldn't do it. They were supposed to be up there and in position when the cats came by. He was in a great sniper position. It would have been two shots and two kills. Or, at least one shot and the other cat running away.

It was a good ambush plan to get up on the cliff and snipe them from safety, but now, they were snipers without a gun. It was a good ambush plan, to launch a surprise attack, except they were the ones surprised, and it was a good ambush plan, to sit and wait for them, except now, the cats are the ones waiting below. But other than that, it was a damn good plan.

He looked over the edge again and a cat leaped at him, falling short and sliding back down the cliff. Maybe if he waits long enough, they'll get bored and move off and he can get his weapon back. Hopefully, they'll figure out that they failed.

Jason and Bo sat. The rain poured, the thunder cracked, and the wind blew. About ten feet above where they sat, there was an overhang that gave them partial protection from the rain. Down below, the cats snarled and leapt and roared and made repeated attempts to get at them.

Jason, armed with his knife, would peak over the edge to size things up sending the lions into another rage. One time, he thought one of them was going to make it up, but the soft face of the cliff couldn't hold its weight and gave way.

They seemed to wander off from time to time, but only for a short distance, and then come back with renewed energy. Eventually, they will have to leave. They will have to eat, and hopefully, they will have figured out that they were not going to eat Bo and Jason. It was just a matter of time before they would have to hunt again.

Each time they wandered off, Jason would study how long it would take them to come back when they notice his movement. He calculated how much time it would take him to get over onto the tree, wrap his legs around it, swing down to grab the rifle off the side of the cliff, and get back up to safety.

The last thing he wanted was to misjudge that and have his head dangling low enough under the tree for the cats to grab. He would wait until they walked a short distance and time them, imagining the movements he would make. Eventually, he stepped out onto the tree to see if that would make them react any faster. It did and he would take that into account.

Each time they left, they would get a little further away, and he would get closer to grabbing his weapon before they would show up for a new attempt. Bo and Jason watched them slowly wander off, this time nearly out of sight. One of them curled under a brush and the other seemed to go off back up the river.

Bo was told to stay and Jason crept onto the tree one more time. No cats yet. He looked around and saw nothing coming at them, wrapped his legs around the tree and swung upside down, grabbing his gun. As quick as he could, he grabbed the trunk of the tree and, while holding the rifle, tried to get himself back onto the trunk, instead of under it.

The motion alerted the cat that was napping and it came running. Seeing the best opportunity yet for it to get a meal, the cat leaped with new energy and spirit at the tree, raking at Jason, leaping at the cliff wall trying kick off it to get more height.

At one point, Jason felt him nick his vest with its claw. It was only a matter of time before it succeeded. He couldn't hold the weapon and right himself at the same time.

Jason got himself as tight as he could to the trunk of the tree, and shimmied upside down toward the cliff. When he thought he was close enough, he held the gun by the barrel, and slid it as far as he could toward Bo, then he told her to fetch. She grabbed the gun by the strap and dragged it onto the ledge.

Success!

He flipped himself on top of the trunk once more and scrambled over beside Bo. The cat went wild. He took up the rifle and looked over the edge. There was only one now. He flipped the safety off and leaned over the edge again, put the stock up to his cheek and tried to look through the scope.

While it sat in the rain with the cats jumping and stirring up dirt, and Jason and Bo knocking dirt off their perch, it had gotten so wet and caked with mud that he couldn't see through it.

Again, he pulled back to the cliff wall. Wiping the lens off and checking through it to make sure he could see, he wondered where the other cat is. Maybe it did give up. Maybe it got hungry and went away to hunt. Maybe it forgot them.

Once again, he poked his head over the side. The other cat was gone too. He looked through the scope toward where it had found shelter earlier. It was wet again, and in the dark, with a wet and smudged lens, the scope was useless.

Reaching his hand into his vest, hoping he might have put the lens caps there instead of the backpack, he found some tissue and cleaned the scope and checked through it. It was dark and difficult to focus on anything, but it was better than it was.

He put the tissue back in his pocket and thought, "No. If there were two cats, one wouldn't leave the other. They would hunt together, the mother teaching the nearly full-grown cub."

"Where was the second one?" he wondered as he sat with the rifle across his knees and a hand covering each end of the scope. Catching some food for the two to share? No. They would work together, and their food was right here.

The rain started to let up as the night wore on into the early morning. After hours of sitting on the cold wet stone, he was feeling cramped and decided to adventure out onto the tree again and see the reaction he gets. The cats had been there so many times without any counter attack or reprisal that they must feel comfortable now about it. They would feel that it is safe. But he has his rifle now.

If he could get the one out here now and get him under the tree, he would shoot it and leave only one. The sky was beginning to show signs of light. He could make out trees and rocks. He checked the scope to make sure it was light enough to use, rose to step out onto the tree and it came running at him once more.

Straight down, he looked, raised his weapon to his cheek and pulled the trigger. "Click" was all the sound it made.

As the gun was wedged between rocks on the cliff face, the rain poured down the barrel and ran into the magazine, soaking the ammo. He leapt back against the cliff wall, pulled the bolt back and ejected the round and slid it forward again, pulling a new round from the magazine.

That's when the second mountain lion appeared on the tree that was their safety.

While Bo and Jason were being kept in their perch, one of the lions went back up the river, climbed up the cliff and approached them from the plateau above. No, they wouldn't hunt alone. Not when there are two of them to work as a team. Now the second lion was three feet in front of him. The thought crossed his mind to hit him with the rifle and grab his knife. He might be able to knock it off the tree.

Bo was up front barking and biting, growling and snapping until the saliva was spitting out her mouth. The cat curled its gums back showing her huge teeth that might soon be sinking into them. With ears pinned flat against its head, it slashed at Bo. She pulled back and snarled and snapped at the claws.

The sound was like nothing he'd ever heard before. It was deafening. Bo held her ground. He'd never heard her make noises like this. Jason was yelling at the top of his lungs too. The cat would make a ferocious attack and Bo would stand her ground. Dog and cat, a huge cat, in mortal combat. Fangs flashing and claws flying.

Jason stood up and pointed the weapon at it and pulled the trigger again. "Click" was all it would do. He ejected it and loaded the next, hoping the water didn't seep into the magazine that deep. "Click". Should he take out the magazine and remove the bullets and put in new ones? Would he have time before it killed Bo? He ejected again and slammed the bolt forward. This was his fourth round. "Click". Only two left now.

The cat below was spinning in circles and running back and forth in case one of them fell or tried to flee. It's how they hunt. They make something run and then they catch it. It's what they do.

He raised the gun again as the big cat in front of Bo was about to make a final lunge and grab her and pull her down, got it in the sites, pulled the trigger, and BLAM! The round hit it in the head with such force that it went in summersaults through the air and onto the ground a few feet from the cat below.

The animal below bellowed and roared at the sight of another of its pride flying through the air and landing lifeless. It went over and nuzzled it and sniffed it, and then, it just ran off, bounding back up the stream.

Jason watched the muscles rippling as it took giant forty-foot leaps across boulders he would have to climb over. Jump from one side of the stream to the other without even touching the water. Trot up a log to the top of another boulder and leaping into the air onto another. Then, it was gone.

Jason pulled Bo over to check for injuries. He couldn't see any blood on her face or paws. He checked her back legs and they were fine. He sat down to catch his breath after the ordeal, grabbed a bottle of water from the backpack and twisted the top, not even noticing it was empty. He grabbed another and shook it. It was empty.

He loosened the backpack from Bo and held it up to look at it. It was shredded, just like the jacket up the trail. He looked it over, turning it this way and that. The backpack had protected her. The only thing stopping those long nails from killing his dog was that the nails didn't get through the water bottles.

It was getting light now and he could see the dead animal below. Bo wanted to get at it and was looking down, anxiously whining. Getting down would be another problem with the cord being cut and lying next to the cat. If he hung down from the tree, he would only have about a one-story drop. He could do that and hopefully not sprain his ankle.

He climbed out on the tree and began to swing down. Bo got excited and, not wanting to be left behind, crawled out on it as well. The weight of the two after the thrashing of a full-grown mountain lion was too much for the roots and it fell, giving both Jason and Bo a bumpy ride down the cliff. Jason landed with one foot down and his back against the trunk and rolled. Bo jumped when she saw she was going to hit the ground and immediately ran over to the cat and sniffed it.

He walked over to the animal and stood there looking at it, got on one knee and lifted up the gums to reveal its fangs. Then picked up and pressed on a paw and watched the claws pop out. "Big cat," he said and then stood there looking while Bo sniffed and examined every part. He let her. She earned it and she deserved it. Jason took a step toward the center of the gorge and looked up to where the last cat ran.

"It ain't comin' back, Bo. It's the only one left and we just thinned out its herd. I don't think it'll want any part of us," and then he yelled up the canyon, "You better stick to rabbits, you son of a bitch!"

With a short whistle to Bo, they headed toward the boat. Every now and then, he looked behind him, just in case. The going was a slow, even pace. How would he deal with this? Gizmo? He would talk to the ranger and let him know what happened and where; he would call the office and let Terry know the bad news about Gizmo; he would see if the ranger wanted him to hike up there with them; he would talk to Gizmo's wife; he would get good and drunk, and he would quit his job – again, and permanently.

Chapter Thirteen

The rear of the boat was nearly under water from rain throughout the night. His gas can was floating near the seat and was being held there only by the gas line. The cushions would have been gone if they hadn't been velcroed.

He called Bo up onto the bow and reached under for the bucket and started bailing. The tree to which he tied the bow had held and he was glad he beached it the way he did or the downpour from the night before might have filled it so much that the stern would have been fully below the water.

While he was bailing, Jason stopped and looked around and wondered where Gizmo might have put in. There were plenty of ponds he could pull into, but usually they are pretty close on choices of where to put in, and Gizmo's boat was nowhere around.

Finally, the boat was floating again. He jumped in and cranked the engine over and it fired right up. "Good ole' American made," he said, and jumped back out, untied the bow and gave it a shove off the sandy beach, hopping onto the bow.

Once they had navigated through the ponds and marshes and were into the actual lake headed for the motor home, he figured there would be signal and reached for his cell phone. "Darn it. It's in the backpack," he muttered as he looked back to the trail and stared for a minute. He could have sworn he saw movement before he lost the view up the Gorge.

With the boat tied up at the dock, he and Bo walked to the motor home exhausted. It was 7:00 in the morning and they had been going since 4:30 the day before. Too tired to jump up above the driver's seat, he shoved the bags and gear that didn't fit anywhere in the small RV that was lying on the rear bed aside and slumped down into it with Bo following, lying down at his feet.

Trying to piece it all together as he started to drift off was difficult. What happened? Too many things didn't make sense. Why all those rounds were fired from the Bushmaster, for starters. He had to be drunk or something. Except there is no way he would haul booze up that hill.

Unless he had some help, maybe. But they definitely don't bring vacationers with them. Gizmo was a good shot, as good as Jason. They'd been to the range together. It just wasn't right. It took one shot. One shot per animal.

But then, maybe he was there with someone else. Or maybe more than one. Then, if he was in a shootout, it makes sense to have that many rounds. A firefight, maybe. He found the .308 casings, why didn't he look farther out for shells for return fire?

Panic. That's why. He panicked. Dammit, why did he panic? He even told himself not to panic.

It was the missing person flyers, the ones on the notice board. Then there were the ones Gizmo left him. Then there were all those notices; danger this, danger that, danger rock slides. Danger! Danger! Danger!

It skewed his thinking. Dammit! Then the camp that was destroyed. Then the damn cats. Of course. It made him panic. He should have checked the other side of that boulder to see if rounds were hitting it, if someone was firing at him.

As he drifted off, he thought about panic and firefights while he fell into a dream.

"I gotta go," he yelled as he swung the door open.

"Hold on. Someone has to come with you," the Lieutenant yelled. "You can't go out there yourself. You'll get lost," then, looking around, "Huggins. You!" he called.

Huggins jumped up, rifle in hand and was at the door with Jason. They stepped through the door, and there they were, in Iraq, patrolling outside of Ramadi, stuck in a sand storm. A brown out, they called it. You couldn't see your hand in front of your face. They spotted a blown out building just before it hit and pulled in for shelter.

Eight of them jumped out of the two Humvees and took up positions. They cleared the building, set up a perimeter, and sat against the walls to wait out the storm.

Jason didn't mind. It might be the best sleep he's had in a while, and they've been getting precious little of it lately. The new Lieutenant had a real hard-on for his next promotion, so he volunteered his guys for every mission he could - sleep or not.

That's what got them here this time; volunteered after three missions in one day. They were supposed to do a patrol, meet up with another bunch of officers wanting their precious Combat Badges and bringing their own volunteers, but he guessed those guys couldn't get their panties on in time. There was a report of Haji movement coming this way. The idea of finally getting some actual action got them all wet.

Then the storm hit and they were blind. If they can't see Haji, Haji can't see them either, the lieutenant would say. "Screw this nozzle" Jason thought, "Wait till he gets some real contact. Throwing out words of wisdom like that won't help him a bit."

There they were, another asshole looking to get a promotion at their expense, waiting for some other assholes to get their promotions and badges. "At least this time, they stand a chance of getting their asses shot off like the rest of us," he thought in his dream.

So there they were, in Jason's dream, and he had to take a leak, and that is why they were outside now. Across the lot was a row of Port-A-Potties in this dream, much like they had in some Forward Operating Bases he was in, if they were lucky. His mission now, the most important mission so far today, was to make it 30 yards across this lot in a blinding sand storm and take a leak.

They stepped into the dirt lot, Huggins left hand on Jason's right shoulder, weapon up. Stepping in unison into the mud they call air. Humid. Dirty. Smelly. Filthy. They would breathe this hot brown mixture of filth and choke on it.

It got in their clothes, and when they sweat, which was always, and it dried, their clothes could stand by themselves. Huggins would take his jacket and stand it at a window or opening and put a helmet on it to see if he could draw fire.

They would even give it a name sometimes. For a while it was Lt. Dan. Other times it was Pyle. It was foul, this place. It's in your eyes. It's up your nose. It's in your mouth. It works its way into your weapons, your equipment, your vehicles, everything.

Jason thought he heard a sound and dropped to one knee. He listened. The howling wind could play tricks on you. The muddy air could make you think you see something that you don't. But then, it could also hide something you should see, like Haji, and it can drown out something you should hear.

Haji could be here, and Haji doesn't have weapons that jam up with sand. He has AKs. You can bury them in sand and then crap down the barrel and they'll still work. Haji lives here. He lives in this. He's eaten and breathed this muck his whole life. He crawls through it.

They stayed there for a moment, waiting and watching and listening. You can think you see things when you look through a wall of flying mud. You can think you hear things through the howl of the wind. You can do that, and you may be mistaken, and maybe not. But the bigger mistake is to think you didn't hear it or see it when you did.

The first mistake can make you do things like drop to your knee and scour the area and wait until you know it's safe, like they were doing now. The other, it can make you drop dead from a bullet or a properly placed knife. It is your choice, and Haji is there to give you either.

After a while, Jason got up again. He really had to go now, and he was half way to his destination. They stumbled through the empty lot,

Huggins trailing behind, feeling his way until he ran into the burn barrel. "Shit! I'm too far north!" Jason called.

The barrel was about twenty yards from the first shithouse. They'll never find it in this mess. How would he ever get back? He's already lost his sense of direction. He tried to wipe his goggles clear. It made no difference. If they were clean, he would still not be able to see through this wall of brown blowing sandy sludge. "I can't see!" he yelled.

He felt his way around the burn barrel to try to get a sense of direction when something hit the barrel. It was a bullet. It ricocheted off the side. He spun and drew his weapon up ready to fire. "BAM" another shot fired and hit the barrel again. He shot in the direction of the rifle sound. "I can't see!" he yelled again. Then, bang, another one and then another.

He returned fire into the muddy air without any idea of where the enemy was. Bang! Bang! "I can't see!" he yelled again. Bang! Came another round. He could feel liquid on his face. Was he hit? No. It must be Huggins blood.

Panic struck. He yelled again, "I can't see!" and fired some more. "Huggins!" He went to wipe the blood from his face, and the firefight started. Rapid fire. Bang! Bang! Bang! Over and over.

Something knocked him over. He was down. He could feel himself lying on his back. Where was Huggins? He couldn't see. He tried to roll over and he lifted his weapon and pulled the trigger. It jammed. He pulled his knife and crawled around the barrel. He felt someone. Was it Huggins? Or was it Haji?

The firing continued. He grabbed the person by the shoulder and got up close to look. "I can't see!" he screamed again. He tried to decide what to do, he was panicked. Were they in the compound? Should he knife him? What if it's Huggins? He can't see either. Will Huggins knife him by mistake?

He whipped around after some more fire hit the barrel and pulled his 9 mil and fired into the dark mass.

But something was wrong in this dream. He wiped more blood off his face and reached for his rifle to try to get it cleared. Something was wrong. The firing went on. How could they get into the compound? They weren't in a compound. They were in an abandoned building. They were in the front yard. There were no burn barrels.

Bang! Bang! Changed to Bark! Bark! He opened his eyes and Bo was licking his face and whining, then stepped back and barked once more. He sat up and looked around, getting his bearings. He looked at Bo and said, "Let's go outside. I gotta take a leak."

Chapter Fourteen

He was standing outside the RV when he heard some chatter down near his boat and turned. It was a family standing on the dock, the kids throwing stones in the water. The woman looked up at him and quickly turned her head. "Oops," he said to himself. "Should have looked first, or used the bathroom in the motor home."

He caught a glimpse of their car, piled with their travel things stacked around and tied to the cargo container from some auto parts store.

That's when it hit him. "Where is the truck?" and looked around in every direction as he pulled up his fly. "Gizmos' truck, where is it?" It never crossed his mind when he first arrived. He never looked. No boat. No truck. No Gizmo. It was the panic that did it.

It was the fear that the missing persons notices and danger warnings put into him, into his mind. It denied him logic; denied him objectivity; denied him the fruits of observation. He was on the road to hell; the road to panic.

He bolted for the RV and jumped in with Bo right behind. "We can find the truck. His truck...the cops, they can find it, we can tell them and they can..," he stopped, realizing he was speaking to a dog.

They keys. Did he leave them up the trail in the backpack? They weren't in his pockets. "Shit!" He yelled, checking his vest pockets. Only bullets. He darted out the door and was about to force the vacationers to take him to the station.

He turned to lock his RV and realized he didn't have the keys to do it with. It was habit. "Wait," and reasoned it out, he had opened the door after they came back across the lake. "The keys are here," he thought. He looked in the lock on the door in case he left them hanging there. He checked the ground around the door in case they fell.

He went back inside, looked on the table. No. Looked in the ignition. No! Did he drop them on the way from the boat? No! He got into the RV, so he had to have them. Then he stopped and thought, went back to the bed he almost never sleeps in and moved some of the strewn items around and heard the jingle, lifted the corner of a sleeping bag, and there they were.

Grabbing them up and racing to the front to start the RV, he berated himself. "What the hell, Jason. That was stupid. Use your head. Use logic." But he knew it wasn't logic that was at fault. It was panic. It was panic and panic denies logic. Panic denies all.

The RV fired right up. Shifting gears as soon as he heard the motor catch, he stopped. "Think," he told himself, "Don't panic," and slammed it back in park, jumped up and ran out of the RV, leaving Bo inside. He ran to the back of the vehicle and started cranking the jack on the trailer.

"I'll leave this here. Nobody's going to take it. Nobody around here anyhow, and so what if they do?" as he furiously cranked the jack and glanced over at his boat and thinking of someone grabbing it. "That would suck," then he flipped the lock on the hitch, gave the trailer a shove, and it was free.

Heading down the washboard road again to the ranger station was much easier and faster without the trailer. "That's it. Cool head. Think about it before you do something. Plan. Use reason."

Now he was putting it all together again on the drive. It started to make sense. He was using his head again. There was no panic. There was a firefight. Lots of firepower from Gizmo's side. So they must have been well armed. "Wait. Just wait there, Pal. You don't know that," he thought. What did he know? What exactly did he know?

He knew there was shooting. Quite a bit of it. He knew it was from behind a rock, so it was likely for cover, but he didn't know that for sure. Could have been anything. Someone taking target practice and using the rock to steady his gun.

"Don't be stupid. Gizmos' truck is gone. His boat, you never saw it. Maybe it's gone. Gizmo - no Gizmo. The EPA sack torn and shredded. Lots of rounds fired." Those things were all real and he saw them, he told himself.

Then there were the animals. At least three of them. But he put two of them down with one shot each. You can argue about the best round, .308 or a 30.06, and he and Gizmo often did debate which was best. The fact is that they are both bad-assed rounds. Either of them could do the job.

Jason chose the rifle he has for the weight and accuracy. Gizmo chose his because he wanted an automatic. They were pretty equal shots, he and Gizmo. No way he took all those shots and missed. Not at a mountain lion.

But what does he know. What was actually there? There was camping gear torn up, lots of brass lying on the ground, and the EPA emblem. Then, coming down the hill, in this order: the gun, lying on the ground, the backpack, lying on the ground, the knife, lying on the ground, the shredded clothes, lying on the ground.

These things he knows. He also knows there is no truck and trailer at the launch and he saw no boat at the mouth of the river.

They pulled into the visitor center and he wheeled around the parking lot looking to see if there was any place the missing truck and trailer could be. No, it was pretty open. It wasn't there.

How was he going to tell these guys the bad news? How was he going to word it and not sound like he just panicked and killed some wildcats? He had to be rational and sound rational.

He parked, walked to the back and got some food and water for Bo and put it on the floor. "You stay here, girl," he said and patted her on the head.

Inside the Visitor Center was like most of any others that he'd been in. There was a counter with a cash register, maps of the area, and books for sale with the history of settlers and pioneers. Then, of course, there were the hats and shirts with "Ruby Lake" written on them. He turned from the counter and looked to the side. There were the usual snacks and sodas and bottled water.

Thinking more of what he was going to tell them, he thought about whether they would think he just panicked. A picture of the cat in front of him on the tree appeared, ears pinned flat against its head, fangs showing, roaring, and Bo growling and barking and snapping, him yelling at the top of his lungs until his rifle finally fired. Panic? "No way," he scoffed out loud at the idea.

"Be right out," someone called from the rear.

"No problem," he returned. Still glancing at the items in the store, he strolled absent mindedly toward the wall. There were some bags there that caught his attention. He walked toward them and lifted one to the side to see what was on them. "Environmental Protection" is what it said, and there was a circle of blue, and inside the circle of blue was written, "It's your job too".

It was the bag he saw shredded up the trail.

His head began to swim. He was confused. What did he actually see? What did he actually see that was there? He had trained to do that. You look and see. You don't assume.

Did he let assumption cloud what was there? That wasn't an EPA bag. It was a tourists' bag. What else did he assume?

He thought about the package. The one Gizmo left for him, and that he assumed things about it. That it was the usual package. That it was the same things he had already seen; the same maps; the same satellite photos; the same missing persons. He darted out the door and into the motor home. There they were, scattered around the table and onto the seat from the drive.

Gathering them up and putting them on the table, he sat. He was going to look this time. He was going to really look. There was a reason he was left this package. He was going to look and he was going to see why, starting with the maps and satellite images.

They always took maps along with them; always placed in a clear plastic envelope to protect them. The map was the same as his. It looked the same. "There might be something different," he muttered to himself, "Just because it looks the same, doesn't mean it is the same," and after studying it put it aside. His map was up the trail, so he couldn't compare now.

Next were the satellite images. He found the mouth of the river draining into the lake, put his thumb on what appeared to be the place he tied up his boat, and followed the gorge with his finger. The image didn't show the recent rockslides, but he could see where some of them were from memory of the twists and turn of the trail.

It was a series of photos, each one capturing one area. His finger was at the top of the photo now. The bottom of the next photo would show the top of the last frame and continue on up the trail, then another one. Taped together, they would show the entire trail. He ran his finger up to where he shot the first cat. He saw the rock on the side of the canyon before it fell off in the rain, causing the water to dam up.

Tracing the trail further with his finger, he slowed the movement to where the first sighting of the shredded clothing would have been. "That's it. The tree it was by," and continued up to where the knife was, the backpack was, and the Bushmaster was.

He followed it up, picturing in his mind every step he and Bo took, and sighting it on the pictures, matching them up. Up the rise he went to the flat area where the camp was destroyed. But there was no camp in the photo. There was no flat area either.

He sat up and looked again. He ran his finger up the trail again. He recounted every step along the way. No flat area. He rifled through the papers for more photos that he might have missed and looked on the floor for another dropped picture. Then he did it again. No, he had it right.

Then he pieced them all together, lining them all up on the table end-to-end to make sure he was looking at them correctly. They matched end to end perfectly and none were missing. There was no flat area on the satellite images.

"That is a big piece of missing real estate," he thought. "There is no way that is new. Been like that, probably hundreds, maybe thousands of years. Maybe more."

He grabbed the map in the plastic covering. "Look, Jason, look," he thought to himself. "See what's there, not what you expect to see," and was about to follow the map from the mouth to the top of the trail when he noticed another piece of paper behind the map. He could barely see the edge of it.

It was nothing unusual. They both usually stuck another piece of paper behind the map in the folder. It makes it clearer. It helps with the definition. It helps keep the sun from coming through. Then he turned the folder over and saw "JASON" written on the back.

Now that was not something usual. He cursed himself for not seeing it before. But he didn't have a reason to look before. There was nothing wrong before. "Stop making excuses," he muttered to himself, "There was a reason he left you this," and cursed himself again.

He pulled the papers out. There was a note. "Damn!" he cursed himself again.

"Jason. Don't go up the trail. Too dangerous. Bad stuff up there. Wait for me. Will be back in three days. Will meet you at the visitor center about noon. Listen to your messages some time, will yah? I left you a message, but I know you never check them. Butthead. Gotta go. Explain later," and the note was just signed "G".

"Son of a...," was all Jason could say. But as he sat, a great feeling of relief hit him. He smiled at first, and then laughed. "Son-of-a...," he said again, putting his hands on top of his head as if to keep it from flying off, "Son-of-a-bitch!"

Bo, sensing some excitement, came over with her tail wagging. "Bo!" he said while rubbing her all over, "Your buddy, Gizmo, is gonna be here tomorrow." She had no idea what he was saying. "Gizmo", that was a word she knew, and she looked around and turned to run to the door as if he were about to come in, ears up and tail wagging.

The few hours of sleep he had that morning was not enough. Once the tension was gone, once the relief hit him of finding his friend was alive and had never even gone up that trail, it set in. The muscles relaxed. The exhaustion took over.

He could sleep now. Real sleep. He would have a snack. Talk to Mr. Ranger Sir, and sleep, and he thought he'd better get in there and talk to them while he still could, before he would fall asleep.

Back in the Visitor Center, he stood at the front desk as before and called, "Hello!"

A girl came up from the back and said her hellos, smiling and saying, "Welcome to Ruby Lake. What can I do for you? Is this your first time?"

"No. Well, yes. Got here yesterday. No, wait, the day before," he fumbled. "Been up the gorge. The ranger around?"

"He's out back working on the boat. About to go out on the lake. He'll be back in four or five hours. But, if you hurry, you can catch him."

With that, he shot out the door.

Chapter Fifteen

Behind the center were thick marshes growing all along the bank, gradually thinning out as it went out further into the lake. It was a perfect place for migrating ducks, perfect for nesting. There was one clear area reaching from out in the lake all the way to the shore, and that's where the small wooden dock was.

The ranger was there, crouched down with the top off the outboard. It was amazing, Jason mused, that it was probably just the little outboard coming in and out at the same spot that kept the marshes from overgrowing that little area. It doesn't take much. But, as he looked around he could see there was plenty of room for the wild animals and birds still.

The ranger looked up as Jason approached, "Oh, hey. Um, Jacob, right?"

"Jason. How ya doin'?" he asked.

"Well. I think this thing has had it," he said, looking down at the motor. "Just a little too old and tired. I can get it rebuilt again, maybe, but... I guess it's just time for a new one. No good getting stranded." He tapped on the head a couple of times with a screwdriver and looked over at another boat. "Guess I'll have to take that. It's junk too. Haven't used it all year."

"I just came down from the gorge south of the lake. I figured I'd better tell you about it," Jason said.

"Was just headed up there," the ranger cut in. "Heard shooting, I thought I'd better go and see."

"Yah, well. That was me if it was last night or early this morning," Jason started in, trying to think of how to begin the story. "Ran into some animals up there. Had to put two of them down. They came at us and it couldn't be helped."

"Us? How many of you were up there?" the ranger asked, now stepping onto the dock. Shooting wildlife is strictly illegal, unless you had a license. Even then, you can't go hunting on Government Land.

Jason watched the ranger take on a serious air. He had broken one of his rules. Don't come here and kill the wildlife he was there to protect. He looked him over quickly and saw he was wearing a side arm.

"Just me. Me and Bo, my dog," and checked for any other dangers the man might represent and wondering things like, when did these guys get issued side arms? What is this country becoming when a guy like this could arrest or shoot someone out in the wilds?

Worse yet, when did they start feeling that they needed to? That was the real issue. He could understand this ranger needing a rifle, but his sidearm, that was for people, and Jason was becoming uncomfortably aware of the fact that he was that - a people.

"Right, right. I remember. Nice dog," and looked around, "Where is she?"

"She's alright," and pointed in the direction of the parking lot. "She's in the RV." The ranger came closer and Jason continued, "Ran into a couple of cats. They came at us," he started to explain, all the while watching any movement the ranger might make toward the gun.

It was how he lived for years. Watching and seeing things like that. Noticing anything out of the ordinary. Seeing what's there, not what he thinks should be there. His body tensed.

He'd already devised his plan. If the ranger made the wrong move, he would be disarmed and on the dock before the gun would clear leather. His weapon was in a holster with a flap snapped over it to hold it in.

The man would have one arm committed, his best and strongest one. It would be committed to pulling the weapon, and therefore, useless when Jason went for him. The ranger would never stop to think of abandoning his reach for the gun before it was too late. That's not how people think.

He would be like a monkey being trapped by a fig. You put a fig in a box with a hole. The monkey will reach in to grab the fig, but he has to make a fist, wrap his hand around the fig to pull it out. But his hand won't come out of the hole when it is in a fist. So the monkey is trapped, never thinking to let go of the fig. It panics, and panic is the enemy. It will scream and bite and jump and pull, never thinking to let the fig go and simply run away.

Jason would have both arms free. Play the man, not the puck, he'd always remembered from his hockey days. That rule served him well. Play the man, not the puck. Play the man, not the gun. It was what he did for a living for years before this, and he had become very, very good at it.

It's the rule you use when the hockey player is up close and has the puck. You play the man, and take him off the puck and kill his play. Then you take him out of the game. Play the man and see if he panics. If he does, he has lost.

Jason watched his eyes. If he looks right, he will go for his weapon that he carries on his right side. He's playing the man now and watched and noted every movement while looking directly into his eyes. The eyes would tell him. "I'm about to start a war between Government agencies here," he thought, wondering who has the most authority right now. He is a federal agent, but he is in a park.

"Yah, they were right up to us, one of them three feet away. Damn hungry looking, too," he added. "There's another thing. There was what looked like a camp up there that was destroyed. A back pack, camping gear. There was even a Bushmaster lying on the trail."

The ranger reacted, but not how Jason expected. He reached out for Jason, but it wasn't aggressive at all. "A bushmaster? No!" and he looked at the dock. "No one around?"

"No. Just some shredded things, looked maybe like clothes." Jason was sure now that there was no threat. The ranger was obviously shaken by the news.

"Come," was all he said, was all he could manage, and headed toward the Visitor Center, Jason right behind. He led the way to an office in the back and stepped behind his desk. "Missing for three days," he said as he threw a picture down in front of him.

Jason picked up the picture and looked. It was a man dressed the same as the ranger.

"He worked here. We worked here. More than twenty years." The man was clearly distraught. "He lived here, we lived here. All our lives. Grew up together. Went to school together. He married my sister and I married his." He sat down at the desk and said, "He owned a bushmaster."

Jason sat down on the other side of the desk and looked at the picture again. "Sorry," was all he could say.

"What happened?" the ranger asked. Then, before Jason could answer, added, "Look. This ain't no green horn. He knows this place...these parts. He's been around it all his life. It ain't like he's gonna go up and get eaten by cats. He's smarter than that. He's better than that."

"Sorry. Sorry." Jason couldn't think of how to reply to that, knowing the feeling he had thinking that Gizmo had just been served up for dinner. "I'll tell you what happened. What I saw. That's all I know."

"I was sent here to find out what's killing the fish. See what we can find here. Test the water, get some soil samples and get it to the lab," Jason began.

He went on to tell the story from when he arrived up until the meeting on the dock that nearly turned into warfare, a part of the story he left out for obvious reasons. The ranger sat and hung on every word and every detail not interrupting once, barely taking his eyes off Jason, and barely even blinking.

When Jason was done telling him the whole story, the questions started, "So you got into your boat, and where did you pull in?" They walked up to the map on the wall showing the entire area and Jason pointed out as near as he could where he thought it was. Then they sat back down.

"Then what? You moved where?" and the ranger made him go through every part over again, beginning to end, only this time asking questions, lots of questions. What time was it? Where was the sun at the time? How many rockslides he passed? How did he know if the slides were new or old? The size of the cats? How did he know? How did he measure the claws and teeth? On and on they went.

They sat now, silent, the ranger deep in thought. As if already in the middle of a sentence, the ranger began, "Because three days...there's no way he'd be gone for three days unless something bad happened. No way," He sat for a while longer. "You're sure it was a Bushmaster?" he asked.

"I'm sure," Jason replied. "Pretty familiar with that," and then got back up and walked to the map. "You know? This county road here, I must have been pretty close to it. Maybe we could go up there and come back down. You know, drive up there and come back down. He might have come from that way," and paused for a moment. "And you know what? I never saw any boats out there. I was looking, too. I might not have looked in the right place, but I looked in a lot of places. The obvious ones."

"Might 'a," the ranger answered. "He might 'a gone out that road. Might 'a done that."

"I have a boat. It's on the south end. We could go if you want, but I just came from the lake, and just came this way. I mean, we can do that if you want. But I say we go to the old road and come down. Think we can drive it?" Jason asked.

"Maybe. Could be right about that. We gotta find him. My sister is losing her mind. Hell, my wife is losing hers." Then he said, "Yah, definitely. You been there already. We'll come down the other way from the old county road. One way or the other, we need to find him, or what's left of him."

The ranger grabbed the phone, looked at Jason and said, "I'm calling for some help. People to come with us that know what they're doing, and my wife, and my sister. God, I hope he's up there."

Jason sat back when it struck him. He was doing exactly what his partner told him not to do. Twice he was told, "Don't go up there. Too dangerous," and now, he was about to go up the second time.

But this time, he would be with other people; people who know the place. They knew the country. People the ranger knew, and the cats were dead, except one. How dangerous could it be? It's simple search and rescue.

The ranger got off the phone and looked at him. "You know, I'm sorry, never thought to ask. But you don't have to come if you don't want. It's not something you...you know. He's one of us. You don't have to come."

"Wouldn't miss it for anything. You couldn't stop me," Jason said, getting up and looking out the window. "I need ammo. I need some 30.06. Just in case."

The cabinet was unlocked and a drawer pulled open. He grabbed two boxes of ammo and looked deeper inside. There was a supply of air horns and cans of pepper spray. He thought about the budget meeting, and thought about how handy the pepper spray would have been out on that ledge.

"Screw it. You never know," he muttered, and angrily shoved them into his vest pocket.

He would be back by tomorrow, safe and sound, and he and Gizmo would have stories to tell over beer. More war stories. It's how they met, over there. Clearing out bunkers of all the chemical and biological weapons they found in Iraq that nobody will say were there.

"No weapons of mass destruction! What ass holes!" is what Gizmo would always say if he heard it on the radio or television.

"What do they want? A nuke? When will they finally admit it?" and he'd always look at Jason the same way and shake his head. "What did they think they were firing at us? Nerfs? What do they think they used on the damned Iranians?" They'd talk about the death and misery Saddam caused to his own people and almost every country around.

They'd talk about how he gassed entire towns and killed everything in it. There were mothers, holding onto their children, walking down the streets, now lying there dead, still clutching their dead child. Birds dropped out of the sky. Dogs lying in the gutters. The entire town, lifeless.

Then they'd have to listen to people calling it an "unjustified war", and saying it wasn't deserved, and they'd ask each other, so what would justify it? A nuke in New York? In the end, after too much beer was consumed, one of them would say, "If anyone on Earth ever deserved this, it was that son-of-a bitch."

It was a secret, he guessed. That the weapons of mass destruction were there, it was a secret. They didn't know why, but it was a secret.

They burned them, he and Jason. Tons of chemical and biological weapons. Tons of them.

Before they went in, before the invasion, even more of the bunkers were spotted by satellite and by spies. They could see the people with their little Iraqi bio-suits on, carrying guns and going in and out of the mouth of the underground bunkers that could go for miles; huge, colossal caves.

They went in with bombers and blasted the hells out of 'em trying out their new Bunker Buster bombs. They had no idea how many there were. Hundreds, possibly thousands, and the ones that didn't get blown to hell, they had to go in and destroy them and the chemicals the old fashioned way - on foot.

By then, most of the Iraqis had given up or just plain old gone home. They'd just leave everything there and walk away. They found over five-hundred barrels of yellow cake, used for making nuclear weapons, packed it all up nicely, and quietly sent it off to Canada. Nope, no weapons of mass destruction.

Then there were the convoys that went into Syria. Hundreds and hundreds and hundreds of truckloads of who-knows what. They stretched for miles and miles beyond what the eye could see. A solid line of trucks went into Syria night and day for days after the invasion. Filled with what? That was the question.

But the news kept on saying it - no weapons of mass destruction found, over and over. "No weapons of mass destruction here!" Gizmo would always joke as he walked into a bunker filled with them. "Nope. Not a damn thing." They had both come to despise the media for it. All of it. "Liars and traitors," he would say.

At times they would get philosophical, as much as you can when beer is involved, and discussed what they had actually accomplished in Iraq. An entire population of a country was freed from tyranny. "Not bad," Gizmo would say. "Not a bad thing at all. I just hope they don't mess it up."

They would discuss the elections they were having, that they may end up with some sort of Representative Government in that country, that is, if they didn't let that religion of theirs screw it up.

"Hey," Jason told him once. "So, they were having that election. You know. Dipping their fingers in the ink and the whole thing. I was out doing a patrol, and there was this Iraqi I knew, and he was at home and not going to vote. So I went up and asked him, 'What the hell. How come you're not voting?' and the guy was shit faced. Drinking whiskey. I told him this is his chance for freedom. He is free. He can elect whoever he wants. This is his chance."

"This is free country now," he tells me. "Free from Saddam and his filth. Pigs! I don't have to vote if I don't want. It's free country now." So he looks at me and smiles a big toothless smile and holds up his finger to show me he had already voted. "I vote," he says to me. "I vote, and now I get drunk.

"So I asked him why he is so drunk, and you know what he told me? Because he can."

Jason was trying to get some more sleep when the knock on his motor home door came. He opened it and Ranger Jenkins was there with some food. "Thought it might have been a while since you had a decent meal. Had the Mrs. put something together for you."

"Come on in," Jason said. "Have a seat and watch this get inhaled. I was thinking of going back upstream and roasting that cat," he laughed. "I was going to whip up a can of something, but this looks so much better."

They sat and talked while Jason ate and tossed Bo a taste of something now and then. They went over the trip again. Jason pulled out his maps and images and showed him the spot on the map where the camp site was and then lined up the satellite images to show the spot was missing. It was filled in with rocks and shrubs instead of being the flat area with a body of water, The images went south all the way to the old road they were about to take.

"That road. Been a long time since I've been on it. It was in pretty bad shape the last time I was there. There's a road block with chains. One of those steel poles going across the road. You know. All the parks use 'em. We'll just cut it and go on through. Hell, I'm the Park Ranger, they shoulda given me a key." Just then two trucks pulled up with two men in each truck. "Let me introduce you to the guys," Jenkins said.

Jason wiped his mouth and stepped out behind Jenkins. "Guys, this here is Jason Brand. Says he had some cat trouble up between the Old Road and the lake. Put two of them down. Also, says he's been to the camp site that I was telling you about. This is the guy. Seems to know what he's doing and can take care of himself, so I don't think he'll be slowing us down."

Hands shaken and names exchanged, they were ready to move out. "I was going to invite you and your dog to come along with me, but I think your rig will do better than my pickup. Do you mind, Jason?"

"No. Hell no. Glad for the company. Hop in and we'll get going," he said.

Off up the washboard road they went again. This time, it was with a guest to ride in the big doghouse with Bo. Jenkins sat in the passenger seat and scratched Bo behind the ears for a good part of the ride. They turned onto the main road and drove slowly so as not to miss the turn off. Jenkins spotted it and pointed. "This is hardly even a road anymore. It goes off to the Indian Reservation," he said.

It wasn't, either. It's more a trail than a road. A dirt bike or two might get on it now and then, but hardly ever would a four-wheeled vehicle try it. The sun was high above them now and would be going down in eight or nine hours. Jenkins brother-in-law, the missing ranger, had been up there three days. Two of those were in bad weather. If he were still alive, it might be barely. He could die just from exposure.

But Jason was more worried about the cats, and worse than that, he was worried about all those shots that were fired. Whatever happened, the man was clearly in trouble. That is, if he's still alive.

That is why they decided to just get in their trucks and head up there and not wait until they had a full day of light. Every minute could be his last. They bounced along the trail, Jason kicking up so much dust sometimes that he would lose sight of the other two trucks behind him.

They were in four-wheel drive as soon as they got off the main road. Up ahead was the last hill they had to crawl up before going down into the gorge where the stream crossed. Any signs of tire tracks were washed away days ago.

They climbed over the crest; almost going sideways from the slant of the road carved from the run-off, and started the descent. "There's the truck. Son of a...you were right. That's Johns' truck, alright. Can't believe he'd come up here by himself. We always have at least another person along in case you get in trouble."

Jenkins leaned forward in his seat to get a better look. "Even if we just bring one of our kids. I would have gone with him if he would have asked. What the hell were you thinking, John?"

They all stopped in the middle of the trail and turned their vehicles off. No worry about blocking traffic here. There would be none. Gathering around the missing man's truck, they looked for any sign that would give them an idea of what happened or what John had in mind when he came up here. The windows were covered in dust, then, after the rain, it ran in a muddy cascade over the glass, blurring any decent view.

They checked the doors and found the driver's side unlocked. This is pretty typical in these parts. No real reason to lock doors. Inside was a stack of papers with missing person's descriptions on them. There was one sheet sitting on the dash above the steering wheel.

"You know. John and I been discussing this rash of missing persons we've been having. It was more than normal. Usually, the people show up somewhere, but lately, well, it's just been more than regular." Jenkins looked at the description left on the dash. "Maybe he ran across something and came up to check it out or something.

"Seems to make sense," he added after looking over the missing person sheet. "I would too under the right conditions. Even if I were by myself. We're only a few miles off the main road. Maybe he was checking something out and just got deeper and deeper and further and further away and then, well, found himself in trouble."

Jason, trying to add a little humor to a serious matter, inserted with a snicker, "Yup. Never happened to me before."

The six of them diverted their attention to the task at hand: the gorge. They peered over the edge of the old dirt road, deep into the canyon, with their weapons strapped in various ways around them. The rains had dug out a steep drop over the years.

The choice was to climb down, or go around. Since going around might be just as bad going down, they all agreed to follow beside the stream that emptied from a large culvert that ran under the road. At least they could see what they were getting into on this route.

Chapter Sixteen

The sides were steep and barely manageable for them, but Bo had to be helped in a few places. Reaching the bottom, Jason and Jenkins stopped and looked back up. "It's gonna be a lot harder getting back up than it was coming down," Jenkins said.

The six men turned and began the march into the descending canyon. "This water," Jason announced, "There is something in it. You've all seen the dead fish. It's just that we don't know what it is yet. So, I wouldn't go wading in it, if you can help it."

The destroyed camp Jason had described to the ranger was approaching. The falling water that cut into the rock and soil over the years was getting louder and louder as they got closer to the small lake it created.

There was an animal trail to the side where the vegetation was worn off. Although it wasn't easy, it was clear of brush, so they could at least see where they were stepping. Bo, of course, bounced down the trail without even a pause.

They were down, and it was just as Jason described it except that Jason's backpack was now torn to shreds. He rummaged around for what could be salvaged and found very little. The dried food was gone. Packages ripped open.

Any protective clothing he had was shredded. There were some containers and plastic bags that he would have used for taking samples of water and soil lying about, but taking samples right then was the farthest thing from his mind.

His waders were torn with similar claw marks he'd seen on the clothing he'd first found by the trail the day before. He lifted them into the air and looked with the other five members of the search party gathering around to see. "The Bushmaster was over here." He pointed at where he had left it and his backpack about fifteen feet or so away.

They walked over and found the rifle lying partially in the water. His cell phone was lying not too far away. "Hmm. Must have fallen out," he said as he picked it up and checked for signals. "Nope. No bars here." He stuck it in his pocket thinking that he would listen to Gizmos' message as soon as he gets signal. "Let me show you the rock."

They all walked over to the rock where the firefight happened. "Check this out. Check out the brass lying around here." He explained his theory of digging in with his toes at that spot and putting up a fight.

Then he went around to the far side of the rock to do what he didn't have the presence of mind to do before. That is, to check for return fire. There would be signs of rounds hitting the rock on the far side. Nothing. Not a single mark or scrape.

"Well. I thought for sure we'd see something," and looked around a bit more. "I'll show you the pack and clothes. It's down this way."

They all trailed behind Jason, down the path, stopping at the backpack. He explained where he had found the gun and pointed to the spot where the knife was. Then they all walked down to the shredded clothing.

"The way I see it, someone got into a firefight and unloaded his weapon and then reloaded a few times and did it again," pointing toward the camp, "Up there." He then started walking back up to the camp while talking. "He emptied his weapon up there. I don't see any casings down here along the trail. I found a box, right about here. It only had two rounds left in it."

"So here's how I see it. One, a firefight at the rock. Two, ran down the hill here, and dumps his weapon right about here. Three, drops the backpack about where it is now. Four, pulls his knife and then loses it about by the bush there. Five. Five, well. You saw the clothes." He looked at the ranger and said, "Sorry Jenkins. It's not looking good for your pal. Sorry."

"No. It's not. I think you may be right," and hung his head. "Son of a gun, that's too bad."

Then Jason started again. "There's only a couple of things that bother me. Well, a few things. Maybe more," and started toward the camp again. "Let me show you."

"He stopped at about where the gun was dropped on the trail and looked at Jenkins. "Okay. Let's say you're in a fight, a firefight. The guy drops his weapon. Way out here in the middle of nowhere. What does that gun cost? Fifteen hundred bucks?"

"Yah, maybe more. Sixteen. Then the scope and such. It's a pretty penny," he answered.

"So. Why didn't they take it? I mean, that's a lot of money to leave on the trail." He looked back up the trail and then back down again. "The gun. The knife. Why would they leave it? Then this," he said as he started again toward the camp. "Look, all those rounds from behind cover here. But no return fire. That is a nasty, mean, deadly round that .308 is. It'll put a cat down, no problem. Mine did. One shot. His would have done the same.

"So we can assume it wasn't a cat. Or a bear," and started thinking out loud to himself, "What do you see, dammit? What do you see?"

Then, he started again. "His foot was dug in here. So I figure he was like this firing, and his brass flew there." Then, for the first time, Jason put himself in that exact same position, "and he would be aiming right out there somewhere."

All six of them looked in the general direction, taking the covers off their scopes and looking through, scanning the range he would have shot in, studying it.

"Look at that," Jason said, pointing toward an area about a hundred yards away. "Look at that, you see, that rock there? Up on the hill right by the edge of the cliff? Kind of grey? Big?" A few of them affirmed they could see it. "Right below that, right about a third of the way up the cliff, you see that bush there?" Once they all agreed they were now looking at the same spot, he said, "So. What is that in there? Behind the bush there. Is that a cave?"

Now, they all began looking more intently. First Jenkins muttered, "Son of a…I think it is. In behind the brush there," followed by a couple of others, "Son-of-a gun. Never would have seen that. Maybe he crawled up in there."

"I'm going up there. I'll take Bo and we'll check it out. One of you wanna come?" Jason asked.

Jenkins looked at the others and said, "I'll go with Jason. You guys, you see anything, anything that looks like a cat or bear, you shoot the bastard."

That being agreed on, he added, "Just don't miss."

"Heel, Bo," Jason commanded and reached down and touched her on her head.

Jason had grabbed another four magazines from his motor home before they left. He dumped the rounds he had in his vest that were wet and loaded all the mags with new rounds, putting them all into his vest pocket. He reached his hand into his vest now for reassurance and they started toward the cliff. Jason slowed and looked down and checked his breach. Jenkins did the same, and then the other four did as well.

"I'm gonna go…let's…let's get in there, and maybe…maybe see if we can find some casings. Maybe up on the rock there too," Jenkins stammered.

They had gone about twenty paces when Jason pulled up to a stop. He raised his weapon and looked through the scope again. Jenkins did the same thing.

"I gotta tell ya," Jenkins said. "I hope we find some shells there. Cuz if there aren't, I don't know what he was shooting at, but he sure as hell fired a lot of lead at it."

"You and me both, Pal. You and me both," Jason replied.

101

They crept along a little further and stopped again to look into the cave and scan the top of the cliff around the rock. Jenkins noticed Jason looking back toward the rock and he glanced back with him. The men by the rock gave them a thumbs-up and they turned and continued inching toward the cave.

Bo was alert, ears straight up, and eyes on the cave when she stopped and growled. They both stopped and checked through their scopes again at the entrance.

"Let's make sure we don't get in their way if they need to shoot," Jason said, talking about the people behind them. "Maybe we'll come down from the left there. Get up on that flat spot and get in there. Keep out of their way. Give 'em a clear angle. Don't want to end up getting shot, end up on one of their mantles."

"Good plan," Jenkins replied. But neither of them moved. They stood and looked through their scopes into the cave. They could actually see inside the cave now. They couldn't really tell how far. It was too dark inside for anything to be clear looking through the brush in front, but they could see inside now and they studied the walls and floor and roof through the scopes.

"Your dog doesn't like something in there. I don't know. You ready?" Jenkins finally asked.

"Yah, I guess." As he brought his weapon down, he thought he caught a glimpse of something move. "H...," he almost got the word "Hey" out, cutting himself off, when he brought the scope back up and tried to get it focused back on the mouth of the cave.

Bo started growling and staring intensely into the cave entrance, hair standing on her neck and back, ears pointing to the cave. Jason and Jenkins both trained their weapons into the dark, trying to see any movement. "Something there. Thought I saw something. Just inside...," Jason said.

They stood, frozen, barely breathing. Except Bo. Bo was growling now, and Bo never lies. Something is there.

Association and familiarity, that is what limited what they saw. You see a form of a body, and you know it's a body. You don't have to see it all. Not every part. But you know what it is. The mind fills in the rest. That's how people see forms in clouds. They see something they are familiar with, and the rest is put there with their minds. It's the shape of all or part of it that initiates recognition.

But these shapes were not so easily recognizable. That's why they missed it. They expected a cat. The form of a cat or part of it. The head. The tail. They could, in their minds put the rest together. Or even a bear. Anything.

They did see the movement though. They saw the movement and tried to study what did it; an unrecognizable form. That's why they hesitated. Then a shot came from behind.

The first one ran out, all the way out, and headed straight for Jason and Jenkins. Then more shots from behind the rocks. Jason focused on it and fired his Savage with a loud bang. Nothing. He pulled the bolt back and did it again. Nothing. Was he missing? Was his scope out of zero?

Jenkins was firing in rapid succession and it was doing nothing to slow the approaching target. A steady volley of fire was coming from the men behind the rock when the second one came out of the cave. Then it hit Jason. The firefight. It wasn't a firefight at all. It was these. These…things.

"Run!" he screamed. But he didn't need to tell Jenkins. He was already running, heading for the security of the rock. "BO! COME!" He yelled as he turned and followed. He and Bo almost passed Jenkins getting behind the rock when he skidded to a stop and whipped his rifle back around toward the charging monsters, taking aim and firing, pulling the bolt back and recharging and doing it again.

The volley continued. There were six high-powered rifles, with six people who know how to use them, and it did nothing. They didn't stop. They didn't even slow down. One of the men decided to run. The man beside him turned to go with him and changed his mind. The monsters charged up the hill toward the rock.

A roar of gun fire began. A deafening roar. Jason dropped his mag and let it fall to the ground while he was slamming the next one in, cocking the rifle and firing over and over until he dropped the next mag. "That was two," he thought. "Two more, and that's it." That would be it, too. Two more magazines and his rifle would turn into a club, out of ammo and otherwise useless. The things were coming too fast for him to refill the magazines.

He emptied his last mag and yelled, "I'm out!"

"Me too!" came a reply, and then another one, "Me too!"

Jason grabbed his knife, getting ready for the inevitable, knowing that, if his 30.06 didn't do anything, and the five other rifles didn't do anything, he and his knife would not last too long. Yet the sound of gun fire was deafening. It seemed more than was possible and certainly more than would come from six guns. It was more than would come from six guns with three of them out of ammo and one running away.

He turned and looked behind them. There were about three dozen men standing and sending a volley of lead toward the things as they were coming up. They started to fire and move forward, fire and move forward. They were using shotgun slugs. The volley of slugs could be seen with the eye as a grey mass heading toward the beasts and knocking them back.

They would run forward again on command and fire again and repeat it over and over, driving the enemy back. But it didn't kill them. It didn't hurt them. It just knocked them back with the pure weight of the combined impact.

Three more men were off to the side watching and yelling and pointing. They continued while the wild monsters howled and roared and screamed; a hideous scream. "What are they?" Jenkins yelled.

They were being driven back by a solid blow. They were being herded; driven to a particular spot. One of the men on the hill yelled "NOW!" and three explosions went off. Jason spun in that direction and saw three projectiles launch into the air dragging some netting with it. The animals screamed again, flashing fangs and claws. The netting went over them and the men rushed forward in unison.

Jason and his crew all stood up and looked in awe, eyes wide and mouths open. Four riders on horseback were already charging over the hills behind them and barreled full bore toward the captured thrashing and clawing abominations. They grabbed hooks that were affixed to the net and started dragging, drawing it tighter and tighter around their captives until they were secured.

The men on foot charged toward the net, surrounding it, guns pointing. The three men who were off to the side ran toward it and started issuing orders. The horses bolted away dragging the beasts behind them, kicking and screaming and clawing back toward the hill with the three dozen men cheering after them and disappearing over the hill.

Jason, Jenkins and the others stood, silent and stunned. Bo began barking and prancing. Jason looked at her. She had been told to heel and was not released from her duty. But she would not stop dancing and squealing, excited and happy. The three men who directed the charge were approaching and Bo became more excited. Jason looked up and realized why. It was Gizmo.

"Hah! Gizmo! Go." It was all he had to say, and she darted off and leaped on him. She licked his face while he rubbed her neck and back. Then she got down and spun in circles with squeals of excitement, now and again jumping up for another greeting.

Chapter Seventeen

Bo settled down a little as the three men continued their approach. "Jason! What the hell are you doing here?" he said, walking up to him, "Didn't you get my message?"

"Well. Yah. I got it. Doesn't mean I read it," he answered.

"Good to see you. Almost got yourself killed, dude." Gizmo looked at him and saw the dazed, overwhelmed look on his face, looked at the others who looked the same and said, "You okay, there Pal?"

Jason didn't quite know how to answer that. The many definitions of "okay" made it hard to find the answer. If he meant, was he hurt? That would be one thing. But besides that, he was anything but okay.

"So, what was that? You found a new species? They live in caves or something?" he asked. "That's going to make some scientists happy."

"Well, something like that. Let me explain, but first, Jason, let me introduce you. This is Eric Runningsprings, Sheriff on the Reservation just over that hill."

"Well, damn. You have no idea. Good to meet you. I can't tell you how good," Jason told him and shook his hand. "Those things…that could have been bad. Thank you. This is Mr. Jenkins…," and was cut off by the Sheriff.

"Mr. Jenkins, Tom, my friend, glad you didn't get eaten. Good to see you. Been a while. How's Mary?" and continued shaking hands with the rest of Jenkins's crew and calling them by name.

Jenkins was a little flustered at the two being so calm and friendly after the near catastrophe. "Good, Eric. Good. Was asking about you and Hellen the other day." He shuffled on his feet, looked to the left and then to the right. Gathered his wits, and exploded, "What in the hell? What the…what was that?"

Gizmo laughed, slapped Jason on the back and said, "Wait 'til I tell you this. I have to show you something. You won't believe it. Have I got a story for you!"

"I already don't believe it. What were those things?" Jason asked. Looking in the direction the horses had dragged them, "I shot them," he said. "We shot. Nothing. Didn't do anything. Shit. What were they? That was crazy."

Gizmo and Eric looked at each other and laughed. "We did it." Eric smiled and added, "You did it."

"I think that was the easy part. That was step one," Gizmo replied. "Now comes the hard stuff." Then he looked at Jason, "But maybe we can figure it out."

"What? Figure what out?" Jason, still a bit shocked, but beginning to get his bearings realized he was about to be dragged into something.

"Listen," The Sheriff joined in. "This is a long story and we have a lot to tell you and a lot to talk about," and he looked around quickly, "I don't want to be standing around here with just us. You never know. But I'd like to get the hell out of here.

"We have two. We caught those two. I don't know how many there are. But we have two." Waving his hand in the direction of the vehicles, he continued, "We parked a little bit down the road from you. But you took the hard way down. Why don't you come with us and get our trucks and get the hell out of here. I don't want to be here if there are more. There's a trail over here."

The hair started to stand on Jason's neck at the thought of those eight standing off an attack of even one of those and he agreed, "Right. Yah, let's go." He began rushing to pick up his magazines, refilling them, loading his rifle and shoving the rest into his pockets as they walked.

Eric started to explain as they made their way up the trail. "We started losing people. You know, out of the village. Not a big deal at first. People come and go. Usually, they come back. It's pretty loose. But someone always knows where they went or at least that they are going.

"But people started disappearing. Well, they were leaving and doing dumb things, weird, like not taking things they would usually take; cell phones or tools, even leaving money lying around."

"Yah. Same with the ranger here, Right? They have a bunch of missing people." He looked over at Ranger Jenkins. "Don't you, Tom?" he asked, then noticed the ranger was walking with his head to the ground looking glum. Then it hit him, his brother-in-law. The reason they came up there to begin with. "Oh, shit," he said. He stopped and turned to Jenkins. "Sorry man. I'm real sorry about John."

"What? What about John?" Eric asked.

"Well, we came up to find him. His truck is over there and all we found is shredded clothing and a bag from the store." Jason glanced around at the group and continued, "Guess he didn't make it."

"Guess so." Jenkins looked down at the ground again. "It's tough. I'll have to tell my sister. My wife. You know, maybe he went South of the road. Maybe we should hike up there a bit and see what we find. Hey Eric, are there any of them things south of the road you know of?" Jenkins asked.

"Don't know. But I'll tell you what, I wouldn't go. Not if I were you. I'll send someone. They'll know how to get up there and not get themselves killed," Eric said.

They got back up to the trail as Eric's men from the village were loading the beasts onto a flat bed. A cloud of dust rose around the feet of the men and the thrashing of the animals as they connected the net to a winch and dragged it up onto the truck where a cage had been welded together to hold them.

Jason could see that this wasn't your ordinary hunting party. This took training. It took drilling and planning. It took money and execution, and it took a lot of guts.

"You guys. You really had this figured out, didn't you? All the details, I mean. You been planning this for a while." He watched as the beasts were hauled to the front of the flatbed by the winch and four men closed the back of the cage and secured it while five men stood on either side, the rest at the rear, arms ready.

This was a perfectly drilled and executed exercise. The men who secured the back – they weren't just men who secured the back. They were the men who had practiced and drilled securing the back over and over again. The men who stood to the side, they weren't just extras. They weren't just men standing at the side. They had an important function, a part of the whole. They had drilled and drilled what they would do.

"So, what now? You sending them to a Zoo or calling National Geographic?" he asked.

Repetition. That's what it takes. Repetition. You do something over and over again until you no longer think about it. You do it until it becomes muscle memory. Then, you make it harder, throw in a variation, and do it again. Do it again under pressure. Under stress. Under fire. You do it until it is in you, part of you. Then, when the real thing happens, you at least have a chance of success.

People can get thrown off what they are supposed to do by the unexpected. It is their worst enemy; panic. He recalled going across the ocean in a convoy. He was about to be dropped off in a secluded cove, he and five others, and was up top late one night during a storm. Waves, thirty or forty feet high, were crashing over the bow. It was pitch black and in the middle of nowhere. Complete blackout. Complete radio silence.

As he stood up on the deck, waiting to get transferred over on a breeches buoy, a device with a seat you get strapped into, he watched the silhouette of a ship pull up. It was like a ghost ship. It pulled up beside them in the crashing waves, completely dark and silent. Men were on deck and they shot a line over across the waves where other men were waiting for it. They grabbed it and hauled it in. With it came a fuel line. They hooked it all up and refueled, sent over a couple of packages, transferred Jason and his men, pulled the line back, and steamed off, disappearing into the night.

The whole thing took minutes. They were gone and the ship he was on never even slowed down. It was like it never even happened. He marveled at the training just that one thing must have taken. The drilling, the repetition. Doing it over and over and over until it was natural.

Muscle memory. It didn't matter that they were in a storm. It didn't matter that they were in waves that could sweep them away. It wouldn't have mattered what was going on. They drilled it and every part of it.

It gave him pause watching that. He might not bag on the Navy so much after that. Well, within reason anyway. On that ship, out there in the middle of nowhere, you are it. There is no gas station. If you run out of gas, you are your own gas station. There is no fire department to call. You are your own fire department.

You are it, and you can't park and walk away like you can a car, a Humvee, or a tank. You can't step out or step off. No, you can't do that and you can't call Mom for help either. No AAA. If you have a problem, you either deal with it or you swim.

It made him think about his own team; all the drilling; all the training; all the repetition. They were trained to do what they do under any condition, and much like the sailors he watched that day, they trained to do a job, and if you weren't watching right at that exact moment, you would miss the whole show, and they'd be gone, and hardly anyone knew it even happened.

That's what he was watching now. It was the result of training that he was watching. It must have taken weeks. Trained to do this one operation – catch the beasts. If he hadn't been there right at that moment, he would have missed the whole thing. He would have gone on thinking that mountain lions had gotten the missing persons.

Mountain lions! Ha! They were nothing compared to these - things.

"National Geographic? Well. We had other plans," Eric answered.

Two horsemen were in the lead, a pickup truck with six men in the back were next, followed by the flatbed with a man on horseback on either side, then a bus with the rest of the men, six up top on the luggage rack. Every part was thought out. Where they were and what they would do was thought out and planned. Every man knew his place and had practiced and drilled for this one event.

Jason watched the well-orchestrated happening and turned to Gizmo and the Sheriff and said, "Respect," knowing what they went through to plan this and to pull it off.

"I'll ride with him; see you back at the ranch," Gizmo called to the Sheriff as he darted toward the motor home. "Come on, Jason! Gotta go!"

They raced to their vehicles, Jason, Jenkins, Gizmo and Bo to the motor home, the rest sprinting to their trucks, and they moved off behind the cloud of dust keeping a safe distance from the convoy ahead. Gizmo was in the passenger seat, Bo beside him with her head on his lap while he petted her, pulling off the odd clump of hair. Jenkins was on his knees in between them with a hand on each seat to keep from falling over.

"So...," Jason began. "Thought you got eaten by mountain lions," was all he could think to say.

"Yah? " Gizmo laughed. "Mountain lions. Nope. No mountain lions." Then he added in a lowered voice, "I only wish it were lions."

"So," Jason started again not knowing how to ask the million dollar question. The one that would answer the thousand questions he had. "What? What the...those things. What's goin' on?"

"Jason," he shook his head, "Where do I start?"

The two others just waited for him as he gathered his thoughts and organized them before he spoke. "Remember Catskill?"

"What's a Catskill?" Jenkins asked.

"Yah. Catskill. I remember them. Back at the chemical plant. Pharmaceuticals, right?" and Jason told Jenkins about the explosion at the chemical plant, and how they had to go in there, but in the briefest way he could, leaving out most of the detail.

"Them, those people, those freak Frankenstein, zombie-making assholes. They are involved in this. I seen 'em," Gizmo started to froth.

Jason looked straight ahead allowing that bit of information to register. What the mind will do to rationalize events is well documented. It will find a reason for something that will put everything in a place that makes it make sense. It will align information to fit with other information it already has.

It was easy to think they had discovered a new species, one that crept out of a cave from deep below the Earth, never before seen. It could be shocking. It could be frightening. It could be surprising. It could be a lot of things, but whatever it was, the mind would align the information it received, such as seeing the monsters, with other information he has received, like in Nature shows, National Geographic, and even fiction.

It was easy that way. It was painless. His mind was prepared to align it in the right spot so that it makes sense. It would be filed neatly amongst those other files. It was a nice, comfortable fit, made comfortable and conforming with reality.

What he didn't know is that as this day went on, he would find it did not so comfortably fit. In fact, it would shake his reality in a way that would be numbing at times. Gizmo knew that. He had just gone through it.

He knew that too much input at one time, too many parts and pieces, input that he could not align with previous input with which it could be compared, would make it near impossible to understand the whole. He also knew that talking was useless. Only seeing would be believing.

After what Jenkins had seen today, his world, his understanding of reality, had already been shaken. He'd never seen or heard of anything like what he saw today and was still traumatized by it. The word caught his attention, "Zombies? What do you mean, zombies? Those weren't them, they were... they were..."

"Yah. Those weren't zombies. But those people made zombies before. We seen 'em. Me and Jason. We seen em." Gizmo turned around to look at him, "Psycho, flesh eating mindless zombies, for real!"

What he was seeing, the capturing of the animals and the trained team to do it with, was not what was really going on, Jason started to realize. There was more to this and the capture was only the part that he had seen, and he knew Gizmo well enough to know when he was not answering a question.

He waited for Jenkins to hear more about the Catskill Chemical plant, but not seeing how this line of discussion was answering any questions, he cut back in, "So then, what about these things? There's more to it than just finding a new species, isn't there?"

"Those? They call them 'The Evil Walkers' back on the reservation. You can call them whatever you want. I don't think they have a name. Oh, and yah. Mountain Lions? I saw those assholes airlift them. Helicopters, with that piece of shit Catskill logo on them, flying in the cats. They are studying the 'Walkers', watching them fight. Freaks. They bring in goats and cows too. Just fly them in and watch them hunt."

The cloud of dust rolling along now entered a large clearing with some houses and two large metal buildings. The doors were open on one, and two men were standing on each side of it. The flatbed turned and began backing toward it.

The horsemen who had lead the way leaped off their mounts and disappeared into the shed, reappearing with another cable with a hook at the end. That was their thing, obviously. It is what they were trained to do. Do the hook. Attach the hook. It was drilled and executed without hesitation, without thinking.

"Dangerous job," Jason said. "That takes some real guts." The men had to be the closest of anyone to the murderous monsters. They had to ride right up to them and get within feet, put their hooks around the net, an untested and untried net at that, while they howled and roared and slashed, and then drag them into position.

Gizmo had already leaped out of the RV without a word before it had even come to a stop. Jason had to grab Bo to keep her from following. Now was the important part. Now is what all this was done for.

What was coming next would make all their efforts pay off. This is where they contain the beasts and hold them. It was the entire purpose of the day. If they blow it now, they are all in trouble; they would be loose right inside their Village.

Jason grabbed his rifle and he and Jenkins were out in the lot, leaving Bo inside the motor home barking at the excitement. They were running toward the monsters when Jason realized that this was not his gig.

It wasn't his call. It wasn't his plan. It wasn't his operation and he had no idea of what they were going to do next. He could screw it up just by standing in the wrong place, getting in some one's way, messing up their timing and cause a catastrophe.

So, he contained the urge to jump in. It felt odd, but he forced himself to do it. He grabbed Jenkins and led him off to the side to watch. They stood, tense and ready, but only watching. He could see, now that he was close enough, what the net was made of; stainless steel cable. The kind they use for rigging on sailboats. "Strong. Real strong. Good idea," he said to Jenkins pointing and then glanced at Gizmo, thinking it was probably his idea.

The cage was something they made and had collapsible sides and ends. The trick was this: How to get the new cable attached to the hooks, when the hooks were pulled tight against the back of the cab. Then, drag these things into the shed and cage them again without them getting loose. Or maybe they were just going to drag the whole cage inside.

Men were running in and out. Most of them were not even looking at the beasts. "Why would they?" Jason thought, "It's not their job." It wasn't, either. Other men stood watch with their weapons. It was their job to watch. It was a well-oiled machine, this group. Everyone knew his place and did his specific duty. Barely a command was given. "Indians," he thought to himself. "How did Gizmo get freaking Indians?"

He turned to look behind him, where there were even more men behind a wall. Some held weapons, some held chains, and some held little boxes. He stumbled on something when he moved and looked down. They were on a pile of chains. Snow chains, they looked like, and this must be a garage of some sort used for sand and salt in the winter. "Big garage," he nervously muttered to Jenkins.

Then he noticed what the little boxes were for. He looked under the flatbed and saw explosives wired and attached to the bottom. If all goes wrong, it would be the failsafe. Run and blow it. Blow the monsters to hell with it. The little boxes were the detonators. No doubt it was another Gizmo design.

One of the watchers called out, "The cable is fraying!" and sent everyone into a flurry. Contingency plan "B" was going into effect. It was a "What if" plan. They had to have them. What if this happens, what if that happens. They had to predict everything that could go wrong and have a plan. Otherwise, they didn't have a plan at all. They would only have panic. They would be knocked off the puck and taken out of the play, and maybe even out of the game entirely.

Someone was instantly in the cab and began tilting the bed. One of the horsemen reached behind the steel plate behind the cab and attached a hook to the cable. The bed tilted more and there was a crash in the garage. Jason and Jenkins knew what that could mean. Trouble, that's what. They stepped forward, both looking for an escape route.

The truck rumbled and the entire cage flipped over, doing a half summersault, and landing on its top. Then there was another crash, and the beasts were flung to the front of the cage, pulling the wall completely off and dragged, wall and all in through the garage door before they had time to blink.

Everyone ran now. They ran into the garage where four men were standing on top of another larger cage, dropping the end shut and clamping it down. As soon as the signal was given, they were down and the cheering started again.

The monsters were screeching and howling and thrashing inside the netting, but couldn't break through. They were pulled to the far end where a weight attached to the cable had been dropped, pulling them, yanking them, hurling them across the garage floor and pinning them against the far wall.

Success!

Chapter Eighteen

People started coming from all around the village to look, hundreds of them. They came in and stared and got as close as they would dare to them - The Evil Walkers. Some of them taunted the monsters. Some people jeered and sneered as the beasts snarled and thrashed at them.

Some of them, especially the older women would walk by and look and then spit on them. Someone would put their arm around them and they would walk away. They were the ones who had lost family, Jason supposed, lost them to these monsters, the Evil Walkers.

He walked around the cage admiring the construction; a cage made of railroad track, welded at the tops to another track. Then, on the corners, there was thick metal plate welded to the side and along the top on both the insides and the outsides. It was sturdy construction, and just in case, the entire cage was set inside another cage with a two-foot clearance. Under the cage and on the top corners were the failsafe, the explosives.

He walked around the cage examining those when Gizmo walked up and pointed to the top ones and said, "Phosphorous. Burn those bastards to hell. It'll burn these tracks and anything around it. Can't be too sure."

"You've been busy. What next?" Jason asked.

"We'll, we need to talk about that. I guess next, we'll all go and have a proverbial powwow." They continued to stroll around the cage looking at every part, every seam, every weld, and every explosive device until there was no doubt that it was intact. It was something that Jason was sure they had already spent hours upon hours doing before the capture. Then Gizmo turned to Eric and said, "What do you think? Turn 'em loose?"

"Yup. I guess it's time." He yelled out that it was time, and the well trained and drilled army took their positions around the cage. Some holding weapons, some holding detonators. One of the horsemen went back behind the cage and released the cable. Instantly, before he could blink, the beasts flung themselves at him, reaching and thrashing at him through the cage, falling just short of their target.

One of them spun and, in one leap, was on the other side snarling and thrashing. They continued, jumping, throwing themselves against the sides of the cage, howling and screeching and trying to get at them, to kill them, to rip them to shreds. An hour of watching them went by. They didn't tire. They didn't slow down. They never paused once, and man, they were fast.

"Remind you of something?" Gizmo asked.

"What do you mean?" Jason asked back.

"I mean the mindless and endless attack. Remind you of something?" Gizmo asked again.

"It does, actually. It does. You're not thinking what I'm thinking, are you?" The mindless and endless attack reminded Jason of the reactions of the brain damaged Zombies; the attacking, the rage, the response to stimulus with no reason.

"You know I am," Gizmo replied. "You know I am, and you know we are right too. Catskill."

Eric was calmly giving out instructions as they approached. Advising them on safety and not taking chances. Not to taunt the animals or allow anyone to do it unless it was a supervised test, and the last fail safe, if they ever did escape and all was lost. "Blow the whole freaking place."

Video feed would be set up, four regular and four infrared. All angles of the cage would be covered. The feed would go to a table in the room with eight screens set on it, and the signal then relayed to a set of screens others could watch from other rooms and buildings in the area.

The beasts never stopped, never slowed, and never tired as long as they were there. Finally, Eric looked around and ordered everyone out except the guards. "Time to get down to business," he said, leading the way toward the next shed, stopping at the exit and putting a little black box in a guard's hand and pointing across to the back, he said, "He's got the other one," and waved it in the air making sure they both had eye contact and each knew the other had a box. "You okay? You know what to do, right?"

Jason was jolted to an abrupt stop as he walked through the entrance of the next building over. The shock of what he saw froze him in spot. Maps on the walls. Pins marking locations. Rows of chairs with a podium set up and a screen behind that. People on the side poring over reports. "What is this? What kind of Indians are these? This is a War Room."

"Yup," Gizmo said sauntering past him as if it were an every-day thing for him to see a bunch of Indians sitting in a War Room. "Come on. This is going to be good."

They walked in and were about to take a seat in what he thought could be the briefing room, yet still part of the same room. A man walked up to Eric and reported, "Colonel! We're all ready."

"Colonel?" Jason asked. "What is going on?"

"Just hang on. You're gonna like this." Then Gizmo reconsidered and said, "Well, you probably won't LIKE it, but I guarantee you won't be bored."

Eric looked at him, "That's right, Colonel Eric Runningsprings. This is Gunny Brent Stonefish."

"Semper Fi!" the Gunny called out.

"And this is Lt. Branford."

"Branford, 101st, sir. Glad to meet you."

It went on. Cav Scouts. Marines. First Armored. Infantry. Navy. Air force. Special Forces. Intelligence. Coast Guard. An endless line of introductions as men poured in.

Jason was again reeling from shock, a new shock. "You have a freaking army," he said after finally admitted it to himself. All that was going through his mind was the word "INDIANS!" being screamed in the hundreds of movies he'd seen of massacres and battles. It was where this information was aligned to make it fit and make sense.

"Yes I do, Colonel Brand, and we are at war. Have been for some time. I was hoping you might want to join us," Eric told him.

Jason was stunned. "Colonel? That was a long time ago," he said. "Are you thinking you're going to war? You can't win. Are you crazy?" and he turned to Gizmo as if he had completely lost his mind to be part of this.

Gizmo grabbed him by the arm and led him to a seat. "Let's sit down. Wait. I don't want to spoil it for you. Wait until you hear what's going on. It's not what you're thinking."

The seats filled up and more men came, filing in along the walls and they still came, and any remaining standing room was filled and spilled to the outside. The noise of shifting feet and shuffling chairs and coughs and low voices and whispers subsided and Eric, Colonel Runningsprings, walked to the front of the room and turned to address them. He drew a breath to begin but was not allowed to start.

The room broke into applause and cheers that went on and on. The noise drifted through the walls to the shed next door, where the beasts were driven wild by it, which made the crowd cheer even louder and longer. At last, the crowd gradually became silent, and all that could be heard were the snarls and screeches of the killers next door.

Eric looked in that direction, turned back to the crowd, and spoke. "So I guess you've all heard the news." At which the crowd stood up and again cheered and applauded, and again the beasts reacted.

When the noise dropped enough that he could be heard, he yelled. "We are the first to do it!" sending the crowd cheering, with added howling now while those who were sitting began pounding and stomping their feet on the ground and chanting, "PAIUTE! PAIUTE! PAIUTE!"

Waiting for the noise to subside again, he started to take a more serious air, looking down at some papers and flipping through them on the podium. When there was silence other than the odd comment followed by an uproar of laughter, he started again. "But, while we have made a tremendous accomplishment today, we are falling behind in a couple of areas that I want to address and this is something we must rectify."

Everyone was listening now and he went on. "First, an acknowledgement to the fine work done today." The crowd started cheering again, but before they could get carried away, he shouted, "Would the men on mission today stand please." Again, there was uproar of applause.

"And I would like to say a special thanks to Jerry Crozley," and he looked at him, "What does your friend call you? Gizmo? Good name for you. Do you mind if I use it?" and after getting approval, went on. "Colonel Crozley, or, excuse me, Colonel Gizmo. Well, what can I say? He made pretty much everything we used today. Smart guy. Thank you," and he stood back from the podium and started clapping his hands, joined with the rest of the men.

"But what we need to do now, what we are behind on is this: We know there are more of these things. We have an idea of where they are." He walked to the large map on the wall and pointed. "Every mark on this map is an area of mountains with a reservation not too far away, and they have had a rash of ills, the same as us.

"Our brothers have reported similar sightings to ours and have had catastrophic failures in discovering what the predators are," and he looked around the crowd, "The same catastrophic failures we've had, until today.

"What we have to do is find their origin. None of us know this yet. Not any of us in the Nations know this. We only have ideas." Walking back to the front of the room now, he picked up some papers and started, "We need intelligence. We need eyes on Intel. Because, all across the country, these things have been set upon us, the People of the Nations.

"Needless to say, we are going to be studying our new guests next door. We will be prodding and poking them and seeing what makes them tick. We know they are fast as hell. We know they are strong as hell. We know they are tough. We know some of their strengths.

"What we'll be studying them for is their weaknesses. We hope to find everything we need to deal with this new enemy of The Nations within a short time. What we need from you is to find where they are;

where they originate. We are assigning recon missions that Gunny Stonefish will be handing out and coordinating. Gunny, would you take it from here".

He began walking away, but changed his mind and turned back, "Another thing. We don't know who or what is behind this, but we all have an idea, don't we. Remember, loose lips sink ships. You talk on the phone, nothing is secret. Assume someone is listening.

"You send an email; you might as well put it in the newspaper. Watch where you have your conversations in public places and who is in earshot. Use your native tongue when you can. Pay attention. Watch yourselves," and turned and said, "Gunny Stonefish."

The Gunny took over, looking like he could wrestle a Bradley tank and win, he got up and started calling off a name and the assignment to go with it and handed the papers with who was assigned to them along with maps and locations.

"You will go to these locations and bring back intelligence. Branford!" he called first.

"You will take your men. You will go to Ruby Ridge. You will take the route marked on your map. You will not be seen. You will not be heard. You will not be caught. You will go, you will see, and you will come back and report. Any questions?" Of course there weren't, and he went on to the next group.

Chapter Nineteen

Eric, Col. Runningsprings, walked up to Gizmo and Jason and said, "Let's go."

Jason stood up and turned toward Jenkins, making sure they had eye contact and looked at his rifle slung across his back. Jenkins did the same thing and they both nodded. They were on the same page and they knew it, they had to get out of there. Indians! They have an army and they are preparing for WAR!

"Don't panic," Jason told himself as he followed the two toward the door. "Don't react. You are surrounded and there are too many of them." There were at least five hundred there, all armed. There were others that weren't there. He estimated there would be somewhere around six thousand in and around the entire village. He started doing the math.

There were over a hundred pins on that map. Add all the rest of the reservations and tribes, their army could easily surpass the United States Military in size, and they are already in country – this country!

As they went through the opening to the outside, some of the men slapped Gizmo and Eric on the back and then turned back to the Gunny. There would be too many now, and they are all armed. He wouldn't have a chance. He would walk toward the next shed, wait until he got far enough away from the crowd, and then he would make his move.

Jenkins was in step with Jason, eyes darting back to the shed and then to the men in front and waited until they were out of earshot. They both stopped and took two steps back, drawing their weapons from their backs and holding them at low ready.

Eric and Gizmo recognized what was happening and turned to them and waited.

"Tell me, Eric. The Army. What is your objective?" Jason finally asked.

Eric looked at Gizmo and shrugged, turned around and kept walking as if nothing had just happened. "Mr. Brand," he said. "I took the same oath as you. Uphold the Constitution. Protect the country from all enemies both foreign and domestic. I know what you're thinking. Are the Indians going on the War Path?"

"Are you?" Jenkins asked.

"Tom. You know me. How could you think that?" he answered.

"You saw those things," Gizmo added. "That's what we are talking about."

"Okay. But there is only two, and you have them. Why the army? I mean, you guys are gearing up for war in there. Why don't you just call the Government, Fish and Game, something like that?" Jason asked.

"Look. I know this is a lot to digest in a short time, and nobody is holding you here," Gizmo said and looked at Eric briefly and continued. "But, Jason, I think you need to see the rest. This is, well I know it's overwhelming. Shocking even. I get it. But there is more."

"What do mean by more? More Walkers?" Jenkins asked.

"More of everything. More information. Things we saw, things we know. Even things you know," Gizmo said.

"I guarantee we are not the enemy. But I also guarantee that there is one," Eric told them. "We are just now, really, finding things out ourselves. So I can't tell you all you need to know because we are just finding out. But I'll tell you what, something is happening. Something is happening and it isn't small."

Gizmo added, "And I would call this an environmental threat, wouldn't you? We're doing our job. Kind of."

Jason lowered his weapon a little more and felt foolish now. Of course Gizmo wasn't a threat. What was he thinking? It was all just too much information too fast, and there was nothing that he could align it with because nothing was fitting.

"Let's take a look at these Walkers one more time," Eric said as he poked his head in and had a few words with the guards before starting for his office.

The Sheriff's Office was about what he expected in a small village like this; one room in the front and a couple of cells off behind it. The floors were worn and the building was old, but it was kept tidy and professional.

A drunk was locked up and started coming to as they walked in. "Sheriff," he slurred and made an effort to sit up. "Sorry man. Sorry. I didn't mean to take a swing at you. I really…I apologize. I won't do it again."

Eric sighed and went over to the cell and unlocked it. "Jimmy. I don't have time for your bullshit. Any more trouble from you and I'm gonna drive you off the reservation myself and dump your drunk ass in a city. Let the local cops beat the shit out of you and lock you away in Federal Prison for assaulting them."

"No. That's harsh, man. You wouldn't do that, would you?"

"Look at me! Have I ever lied to you, Jimmy? I've had enough. I mean it. I'm letting you out, and you better go home. Get yourself some help." Then he opened the cell and watched the young man stumble out through the door.

Eric sat at his desk and shook his head. "So, you saw the map? You see how many locations we're talking about? One hundred and twenty. That's how many marks are on that map. Those are just the ones we've heard from.

"Not all The Nations talk. So there could be a lot more." He leaned back in his chair and said, "Imagine this. Imagine if one of those got into a city full of people. Imagine the damage it would do. What if a dozen of them were let loose? Or a hundred?"

"It would be a slaughter," Jason replied. "They would kill...so many people. But what makes you think..."

"What? That they will get into a city? Get let loose?" He got angry and slammed his fist down on the edge of his desk, stood up, and took a couple of steps away from it, then turned. "I'll tell you why. This reservation, all of them – all reservations are under the Department of the Interior. That's who we all come under.

"You know, funny thing. I thought we were having a problem with animals. I mean bear or cats. That's what I thought. So I called the Department of Interior and told them that these animals have to be hunted. That we were, well, we were missing some people.

"It took days. They called back and gave me some bullshit story. I gave them names of people. They said they found one of them, that he was in jail up in Salt Lake City.

"So, someone here has been there before. He knows one of the guards. He calls and has him check, and you know what? It was a lie. Then the other day, I saw it. They were airlifting these cats in. Gizmo was there, weren't you?"

"That's right, Jason. Saw it," Gizmo said. "They were airlifting them. Dropping them right there. Right about where you said you shot a couple of them. They dropped cows, sheep and goats too. They're studying them. Watching them. Watching them hunt. Watching them kill."

Eric cut back in, "They dropped some horses, maybe to see how fast they were. You should have seen it. These things, if they get out of hand, could cause a lot of damage. I don't know how many there are. But I know we caught two out there. I'm glad it was only two. But there are a hundred and twenty places around reservations that are all talking about the same thing. That means at least two hundred and forty of those things."

"Yah, Jason, and here's the other thing: Are they reproducing? This could be worse than an Aliens movie. They are hard to put down." Gizmo paused and laughed, thinking about the capture. "Man! That was intense!"

"It sure does bring up questions," Jason said.

Jenkins spoke up, "This is like a bad dream; these things, and then John getting killed and everything."

Jason stood up and aimlessly walked around the office, deep in thought, trying to reconcile what he knows, what he's been taught and told to think all his life with what he is seeing now. The problem is that it wouldn't reconcile.

The satellite images, the Walkers, the army of Indians, the poisoned lake, none of it could be categorized so it fit properly, so it fit painlessly and easily and comfortably in his mind with everything else he knows.

He had to get it all to start making sense. Science. That's what he needed to use. Logic. If data won't reconcile, one or more of it is wrong. It is false. He needed true data. What did he see? What does he know?

He would have to erase any preconceptions and start anew. The idea that Indians were a threat was a preconception. It was false and it clouded his observation. It slanted his conclusions. That was a good start.

Nobody spoke, they just watched. He walked over to the window, but didn't really look out. He turned and took a few steps back toward the desk and then turned toward Jenkins. "No. No, they're right, Mr. Jenkins. They're right, I'm sorry to say. There is something going on. It makes more sense now."

Jason was still pacing with his hand on his chin. Then, he started. "Alright here is what we do. First, Jenkins. You go and get some of those dead fish and a sample of the water. Don't get it on yourself."

"We find out what's killing them. It'll either be biological or chemical. We need to find out which. If it's waste from the Walkers, we can find out a lot from that. While you're doing that, Sheriff, can you get DNA tests done?"

"Sure. But how are we going to get a DNA sample from them. Their skin, I mean a bullet won't even penetrate," he asked.

Jason turned to a mop and a bucket, grabbed the mop, wrung it out and left, saying he would be right back.

"Okay. What did I tell you? Just watch. This guy has a mind like nobody else," Gizmo started bragging.

A minute or two later, Jason walked in with the mop. The head had been chewed in half and what remained dripped wet with saliva. "Here," he said, handing it to Eric. "I got a swab for you. That should be enough. Find out what they are made of.

"While we are getting the samples tested, we can run some other tests. Important tests. Things we can do here with things we have here."

Then he stopped. He turned and again went into thought. "Look. You say the Department of Interior? If that's the case, we can't alert anyone to what we are testing. We need private labs. Nothing that can go back to the Government.

"What resources do we have? I can get some water tested by someone I know – checks water quality. Some hippie type conspiracy theorist. But smart. The only way anyone official will know is if they are watching him. But wait, he swears they are."

"I think I can get the DNA done. I'll make a call," Eric said. "Oh, wait. No calls."

"What you said. Loose lips sink ships. I think that, if who I think is behind this, actually is behind this, we may be in for a hell of a ride. Ranger Jenkins, how about you get yourself a ride to the lake and back from someone out there while we tell Eric a little story about zombies. You've already heard it."

Jenkins was up and out the door. Jason yelled out at him, "And don't tell anyone! Not even about John!"

"We're gonna need a squad of runners," Jason told Eric. "We need runners who can come and go and not talk and not get into trouble when they are gone. They'll have to go into town, get tests done and returned. No phones and no emails. Relay messages, things like that. Maybe six or eight of them on standby."

"Okay." Eric stood up, picked up the phone and told someone to come to his office right away, then, looking back and forth at Jason and Gizmo. "Okay. But Zombies?"

That made both Jason and Gizmo laugh. They started to banter back and forth pretending to argue over whether were in fact zombies. "Okay, okay," Jason finally capitulated. "You're right. By all definitions, they were in fact zombies."

Eric was staring at them in wide eyed disbelief. After what he'd been through and seen in his little out-of-the-way village recently, you could tell him Santa was coming next and he would wonder for a moment if it were true. Now zombies! Jason and Gizmo saw the look on his face and broke out laughing again.

"Wait, Eric. Let me explain.' Jason said. "They weren't real zombies."

"What do you mean, weren't real zombies. They were mindless, insane, flesh eating used-to-be-people zombies. That's what a zombie is," Gizmo retorted.

"Zombies? Real zombies? Zombies aren't real." Then he looked at them, "Are they?"

"Okay Gizmo. You tell him about the zombies," Jason said.

Eric sat while the story was told about Catskill and the explosion in the factory. Every now and then, Jason would add something to the story like, "The acid ate away any mucous membranes first." Or "The eye lids were gone completely, so they looked like they had huge, bulging eyes."

When it seemed like the story had been told, Jason looked at Gizmo and finally admitted, "Yah. Alright. They were actual zombies. Fine, fine, fine. Can't believe we actually saw zombies."

Eric sat astounded. "So, these are the guys that have been dumping here? Catskill. These are the ones…did they…make those things out there?"

"We have to find out. If they are the ones, I mean, if they actually made them, they are in deep with the Government. DEEP. In fact, I think that in some cases, they give the orders to the military. That's what I saw; what we saw," Jason told him.

"So Jason, what is the plan? What can you do with these tests?" Eric asked.

"Simple. We find out what they are made of, we will know how to kill them. We can't do it with bullets. Take the human body. Put simply, it is a carbon oxygen machine. It is made up mostly of carbon, oxygen, and hydrogen. We've known that for a while. But we can tell things from DNA.

"If you disrupt one of those, the hydrogen, the oxygen, or the carbon, the human body dies. Most people concentrate on oxygen. You disrupt oxygen, the body dies. But look at hydrogen. Look how much hydrogen is in the body. H_2O. Hydrogen and oxygen is what makes up water, which makes up most of your body. So, we have hydrogen, carbon, and oxygen.

"But if you change how they combine, you can make poison. Like carbon. Carbon is good stuff, but if you mix it wrong, you get carbon monoxide. It's a different mix of carbon and oxygen. It'll kill you dead. Yet you have those molecules in your body, just combined a different way.

"We need to find what they are made of and we can determine what will kill them. Otherwise, we have to start trying things until we hit on something. But there are lots of things we can do in the meantime, until we get results back.

"We can start testing reactions to senses. How do they sense things? Do they see and smell and feel and taste the way we do? Are some senses detrimental to them? Waves. Sound waves. Light waves. Electromagnetic waves. What frequencies will do what to them? Make them sleep? Make them crazy? Make them die?

"You can kill things with radio waves. People have been doing it for years, killing bacteria and viruses with it. The Japanese were working on it in World War Two. There are a lot of tests we can do. All of them or any of them could be important. I say we work on it until the penny drops. Gizmo can make things almost as fast as we can think them up."

"Good idea," Gizmo said. "Radio waves. Never thought of that. Waves. I can do that in a few hours."

"Right. Let's build a gadget to adjust the pulse width, and… you know what we're going to need? We need a programmable controller. So we can regulate the duty cycles and frequencies. We can use the same set up over and over and start checking out frequencies, run electrical pulses through it, for example, then sound, light, electromagnetic, radio, and we can even have combinations if we get a decent controller."

"I'll send one of the runners for a supply run as soon as they get here," Eric said. "I don't know what those things are that you're talking about, but why don't you make up a shopping list for me to give them? You know, I never asked, you guys need anything? I mean, we've kind of stolen you away from your life."

"Is there a store here? We could get a few things, snacks, ammo and such," Jason replied.

"Yes, we do have a store. You'll like it. It's duty free. I'll make sure they set you up with everything. Actually, it'll be on us, the village."

"Gizmo. Eric. Gentlemen, what do you say we go out and take another good look at these bad asses we caught? Oh, and we'll need a vet. We are going to figure out how to kill one and then get him to dissect it, maybe we drown it or suffocate it somehow," Jason said. "We'll have to make a big tank."

They met the runners half way to the shed lined up with eight identical Ford SUVs, the Edge, all brand new. "Man, where did you get those? Sweet!" Gizmo said.

"Little secret we've had. Most of the tribes have their own casinos. We have three. Tax-free money. Lots of it. Anything you guys need, we can probably get. Most of the Nations have committed to this.

"They all fear the Government is doing what they always do, betray us. But they may be betraying everyone this time. That the Government is involved, that is our fear. They are strong. We've all been in the military, you and I, we know what they can do," Eric said.

Chapter Twenty

Pete Goodwell stood in front of the men lined up in front of the vehicles. He was the one who ran the runners. Two of them had the traditional long hair. The others looked just like anyone else, short hair, piercings and tattoos on the two younger ones. One of them had reddish hair and a short beard. You would not recognize them as from the Nation.

The list of electronics Gizmo made up was handed to Pete, who looked at it and turned to his men saying, "Electronics" which called two of them forward, handed it to one of them and said, "Make a copy and split the list.

"The diodes and resistors, the common things, get at the local electronics shop. Wiring, bread board. Yah. Easy." Then turned to one of them, "This stuff here," pointing at some of the items on the list, "You seen these?"

"Sure," he replied. "I know where I can get them." He was about to turn and take off when he changed his mind and said, "Can we look?"

He was talking about the beasts, the Evil Walkers. The runners might not get another chance to see them alive. Pete turned to Eric with a questioning look.

"Of course you can," Eric said.

They all started toward the shed again, the runners in tow, when he commented, "Two of them lost family to those things. But then, most of us are family here. We try to have events with local tribes, you know, powwows, picnics and such, for the young people to meet. So, lots of relatives here. First cousins, second, aunts and uncles. I'm sure they lose track after a while."

Jason changed the subject. "Gizmo, you never did come up the gorge like we planned on the maps, did you?"

"No. Never got a chance," he said.

"So you never got to compare the map to the satellite images, and compare them to what was actually there?" he asked.

Gizmo looked at him quizzically and said, "No. Never been there, except for that one spot. Never seen it. Why?"

"Because the satellite had that part of the gorge missing. It was filled in. Airbrushed or something or copied and pasted terrain," Jason told him.

"You see," Eric cut in. "I knew it. The government IS doing something. I knew it. I was thinking we were just all getting paranoid. But it's too much. Lying about people, missing people. The airlifting. I was thinking maybe it was all that Catskill bunch, but now...I want to see them. The satellite images."

"Sure, they're in the RV; you can come over any time. But there are lots of privately owned satellites too. Look at Google." Jason continued his train-of thought. "But the loose lips lecture. I think, now, maybe it's more important to talk about it. The satellites, they do everything. Phones, images, television. Everything.

"If the government is involved... well, I can't say that anymore can I? How about this: Since the government is somehow involved, I think you are right, we have to watch ourselves. We have to watch our calls. Just assume they are being monitored too, since this is now a hot area, and if a private corporation is involved, well, that's worse."

"And we have two of their pets now," Gizmo added.

At that, Eric spun and addressed the Runners. He told them what he told everyone else. No talking on the phones about what they were doing, no emails about it, no texting. Assume someone is listening.

Two of the Runners made runs to electronics shops routinely for parts for the slot machines in their casinos. They picked a name for one of the games, and that would be the code name for anything having to do with the Walkers. "Wild Times" was the code.

That being settled, they were about to start the tour when Jason spoke. "The biggest security risk you have right now is Gizmo and I."

"What do you mean?" asked Gizmo.

"We've been gone for two days and haven't checked in with the office. They'll be sending a search party out soon. We'll have to make up a good lie. A convincing one. Buy us some time," he said.

The Walkers went wild when they entered the building. "They been doing this the whole time," the guard told them. "But they really go nuts if one of us moves. Otherwise, they just keep charging at us pretty much non-stop. Crazy. You'd think they'd be tired by now."

The Runners apprehensively walked over to the cage, slightly behind Jason and Gizmo. As they gained courage, they got closer and closer, looking intently at their make-up. "Hey. This guy has a slug stuck in him," one of them called out.

"Where?" all three of them asked, but the beasts had stepped back and made another charge before he could point it out to them.

"Right under the jaw. Right on the neck. It's sticking in him. I can see it. That one." He pointed as one of them moved back to take another wild spring at the cage. "That one."

They all strained to see. One by one, they followed the charging monster, trying to get a better look. It was there. One by one, they saw it.

"I don't know if it's stuck in there, like just wedged, or if it actually penetrated its hide," Jason said.

They watched some more and started searching, scanning every part of them to see if there were any others. They all agreed there might have been one on the inner thigh of the other. But none were sure.

The runners came in slowly with their guides, but when they decided to get on with their mission, they left the building much more quickly. Whether it was out of purpose or out of fear, Jason couldn't tell. They were off for Wild Times, an appropriate code for their mission and anything to do with the beasts.

Next they went to the monitors and watched. They turned off the lights to watch in infrared. "Imagine the density of the hide. These slugs will go through an engine block," Gizmo said, looking at the screens, "Well, they show up on infrared, but I don't know if it's just from the friction or not. Are you recording this?" he asked.

"Every minute," said the guard.

Watching the video now in the dark, Gizmo again spoke up. "Can you play back this feed?" pointing at one of the monitors. "And blow it up. No, maybe put it on the widescreen."

That being done they watched again. "There. Right there, back it up. That right there. Look under the chin. It's brighter. So something is going on there. Right where the slug is. It's blood, some kind of blood. Rushing to repair the damaged cells. It shows up as more heat on infrared. He's hurt." He stood and looked at them. "We know something else too."

"It's warm blooded," Jason said. "Good job, Giz. Good job." They stayed, looked at other feeds, and tried to find the thigh injury with no success. "Maybe it's just not there," he eventually said.

"We better get moving. You and I need to get inside that cave and take a look. See what's there. See if there was a supply stash or something. See what's in there, something that would poison the fish like that. Maybe… maybe they keep something, like something to maybe…, I don't know, maybe keep them at home in the cave. Keep them returning. So they can watch.

"But we need to get in there. Go in that cave. Before we do though, we need to phone home, call Terry and let him know we're okay. I wonder if they know. I wonder if he knew," Jason mused.

Back in the Sheriffs' office, stopping first to let Bo out, they made up a story and called. It was the end of the day and everyone would be rushing to get out of the office. It was a perfect time to phone. Friday afternoon. The call would be cut short and weekend planning would be resumed. They wouldn't need to make contact again until Monday, and, if they played it right, not even then.

"Terry! It's Jason," he called into the phone as if nothing was wrong.

"Well. Nice of you to check in. We were about to send a search party. I just got off the phone with the ranger there trying to find you. What the hell?" Borden said.

"Awe. That's sweet. Did you miss us? We love you too," Jason ribbed.

"Asshole. So, are you done?" he asked.

"Hell no. Haven't even started," Jason began the tale. "You know what? You should have seen it. Pouring rain. Pouring!" he knew Terry had access to satellite images and anyone can check the weather, so that part had to be true. "And hail!" he continued, "It was amazing. Hell, no. Nope, we didn't even get started, but we'll get at it next week."

"Next week? Why next week? Is it raining now?" Terry asked. "Just go and get the samples and get back here." Then added, "Why the hell don't you guys call? I was getting worried."

"Couldn't. We had no reception where we were. We decided to go up in the hills and wait out the storm. Beautiful up here, Terry. Almost makes me not want to quit my job," Jason said.

"So you couldn't call? You have a phone now," he asked.

"Yah. Well, it's a land line. We got nothing where we were. Hey, we have some vacation time. We want to hang for a few days. Do a little relaxing. Hiking. Look around a bit. Let the rain run out of the hills before we go up there. You should have seen it, Terry. Intense, man. Really something to watch. You know, you really should get out from behind the desk and come with us now and then."

Terry was silent for a minute and then said, "Look. Go get the samples and overnight them to us. Then take your time off. It won't take but a few minutes to get there and..."

Jason looked at Gizmo and they both shook their heads in disgust. "No can do. I want the water to drain first. Too dangerous, Terry. Too many rockslides up there. They had warnings all over about them. They have rockslides all over here after a rain. Missing people, people getting killed by them, buried."

"Well. So Monday then. Right?" Terry asked.

"Um. Well, we were kind of thinking of taking a few days off too. Some places up there we wanted to go. Hey, I have tons of vacation time. Same with Gizmo. And we need it. You been slave driving us, man. You're a tyrant, a TYRANT I say!" Jason continued.

"Asshole. Yah, well. I guess you have time coming. Just that, I just hate it when you don't call. We don't know what the hell you're doing."

"Alright, boss. Alright. I'll call. Maybe not right away. But as soon as we get out of the hills, we'll call. Promise," Jason told him.

"Alright then," Terry said. "Talk to you soon - next week. But next week for sure, right?'

"Oh yah. I can't imagine staying cooped up with Gizmo for more than a week. But don't get all clingy. If we don't call, you know, we're having a little vacation," Jason played along.

They both said their good byes and hung up the phones. As soon as the receiver hit the cradle, Jason and Gizmo both started, "That lying rotten sack!"

"Two face back-stabbing piece of crap!" Gizmo cried out. "He knew, the bastard!"

"What?" Eric asked with a bewildered look. "How do you know?"

"Look," Jason began. "We do dangerous stuff. He would never want us to go someplace if there was any unnecessary risk. Any unnecessary risk!"

"He knew. The bastard," Gizmo added. "He knew. Did you hear him? He said, what? That we're only a few minutes away. He knows! They know exactly where we are."

The three sat, considering the implications, thinking about the conversation, then going over each word again and again. Considering the significance of it all and discussing it, every word and every inflection.

Jason watched Bo walk over to the empty bucket and shove her nose in it to take a sniff. "She must be hungry," he said, and realized how hungry he was. Wondering how long it had been since they had eaten, he said, "Let's eat."

Chapter Twenty-One

The woman behind the counter of the local store always had a pot of stew and another pot of hominy soup going and would serve it up to customers throughout the day. She was an older woman who kept her hair tied back and wore a colorful dress with an Indian design. Jason studied the lines on her face as she served up their food, lines from the weather, the sun, and age.

The edges of her mouth turned downward and her eyes were dark, making her look sad. "I have a feeling you are going to need your strength," she told them, and filled the bowls to the top. As she was passing the bowl to Jason, she took hold of his hand and stared deep into his eyes. "I heard about what you did. The spirits told me you would. So I was not afraid.

"They showed me the Evil Walkers some months ago and told me you would come. They told me to tell you to have courage. More depends on you than you know. Secrets. There are secrets and you must be cautious. Prepare for travels, they said to tell you. Your courage, it will guide you to the right decisions." Releasing his hand, she turned back to her duties.

They took their bowls and some bread and sat at a corner table eating quietly. Finally, Gizmo spoke. "Nobody going to say something? What was that?"

Eric swallowed a mouthful of stew, looked up and took a breath, "We, well, some of us speak to spirits. The ancestors. Some of us still do that."

"What exactly do you mean by 'Speak' to them? I've never understood that." Jason sat back in his chair and continued, "I've always wondered about that. Do they come to you? Is it a vision, like some idea of it, an impression? Or do they actually come and, well, come and speak?"

"Both. I've had both. Not so much until lately." He looked back at the woman behind the counter. "She's always had them. The ancestors, they speak to her, and then, there are wise ones. The Ancients. They know. They can come and speak and can guide."

"What do they say?" Gizmo asked, and then added, "I don't mean to be cynical or offensive, I'm not meaning it that way, just curious, but, if they speak, what language do they use? Especially the Ancients. Is it an ancient language?"

"These are good questions," Eric replied. "I take no offense. I'd ask the same questions. Some are powerful. They are strong spirits. They can will people. They guide them this way, with their will. If you are in touch with the spirits, you know it and you let them guide you.

"Others who are not in touch are still guided. They just don't know it. But some of us, it's a little different. We speak, some of us. We can have conversation and reason things out with them." He looked over at the woman again. "She has always spoken with them. That is Singingbird. It's what she was named by her parents.

"Her parents said that they called her that because the spirits sent that bird. It was custom to name a child after something that appears soon after birth. So she is named Singingbird, although almost everyone calls her Hellen. I forget why.

"She has always spoken to them. Ever since she could speak she talked about them." Eric swallowed a few more bites of stew while Jason and Gizmo sat waiting for him to continue. "I used to. Not like her, not as clear, but I used to.

"I wondered if it was imagination. But one day they spoke to me. They told me about a bear over in a place I used to play when I was a kid. They spoke to me and they showed me the bear as a warning not to go there. It was huge. Of course, I being smaller made it appear that way.

"I spoke to Singingbird that day, and she had the same conversation. So, we talked about it and decided to go and see how dependable…" He said with a laugh, "How dependable these spirits were. Yah. I never doubted again. I don't know if she ever did doubt, but I sure as hell never doubted again.

"We spent, oh, I don't know, hours up a tree. Hours. You know bears can climb, right?" and they both nodded and mentioned that they found out the hard way. "Well. It was the exact same bear they showed me. I guess they wanted to teach us a lesson. They let us stay up there for quite a while before sending some villagers to the rescue.

"When I got home and told my parents the story, they tanned my hide for disrespecting the ancestors. I never doubted again."

"Wow. I wish I had some of those," Jason started, "Maybe would have warned me about coming out here, about Terry and trusting him."

"Who says they haven't influenced you? You had plenty of opportunity to turn away. A message on your cell phone. A written letter. A storm. You still came. You even quit your job, but still, you're here.

"I used to speak to them fairly often. Don't really like talking about it. Except for people that live around here, if you mention it, people will think you're crazy. Even some of our own people are starting not to believe. Then I joined the military. Now, I guess, I don't know. We don't talk like we used to. Maybe I'm on a different frequency. I don't know. I did some things, I think it changed me. Bad things. Maybe they're mad at me. Maybe they gave up on me – a lost cause. Lost soul."

"We all did bad stuff," Gizmo came to his defense. "But we did right. What we thought was right. Did our jobs. I mean, look at us. All three of us, Colonels. You know how it is. As you rise in rank, your mistakes are magnified, and I guess, your feeling of guilt with it. They impact other people more and more – your decisions. It's natural." He looked down at the table in reflection, then snapped out of it and asked Jason, "So, you never said. What made you go civilian?"

"I don't know," Jason replied vaguely. "You know, I was a sniper. Good at it too. After a while though, you don't think about the life you're taking. It's just an image in the scope. Kind of get numb to it all. Then, I guess, somebody found out I was smarter than the average, not bragging or anything, but, you know what I mean. Found out I went to school, studied Physics and Quantum Physics and such."

"Oh," Eric said. "So you really are smart. He wasn't just bragging. You do know this stuff."

"Well, look," Jason explained, "Educated doesn't mean smart. So I wouldn't hang that on me. I've done plenty of dumb things, without a doubt, so I'd never admit to being actually smart. But I did get some education. Gizmo too. It's how we met. I guess someone somewhere found out I went to school, and got me edumacated. Next thing I knew, I was in a bio-suit, crawling into caves and holes and bunkers with Gizmo here in the Middle East. Checking out chemical and biological weapons mostly, but some nuclear."

"Yah. So what made you decide to get out?' Gizmo asked again.

"I don't know. I was sitting there one day when some newbies came in and I just looked and thought that these guys had it covered. They could take over. My job was done. It was just a feeling, that's all. I was done with this job. That's all."

"Me too. That's almost exactly what happened," Gizmo said.

And Eric looked at them and said, "Me too. Almost exactly that same feeling. They had it, they could take over."

"You have to go to the cave now." All three jumped when they heard the voice. "Didn't you hear me?" They turned to see Hellen standing at the table. "I've been talking to you. There is something waiting there for you in the cave. You have to go now." She began picking up their bowls and turned back toward her counter.

Jason stood up. "Yah, really. We have to go to the cave. We should wear suits. I've got my spare in the RV, you got yours?"

"Never leave home without it," Gizmo replied.

"I should come too. Bring a half dozen braves with us. Just in case," Eric said.

"I have a spare suit. Ever been in one?" Gizmo asked.

"We all trained for gas attacks. But never been inside one of those, not the full-on space suits I think you're talking about. No," Eric answered, thinking to himself, that's the first time he'd ever referred to his men as "Braves". He turned to look at Singingbird watching them leave.

Bo was happy to be moving again. She would still look toward the shed containing the Walkers with her ears perked up and the hair on her neck standing up. Then she would look at the men getting their gear ready and get excited again. It was another trip with more duties and commands for her to follow and new ground to cover. Maybe even more excitement like they had with the cats. Exciting!

There were nine people in the party and they all piled into three trucks. There was some discussion about whether or not there could be more Evil Walkers in the canyon or in the cave.

They decided that, if there were, they would have been out and attacking with the other two during their capture. However, not knowing what they would find, they would still go armed with shotguns, the twelve gage pump, loaded with slugs, and have whatever usual weapons they would carry for an assault or defense.

In a cloud of dust, they headed for the same trail the horsemen had dragged the monsters up to their cage. They started down the trail, all men listening as the protocols were discussed. Nobody should go into the water. Nobody should go into the caves without a suit. Try not to touch anything that the Walkers may have touched. Stand guard and warn the people inside if anything approaches. They didn't want to be trapped inside the cave.

Jason had to assign someone to Bo. Someone who would take care of her in case something bad happened. He tried to choose who it would be all the way down into the canyon. Bo couldn't come into the cave. She could get poisoned. She couldn't go into the water, and if they didn't come back out, she would need a new companion.

He saw one of the men reach to pet her several times. He obviously liked the dog, and Bo would allow him to touch her, so she liked him. He would give her a command. This command, like most of her commands were, was one that she would follow until released from that duty by Jason himself.

The man's name was Gary. Jason introduced himself and then asked, "If something happens, like if we don't come back out. Would you take care of my dog?"

"Of course," Gary answered. "She is a good dog. You know how to tell if they are good dogs? Loyal? You look at the roof of their mouths. If it is dark, they will be good. The darker the better, and she has a black mouth. Don't worry. She'll be alright."

Jason walked up to Bo and stroked her head and pointed at Gary, "Bo," he said as she followed the direction the finger pointed. It was the tone of voice that did it, alerting her to pay particular attention because she was about to be told to do something. "Bo, protect," was all he had to say.

She ran to Gary's side and sat, and she would protect him for the rest of her life if Jason never returned and she would be in good hands. "Good girl," he called.

"Nice dog," Eric said as they walked toward the cave. "So what's the plan? We just going to walk in and yell, 'Hello'?"

"No, Eric. Where's your manners," Gizmo took him by the shoulders and slowly turned him to inspect his gear. "You ring the doorbell and wipe your feet first," patting him on the leg to check for positive pressure in the suit. "Your ears popping or anything?"

"No. I'm good. I think. Unless…should they be popping?" Eric asked.

"No. Right here. That's your pressure gage. You want more pressure inside than outside. Keeps the bad stuff out. If you need more air, turn this, right here," and grabbed his hand and put it on the gage. "Righty tighty, lefty loosey. Okay?"

"Got it. Left for more air," Eric said.

"Correct," Jason said. "Look, just leave if you think you're in trouble. Get out and we'll see you outside. First sign of trouble, especially a Walker, you turn and move and get out. Don't look back. You'll trip and fall. Watch you don't tear the suit. We don't want you getting yourself sick breathing in something."

The three approached the cave entrance. "Why am I doing this?" Jason thought. "This is dangerous. This is stupid. The Government should be here. That's what they get paid for."

Then he realized that he was the government. Part of it, anyway. Maybe not the right part, but part. Who would he call? Who would come? The Department of Evil Walkers? No, he was it - he and Gizmo. Their jobs were never easy. It was never the easy stuff they did. Once again, there they were, doing the hard stuff.

First Jason stepped to the side of the entrance to look in as far as he could; slicing the pie as he stepped around to the other side. Gizmo stayed on his knee prepared to enter. It was the same system they used in every bunker and cave they went into in the Middle East, and it kept them alive so far.

They both took a step through the fatal tunnel, the mouth of the cave, and checked to the corners and stopped, letting their eyes adjust and moved to the sides again.

"Dark," Gizmo said. "Ready?"

"Ready as I'll ever be." Jason checked the breach on his rifle to be sure a round was in there. Something he had done at least six times since they put their suits on. The other two did the same. He looked around at them as best as he could in the suit and took another step inside. He reached up to his helmet and flipped the light on, then turned to Eric who was feeling around for the switch and flipped his. "There. You see okay?"

"Yah. I mean I can't see much. I'm looking out a hole. How do you guys do this?" Eric asked.

"Just be careful," Jason told him. "You don't want to trip and fall and tear your suit." With that he turned to shine his light on the back of the cave.

Jason and Gizmo panned their light back and forth towards the back. Then they did the same on the floor, looking for trip hazards. When they were satisfied they scanned the roof of the cave, and they moved in.

Chapter Twenty-Two

They took two steps forward and paused. It was a routine they developed, so they knew what each other was doing and thinking most of the time. Eric followed.

"Look," Eric said. "Is that a cave-in? Way in the back there. You see it?"

They all stood and looked. Jason and Gizmo scanned the rock fall first, then the sides around it and then in front of it and above it. "Looks like," Jason finally replied. "Don't want to be under that stuff, huh Giz?"

Gizmo didn't answer. Instead he put his hand on Jason's shoulder and then pointed to an area of the cave. They walked to it and bent over, directing both their lights to the spot.

"Know what that looks like to me?" Gizmo finally said. "That is a nest. Or a bed. Looks like they were lying down here. Kind of burrowed in a little bit. Like a dog does, kind of. Digs a little bit and gets down inside."

"So, I guess they do get tired eventually. I guess they sleep," Jason muttered and then looked around. "No bones or anything in here. You see any? Nothing that looks like they dragged something in here and ate it either."

"I guess they dine out, huh?" Gizmo said.

Eric walked up with them now and looked it over. "I'm just glad we're not seeing eggs or hatchlings or whatever. Babies. A litter. Whatever they have."

"Me too," Jason said. "Let's look around some more. Nothing alive in here. Let's split up. Eric, You and Gizmo go up the left side there to the entrance, I'll go up the right. Then, we'll all come back down the middle. Anything. Anything you see. You call out, okay?"

They moved slowly up the sides. Jason stopped and looked at the other two and thought, "We're missing it. Something is here and we're not seeing it. I have to see. Not look. See. See what is actually there. Looking is only pretending. Seeing is the real thing.

"We can look all day long. But without seeing, it's a waste of time. People, they look for answers their whole life. They never see it. It could be right in front of them, but they only looked and never saw."

He panned the light again from where he stood on the side of the cave. He panned all the way to the back, then across the rear where the collapse had happened, and then started up the other side. There were some rocks jutting out. Under it was an open area.

"Why didn't they make their burrow there?" he thought. "It's more protected. It's what a dog would do. There would be less possibility of attack from above and all sides except the front. Why did they nest here?"

The other two had stopped and were watching Jason now. He went back to the nest. "Look, Jason, look. Look and see," he told himself. "Rocks. There are rocks here."

Then he spun around to look at the other side. "But there are rocks there, too." He stood there in the silence of the cave. All he could hear is his breathing and his heartbeat. It was something he'd become used to, his solitude, shut off from the outside world.

He could think inside his suit. It was his very own private cave, so to speak. A cave inside a cave. A place to focus and have uninterrupted thoughts. No one dares to follow. Nothing gets in, but he can see out. A place where he can look. He can look out the opening and see.

Eric and Gizmo were curious now and started to approach.

Jason walked from the nest toward the back of the cave again. "Are these rocks any different?" he asked himself. He examined them, then walked to the other side and examined those. "Just rocks, that's all they were." Then looked back at the nest and walked over.

"Clever bastards," he thought. "You hid it," and took one of the rocks and lifted it. It should have weighed over fifty pounds, but it was light as a feather. The other two were there now and began checking the other rocks. They were only rocks.

"Come on." Jason brought it to the center of the cave. They rolled it over and over inspecting it. "Feel it." Jason handed it to Gizmo. "Light as a feather."

Gizmo took it and rolled it around and handed it to Eric who bounced it up and down. "What is it?" he asked.

"Fake rock. It's fake. But something is inside it," Gizmo said. "Let me see." Taking the rock and turning it more slowly, he noticed a bump and pressed it. The rock popped open exposing some circuitry on the inside of the lid. "Look," he pointed. "Batteries."

"Not like any batteries I've ever seen," Eric said.

"What's inside there?" Jason said, pointing. "You see that, looks like wax or something. What is that?"

"You know what this looks like?" Gizmo asked. "I'd put money on it. Remember those atomizers? They sold them on T.V. for a while. Used them to send out a stream of mist. They said that it atomized the water. Took one apart once. That's what this reminds me of. An atomizer."

"I remember those. Late night T.V. commercials. I think there was some multi-level marketing thing selling it too," Eric said, "But what's it atomizing. Maybe that's what's killing the fish. Maybe that's the poison."

They examined it even closer now. "But wait! There's more!" Gizmo joked, "What the hell is that. I've never seen one of those before, and that there. Looks like some kind of a chip inside some sort of, I don't know, a capacitor, maybe. Jason, this is something that, well these parts, some of them I've never seen. I have no idea what they are or what they do."

"Agreed. Between us, there isn't much we haven't seen. I think that is what we were looking for. Pull the batteries," Jason told him. "Pull it and let's get the hell out of here – send a scraping to the lab and see what it is inside there."

They watched as the battery pack was pulled and were getting up when they heard it. It came from the back of the cave; behind the cave-in. At first it was just a sound of movement. All three grabbed their shotguns and looked to the rear and directed the light to the rocks.

Then they heard scratching and rustling. It got louder, and they were now standing up straight. Then the screeching and screaming and howling came from behind the rocks.

"Walkers!" one of them yelled as all three darted toward the cave entrance, Gizmo carrying the rock under his arm like a football, moving as fast as they could in the suits. "A lot of them!"

As they ran through the mouth of the cave, screaming a warning to the men waiting outside, fifty miles away, deep in a mountain, a man walked into an office containing a large map. The map was similar to the one in the Sheriff office back on the reserve on Ruby Lake.

It was similar, but not the same. It had all of the one hundred and twenty markings on it, the same as that, but it was marked with lights illuminating each one. It also had several hundred other markings.

A man was sitting at the desk looking over papers and occasionally glancing up to the map when another walked in. "Excuse me, General. We had another signal go dead. Ruby Lake."

"Alright. That's why we have backups, Captain. You know what to do. Get me satellite images and reports and turn the backup on. Why are you telling me about this?" he asked.

"Well sir. We've had several hundred go down now. They do not have a high life-expectancy."

"Neither do you and I, Captain. What point are you making?"

"Calculations, Sir. The expectancy sir. The devices started going down about six weeks ago. That gives us their life expectancy, the average, General. According to calculations, the backups will start going down in the next ten days. Ruby Lake was a backup," The Captain explained.

"That will be terrible, won't it, Captain," the General asked.

"Yes, Sir. There will be nothing holding them back. They will get out and into the population," he said.

"And you think we should do something about it?" The general turned toward the map.

"Yes. Sir," the Captain said, "It seems like we should."

"Well Captain. Ten days." The general turned back toward him and asked, "You have family?"

"Yes, General. A wife. Two daughters," he replied.

"You'd better call them, son. You say they will start failing in ten days? It won't matter in ten days. In ten days, it'll all be over. It won't matter if they fail. We have three. Maybe four," and he walked back over to the map and pointed to a spot with a light next to it.

"I was born right there," he said. "Still have family there. Poor bastards. May God forgive us."

The General turned and asked, "How is the contraption coming, Captain? Any progress?"

"I'm afraid they are not having much success, Sir. I fear they will not be ready in time," the Captain replied.

"Me too, Captain. Me too. Bring me the satellite images and the reports," and he looked at him and said, "Dismissed."

"Walkers!" Eric yelled to his men as he tore at his bio-suit. "Run!" But they didn't run. They all got on one knee and lifted their weapons at the cave ready to fire on whatever would come out.

Gizmo and Jason peeled their suits off and left them as they were running. Jason stopped and grabbed Eric and helped him to the spot the others were intending to defend. He got him out of his suit and let it drop while he raised his gun. Nothing came out.

They listened to the faint growling from deep inside, but nothing came through. "Maybe they can't get through the rocks." Jason paused for another second or two and then jumped up. "Let's get out of here!" and bolted toward the trail. "Come, Bo!" he called.

They all got up and ran with him back to the trucks, piled in, and in another cloud of dust returned to the village. The three of them sat in the cab thinking about what they had just experience. The same thing went through each of their minds.

The noise. How many of them were there? Maybe dozens. Maybe more. Maybe hundreds, maybe thousands, and if it took thirty well-armed men to capture two of them, and they were entirely unable to kill them, think of what so many others would do. One or two of them could wipe out the village and kill every one and every living thing in it. A few dozen of them could wipe out entire cities.

Eventually they got out of the truck. The men who rode with them were already waiting outside. Eric walked up to one of them and said, "I want you to take men and get some dynamite, a lot of it, and I want you to close that cave. Nothing can come out of there."

They were met on the way into the War Room by the Gunny. "Pay dirt, Colonel," he told him. "Looks like we found something of interest. We have photos and Branford is waiting for debrief."

"Good. What did you find?" he asked.

"Looks like there are pretty big plans, Sir. Railroad tracks leading up to and disappearing into a mountain. Two sets. One going in and one going out. Looks like lots of activity." Once in the room he called to Branford. "Come on over here son. Good job by the way."

They sat and studied the photos while Branford and his men explained what they'd seen. They were up on the side of a cliff about a thousand yards off. Two sets of tracks. One loaded with cattle coming in. One empty going out. Guards at the entrances. No need for security where they were observing from, it would be inaccessible unless you were familiar with the area.

They had .50 calibers at the entrances. Up the tracks there was a bunker with six men in it. "I couldn't get much closer, so I couldn't see what munitions they had there, but they had some for sure, and the .50 cals, they had two sets, one pointing in and one pointing out.

I think that whatever it is we are looking for is in there. They have communications set up here," pointing to a photo, "Satellite communications here."

They poured over it again and again. Noise, smells, sights. Nothing was left out. "This mountain here, this range, Ruby Ridge. Right?" Eric asked. "That's what, about fifty miles from the cave?"

"That's right Colonel. Ruby Ridge. That right there where the tracks lead is another old cave they widened and started mining out of way back. It was shut down maybe ten years ago," Branford replied. "Was born around there. Hunted it my whole life. I know every rock over there."

"I think we need to get inside and see what is going on in there. Any ideas?" Eric asked.

"Sure. Lots. These old mines always had air shafts going up at angles. I almost fell in through one once. But I know where a couple of them are that we could fit some people through. Better bring ropes though."

"Well then. Gunny. You get some men together and get them set out in the morning," Eric said. "I think it's time we found out what they're doing."

Jenkins came in during the meeting with a jar of lake water and a fish wrapped in plastic. The Runners arrived with the electronics. It was time to get to work and see what these things are made of.

"Ranger Jenkins, I think we better do something with you that you might not like," Jason said. "I think you might not like it, but I think it is the smart thing to do."

"What's that?" he asked.

"Well. We have one missing ranger, and we don't want two. I'm worried that we are going to draw attention to ourselves before we find out what is really going on," Jason explained. "If you suddenly are gone as well, I'm sure somebody is going to notice. I'm not saying you won't be involved, in fact I think you will be very much involved."

"So, what did you have in mind?" Jenkins asked.

"You are in a perfect position. You have a job that requires you to go places and do things without much notice. You can be on the lake or around it, and really, any place you see fit within the park. You can also go into town and even here if your job requires it. You are perfect to be our eyes and ears and are in perfect position if we need something done or looked into. You even know who is in the park – visitors and such."

"So you want me to be look-out? I have no problem with that," he said.

"Right, and watch for things out of the ordinary. You should put 'Lake Closed' signs around. Just because of the dead fish. So, if you have campers around still, maybe people who don't look like they have families and aren't just pulling in for the night; that would be kind of suspicious to me."

Eric pulled out some of the maps and satellite images. "See here? This is an image of where we caught the Walkers. You know, that flat area? And that little lake? Gone."

"Yah. So it's not like we can call the police or the National Guard for help," Eric said. "We are kind of on our own until we get more information, and it is coming in faster and faster now. Strange things. In fact, Wild Times. That will be the code word for anything related to the Walkers. Wild Times."

Eric looked around the room and saw that it was beginning to fill up and decided to brief everyone on the events and information gathered during the day. Since it is usual to conduct business having to do with their casinos and the slots, Wild Times had become the code, named after one of their machines.

He went over everything. The rock they found, the train tracks into the mountain, the reports coming in from the other Nations, and the cave; the cave with an unknown number of Walkers in it. He told them what they knew now about the Walkers. They sleep. They are possibly warm-blooded. They can be damaged.

Then, he instructed them again on security. Phones, emails, and even private conversations in public would have to be avoided or coded or spoken in their native tongues. Then he scanned the crowd and made his closing instructions.

"That we know of, there are over two hundred of these things. From what we could find out from the cave, the Walkers that were behind the rocks, there could be any number of these things, from dozens to hundreds to, well, even thousands of them. If they were ever to get out, get into the population…I can't imagine what would happen. Los Angeles. New York. Think about it.

"We had thirty men, all good shots, firing slugs at them and didn't hurt them. These slugs will go through an engine block. Didn't stop 'em. It was only the sheer weight of the combined impact that knocked them over and drove them back into our nets. I don't even know if a bomb would kill them.

"Someone has a secret. A secret is only good when nobody knows about it. But we have a secret too. It's an important secret and it has to be guarded. The secret is that we know the secret. The Evil Walkers.

"They have been kept secret. But we know about them now. While whoever brought them to our land and our people still thinks it is a secret, we have to find out more. Exploit it. Exploit that secret while they still think it is a secret."

"Gunny!" he turned to him. "It's all yours."

"Alright!" he got up and rumbled. "Assignments for tomorrow. You are going to need your beauty sleep tonight, so pay attention and NO FOOLISHNESS! No staying up late. No partying! We need you sharp. You will not be seen. You will not be heard," he continued his instructions.

Chapter Twenty-Three

It was getting late and Jason was beginning to feel it. He, Gizmo, Eric, and Jenkins headed to the shed, stopping to put Bo in the motor home on the way. The electronics they requested were piled on top of a table that was set up next to the monitors.

"Okay then. Enough playing around. Back to work." Jason looked the pile over briefly and continued. "So, which do you want, the pulse or the logic controller?"

"How about I do the pulse. It'll take about twenty minutes and then I'll start tinning your wires while you finish up the programming," Gizmo replied.

"What do you want us to do?" Jenkins asked.

"You know what? There is something you can do." Jason turned to him. "I want to see how their vision works. I'd like you to heat something up and we'll hit the lights, I mean turn them off. We'll watch on the infrared while we move it across the room. See if they track it – track the heat."

"No problem. We'll heat up a rock or a piece of metal and pull it across the room," Eric said.

"Or even better, let's hook it up to the gantry, suspend it, and move it. That way we will know for sure. If we drag it, they might be following the sound and not the heat," Jenkins said.

"Good thinking. In fact, do both. We can check vision and sound." Gizmo looked at them and chuckled. "You guys could find out with low tech stuff more than we will. Good thinking."

The two men left the building while Jason and Gizmo started snipping wires and laying out the circuitry they would use. One of the Runners came in and asked, "So, you got everything you need?"

"Looks pretty good. This will do us for tonight, but I'll have to send you for some things tomorrow. Oh, hey, can you get me a good microscope?" Gizmo asked.

"I can get just about anything you need. Whatever we can't buy, we take from somewhere," he snickered, "Like all of that railroad track we made the cage out of."

"Well, in that case, I could really use a Mass Spectrometer. I'll just make another list for you," Gizmo told him.

"Hmm. Mass Spectrometer. Not your every-day shopping item." The Runner stood and watched them prepare the wires and said, "You know, I can do some of that. I repair the slots. I'm pretty good with a soldering iron."

"About thirty pieces of six-inch wire, stripped about a half inch and tinned at the ends," Gizmo said as he handed him a couple of rolls of wire and turned the soldering station around facing him. "Have fun."

They all concentrated on the tedious work, stripping wires, arranging the bread board, putting diodes and resistors where they were needed, and programming the logic controller. Before long, the litter of electronic parts began taking a form.

The runner stood and stripped the wires first while the iron heated up, looking now and then at Jason and Gizmo, wanting to start a conversation, building up the nerve and finally saying, "You know, I think I'll just send Jones to the University for that Spectrometer. He can just get it from there. By the time they know it's gone, who knows."

He looked up at Jason and Gizmo working and continued, "They might not even miss it. Might think someone else has it – some professor. Then we don't have to wait, and they get all the best equipment."

The Runner continued working, the beasts behind them in the cage ranting and screeching. "So. What do you think they are?" he finally asked.

"Not sure," Jason said. "What do you think?"

"I don't know. But they don't look natural," he said.

"That, I agree on. It could be a hybrid. Could be someone created a monster. Maybe mutated too," Jason said.

"Yah," Gizmo jumped in. "Someone like Catskill and their Frankenstein team."

"They look alien," the Runner continued. "They don't look like any animal or any reptile I've ever seen," and looked up to watch their reactions, "How about you?"

"Alien? Gees, I don't know. That's a bit of a stretch. Kind of out there. But who knows, right?" Gizmo commented, enjoying the small talk.

"I don't know," Jason said. "I don't know what they are. But I do know what they aren't, and that's space men," and he pointed the wire stripper in their direction. "Look at them. Do they look like they could build a space ship and fly across the galaxy?"

"Good point," the Runner said. "But that doesn't mean they are from here either," and he got busy again with his work, mumbling, "Sure don't look like they're from around here, anyway."

Eric and Jenkins came through the door pulling a red wagon with squeaky wheels and loaded with items for their test. Jenkins pulled out a rope and wrapped it around a post in the back of the building and tied both ends to the handle of the wagon. They tested it to make sure they could pull the wagon in either direction and yelled, "Okay. Watch this."

The wagon moved across the floor, wheels squealing all the way to the back of the building while they watched the Walkers react, and did they react! Throwing themselves against the cage walls and howling and screaming as it moved.

"Wow," Eric said. "They didn't like that."

Then Jenkins said, "Let's try it without the noise."

They took the wagon and tied the handle to the gantry and hooked up a similar method to roll it back and forth by pulling a rope. Again the beasts reacted. "Okay. Lights off," Eric said. "Ready?" and when everyone was, they flipped the lights and watched the infrared, pulling the wagon through the air silently toward the rear of the room. Again, they reacted.

"What the...?" Gizmo said, "No difference."

Then Jason said, "There's hardly a point to it, but let's heat something up and see what happens. Just to be sure, complete the test, so to speak."

Eric and Jenkins got a torch and heated up a piece of rail road track they had hung on the gantry. Then, put it in the wagon and pulled it as before, both with the lights on and the lights off. The monsters reaction was the same in each case.

The men stood wordlessly in the dark from the final test. Nothing made a difference. Each action was met with the same reaction.

After waiting for some time, the Runner spoke, "Wrong spectrum, eh?"

"What?" Gizmo replied, not because he didn't hear or understand. He was just surprised to hear him say it.

"Wrong spectrum," the Runner repeated. "They don't care if our light is on or off, that is not the spectrum they are seeing. You would have to have total darkness, one hundred percent darkness, and then, maybe these tests would work, maybe show you something. Maybe not even then.

"Right now, I bet the light from the computer screens is enough for them to see clearly, and who knows what things put out that they could be seeing. You know, atoms and such. Maybe they can see something we can't."

"What are you talking about, spectrum?" Asked Jenkins.

"Ever play with a prism?" the Runner asked.

"Well yes, when I was a kid," Jenkins replied.

"All those colors. Different light waves," the Runner started explaining, "Some spectrums we can't even see: like infrared and ultraviolet. We can't see them with our eyes, but they are there. The camera here can catch it, the infrared, and the camera changes it into something we can see. But there's lots of light we can't see."

"Who the hell are you, kid?" Jason asked.

"What, you thought we were all just dumb Indians?" he asked, making them all laugh a little.

"No, no. It's not that," Jason said. "It's just that we could use a little help around here with this stuff and it looks like you might know a little thing or two." Then he looked at Eric and said, "And really, the more I think about it, the more I'd like to get a closer look at that mew cave myself in the morning. The Ruby Ridge cave, and maybe get inside." Turning to the Runner, he said, "I was thinking you and Gizmo… you could be as good a help as I could with this stuff. Pretty straight forward stuff here."

"I was hoping you would say that," Eric said. "I wanted to go there myself. If that's alright with Colonel Crozley, or Col. Gizmo, that is. Mind if I borrow Jason for a while?"

"No. It's a good idea. I wanted to go myself, but that will work out fine," and then looked at the runner, "That is if it's okay with you."

"Sure," The Runner said. "I'd like that."

"And, I ask again. Who the hell are you?" Gizmo repeated.

"This, my friends, is Cody Runningsprings. The brains of the tribe. You met his Grandmother at the store," Eric explained. "He has been doing this kind of thing since he was about five. Probably enjoy the conversation with you guys, instead of talking to us pee-brains," and laughed.

"Good to meet you, Cody," Gizmo said as he shook hands. "Welcome aboard. I'd be interested in any ideas and input you have. Even if you talk about aliens."

"Aliens?" Jenkins exclaimed.

"We were just talking. Jason torpedoed that idea. Pulled that logic thing out that he uses now and then," Gizmo said.

"So…about this spectrum thing. What were you talking about, really? I get the idea. But what can we do with it?" Jenkins turned the conversation back to his experiment.

"Well. I guess we can try different spectrums. I can set something up. Lights and such," said Cody.

"But what about the ones we can't see? How can you set something up that you can't see? You won't know if you have it or not," Jenkins asked.

"Something I've been working on at home for a few months," Cody said.

"Really?" Jason asked. "What do you have going?"

"It's just an idea I had. A series of lenses, sort of like prisms. You know, shine a light through one end, have it refracted to the next one, have that refracted to the next, on and on through a series.

"That way all colors in the prism gets tested in every variable. I guess I could add some more lenses to complete it. It's not the colors. It's the space in between the different colors that I'm interested in. If there is a blank space, it means there is a color I'm not seeing."

"Brilliant," Eric exclaimed. "You can put it on a little motor that turns nice and slow while someone watches the reaction."

"Only one problem," Cody said. "We don't know if it's the same light…Okay, let me put it this way. We don't know all there is about light. We don't know about a lot of things.

"We make statements like, 'Oh, the black holes bend the light. That's how we know that there's a black hole.' and then everyone thinks that way because we can't prove it wrong, and maybe it isn't wrong. But then, they say that a black hole has gravity so intense, and it is so dense, that not even light can escape from it. That's why it's black."

"That's right!" Jenkins jumped in. "Then a couple of years ago they found one that actually shoots out light. So what do we know, right?"

"Then there is the theory that they are worm holes to different parts of the universe," Eric threw his two cents worth in, "and another one, that they are entrances or doors to other universes or entrances to ours. I guess the one with light shooting out is leaking."

Everyone laughed at the idea of a universe leaking into our own.

"But," Cody went on. "What we know about light is so small, really. Different stars have different elements. We only see within the light spectrum our sun has forced us to evolve to see. But other suns, other stars? We don't know.

"For all we know, these black holes could be the brightest stars in the universe. We just can't see that kind of light. Like infrared and ultraviolet, we can't see those."

"So, any idea of how to test for that?" Jason asked. "How to duplicate light from other stars?"

"You see!" Gizmo yelled out, "Now you're thinking of space too. Aliens!"

"Ha. No, no, no, no. I'm not going that far just yet," Jason said. "But clearly we need to do more and check different light. I'm open to anything that will get a result. Two or three days ago, I would have called you crazy if you told me you saw a monster."

"And now, look how far you've come," Gizmo said. "We're all so proud of you."

That got the room laughing again which made the Walkers go crazy.

"You know what. I'm tired," Jason announced. "Let's get some rest and get a fresh start in the morning. We all have a big day ahead of us."

They walked to Jason's motor home and he invited them all to a beer. Bo was happy to get out and bounced around between the visitors outside while they chatted. It was a perfectly clear night and, without any lights of a city, the stars were as clear and bright as they had ever seen. Eventually they had all said goodnight and gone to their homes leaving Jason and Gizmo to themselves.

Jason wrestled a couple of camping chairs out of his motor home that he had stored under the seat and they sat and stared at the stars. Now and then a shooting star would fly across the sky or a coyote would howl, and the only other sound was the pop of a beer can every now and then until Gizmo said, "So. Mountain lions. You thought I got eaten by mountain lions?"

"Yup. Was sure of it," he answered.

He began to tell the story, beginning at the signs of missing persons and continued all the way through every step that brought him to the conclusion that he had been eaten. Then he started to detail his trip back down the canyon.

Every now and then there would be a cry from Gizmo saying, "NO WAY!" with a roar of laughter, or "No shit!", "Oh, My God!", or some other such exclamation, but mostly he sat listening intently.

When he had finished the story, all Gizmo could say was, "Wow. I'll never get eaten by lions again, I promise."

Jason reached over and said, "Poor Bo," while patting her all over. "Those were bad kitty cats. Weren't they, Bo? Bad, BAD kitty cats."

Although they were sitting by themselves while the story was being told, they were not alone. In the little town, in the dead of night, sound travels. Almost everyone in the village nearby was listening by the time he was finished, especially Hellen Runningsprings, and most likely, the ancients that surround her. Perhaps those spirits were hoping this part of the story would be a part of a much larger story that would be told by this tribe and many others for generations.

Both sat silent again, staring at the stars, making a casual comment as the night wore on until Gizmo said, "So. A guy and a girl get married."

"Alright. A guy and a girl get married," Jason repeated after him.

"It was one of those really traditional couples. No sex before marriage or anything. Never even seen each other naked."

"Alright. A fantasy story. But go on," Jason chuckled.

"Right. So after the wedding, they go to the honeymoon suite. The girl gets all prepared and puts on her carefully chosen negligee and is lying there on the bed waiting for the new groom to come in. He comes in and starts getting undressed and he takes his socks and shoes off.

"The girl screams in terror, 'Oh! My god. What is that?' as she looks at the man's toes.

"Oh that. Well, when I was a kid, I got toesellitis."

"'Toesillitis! I've never heard of that,' she cried.

"'Oh, well. You see, all the other kids had tonsillitis. Me, I got toesellitis.' The guy tells her."

"Alright. Toesillitis," Jason chuckled again.

"Then the guy takes off his pants, and again, 'Oh! MY God! Your knees!' she screams.

"So the guy says, 'Well, yah. When I was a kid, I got kneezles.' And again, she says she's never heard of kneezles before, and he tells her, 'All the other kids got measles; me, I got kneezles'.

"So the guy takes off his shirt and she puts her hand over her mouth to stifle a scream and points to lumps that he has all over his chest and back. 'Lumps,' he says, 'Everyone else got mumps; me, I got lumps'.

"So finally he takes off his underwear, and she lets out the loudest scream yet and says, 'No! Don't tell me! Smallcocks!', and with that," Gizmo added, after they both stopped laughing, "I think it's time to turn in."

RUBY LAKE

Chapter Twenty-Four

They took quads most of the way to Ruby Ridge early the next morning. The roads and trails were too washed out for trucks. Horses were considered, but they decided to get there on quads, park them far enough away so they couldn't be heard or noticed, and hike in the rest of the way.

About an hour into the hike, they came to the side of the mountain they had to get up. Trees grew out of cliff tops like a giant stairway all the way up, and where there were no cliffs, there were large boulders and loose rock. Somewhere up that hillside was the air shaft they would enter.

They stood and listened at first. They knew where the sentries were posted from the pictures they saw last night. Then, Jason took out his rifle and peered through the scope, searching for others. He searched the canyon down toward the entrance and then back again. Then he did it again, trying to think of where he would put hidden guards.

It would be somewhere near a path that would be travelled. Somewhere you would be forced to go through. Not necessarily on the path, but near it. Above it would be the most desirable, and that is where he searched again.

He spotted them that time. Deep and hidden. They would never be seen unless you really looked for them. Even then, if you didn't know what to look for, you would miss it, and you would suffer the consequences. It was the dead foliage turning slightly browner in the sun than the surrounding trees that gave it away. They put it there to cover their path to the nest. But he saw them.

He scanned around following the trail, and spotted two more closer to where he stood. He spoke slowly and quietly. "Four guards. I guess we are in the right place. Better be careful."

Then, he turned the scope to the area behind them to see if more were posted. That would make the climb impossible because they would be seen climbing by anyone looking forward toward the entrance of the cave.

Then he scoured the hillside with his scope to look for tripwires or motion sensors on trees and rocks, any cameras, any infrared. Motion sensors would not be used except in certain places. You don't want birds and rabbits to sound alarms all day and night, and you don't want it to go off every time the wind blew a branch around either.

So he tried to rule those out first. They would be directed between solid expanses; areas between rocks. Places you could not help but pass through.

There were two that he saw. Of course, they were placed on the route they wanted to take; the easiest and most obvious route. So that ruled that route out. He looked at the next most logical way to go.

There were no cameras or listening devices or gadgets that he could see, but he did see some disturbed ground, meaning someone or something had been up there, and rocks had rolled down the hill. He pointed it out to Eric and they ruled that route out as well.

It's better to do your homework and pass the test than to skimp on the last bit of homework and fail. After a good hour and a half of looking and studying the mountainside, they decided the safest route to take was the least safe route; up the cliffs.

They all concentrated on it now, studied it more, and all agreed that none had seen any signs of surveillance, even though they could not see the flat areas above them. If they ran into anything there, they would have to deal with it one cliff at a time.

They made their way to the base of the first step and stopped to plan how they would get up. One of the men suggested that they find a cave entrance that was lower, the logic being that there were caves that ran for miles and connected to other caves that network through the mountains.

It was decided that any entrance that was easy to access would be well guarded and they would be spotted. The secret they were trying to keep was that they knew the secret.

So they went up the cliff face, slowly and quietly. Once one man was up and checked for surveillance, he would drop the rope for the rest. Jason would tie it onto the backpack Bo was wearing and haul her up last. By midafternoon, they had reached the airshaft.

They rested by the opening and listened for signs of movement. What noises they heard seemed to be coming from deep inside. Jason and Eric checked for trip wires, motion detectors, or cameras inside the opening, and seeing none, they entered.

The shaft was large enough to crawl through and descended at an angle sufficiently steep to make it difficult on the arms, but Bo had no troubles at all. There was no clearance for the backpacks, so they were left near the entrance and only their weapons, cameras, lights, and extra ammo were carried.

As they crawled through, the light from behind them grew dimmer and dimmer until it was pitch black and they had to use their lights. Jason guessed they had crawled for about a mile when they started seeing a dim light up ahead. All they had encountered so far in the shaft were bats.

They paused and took another break and the men were again warned about noise and detection. Jason gave Bo her duty to be silent, along with a pat on the head from him, and everyone else in the tunnel took their turn. The most noise she would make now would be a quiet whimper.

"You ready?" Jason whispered.

"I'm ready. The opening widens about fifty feet up ahead. We should get a pretty clear view. It looks like there will be some light in there," Eric answered. "You hear that noise?"

"I do. What do you think it is?" They both listened for a bit, Then Jason said, "It sounds kind of like machinery that hasn't been oiled. Lots of it."

Eric tried to turn his ear more toward the opening and shook his head. "Guess we have to go and look."

"Guess so," Jason replied as he turned to get back on his knees to crawl the final stretch.

As they approached the opening, the noise became louder. They could no longer whisper to be heard. The edge of the shaft was built with a lip to divert rain that would wash its way in through the shaft to keep it from falling directly to the floor of the cave or splattering against the walls causing more rocks to fall.

Some of the roof of the cave came into view now, a huge expanse going back as far as they could see from their position. As they got closer to the opening, walls on the far sides of the cave could be seen.

"Man. You could fit a city in here," one of the men said.

They finally got to the edge and saw the entire cavern. Floor to roof was a good four hundred feet. Side to side was around a thousand, Jason figured, and the depth couldn't be seen because it made a curve.

"This is huge!" Eric spoke over the noise.

"I told you. These caves go for miles. It's an entire network. There might be fifty or more miles in here," one of the men told them.

Eric and Jason half slid and half crawled right to the edge and tried to get a look straight down. "Trains," Eric said and pointed.

Jason followed the tracks as far back as he could see with his scope. He pointed to the sides and said, "Looks like corrals. They're loading or unloading animals there."

"Let's get some shots here. NO FLASH," Eric called back. "Hang a camera here on the corner." One man came up and started taking photos while another started hanging a video feed up on the corner.

Jason looked behind him and saw one man still had his light shining. He pointed at it and the man switched it off mouthing "Sorry" when an alarm sounded and they all got down on their bellies.

Jason and Eric watched the floor of the cave as a train pulled up beside the loading corrals and pulled to a squealing stop. Cattle were unloaded and the train pulled away. "That is a lot of cattle," Jason said. "What do you think, a thousand head?"

"More than that. Way more," Eric answered. "Did you see how far back that train went?"

The noise of the train as it was pulling out eventually disappeared below the undefined noise and the bellows of the protesting cattle. An alarm went off again. It was different from the first, sounded much louder and a deeper tone. The side of the corrals facing the center of the cave dropped. A spray of water came from the walls making the cattle move and clear the area and the walls came back up.

"Huh. Pneumatic. Interesting," Jason muttered.

They watched the cattle roam the open area while the men behind them came forward and picked a good spot. Once they were all comfortable, a siren sounded. They all stopped and looked around to see what would happen next. Then a horn blasted out, loud and thundering short blasts.

The men held their hands over their ears for fear of damage to their eardrums. Jason noticed movement at the far end of the cave and prodded Eric with his elbow and pointed, about to say something when he froze, along with everyone else in the airshaft, as Walkers were unleashed onto the cattle.

The mystery of what the sound was had been answered. It was the noise of Walkers. They came from the sides and from the back as far as the eye could see. The men were frozen in place as they pounced on the cattle and ripped them apart. They came leaping over each other to get at them, and when they were mixed within the cattle tearing them apart, another wave came.

They were killing them with nothing but their claws and teeth. Ripping parts off and tossing it in the air. Jason watched as a cow tossed one of the Walkers into the air with its horns. As quick as it hit the ground, it turned and attacked the cow again, tearing it to pieces.

"They're not eating!" Jason yelled to Eric.

"What?" Eric yelled back.

"I said they are not eating. THEY ARE NOT EATING. THEY ARE ONLY KILLING," he screamed back at him.

Eric looked back, still in shock. "You're right," he yelled. "They're not eating, just killing."

Jason didn't hear him, but he knew what he said. Thousands of cattle were slaughtered and lay in pieces on the cave floor while Walkers screeched and howled and pounced on anything they thought might be alive. None of it was eaten.

After twenty minutes there were no longer sounds of cattle. It was replaced completely by sounds of these pure killing machines, leaping from one mass of flesh to the other in hopes of finding something else to kill.

It was some time before they began to eat. It was like an afterthought for them, that is, if they did have thoughts. It started slowly, with one or two running through the carnage and, finding nothing left to kill, picking up a leg and tasting it, then running out of sight into the dark reaches of the cave.

The others followed suit, running howling and screeching, and eventually grabbing a piece of cow, almost disappointed that there was nothing left to kill, and running off with it.

With the exception of blood on the cave floor, it was picked clean within an hour and the beasts had vanished. Jason and Eric's recon party stayed frozen in position, not daring to make a sound and draw the attention of the Walkers.

In the middle of the rampage, one of the men couldn't take it and started to crack, screaming, "We're all dead! We're all gonna die!" until someone jumped on him and put his hand over his mouth. Another had turned around and started scampering back up the airshaft. Eric sent one of his men to go with him, telling him to make sure they stay just inside the entrance to the airshaft and not draw attention to themselves.

The ones that were left looked too terrified to be of any use if they got in trouble. "Don't panic," Jason told himself. "Don't get taken out of the play," He turned back to see the condition of the rest of the men he came with. "Panic is the enemy," he told himself. The others had panicked and now, weren't even in the game.

They were all ready to leave; to turn and scramble back up the air shaft to safety; to put as much distance between themselves and danger as they could.

The mission, what was it? They came for information. Did they do that? They sure got information. They saw what the hidden secret was they had deep inside that mountain. But, was the mission done? He fought the impulse to turn and scamper up the shaft himself.

A game is a series of plays. You bring the puck down the ice, you organize the set up and you make the play. If the other team can counter your attack, they knock you off the play, and then they have the puck.

Did they make their play? That was the question. Did they come and do what they came to do? He composed himself and looked down over the side. The threat was out of sight, but still there. The play was not over. They were still there and still able to gather intel. The others that had come with them were taken out of the play and out of the game completely, but he was still in it; him and Eric.

After several attempts to get their attention, he finally got one of them to snap out of it and pass a camera forward. "Focus," he told himself. "Do the mission. Don't panic." Jason tried to get out as far as he could on the ledge to get a good look at the entrance, but couldn't get out far enough for a good angle.

It appeared to have blast doors, but he couldn't be sure. He took the camera in his left hand and held onto a rock with his right and stuck the camera out as far as he could reach and snapped the shutter several times.

Pulling the camera back in and viewing the pictures on the small screen, he could see that he captured something, but wasn't sure what. He would have to look at it back in the War Room when all the pictures were analyzed. He got Eric to hold him so he could lean out further and get a clearer shot, and pulled back in and looked again. "Good," he said.

They lay there on their stomachs looking at every detail of the cave they could, pointing out the curve of the cave walls, snapping a picture of it so they could plan how to bring the mountain down if they needed and where to place charges along the base; who they might use to do it.

How would they get in there? How could they even get in to place the charges with so many Walkers? Maybe they could suspend themselves from the roof of the cave? Drop down on ropes. Eric got Jason to sit on his legs while he hung over the side backwards and got some straight-up shots up to the roof.

The security inside was the next subject. There wasn't any. Other than cameras and what looked like observation windows at the far end, there seemed to be, after the cattle were killed, no living thing in the cave with the Walkers. They watched and looked for another hour, pointing at things and discussing how they could exploit the angles, these rocks there, that column over there.

"Let's see how comfortable they are in there – see what it takes to get them to come out," Jason said. "Got something to throw down there?"

They discussed what they could throw. They didn't want security to see it on the cameras, so it couldn't be big. It couldn't be a piece of equipment because they might find it. They didn't want to give away the secret - that they know the secret.

"We could throw a rock. They probably fall all the time," Eric suggested.

They dug around looking for a rock or a pebble. Years of rain water pouring down the shaft had washed any loose rocks away. They clawed at the roof and sides and both got the idea to use a knife to pry one loose when they both stopped, realizing it could make noise, especially if it broke, and they could be detected.

"Hey," Jason whispered digging into his pocket and holding up a coin. "They'll never see this. If they do, who cares, they'll think someone dropped it. That is, if anyone ever goes in there."

It was agreed. Jason took the coin between his thumb and his middle finger and flicked it, launching it, sailing through the air. They lost sight of it in the expanse of the cave and both turned their heads to listen to it hit bottom. They would not hear the coin hit the surface, but they did hear the reaction from the monsters as several dozen of them rushed toward the location.

They both turned to see each other with their index fingers to their mouths, a reminder to be very quiet, and began sliding themselves back deeper into the shaft and decided to leave.

Going up the shaft was easier than going down. They made better time and it was less tiring. Jason's fear was that the man that bolted along with the other who went after him might have shot out of the shaft and drawn attention to themselves in their panic.

He met them about three-quarters of the way out, out of breath and resting. They didn't pace themselves. They scampered. They panicked, and now they were sitting, not even a player any longer, barely even a spectator.

They all sat and rested and caught their breath, looking at each other with wild eyed, terrified stares. "Alright," Jason finally said. "We did part of what we needed to do." He looked at each one of them individually, making sure they were with him now. "But we aren't finished."

"Our mission today was to gain access to this shaft unnoticed, get whatever intelligence we could, and get back out." He paused, making sure they were paying attention to him. "But we are only half done. So far, so good. But now - the important part of the mission.

"We have to get out of here, and get out of here unnoticed. We have to get back. We have to get out and we have to get the information that we gathered into the hands of people who need it, who can use it, and who can develop a plan out of it.

"Look. I know you're scared. I am too. I know you didn't expect to see what we saw. Neither did I. I know there are a lot of them things. I

161

know it. But we are the only ones who know it right now. You might think that all is lost, that there is no way we can fight that many of them.

"If we get caught, if we blow it, get rattled and don't focus, well, we will never be able to figure out what to do about it. Then, all is lost.

"It is not your job. It is not your mission right now to kill them; nor is it to figure how to kill them; nor is it to know how to kill them. We just came to get this information and give it to people who can figure it out.

"Right now, you may be the most important people in the entire human race because you saw and you know. But if we blow it now, it will all be wasted. Focus. Gather your wits and focus. Complete your mission."

"Right," one of them said. "Right. We have to get back – make it back. Warn them at least."

"No way," another said. "No darned way can we let them things get out; get at our village. No way." They all agreed.

Eric and Jason sat and watched as one-by-one, the panic left their eyes and was replaced by hard-as-steel determination. They focused. They would finish the play.

Sometimes, you're coming down the ice, players in front, ready to block you, knock you off the puck and take it to your end and try to score. You're coming down the ice, you cross the blue line and set up for a pass in front of the crease, and someone hits you. You get checked into the boards and you lose the puck.

But you get up and you get going and get back in there and you mess up their play too. That's what Jason was thinking; how to mess up their play. You execute enough plays successfully, and kill the play of the other guy enough times, and you won the game.

Up until two days ago, he didn't even know there was a game on. He ran across the game by accident. Then, he became a spectator. Then he did a little practice. He took a little hike and did a little practice on their rink, the gorge, and put down some mountain lions. Someone on the team noticed he could play, and he was invited onto the team. Now he was a player; a player in a game he had to win.

Climbing back up the shaft, they started to see light from the opening. They all shut off their flashlights so as not to draw attention to themselves coming out of the dark mouth of the entrance. They passed the spot near the entrance where they deposited their backpacks and one by one grabbed them as they approached the opening.

Checking first to make sure all was clear; they stepped onto the ledge and stood up. How many hours had passed that they had been crouching and crawling? It felt good and they all stretched and breathed a sigh of relief.

Taking a break now and digging snacks out of their backpacks, they sat as the sun set over Ruby Ridge and looked out toward Echo Lake. "Beautiful, isn't it?" Eric commented. Nobody answered. There was no need.

"Fifty cals, maybe," he said to Jason. He was thinking the same thing Jason was thinking up there on the top of that cliff. How to kill them. How to kill a charging, leaping, screaming, howling horde of monsters.

"Maybe," he replied. "Bunkers. Get in there, maybe. But they have to be in front of it. Maybe draw them in, draw them into line of fire. Maybe." He sat for another minute and then said, "Depleted uranium?"

"Yah, was thinking of that. Lot of rounds though. How to get 'em. That's the problem." Eric sat for a minute more. "Because we can get fifties," he said.

"Any armories around?" Jason asked.

"There's a couple," one of the men answered. "There's a range too. Tanks and everything. They practice out there. Big guns, artillery. Loud."

The men started to get anxious now, wanting to move, seeing the makings of something coming together, assessing resources. It was something other than planning to succumb to the enemy. There was some hope, any hope, and they started to stand.

It was time for Eric and Jason to move. The men were letting them know they were alive and still had fight left in them. They still had their will, and it was getting stronger.

Getting down the steps of cliffs was easier and faster than getting up. They attached the rope and began lowering themselves down, one-by-one, with Jason last, lowering Bo and then coming down himself, releasing the rope and moving on to the next drop.

They crept their way to the quads and were back at the village before midnight.

Chapter Twenty-Five

Eric sent everything they'd gathered from the cave to the War Room to be distributed to the rest of the reservations and told them all to get ready for debrief while Jason went in to see what Gizmo and Cody had come up with.

"I have a feeling that the answer to those things is going to be coming from their work." Jason told Eric before going over there. "I don't know if we will ever have enough bullets to kill them all. Don't even know what fifties will do. We have to come up with something in there."

Once inside the shed Jason immediately noticed all the equipment set up on four different tables. "Been busy, eh?" he muttered to himself. Cody and Gizmo were gone, so he poked around and examined what they had set up.

He was always impressed with how Gizmo could put things together and figure out complex circuitry on his feet. Jason was good, but usually had to draw it out. Gizmo would get it in his head, a picture of multiple complex circuits from start to finish, and could just build it off of what he pictured.

Something was different besides all the lab equipment and electronics and test tubes. Something else he was missing. He looked at the guards who waved at him, and he continued looking.

The light thing – the prisms Cody talked about. It wasn't moving, wasn't rotating like he'd described, maybe they found a spectrum the animals reacted to already. But something was odd.

He looked at the animals in the back of the cage, and it hit him – they weren't going crazy. They weren't jumping and thrashing and howling. "How long have they been like that?" he asked one of the guards.

"Most of the afternoon," he answered. "Man, it's good to get a break, too. I've had a head ache ever since we got them."

Just then Gizmo bounced in with Cody. "Hey. You're back. How'd it go? Get anything?" Gizmo asked.

He didn't answer his questions; he just asked while pointing to the rear of the room, "What did you do?"

"Oh, yah. We found out how to shut 'em up. Interesting. But you were right. Waves. Radio – watch this." Gizmo adjusted a knob and pointed. "Look. It's not entirely radio. It's a captured wave. We send it along a particular light wave."

The Walkers moved around in circles a few times and then lay down. "Sleeeep," he said. "Watch this." He turned the knob again, and they got up and went crazy, even more than usual. "I don't want them to sleep, you know, keep them tired – just in case, you know, in case they get out."

"That's amazing. That's incredible. Hell, yah," Jason shouted his approval.

"Wait until you see this," Gizmo said, pointing to the prism system. Then Gizmo directed his attention upward to a hole cut into the roof of the shed where a telescope was erected to track celestial objects. "Cody. Smart kid. He figured this out. He focused on different stars and directed the light right into the prisms. I'm not exactly sure what we're going to do, I think I get it, but I'm not exactly sure. Tomorrow we'll have it nailed, I'm pretty sure. But it did something, made them react."

"This is good. This is all good. This is really good. Gizmo, you have no idea, but this is good. How far can the signal carry?" he asked.

"Briefing!" someone poked his head in and yelled through the door. "War Room. NOW!" and was gone.

As the two walked into the room, Jason saw the image of the cave on the widescreen. Eric was beside it with a pointer, telling someone at the side to hold the image while he described parts of it, and then telling him to move forward to another image and halt it again.

Then he went to the still shots they took around the blast doors. "This is the setup they have. Here is the entrance," and then would say, 'Next', and the new photo would appear, "These look like blast doors, and this is the control room," and went on describing the cave, the size of it, the tracks, and how the cattle were unloaded.

"We have feed from a video camera left there that you all should see. I know that it is shocking, what we saw while we were there, what we just showed you, but what the Gunny will show you now may be even more shocking. It is not our intention to shock, but we have to know the enemy. You do." With that, he motioned and said, "Gunny?"

Gunny Brent Stonefish stood up and was about to speak when Gizmo asked, "So, any idea of how many of those things there are?"

"We were just going to look at that. We have an idea, but it is just a guess. Not a bad guess. But just a guess," and he turned to the screen. "Put up that still, will you?" and a picture appeared with a small square highlighted.

"We took a section of this shot of a mass of Walkers and did a head count. Next," and the highlighted area took over the screen. "In this one section shown here, a head count shows forty seven. Then, taking that square and measuring the area, we calculated that there were well over a hundred thousand of them, right here in this cavern."

The entire room gasped a breath. "Roll the film," he said. The same scene that they had just watched played showing the carnage again. "Move it to 18:30. After the scouting team left, we captured these images as well." It showed another trainload of animals being brought into the cave. "But you'll see, the train keeps on going deeper into the old mine and stops. You can see the end of it in the light if you look real close.

"It appears to unload in the same fashion as the last one we saw, except much deeper inside and then move off," he said.

They watched as the train pulled away and a short time later several pieces of cattle came flying onto the screen. "Okay, 22:00 now. Alright," as the screen shot ahead in time, "and here is another train with another load of cattle."

The train came in, but neither stopped nor slowed in the cavern, nor past it where the other one stopped, but continued on. Everyone watched as a face appeared on the screen and looked closely at the camera. Then a hand moved up to it, growing larger and larger until the hand covered the entire screen, and it went blank.

"There are 5,280 feet in a mile. Calculating the length of the train and the average size of cars, these three trains were over a mile long, and we could see front and rear with room to spare on either end," and he turned and grabbed some papers.

"These are maps of the mines and caves in that area. They interconnect and go for miles. Someone here has been in 'em. Let's see, who was it?" and panned the room with his finger stopping when a man stood up near the back. "Oh, yah, Jacobs. Supposed to be over fifty miles of cave that connected when he worked in them. Who knows now?

"After the briefing, you will get your assignments. It's still recon. But now they know someone knows. They might not know who knows, but they know someone knows.

"So, men. You will get your assignments, and they will be watching this time. Even so, you will not be seen. You will not be caught. You will carry out your duty. You will get the intelligence we need, and you will report what you find."

"So, what do you think? How many?" someone called out.

"Could be as little as half a million, as much as, well we don't know. Maybe millions. But we know this: we are not the only ones with this. Two other locations across the country have reported similar activity since we sent out the alert about the train tracks and caves. We're the only ones so far to get into one."

Eric could sense the room beginning to collectively spin. They were overwhelmed. Their heads were swimming, and he could understand why. He got up and addressed the crowd again.

"Overwhelming, isn't it? Shocking. It is, I know. Some of you are sitting there, and you might be thinking, 'Why me?' You might be thinking that. 'Why me?' Wouldn't it be so much easier to go home, turn on the TV, open a beer and forget it all for a while? I'll tell you why.

"That we know of, from the Nations we have been in contact with, there are over a thousand people who have vanished. Your people. Our people. Indians on reservations across the land of all the Nations. All of them have spoken about things that appear to be the same animals we have captured next door.

"So let me try to answer this question of 'Why you?' as simply as I can. It's not that a new and fierce enemy has been set upon the tribes. Although it is true. It is not that friends and family members have been ravaged by these things. Although it is true. It is not that it is the reservations that have been targeted. Although that also seems to be true.

"Ten Indians vanish from a tribe. It's a big deal, right? We all hear about it. What about ten white people vanishing? Vacationers? What then? Think about it," and he gave them a few seconds. "Nothing. You won't hear a thing. Oh, maybe a news article or something, but they are too spread out. They are from all over the country. Nobody pays attention.

"What about people from other countries? You've seen them. Renting all those clean-new motor homes. They vanish, and nothing. Sure, sure. The various departments say they are looking and act like it's important.

"But look. How do you build something this size and have beasts that you keep a secret, unless people know? Government people?

"So you're asking yourself now, Why me? Why doesn't the Government come? Okay. What part? The police? The army? Who? Who would come and make everything right?

"We know of over one hundred and twenty areas that have the same problem we have. Think about how many potential Walkers that is. Millions. Are they on other continents as well? This isn't about you and me and the Indians on reservations. If these things got loose, it could mean the devastation of mankind.

"I can't imagine that these things are being kept and sheltered and fed because they make such nice pets. They are there to do what you saw them do on the screen. Kill. Look, if they are going to be released on mankind, mankind had better be prepared.

"So why you? Because you can. That's the best reason. On reservations across the country, we have freedoms that other people don't have. We can move around and do things, communicate and organize and plan.

"Who cares about us? We complain to the Government and they throw money at us and we go away. We are free to move around and speak to each other. We can hunt and fish. We don't even pay all their taxes.

"That's why us. Because we can. Nobody else can. You know that. You've seen these people off the reserve. Fat and stupid. Drugged and lazy. It is up to you and me.

"The Government isn't coming to our rescue. It is you and I. We will be our own salvation. We can work with people all across the country that have the same freedoms we have. We can plan and organize.

"So, why you? Because you can, and if you can, then you must, and if you don't, well, the consequences are too horrible to even contemplate. So that's why. But you won't be alone.

"You won't be without help and without tools and weapons that work." Then he chuckled and said, "We are not going to send you off to wrestle these things by yourself.

"So we are doing this because we must. It is we who are doing it because it is we who can do it. It is our lives. This is our Earth. Our land. I will not turn it over to monsters – to The Evil Walkers.

"They will not take my place on this Earth, and they will not walk with my ancestors. Was it the spirits who sent them to us? Or the other way around, was it the spirits who sent us to them? Guided us. I believe that must be the case. We were warned and brought to them."

He looked over the crowd and wondered if they were feeling less overwhelmed, infused with courage, or if he was just talking over their heads. He decided that, whatever effect he was having, it was better than what he saw in them before he began his speech, defeat, so he added. "And if tomorrow or the next day I am dead, I will walk with pride among the spirits knowing what I did.

"I did it because it was the right thing to do and I did it because I could. I have an opportunity to do it now that I might not have later. Get a good night of sleep. We will have a busy day tomorrow."

"Wow," Jason said standing in the middle of the room. "I vote Eric for President!" he joked.

Some of the men standing by laughed and commented things like: "Eric is right;" "It is up to us;" "It is like he said."

Jenkins had been calling. Said he was having Wild Times at the park and asked if maybe Eric could help him with a couple of things.

This was usual communication, unsuspicious. But the code meant something unusual was happening. Jenkins often called and asked the Sheriff for help, especially if it involved some of this people. It wouldn't draw attention.

The runner who delivered the message had one of his guys go through the park to take a look while Eric and the rest were in the cave. "There were quite a few people there. Campers, some of them. Then there were visitors, too. Just driving through and wandering around.

"So I had him check the motels around and see what kind of business they were getting. The one in the North, you know, the Pakistani place, it was full. Ever been there?" he asked. "It stinks. Can't imagine it being full. But there were some vans there, black ones, and SUVs. Not good signs."

"You're right," Eric told him. "Good thinking. Keep it up. Keep on top of it."

"You guys, you want to pay a little visit to Jenkins?" He asked Jason and Gizmo. "Then you and Cody can fill me in on the way. I understand you've got something for us. I think we are going to need you two to pull a rabbit out of your hats."

Chapter Twenty-Six

It was about the time the Gunny was showing the film and speculating on the possible number of Walkers that it happened. The village had centuries posted. Guards hidden along the routes into town and along the most likely routes a Walker might approach as well as any roads and trails something or someone might slip in.

They went first, without a shot and completely without notice.

With no alarms being sounded, next came any outlying buildings and houses. They fell silently and without a fight as well. The village was divided into North and South down the main road to the Sheriff office with the south side overrun first, leaving the side with the two sheds containing the Walkers and the War Room full of people.

With the force now concentrated, the north side was approached from both ends, clearing out the entire town to the sheds. Not a shot was fired.

"He left some messages and has been trying to get hold of us," Eric was saying about Jenkins as they walked through the War Room to the outside lot.

As they stepped outside the shed into the dark, before their eyes were able to adjust to the darkness, they were surrounded, with no escape route. Men in black camouflage, faces covered, guns pointed, began pouring into the shed overwhelming anyone there. Jenkins was brought forward in cuffs and put on the ground, a black bag over his head.

Then the rest were marched into the yard with their hands in the air, they were cuffed with zip ties, and herded away, stunned and confused as trucks and helicopters began arriving. Rolls of fencing with razor wire were being erected.

Men were barking orders and others were rushing this way and that to do it. It was a well-organized confusion. The Sheriff office had its own fence around it with guards posted, and the village had instantly become a concentration camp.

Particular interest was being paid to the second shed. Jason and the men could only listen and imagine what they were doing as they were held on the ground with bags over their heads. People were running in and out of it to the Sheriff's Office and back.

Within a short time, the equipment Gizmo and Cody had put together had been dismantled and loaded onto a pallet. A helicopter hovered overhead and it was taken away. Then another arrived, and the

171

walkers were flown away, screeching and thrashing and charging the sides of the cage.

Jason, Gizmo, Jenkins, Eric and Cody were hauled onto their feet and marched to a waiting helicopter. They were turned around with their backs to it. For a brief moment Jason thought he could hear Bo barking, and then Hellen calling her over and saying something to her.

He couldn't hear the words over the rotors turning above and the shuffle of people and barking of orders, but he knew it was her. He was straining to hear more when all five were grabbed from behind by the collar and hauled into the chopper like sacks of potatoes and placed on their knees.

In the air now, he tried to determine the direction they went. It seemed like it was North, toward the cave, but he couldn't tell for sure. There was some chatter on the radio coming from in front of him.

He yelled, "Who are you? What do you want?" and was answered by a hard shove from someone behind him with butt of their rifle.

The helicopter, as near as he could tell, proceeded in what seemed to be a straight line when it tried to pull up, to stop moving forward, he could feel it try to stop, but there was no way they could be at the cave by now.

Did they have a facility that was even closer that they missed? They couldn't have missed it. But it was pulling up, stopping in mid-air. He knew that feeling well. Then he heard the pilot say, "Radio's jammed."

He could hear the rush of their captors opening the side doors and yelling back and forth when the empty and cavernous sound of a loud speaker clicked on. "You will land your craft or we have orders to shoot," followed a few seconds later by, "You will put it down now, or we will open fire."

The men in the helicopter were frazzled. There was a discussion of fighting, but the chopper wasn't equipped with weapons, only the men had firearms. He could feel the chopper descending and coming to rest on the ground. Then, he heard men coming up and issuing orders for them to lay down their weapons.

The five of them were again taken, and hauled onto another helicopter, one with a more familiar sound, like some he's been on before. It was a reassuring sound to him in this confusion.

Someone was ordered to free them, and the bags were lifted off their heads and the zip ties were cut. He looked around to see himself in an Apache surrounded by military personnel. Outside were three other helicopters, one with a Catskill logo, and the other two were the same as he was in.

As they lifted off, he could hear small arms fire, then an explosion followed by the fireball you see when a helicopter crashes. "Viper actual, this is Viper one," someone up front was saying. "There is a Santa Clause."

The group was flown to Ruby Ridge and entered the base they had just come from, except they came through the front this time. The helicopter easily flew into a cavernous opening and landed near a dozen other Apaches. Off to the side were Catskill helicopters and personnel loading and unloading.

They were taken and escorted through a seemingly endless maze of antiseptic hallways and passages, through security doors and past guards and military personnel in uniforms. They were being lead down a quiet stretch of hall when a single Catskill employee came from the other end. Two uniformed men entered the corridor behind him while two others were coming from the entrance behind Jason and his group.

They came together midway by a door as Jason and his group was passing through a set of security doors. As they were closing behind him, Jason looked to see the Catskill man shoved through a door while one of the others pulled his blade and the rest pushed their way inside.

"General. The Ruby Lake team, Sir," one of the guards announced as they were led into his office.

"Very good. Two of you wait in here, the rest wait in the hallway," he replied.

The General was silent. There were four other men in the room with him, all eyeing the group. The General watched the five gather their bearings. He paid particular attention to Eric's reaction when he spied the map on the wall and recognized what it is.

"You're right," he began as if in the middle a conversation. "You're right, what you're thinking. It is what you think. Locations. Locations of what you call The Evil Walkers."

"Eric Runningsprings," he said. "I remember you. Out of Fort Knox. Remember you in Afghanistan," and looked over some papers, lifted one out and turned it toward Jason and Gizmo. It was a satellite image of the area near the destroyed campsite. Circled on it were the bio-suits that had been peeled off and discarded as they ran from the cave.

"These, I take it were yours," he addressed Jason and Gizmo now. "Colonel Jason Brand and Colonel Jerry Crozley. Interesting history, you two. It wasn't difficult to find that these suits belonged to you. Who wore the third suit?"

"I did," Eric spoke. "I was in that."

Jason, Gizmo, and Eric knew the score. They knew, at this time, in this place, there was no such thing as rights. No such thing as laws except the most brutal form of Marshall Law. No such thing as due process. They were there for a reason.

They had been captured for a reason. Then, they had been rescued, transported and were alive; alive for a reason. They also knew that if that reason proved false, they would probably not be alive for much longer.

They had been flown to some place important and they were standing at the desk of someone important. A General. Beside that General were other people that would be important. Observers, and it was they who were being observed, which made them important.

For now, it was their task to keep themselves important. They would try to do that as if their lives depended on it, because it did.

One of the observers broke rank with the others and took a step forward and excitedly asked, "Which one of you set up that lab."

Cody was about to speak. He was about to tell them that it was he that did it. He and Gizmo. Jason cut him off. He had to keep everyone relevant. They all had to remain important. If it was the lab they were interested in, if it was the lab that was important, then the rest could be unimportant. Jenkins especially would be marched away and in all likelihood would disappear.

So he cut him off. "We all worked on it. Different parts. We all worked on it." Then, since he had answered a question without protests about such silly things as rights and freedoms, he looked at the General. "Can I ask, Sir?"

"Of course. I expect it. But let me just jump into it. Save us all a little time," and looked at the guards, motioning at them with his hand. "I believe you know the score, gentlemen."

Jason shrugged and gave a smile. "Of course."

Cody and Jenkins stared. They both realized that they were now in a different world; a world of abbreviated conversations; conversations that had meanings and sub-meanings; a world where a slight motion can replace a paragraph of conversation. It was a world they were both unfamiliar with.

But Jason, Gizmo, and Eric were familiar with it, and Cody and Jenkins both concluded to never open their mouths without looking at them for approval first, because Jason had just ensured that they would be guests, rather than prisoners. Guests with guns pointed at them, maybe, but guests never the less.

"I'm going to give you the short version. It may be a little overwhelming to you. We usually introduce people to what you are about to hear a little bit at a time. Let the shock wear off before the next shock is administered, so to speak.

"But I'm going to be brutal with you, so I apologize in advance. We don't have a lot of time and it is a long story. In fact, it starts in the late 1800s with a man named Griffith J. Griffith, also a Colonel, as I recall. He enjoyed astronomy and gazing at the stars.

"Ended up being involved with observatories. One of them, the Griffith Observatory, was named after him, you may have heard of it. He donated all the land for it and gave a park to the city of Los Angeles and all that.

"But, back in the late 1800s, he spotted something out in space and, for the next almost hundred years, it was kept a secret, this thing. We didn't know what it was. We were worried that someone, some other country would find out about it and get there first; send people before us. So it was kept a secret, and that began one of the best kept series of secrets possibly in the history of mankind.

"Our space program. Not the one you hear about; the real one. A lot of good people gave their lives to get to that thing. As telescopes were made more powerful, we got to finally see clearly what it was. It was a transporter of sorts. Space ship, if you like. Floating out there for who knows how long.

"Seems they had some mechanical difficulty and couldn't reach their destination. It was sixteen miles long. Huge. Four levels deep. The destination was here. Earth. Sixteen miles of transporter for an invasion of Earth. That's sixty-four linear miles of deck space filled with monsters like you couldn't imagine.

"Long story short, we catapulted a rocket full of Air force, Marines, some Army, the Navy of course, and a group of scientists out to it. Some of them died on the way. Radiation killed them. But they got inside.

"There were millions of them, mostly dead, but some still alive. Millions. It was an invasion that never happened. It was pure luck they broke down, lost power or something.

"That was when we started trying to figure out their technology. Way back then. They had things that were unimaginable. Devices that we couldn't comprehend. Still can't, and we have the most brilliant scientists working on it. We just can't get it going.

"We didn't know at the time that it was meant as an invading force sent to wipe mankind from the face of the Earth. We thought maybe they were refugees. Maybe travelers. They had no weapons they would carry to speak of, a few hand guns and side arms.

"But now, fairly recently, it's become pretty clear. They didn't need them. We have been able to watch some of their entertainment. I guess you'd call them that, shows and films, instructional videos, which also made it pretty clear that we had no defenses to keep them from accomplishing their plan.

"Their planet came under attack. I guess some of these transporters were called back to defend their planet. This one never made it, and we just don't know why.

"You've seen something similar to the inhabitants of the craft. You call them Evil Walkers. This is where they came from. We made them. From the Invader's DNA. Not us, not we, Catskill made them to fight these aliens after they had destroyed and occupied the world and wiped out mankind."

Jason interrupted, "Excuse me, General. What do you mean 'after' they destroyed the world and mankind? Why after? You mean before, right?"

"No. I wish I did. No, I mean after," he looked down and said.

"That doesn't make sense, why after?" Gizmo asked.

"Because gentlemen. This is the way it is and there is no other way around it. There are two more of those things coming. They are coming and we have nothing that can stop them.

"They are going to come here and they are going to bombard the surface until there is very little left of civilization. It's what they do. We watched hologram after hologram of it and film after film. Worlds that were stronger and more advanced than we are - gone.

"After the Earth is all but destroyed, they will unload their army onto the surface. Tough characters. Millions of them. With otherworldly strength. We watched invasion after invasion of them doing it. They won't need weapons once on the surface. They use their weapons to fight beings stronger than them or ones that have workable and effective weapons.

"But they won't use them here. No need. They will just have their way with whatever remaining people or animals are left. Whatever there is left. It's entertainment for them. You can watch the films, later, that is…," and he never finished the sentence.

Jason, Gizmo, and Eric already knew what the 'that is' meant. That is if they agree to something. That is if they are on board. That is if they cooperated. That is if they are still alive.

There were a lot of "that ises", and he meant all of them. But still, they were there, sitting and getting personal attention from the General; a personal briefing. They didn't understand the significance of their group; they just understood that they were very significant.

"I am going to have these men take you to the library and show you the films. There is no time left for hand holding and guiding you through what you are going to see. There is no time to be gentle. You are just going to have to see it and decide what to do," and looked at the guard and said, "Show them to the library and see that they start with the disks."

"Yes Sir, General," the guard replied.

"Oh, and if they try to escape or anything, shoot them," he added.

On the way to the library, Cody could no longer contain himself and blurted out, "Shoot them?" and Jenkins joined him in expressing his shock. "What's that all about? He didn't really mean that, did he?"

Jason looked at the guard smirk and said, "You are in a base with its own law now. Things will be different and you'd better watch yourselves. There are so many laws governing something like this. The only problem is this: you wouldn't know them.

"New Bill of Rights, new Constitution. They are passed in congress, sometimes secretly, sometimes not. You've heard of some of them. The War Powers Act. NDAA. HR-8791. Things like that.

"It's like Martial Law on steroids. Right soldier?" he addressed the guard.

"That's right, Sir. Steroids and Meth," he said. "Is it true you are a Colonel, sir?"

"Used to be," and they entered the library.

They sat at a table and the guard brought them a stack of discs. "These will show you the bombardments. These will show you the invasions and occupations," he said of the first set. "These ones here, these are our guys, the things you call 'Walkers'. Actually, I'm gonna start calling them that. We have a number for them, 8791-1, but 'Walkers' is better, I think."

"Your guys? Or, rather, our guys? I guess that's appropriate. They are 'Our guys' when you look at it. But how do you know if they are guys? Can you tell if they are male or female?" Jason asked.

"I can't. I'm not sure anyone can by looking," the guard said while handing over another set of disks. "This, you will be interested in. How they were developed. The walkers, and these babies here, they are the Invaders, their ships and some of their equipment," and then backed away. "I'll be right over here if you have questions. Oh, yah, fast forward button, right here, unless you want to be here for a day or two. But from what I'm hearing, it could all be done and over by then."

"Thanks," they all said as Jason slipped in a disk.

The first scenes were as described. It showed the Invaders entering into low orbit and bombarding a planet. The planetary defenses for the first victims looked like energy weapons which were ineffective. The scenes were shot from the point of view of the Invaders, of course. The next showed nuclear weapons as a defense, also with no effect.

The Invaders didn't seem to pay any attention to flying offensives or any orbiting defenses when they first come in for an attack. Once they entered low orbit, they just went along hitting the major cities, then came around on the second orbit taking out secondary targets, and the third time around, outlying smaller towns and villages. After the bombardment was over, any remaining annoyances like flying craft or orbiting defenses were knocked out.

One planet did not have a cohesive civilization. It did not form large cities and towns. Jason found that interesting. They still bombarded large areas, as if there were large cities. That is where they would land their forces. The bombardments were as much for landing zones as they were for eliminating the population.

The complete destruction of the cities and collapse of anything the planets would call civilization would occur in a matter of a couple of hours before the actual invasion. Jason, Gizmo and Eric watched the bombardment several times trying to determine what kind of weapons they were using, with no success. One of them asked the guard what they thought the weapons were and he also didn't know.

They watched the invasion in horror – the landing. The Invaders would descend on the remaining shocked and terrified population and slaughter them. When they were not petrified by their shock and ran, they would be chased down, usually in a single bound, and slaughtered anyway. They watched several of these, all resulting in the same outcome – complete extinction.

There were only two films showing the Invaders equipped with side arms and hand-held weapons. In both cases, the populations of the planets were much larger than the Invaders and appeared to be more capable physically. The weapons they used, however, were no match for the Invader weapons. Once any opposition was eliminated, it showed the weapons being returned to the shuttles.

"They have to return them right away. Don't trust them with weapons, maybe?" Eric said. "This is just sport for them. They just get in there and rumble after the defenses are down. Those side arms they use, they only use them on stronger life forms or if they have effective weapons they use against them. Won't have that problem here, will they?"

"I'm not sure. We'll have to speak to someone and see what they used to kill them. We have to have something that'll take 'em out. There must be a plan. But we'll have to somehow deny them access to their weapons," Jason said. "Once they find out we have something to use against them, they'll be going for the rifles and side arms. We'll have to cut them off from that."

"The scale on this," Jason spoke to the guard again, "How big are these things?"

"About a foot smaller than the walkers," he said. "You'll see them in the next disk."

They did. Hideous creatures that appeared to be somewhat reptilian. Their skin, if you want to call it that, was much like the Walkers; thick, hard, dense, and almost tortoise-shell looking in areas that didn't require movement.

"Are they Dinosaurs?" Cody finally asked. "They look like dinosaurs, kind of. Their skin does. How do you think they made this stuff, weapons and spacecraft, with those big hands and claws?"

Nobody answered, but it didn't need to be answered. It was a good observation from the smart kid.

Next came some hard to make out film from the people sent from Earth to the stranded craft. It started as they got within about fifty or more miles out from it, just outside the orbit of Mercury. Then they filmed the entire exterior of the craft, maneuvering around it and over it, paying particular interest to the engines.

The top level was where they accessed the transporter. There was an opening that the craft flew into and was swallowed with no problem. There were launch vehicles in what appeared to be the landing bay. Row after row of shuttles that would be used to transport the Invaders to the surface were lined up as far as the camera could focus.

The interior of one was filmed showing the controls in the front and seating for hundreds of aliens at a time in the rear. There were hand held weapons in a container, the ones they briefly watched on the film. It gave the impression that the entire top level was for launch vehicles for invasion. The camera went on to enter the main craft.

The door was open, meaning there would be no atmosphere inside, possibly for decades. The camera focused on the dead Invaders. Millions of them, by the time they had surveyed the ship. The crew went around, measuring the hands and legs, the head size, length of the body and got some close-ups of their teeth and claws.

The engine was again of particular interest. Every detail was filmed; every control panel; every pipe and every gadget that they had no idea of the purpose of. What looked to be tool cabinets were opened section after section and filmed.

"Amazing," Jason mumbled, "You know. I wonder why they didn't get in the shuttles and take off. Land somewhere. You know, phone home. They stayed there and died. Maybe they didn't work either. Maybe it's all on one system, powered by one system."

179

"But wouldn't you send out a distress call? Call for a tow truck? Weird. Why didn't they do that?" Jenkins added.

"Their planet was attacked. Maybe there just wasn't any help. Maybe they were under radio silence, a blackout." Gizmo watched more and said, "Lucky for us too. So now they are coming again. I wonder if they're thinking we took out their invading force. Kicked their asses. They could be sending the tough guys this time. If they didn't get help, maybe they couldn't ask for it. Radio black out. Op Sec."

"Maybe. Could be a disease or something, too," Jason said, and then thinking again added, "No, they let the air out. The doors to the bay were open. They were killed. Maybe a revolt? A mutiny, maybe? They keep their small arms locked up. That could be why."

The guard was at the table listening and said, "Keep watching, it'll all make sense."

The filming continued through the derelict ship down into the next level when they came to a section closed off with what looked like frosted glass. Inside, there was some light coming in from outside the craft, a portal, and some shadows were moving behind it. They had found live intelligent life forms stranded in space!

The picture went off, and then came back on showing a person about to knock on the enclosure, like they were knocking on the neighbor's door. One of the Invaders came out with an apparatus for breathing and unceremoniously proceeded to attack the man, instantly ripping off one of his limbs.

There was a volley of gun fire directed at the Invader, none of it penetrating or harming it, until one accidentally hit the breathing apparatus, sending the Invader into convulsions as the instant vacuum of space pulled his lungs through his mouth.

The next shot showed rockets being assembled to the side of the craft with a control module of sorts that two men entered. The rockets fired and the craft was directed towards Earth. Next there was a film of the Invaders entering one of their shuttles with an army of well-armed men surrounding them. The shuttle was towed out of the bay by a craft that looked like an old X-15.

There was then a picture of the shuttle sitting on a floor inside a building. "Is this here?" Jason asked the guard.

"It's down about four levels. I understand you'll be getting the grand tour soon. You'll be seeing it and some of these Invaders. Live ones," he answered. "Don't know who you guys are, but there sure is a lot of excitement here lately. Things were looking pretty bleak."

Jason slipped in another disk, it was an autopsy. They pulled an Invader apart piece by piece, filming every detail, turning it over and over, putting it on a scale and weighing it, then, slowly examining the next before doing the same. They fast forwarded through most of that, but not when they took out the brain.

For that, they used what looked like a concrete saw to cut the outer shell. "Diamond blade," the guard commented. After the outer shell was removed, another saw was used to cut the actual skull. That removed, they were able to take out the brain. They were all impressed and commented at how small it was compared to the head size. Most of the massive head was protection for the brain.

Another man came in and spoke with the guard for a short while and left. "You'll have to come and look through this later. It's time for the grand tour," the guard jokingly added, "Tickets please."

Chapter Twenty-Seven

"And what about that damn dog? What did they decide on that?" the Administrator asked. He was sitting inside the Sheriff Office at the village, sifting through the paperwork, every detail of the people and animals of the Village. Male, female, size, age. Everything had to be accounted for, every reaction and every result documented. "I hope we can just shoot it."

"No. They want it included in the test," the man answered. "They want to see how it does against people, I suppose."

"Yup. They would. You ever see donkeys?" Styles asked, knowing he hadn't. "You should have seen it. It was funny. Hilarious. Just the noise they made, oh my god, you should have seen it. Funniest thing you ever saw."

Jerry Styles, the kind of person you would expect to be tasked with experimenting on animals, and now people. It takes a sick and twisted kind of person to do that. A person who considers he has a right. A person who considers that nobody else has rights.

They were there to do another experiment and he would not let silly things like socially imposed morals get in his way. Concepts of right and wrong were always determined by others, he thought, now he could experience true freedom.

These morals that inhibit and control and restricted him, they no longer mattered. Laws, Ha! There would be none soon. Who would enforce them anyway? In a few days, it was all going to crumble. He was finally free to do whatever he wanted, the way it was supposed to be. As a bonus, he had his place secured in the base.

Yes, it took a special kind of person to do this job, and Catskill saw such promise in Jerry Styles that they had him running many of their experiments now. He was now somebody. It was what they needed, a man who was not fettered by ideas of ethics and morality and would not be plagued with guilt.

"Alright. Here is the breakdown. This is how they will be separated into two groups in the two sheds until we are ready. The dog, I have to decide, eater or eatee. I'll let you know," and he handed him the list. "Get going."

The man took the paper and left. Styles sat at the desk with the two cells behind him and his chin in his hands, looked around at the filth that had accumulated in the office and said to himself, "What to do now?"

He stood up and walked to the first cell where a woman was sitting on the bed and just stood there looking at her. She was about twenty-five, he guessed. He moved his head a bit to get a better view through the bars at the welt on her cheek and the cut above her eye.

Then he moved to the next cell where another girl was, perhaps twelve or thirteen, and studied her; her long, jet-black hair, her big dark eyes, and her pouty lips, so sweet and innocent looking. He jingled some keys in one hand while he pulled his belt through the loop with the other and said, "Your turn, darlin'."

Outside, the man with the list opened the door to the empty shed to get it prepared for the subjects of the test, only to see one of his men hanging from the gantry.

"Three AWOL and two suicides," he muttered to the two men with him. "Yup. Three AWOL and two suicides. Well, this guy was messed up anyway. Should have seen it coming. Did any of you have bets?"

"No. No bets on him," one of them answered. "But I made fifty bucks yesterday."

"Well, let's get him down and move these people in here," he said.

Up above in the rafters, the Gunny watched from a dark corner, war paint covering his face, where the only thing visible was the whites of his eyes, up there behind an air vent wrapped in insulation. He watched as they cut down his latest work; the man who threatened Hellen.

The harmless old woman, she was deemed. She ran the store, so she was allowed to continue working in it so the men of Catskill could get things, cigarettes, booze, and candy. There would be no stew for these animals from Hellen. No home-made Hominy Soup. There would be no fair prices either.

To them, it didn't matter what they paid. It was a joke. Money was about to be a thing of the past. They would pay what she asked, no matter how ridiculous, and if they ran out of money, they would just take it from her and pay it with that and laugh.

Hellen refused to give some chocolate to the man who was now swinging from the rope after he walked in and tried to kick Bo. For that, he was going to march her to the shed with the rest; the shed, where the people of the village were forced to sleep on the concrete for the last two days with no food and no sanitation. Where they were kept like livestock, and treated worse. The shed where anyone who complained or protested were taken out and shot.

Although the man swinging at the end of the rope deserved what he got for any number of reasons, threatening Hellen was the one that got him where he was now. He wasn't the first, and he wouldn't be the last.

Hidden in the rafters, the Gunny watched as they cut the rope and let him drop like a sack of flour to the concrete below. The men stood and gawked for a while, making a few joking comments about the look on his face, and then rifled through his pockets, divvying up the contents and dragging him out to the burn pile while the Gunny pulled a paper out and made another mark.

Chapter Twenty-Eight

Going through a series of corridors and doorways, Jason elbowed Cody and said to the guard that he'd like to go to the restroom. Cody took the hint and told him he needed to go as well. Gizmo, having seen the exchange, elbowed Eric and said that he was good and would wait in the corridor, and Eric did the same.

The guard couldn't be in two places at the same time and splitting the group up like this would give him a chance to speak to Cody and give him direction on how to conduct himself, what to say, and what not to say. There would be a 50% chance that the guard would not make the entire group go into the bathroom at the same time.

If he did let the group split, he counted on him not coming in with them to the restroom. There would be a greater than 50% chance of that. It's a guy thing, he wouldn't come in. The guard walked to the facilities and looked at the group and pointed at the door. "Go," he said.

Until Jason was sure that he and his group was safe, he needed to take precautions. He was pretty sure that Catskill was not to be trusted. He was certain that Catskill and the Military were at odds. This he had seen. But he still wasn't convinced that they were safe. He needed insurance.

Once inside, Jason directed him to take a stall. "Listen. I want you to be very careful. Don't answer questions directly, and if at all possible, direct them to me or to Gizmo. But you can't act like you are withholding information either.

"Common knowledge things, things that anyone would know, you can talk about that and that's alright. Go on and on about that. It'll make them think you are being open."

"Right. So what kind of things should I be careful about?" Cody asked.

"Anything that would give them direction to what you did. Until we know what's really going on. You know, talk about conventional science. That's okay. But anything unconventional, no.

"I saw some of that. What you did, what you and Gizmo did. There was conventional science applied in an unconventional way too. So that, don't talk about unconventional application either."

"What are you thinking?" he asked.

"I'm thinking that there are a group of scientists here and they are going to be in a contest with each other. So everything will have to be based on a proven technique and standards. I doubt there will be any thinking out of the box.

"They'll be challenged. Nobody wants to lose credibility, even though in less than a week the world is going to end, they have to hold onto that precious credibility.

"The other thing I'm thinking is that Catskill and the Military are not on friendly terms. There is a competition between them, some kind of battle between them. Since we won't know who is who just yet, you don't want to take the wrong side. We'll play it by ear, but Catskill, we have to watch out for them."

"Right," Cody said. "But we're going to do something, right? Save the world? Boy, can't believe that just came out of my mouth."

"Of course. Try anyway. But I want to get us some freedom. If we end up working with the same people doing the same things based on the same theories they have, the same things they have worked on for who knows how long, then we are wasting our time. It would be better to try and get out of here and hide in the hills."

"Okay. So I'll keep my mouth shut. Except for usual textbook stuff," Cody said.

"Right, and another thing. No protesting. Be very cordial, very polite. There will be a time for protest, and if you see me do it, then join in. Make it count. Other than that, you're doing great. Just do what we do," that being agreed on, he added, "Alright. Now flush and let's go."

"Wait," Cody said. "I gotta go now."

Jason washed his hands and walked into the corridor. The play. He was setting up the play. They were almost taken out of the game entirely, put in the penalty box, but now they are back in the game, setting up the next play on the fly.

He was invited to scrimmage at the Village, the local game down at the neighborhood rink. Before that, he didn't even know there was a game on. Before he was even able to fully decide on whether he would join that team, the semi-pro's, they'd been noticed by the pros., a talent scout, and they are about to be contracted to play on a team he was not entirely sure was the right choice.

There were too many Catskill employees all throughout the facility. There were men with guns escorting them wherever they went.

He gave Gizmo a nod toward Jenkins. They'd worked together for too long for him not to know that he needed to speak to him.

He elbowed Jenkins and nodded toward the bathroom door and said, "You know, I need to go now too."

At which Jenkins said, "Well, I should too, since we're here," and went inside where Cody listened as Gizmo gave Jenkins the same rundown, Cody adding a couple of points that Jason had mentioned.

Eric and Jason stood in the hall with the guard and began to chit chat. "How you guys holding up?" Jason asked. Intel. He needed intel.

"It's been pretty intense," the guard started, "It isn't easy, knowing what's coming. Makes you want to get outside and see everyone you know one last time. All the things you could have said to them. You know. What you should have said."

"I can imagine. How long you been here?" Eric asked.

"Two years. Haven't been outside in six months. It's that new deployment bullshit. Fifteen month stretches. It shouldn't be. Nobody should be deployed for fifteen months straight. Even though my deployment is right here. Still."

Intel. He was getting it. But it was coming freely. He almost expected something else. Perhaps the General was being upfront. Perhaps he was being asked to join the right team. "Did you get out and see your family?"

"A short visit. Spent most of my time with this girl. Now I wished I hadn't," and he paused and looked at the floor, "Now that we know it's coming - the invasion," and he looked down the hall and all around. "I might never get out of here. Might die in here. Makes me want to get out. Some of my friends, they cracked. Couldn't handle it. Me? I don't know."

"Hang in there. Be still and know, man, be still and know," Jason told him. "I should talk, right? The guy that just got here?"

"No man. You're right. You're right," the guard defended him. "Good point. Thanks, Colonel. Be still and know. Haven't thought about that in a while."

He was referring to a self-help drill for Veterans, although it would help anyone. One of the most effective ones he'd known. "Be Still and Know" was something he found on the internet. It was for treating stress or PTSD, a self-help series of lectures and simple drills. It gave him peace and allowed him to function and enjoy life when he needed it.

After the discovery, he told his friends about it and watched them, little by little, get back into the drivers' seat, or more correctly, not drive into a ditch or tree. They would regain control of themselves. Begin to see the rose instead of the thorn.

He was not gathering intel now. He was helping someone; being a part. Once you are a part of some things, you are never, really, not a part again. You will always be one of them in some way.

189

He considered this for a moment and wondered how these Invaders must feel. They must feel. They are a part, a part of something; a part of something evil, yes, but still a part.

"I've got to keep this in mind. They are a part of something. What is it that keeps them? Holds them?" he thought to himself. "Or were they? They were left adrift in space for how long? They weren't rescued. Maybe they couldn't communicate or send a distress signal.

"But we would never let a vessel go down without a search. We would never let our men vanish without a search. But, here it is, decades later, even over a century later. I wonder how they feel about that."

They continued down the corridors and down flights of stairs until they stopped at a large window. "The receiving room," the guard said. It was a room that the ones meant to survive an extinction level catastrophe would be brought and indoctrinated; a room that was now full of new arrivals.

A screen was on, playing a message from the President, telling them of the coming invasion and that they had been chosen based on knowledge, intelligence, skills, and health. There was no lottery, there was no buying access. There was no luck to it and there was no nonsense. None of that.

Will you be strong enough and smart enough and educated enough? That was what will determine whether you live or not. Will you contribute to the survival of man?

The guard wasn't watching the screen. He was watching four men who had just entered the corridor wearing blue Catskill outfits. "Three, twelve, blue, four," he said into his com.

Jason looked above the door and saw "12" written above it and surmised that the guard had just told someone they were on the third floor by door twelve with four Catskill employees heading in their direction. He was right about a battle going on between the two forces, Catskill and the Military.

A quiet rebellion was happening. Eric and Gizmo were alerted to it with the sound of the guard unsnapping the leather strap of his side-arm and they watched him hand the 9mm to Jason through the reflection in the screen.

On the other side of the double doors the Catskill people came through, there would likely be a guard station. Whatever they were going to do would have to be quiet and fast so as not to alert them. Jason tried to get a better idea of his surroundings. Anything he could exploit.

They were in a long corridor and all he could see as he moved slightly looking at the reflection was that there was a door behind him, and that door jamb wouldn't provide cover for anyone if shooting started.

The four men came closer, and he got that same familiar feeling you get when you are being watched; being stalked. Whatever was going to happen, it was about to happen and it would be fast. The guard stood relaxed with his M-16 held comfortably at low ready, the safety having been flipped off as soon as he saw the men come through the door and approach.

He would wait for them to make the first move and commit themselves. They still think they would catch guard and the group unaware. A distraction is what they needed.

Jason leaned toward the view screen to change the angle of reflection and tried to see what weapons they were carrying. He could see one with a pistol and could not see the others. He would have to assume they were all carrying them.

The men in blue would wait until they were right on top of Jason and the guard before making their move. Their attention was on the guard now, the only one they thought had a weapon. They came within five feet when Gizmo stepped back away from the screen and started pretending to sneeze.

Jason's' hand, obscured the whole time by the guard, held the pistol as he stepped around Gizmo and fired three shots, putting three of the men down. The guard had his rifle at the other's head and he froze.

Eric had already bolted around and taken a weapon from a falling man before he even hit the ground. Gizmo was taking the other two weapons and handed one to Jenkins and shoved one under his shirt while Jason took the pistol from the one left standing.

Four men bolted into the corridor from either end with weapons drawn and rushed toward them. Seeing the men on the floor, one of them called for a cleaning crew and the others opened the door Jason had seen in the reflection while the dead men were dragged in and out of sight, with the one left alive being marched in last.

"Idiots. So, I guess you are important. Shall we continue?" the guard asked.

They did continue, down even more corridors and stairways to a guarded double door. "This is where it gets interesting. It's all in here." The guard pushed through the doors into an open room the size of a football field.

The floor was coated and the walls were white. Spectacled scientists in smocks were either at stations or walking with clip boards and testing equipment. The guard pointed toward the alien shuttle and said, "The main event."

"How did you get it down here?" Jason asked.

"Parachutes," one of the scientists walked up and spoke. "You must be the new arrivals to the team we were told about. We put the Invaders inside and dropped it like a rock from space and pulled the chutes. Then we just picked it up and airlifted it here.

"The beasts are pretty tough. They must have been jostled a little, but I don't think the fall even hurt them. You're going to see some of them later.

"Names Stanford," and held out his hand for introductions. "I am the...well, I guess you'd call me the project manager for this research team. I understand you are the ones that did something we haven't been able to do yet. Did something with the 8791s."

The guard cut in, "We just call them Walkers now. Easier," and leaned over speaking in a lower voice to Jason, "Dr. Stanford is one of ours."

"Walkers, eh? Alright, but you did that. How'd you do it? You're going to have to show us," Stanford said. "The exterior lights blinked over there too. Never got a single thing to go on, ever, in decades. You have to show us what you did."

"No problem. Right after the tour," Jason replied. "I understand you have some Invaders here. I'd like to see that. Maybe get inside that shuttle too."

"Right. There is one over this way," and started to walk toward it, "It is one that we have separated. You can see the rest, but this is just one of them." Then he added, "So, how'd you do it?"

"Waves," Jason said, telling him without telling him.

"Waves, of course, waves. But we've tried every wave there is that we know of. What did you do different?"

"It's hard to explain. Just a kind of half-baked theory, but I'd be happy to show you," he said. "Looks like we'll be spending some time down here with you, right?"

"Well Drs. Brand and Crozley, it'll be a pleasure working with you, I'm sure. Could use a fresh mind or two. The rest of you too. We've been grinding too long with little result and we are just plain running out of time, and worse, running out of morale."

"I can imagine," Eric said. "I just got here and I'm already depressed."

"Wait 'till you see what we're going to be up against," the scientist said as they approached a large viewing screen. "Gentlemen. The Invader."

They all stood silently looking at the beast, studying it, and sizing it up. It sat in a room by itself, morose and despondent, as hideous as the Walkers, just slightly smaller.

"It thinks he's the only one left; that the others on the ship are all dead. We made up some pictures. I can't tell one from another of these things. But there are differences. Like the spots and coloring. Shades. That's how they know one from the other, I'm pretty sure.

"So we made up some pictures. Cut and paste them. Put them in piles with the other dead bodies. Simple Photoshop. He fell for it. Or she. Been a little sullen ever since."

"And the rest?" Jason asked.

"We have another two in solitary. One that thinks the same as this and one that is just sitting with no input at all. We have no idea what they think; what's going through that thick skull of theirs." Stanford motioned for them to go further.

"This is the rest of them. We had around two hundred live. Killed a handful, tested weapons on some. You know. Tough characters. No way we can fight them when they land," and he paused and thought about it before speaking, "With millions of them. No way. We're done."

"Well, we'd better think of something. Figure something out," Eric said. "I'm not lying down for them. Ugly bastards. No way."

"That's what I like to hear," they heard a voice from behind. They turned to see the General standing there. "That's what we need. A fresh horse. Or horses."

"Good evening, General. Or night," Gizmo greeted him. "Not sure what it is down here."

"Doesn't matter any longer, does it? Time is running out. But it is night," he said.

"General. I get it," Gizmo said. "We're here for the duration. I get it. I have a family. I really could concentrate better…"

The General cut in, "Already taken care of, Colonel," and turned to one of the men standing beside him. "What time do they arrive?"

"Should be in receiving with the next batch, Sir," he replied. "You'll be able to see her in two or three hours."

Jason gave Gizmo a pat on the shoulder. It was his wife he was asking about. He wondered if he should ask about Bo. Would they let dogs in? "Do you let in animals?" he asked.

"Just food. No pets," he replied. "We have a zoo set up. I guess a sort-of Noah's ark. You could go look if you had time. But, sorry. No pets."

He turned toward the shuttle. "Have you looked yet?"

"No. Just looked at the animals, so far. Interesting from the outside, though," Jason answered. "What kind of drives do they have?"

"That's the problem. We can't figure it out. We were hoping you could do something with it. Right now, it's the biggest damn paperweight on Earth."

"We'll take a look and see what we can figure out, General," Jason said.

"Good. That's what I was hoping you'd say," and turned to them. "I imagine you are going to need a little help finding your way around. I don't want you to waste a minute getting lost. Any of you.

"I'm assigning a person to each of you. I don't care what it is, if you need it or if you need to get somewhere, use them. If they could take a piss for you they would. We have not even a handful of days left. Don't waste time," then added, "And get in uniform. You just re-up'd. We meet in two hours."

Next on the tour was the shuttle. After the outside was examined, they went inside to the cockpit. "We haven't got a clue, to tell you the truth," Stanford began. "Everything we have is based on electron flow. It's pretty much everything on Earth, except for internal combustion and rockets and such. But any other energy, it's based on electron-flow theory. This, we haven't gotten to square one."

Stanford explained what research they have done and all the failed attempts to get some response from the equipment. A suggestion or two was brought up by the group, but they had been tried many times in many variations. But they were all good ideas, Stanford told them, and invited them to come up with more. They did and they had been tried as well.

They all came out and walked around the craft again asking a couple of questions and then went back inside. They racked their brains, looking at different pieces. Every now and then Gizmo, Cody or Jason would look at something and say "This looks like a…" and it would end there. Stanford would watch and make encouraging comments like, "I like the way you think," until it was time to leave and get ready for the meeting.

Chapter Twenty-Nine

Jason was quiet on the way to the meeting. Stanford was a smart guy, and they couldn't come up with even a theory on the alien systems. Nobody had in decades. He began formulating a plan. "Play the man, not the puck," is what he was thinking.

He was formulating a plan that could change the momentum of the game. Without doing that, the chances of the human race surviving were slight, even if they were hidden in caves. It would just be a matter of time before they were discovered and dug out.

The plan wasn't complete, but it was starting, and the thing about Jason's plan that was different than the Catskill one they heard is this: it didn't include losing. It didn't include hiding. It didn't include the destruction of society. It didn't include the extinction of mankind.

Another part of the plan, an important part, would include getting Bo.

They were escorted to their berthing where uniforms had been laid out. Waiting for them were their assistants. Cody didn't quite know what to do with his and felt uncomfortable with the idea of having one. Jenkins had usually had someone working for him while being a Ranger and took to the idea easier.

Jason, Gizmo and Eric were used to having a chain of command and each made fast introductions and began putting on their uniforms. Jason was deep into formulating his plan, a piece of it at least, while the man stood uncomfortably and nervously asking questions. Did he need anything else? Is there something he could get?

But Jason was deep, deep in thought now. His plan was coming together. So deep he did not hear the man speaking. He stood up and said, "Brenner? It's Brenner, right?"

"Banner, sir. Banner, and if you need anything..." and he was cut off.

"Get me a wide screen TV and put it down by the Invaders, the one we saw today. You know the one I'm talking about?"

"Yes, I..."

"Go, and bring some DVD players and get it all hooked up," he told him and turned to Gizmo. "Get your guy to get us disks of the Invaders home planet. Get disks of the bombardments, the stuff we saw in the library. Then, get me some Star Trek shows, and Aliens. Star Trek with battles, not that talking bullshit. Fighting Klingons and Romulans. Space wars. Meet us down at the cage."

The man was standing next to Gizmo bewildered. "Get going. Hurry," Gizmo told him. "I know what you're thinking. Brilliant," he said as the two men scurried out of the berthing.

"Well," said Jason while smoothing the front of his uniform, "Meeting time. Don't we look purdy?" And they all looked at Eric's' Yeomen.

"Ready when you are, son. You do know where we're going, right?" Eric asked.

"Yes, sir. Right this way," and started walking without hesitation.

The General was sitting at his conference table surrounded by scientists, officers, and his personal staff going over details of the coming invasion, the transport of people to the bases and food storage, medicine, and security.

He looked as if he were in pain having to sit through it; all the endless details in preparation for the inevitable outcome. It was an outcome he had worked years to avoid. Now, he was going over the endless details of an apathetic defeat.

They all stood and listened to the final last stand of mankind being planned, being backed further and further into the caves, blowing the top down as they retreated deeper and deeper, setting up a new defense, and blowing that once they were again overrun, and moving further back, until there was nowhere else to go, and no deeper part to retreat.

Jason listened to as much as he could and exploded. "Sir. Hate to interrupt, but we have a war to fight. To win! I think I can get those machines running. Interested?"

"Hell yes!" The General yelled as he jumped out of his chair.

Jason was already heading out the door talking a mile a minute when he turned and looked back and motioned toward the exit. "General?" he said, inviting him to come along.

"I'm going to make that son-of-a-bitch turn on his equipment," Jason started out. "I'm gonna make him do it and it's going to show us how. I'm gonna get in his piece of shit space ship and I'm gonna go and blow the hell out of his planet. I'm gonna kill them and I'm gonna destroy them and they're gonna get no mercy."

The General started to laugh. "Okay. You have a plan. We've been working on this for years. Tell me something we haven't tried."

"Star Trek," Jason said.

"What are you talking about?" he asked.

"I'm going to show him movies. Show him our space ships. The Enterprise. Aliens. Things like that. Show him we have potential for an assault. Show him battles," he said. "I'm going to show him his home planet and his ships. Then, I'm going to show him a movie of his planet being destroyed."

"We don't have that movie," The General said. "Wait. I get it. Then we show who killed his planet, right, and show Captain Kirk going and fighting with them. Now he'll want to help us. He'll have a common enemy. Might work. Might work."

"We can do that, right? Make up a film. I don't think it has to be perfect quality, but believable. We can do that, right?" Jason asked.

The General stopped in the corridor and issued orders. Two of his staff ran off to get the project started. "We've been making these videos for a while now for the incoming instruction and indoctrination. I'll have you a movie before the day is out. Their planet will have the hells blown out of it and we will be chasing the bad guys."

"If we can do this fast enough, if we can get their transport going and start bombarding their home planet. The attackers will have to return to defend it," Eric said. "That's what they did before."

"How do you figure? They might do that. How can you know that they will break off an attack here and defend it?" the General asked.

"We hope they will," Jason said, "They left their own guys drifting in space when their home planet was attacked. We know that. They were at war. They pulled everyone back to defend it. I hope they will. They have to."

"You're going to have one ship and no experience running it. You think you are going to destroy their whole home planet?" the General pointed out. "I like your attitude, Colonel, but I think you're expectations are a little unreal."

"Well, sir. I haven't got everything figured out. But it's a start. Better than sitting here and being a target. But we have the shuttles too. How many? Couple hundred? We can load those up too. Fly them and they'll never expect it."

"No," the General said. "There are sixteen miles of them things sitting up there. They had to transport sixteen million Invaders. No, it's a little more than a couple of hundred shuttles. There are 2640 of them. That is a total of thirty trips for each one by the end of the invasion before the transport lands."

"Wow. They must have different economics than we do. Imagine. How many planets do they have?" Jason said. "But it'll buy us more time if it fails, their invasion, I mean. We can figure out everything, their technology, defenses, and their weapons, all of it. By the time they come back, if they do come back, and if we have it figured out, they will have a really bad day in store."

"You're counting on a whole lot of maybes, Colonel," the General said.

"True, General. But there are some things that are certain. The extinction of the human race is one of them if we don't do this," Jason replied. "There is one thing that will win us the War. One thing we have to find. It'll be on their home planet and will be guarded better than their Fort Knox. We'll have to find it and destroy it. Then, it won't matter if the Invaders return to their home planet or not.

"If I'm right, and we can knock it out, the Invaders will be stuck again with no power and no weapons. I don't have it all figured out yet, but I'm pretty sure I'm right on my theory. If I'm wrong, well, the end is almost here anyway."

"That is a fact. That is a sad fact. You let me know anything you need. Anything." He turned to one of his aides and said, "You go with him. You inform me of all progress and you get him anything he needs. Anything. I'll be in my office," and started to walk away.

"General, there is another thing we need to discuss, an important thing: Catskill," he called to him.

The General looked around quickly to make sure no Catskill personnel were around, walked up close to him and said, "Watch what you say and to whom you say it. These people have the President under their thumb, drugged. Spies everywhere. They practically run the place. They've been involved from day one with the planning."

He looked around again to make sure it was clear, "We'll have to compare notes. But later. They still think that helicopter crashed with you on it, so don't talk about it. They still don't know who you are, and right now, you're just another guy in uniform."

Jason was starting to like this General. He looked at the aide while they walked away and said, "I think that I may need to go to the moon, take a look at that ship."

The aide's eyes grew wide in shock. It was an unexpected request. Could he do that? Go to the moon? The General did say "Anything he needed." He got on his head set and started speaking.

"Oh yah, and get me some of those headsets. At least eight. Maybe some spares too," Jason added.

Jason had a growing crew, Gizmo, Cody, Jenkins, Eric, all their assistants, and the aide. He would need to communicate with them all. Time was running out and he didn't want to waste a minute trying to get hold of someone. Taking an extra two minutes to contact all those people over two days could add up to hours. That would be long enough to wipe out every city and town on Earth and begin the invasion.

"It's great having a General's aide here with us," Gizmo started chattering about a half hour later down at the viewing screen. "You don't have to wait for anything, and the guy never leaves. If we need something, he can just get on his head set and, presto! It's done. We should have gotten us one of them a long time ago." He picked up a disk labeled "Home Planet" and looked at it. "All set?"

"Let it rip," Jason said.

The movie played, showing the alien planet, while Jason and Gizmo watched the Invader. This thing hadn't seen his home in over a century and had been lead to believe he was alone on this planet, a captive. They studied the reaction. It went from what appeared to be morose resignation to something else. They weren't sure what it was, but the Invader's spirits had lifted.

"Seems like a reaction. How do you think it feels? Is that happy? Longing? Loneliness? I can't tell," Jason said.

"Me neither, but it's coming to life," and he picked up another disc, "Next."

This was showing bombardments of various planets by his kind, maybe even him. It was a shortened version of four different civilizations destroyed and planets overrun and occupied. It stood up and watched these. While it was watching, Jason and Gizmo were watching it.

"Star Trek," Jason requested next.

"I remember this one. Good choice, pal," Gizmo said, looking at his assistant.

Eric, Cody and Jenkins had joined them now, watching its reactions.

"It likes this," Cody commented. "Ooh! It's checking out the engine room. Look at him. I think it's hot for Scottie."

It watched the entire episode paying particular attention to the engines and engine room. The next one showed more action. It was a battle with Klingons and the Enterprise. It stood up when the phasers were fired and almost leaped up when the photon torpedoes were deployed and started excitedly pacing side to side.

"Brenner," Jason called his assistant over.

"Banner, sir," he said.

"Right. Did you bring popcorn?"

"No. Sir," he answered.

"Well, that's unfortunate, because I need you to sit here for a while. Just play a couple more of these Star Treks. Then plug in Aliens. Okay? Get yourself a clipboard and note down its reactions and what it is seeing at the time. Just like that and call me when you're done."

The invasion was only one issue to deal with. Almost as important and threatening as the invasion, were the Walkers. There were millions of them across the world, with no way of killing them without rendering Earth uninhabitable, and he and Gizmo and a kid had made more progress than the group of scientists who had engineered them had made in years.

Something was wrong with this picture and Jason needed to find out what it was. It wasn't making sense. They were on their way to the library to see what records they could find when he began to think about the village and the Walkers being released onto them. The village was burning in his mind.

Pete Goodwell sat on top of a hill overlooking the valley. The lights from the village sent off a dim glow behind the rocks obscuring him from security. He balanced with the other runners on the boulders and watched and waited until a person came to them out of the dark. It was Hellen, Singingbird, just like his vision had told him.

"I brought you some corn soup and bread," she said walking up the path. "You have lots to do and you need your strength."

"Thank you Hellen," they all told her, and Pete asked, "How are things in the village?"

"Oh," she said. "Don't you worry about the village or the people in it. They'll be fine. They are protected and so are you. But the Gunny, or rather, Mr. Stonefish, asked if you got the packages out to the other Nations and tribes. He seemed a little worried about that. I told him that it would happen if it was meant to be. No use worrying. That'll never change anything."

"Yes Ma'am. You can tell him they have all been warned now. They will be moving to higher ground, above any caves. This is really good soup," Pete told her.

"Hominy soup, corn soup, we have been making it since way before the White Man came. Even before those Spaniards, those heathen rotten murderous devils. We should be able to make good soup by now," she laughed. "I put a little pork in it for flavor. It's always better the next day, you know. So I made a lot of it."

"Have we heard anything about Eric and Cody and the others?" Pete asked.

"Oh yes. You would be so proud of Cody. He is turning into quite a brave young man. Eric is working with those two gentlemen, Jason and Gizmo. Mr. Jenkins is with them too. They are all together and they are well."

"I have to ask you something," one of the runners said. "How do you get past the guards in the village?"

"Surely you must know. I just walk out. I go where the spirits tell me to go. They do everything else, make the guards look the other way just at the right moment or make them sneeze at the right time. All I had to do was make you some soup and bring it where they told me. It was a nice walk too."

"I've been having visions too," Pete said. "How is the man's dog? I've been thinking a lot about her."

"The dog is fine. She won't leave my store! Just lies on the floor like she is waiting for something. I like having her around, it's comforting. But you will have to bring the dog to Jason when the time comes, they told me. But not just yet.

"He will also need that gun of his he has in his motor home and something he puts on the dog; it goes on her back to put things in. But don't you worry about that just yet."

They all thanked her again for the soup and when she was about to leave, she handed Pete a piece of paper. "This is from the Gunny, or um, from Mr. Stonefish. It's a little dark right now, so I guess you can read it in the morning." Then she disappeared back into the night.

Pete and his runners sat looking at the stars when a hoot from an owl broke the silence. They all looked in that direction and moved toward a large smooth boulder of sandstone, and climbed it. Peering over the top, they could see parts of the village, the razor wire glistening in the moonlight and a few people moving in and out of the shadows.

"Look. It's Hellen," one of them pointed at a guard stationed near the end of town picking something up that he had dropped, while she casually strolled by.

Pete Goodwell felt for the note from the Gunny in his shirt pocket and had a growing concern that it might fall out and decided to transfer it to another pocket that was more secure. "Glad we helped Mr. Gizmo make those rockets," he casually commented, "I think we are going to need more soon."

"Glad we have firework stands all over the county," another said. "I was surprised how much powder they used. But man, did they work or what! That was something to see."

They spent much of the night telling stories, each one his own version of the capture of the Evil Walkers, each from his perspective. One, a rider on horseback, galloping up to them, worried that his horse would rear up and buck him off. Another in amongst the thirty on the ground firing round after round of slugs, never knowing if it would succeed in toppling them over.

He described how it looked firing so many slugs at one time, and from where he was standing, it looked like a grey ghost blanket being thrown over the beasts, and then disappearing as the Walker stumbled or rolled backward until they fired another round, over and over.

They all told their versions of the capture in great detail, each one from where they were and what they were seeing and who was beside them and what they were doing. It was pure luck that Jason and his group had drawn the monsters almost to the precise spot they needed to be in to be draped with the net.

Into the night the tales went on until eventually they were silent, watching the night sky for shooting stars, and then falling asleep, dreaming of other brave deeds, acts of courage and valor, and the most beautiful Indian Princesses as ever there were.

Chapter Thirty

Jason and the rest were in the library finding what they could about the Walkers, going through disks labeled 8791 and 8791-1 when Eric came up with a disk of photos and some surveillance labeled "Ruby Ridge" they hadn't expected. It was their own photos and film that they had gotten from the air shaft that had now been added.

They fast forwarded through the trains coming in and unloading the cattle and the horror that followed. The stills were next and were of particular interest to them. They had seen them, but never really studied them. Not knowing if they would ever get back inside the Ruby Ridge mine, they paid close attention to the details of what their village might be forced to deal with.

The photo of the blast doors, the columns, and the viewing platform were all there. They had never paid much notice to the people behind the thick glass, but something caught Gizmos' eye and he enlarged the picture.

"Look!" he said with some surprise. "You recognize that?"

Jason got closer for a better look. "What?"

"Look at who that is," he said.

Jason got even closer and stared. "Is that…who I think it is?"

"Frankenstein, it's him. Look at him, he was there," Gizmo sneered.

Eric came up to the screen and looked, blocking the picture with his head. "Who? What are you looking at?"

"The guy. We ran into him. Look," and Jason put his finger right on the screen, "This guy. He was at an explosion at Catskill Chemicals. The same piece of …" and he thought for a moment and said, "Hey! Catskill. Aren't there Catskill Mountains back East? Eric, see if you can find something on Catskill Mountains."

As Eric searched the files and disks they told the story again of the explosion at the chemical plant and how they ran into Dr. Bradley, how the other scientists nearly beat him to death, and how he tried to blow the whole facility.

"Man, there is a lot on Catskill. Let's see, Catskill Mountains, Catskill Pharmaceuticals, Catskill…there's a lot," Eric called out to them. He brought them a stack of files on disks and went back for second load when he called out, "Hey! Did you say it was Catskill Chemicals? Because there is one here labeled 'Security Footage – Catskill Chemicals Explosions'. You want it?"

"Yes!" Jason yelled. "Let's see that," and he shoved it in the drive.

All eyes were on the screen watching scenes that looked like something from a "B" Horror show. An elderly man wearing a smock came on the screen and a label underneath saying "Dr. Gruber", and a few minutes later showed him talking to what looked to be his assistant.

"That's him. Bradley. He was a bit younger then," Gizmo commented.

They were showing something now labeled "8791" that looked like an embryo with a needle being stuck into it under a microscope. Then it showed the embryo growing to a form, the form of a Walker. Then the walker grew and as it grew larger, it showed Gruber and Bradley beside it from time to time, feeding it, petting it, and playing with it. Bradley, the madman they knew, looked filled with the joy of accomplishment and proud of his new pet.

"Doesn't look too dangerous to me," Eric said.

Then there was Gruber being filmed with the Walker lying on a table. Bradley was standing off to the side with a disturbed look on his face. Gruber was cutting into the head of the beast and was about to remove the brain.

"Wait!" Jason yelled. "Back it up just a couple of minutes," and they watched it over. "Do it again. Watch Bradley. Is that a scalpel in his hand?"

They played the scene over and over until there was no doubt. "Look at him," Gizmo said. "He's gonna kill Gruber. Look at his face. He's gonna do it. What a psycho."

The scene played out a few more minutes showing the brain coming out and placed onto a tray while Gruber looked deep into the cavity. Bradley had become agitated and made movements toward Gruber and would appear to change his mind and think better of it until he seemed to excuse himself and left the room.

Another scene came up of several of the animals with Gruber doing tests on them. Bradley was standing to the side participating only when Gruber told him to do something, watching, glancing with hatred at the doctor.

Several large gas cylinders were shown on the screen. They were about ten feet around and standing a couple of feet above Gruber's head as he looked at the direction of the camera. This was different. This was not actual film. This was the actual security footage. Gruber had a horrified expression when he looked in the direction of the camera, then he yelled something out, and then the cylinders behind him exploded, killing him instantly.

The security footage showed the gas from the cylinders being drawn up into the ventilation and air filtration system. The film went on while the canisters emptied into the facility, when another explosion went off out of sight of the camera, and the screen went blank.

They played the video over again from the beginning. Gruber walking into the camera view, turning and walking back the way he came and returning into the camera to look at it.

"I bet he got locked in. He comes up, turns around, checks the door and sees that it's locked," Eric provided the running commentary. "Look, now he knows he's in trouble and he screamed at the camera. What's he saying? What was that guy's name? Bradley? It looks like he screams that and at the end, just before it explodes, look, he knows, and he yells 'NO!' and then, he's dead."

"I think you're right. Looks like he might be yelling 'Bradley. NO' to me too. That's harsh, man. Knowing that is the end," Jason said. "But maybe we're just seeing what we think, reading into it."

Cody had fallen asleep some time before, so wouldn't have the same input they had already had. He hadn't even heard the man's name yet, so Jason woke him up and asked what he thought the man was saying.

He rubbed his eyes and squinted at the screen and tried to speak along with it. "Ball, eee, nooo. Bally, baily or something, then, but definitely a 'no' at the end. Let's see it again," and it was replayed. "Looks like something starting with a 'B', then followed by an 'E', but long and drawn out. Then, I'm pretty positive that's a 'no' that he's yelling."

"We're thinking 'Bradley, No' was what he was yelling," Eric told him.

"Oh, yah. For sure. That's exactly it. 'Bradley NO!' Makes sense. Who's Bradley?" he asked.

With a short explanation, they continued the security footage. "Hey, that's us!" Gizmo got closer to the screen to watch himself and Jason wander through the dark corridors. "Look, what did I tell you? Zombies," he said, drawing them all closer to the screen.

Next were some more Invader video, or rather Invader vs. Walkers. The first short scene was a Walker being released into a room with a captured Invader. It was short because the Walker instantly ripped him apart. Although the Invader fought back, the fight only lasted about thirty seconds before it lay dead and in pieces.

The next showed three Invaders having a Walker released into their room. The Walker threw them about and slashed and ripped them apart in less than two minutes and continued to pounce on them after they were dead.

It is one thing to have them trapped in a room doing battle. It is another in an open space. So, eight of them were put into a large open area. It showed the Invaders organizing an attack after the first of them were killed.

The Invaders, huge themselves by human standards and possessing other-worldly strength, were able to finally kill the single Walker, but not until after six of them had died and the other two badly injured.

More trials were done using two Walkers against various numbers of Invaders. Then three. Rudimentary weapons were provided. Clubs, metal bars, rocks. The results were the same. The Walkers, in their mad uncontrolled rage, were stronger, faster, larger, and were superior killers to the Invaders.

They all sat silent for a while looking back and forth at each other, trying to digest all they had just seen. Catskill Chemicals. Catskill Pharmaceuticals. Bradley had made these monsters into monsters. It was to fight the Invaders. That's why they did it, was the conclusion they all arrived at. They had made things of nightmares.

"This is nuts, it's not going to work," Eric finally spoke. "The Invaders have weapons, we've seen them. They'll just grab their guns, or whatever they are, and wipe out the Walkers. Then...us."

"I think the Invaders are counting on the bombardment wiping out most of everything. Then they land in the shuttles and get out and have a little fun. Go on a killing spree. That's what they always did in the videos," Jason said.

"We must be counting on them all being out of the shuttles when the transport lands and opens up. That's probably the plan now. Then, they want to release the Walkers and at the same time stop the Invaders from getting to their weapons. Blowing up the shuttles, coordinating an attack. Something like that." He sat for a moment and then added, "Yah. I agree. It's a long shot. But it's the only play they have left."

"What's to keep us from jumping into their shuttles once they land?" Cody asked and then answered his own question. "Oh, yah. We can't get them to work."

"And that is what we need to work on next," Jason responded, "and we'd better get to work. Time is not on our side. Ready? Ranger Jenkins, I wonder if you could spend a little time here, get on the internet, look through the files they have and see what else you can find out about Catskill. Cody, I'd like you and Dr. Stanford to build something. I have a little plan I've been doodling out," and handed him a sheet of paper.

Jason, Eric and Gizmo watched the new film they wanted to play to the Invader, a film of the destruction of the Invader home planet, and watched the chase scenes of spliced Star Trek shots chasing and killing the perpetrators with phasers and photon torpedoes. It would suffice and served the purpose of showing the Humans as having a common enemy with the Invaders.

He walked over and looked at the reactions noted on the clipboard from various scenes while the earlier shows were played. The most response came from the movie Aliens, where dialogue was not required to follow a plot, but the beast was still intensely interested in the weapons of the Star Ship Enterprise and its engines. This was good.

Jason walked over to the machine and plugged in the shot of the Home Planet once more, letting the thing watch again. Then, he plugged in the new film of it being attacked. The Invader jumped and howled in protest as its defenses were destroyed first. Then it showed satellites being blown up in space. Then their cities being blasted.

It was decided that, if this were to really happen, some of the Invader cruisers, the Transporters, would most likely show up to defend their home. This turned out to be a brilliant addition to the film. It drove him wild as they were hit and destroyed as well.

The enemy ships, the make-believe enemy ships, were copied from a recent Sci-fi film, and all enemy ships had similar design and similar made-up weaponry which the Invaders were not able to defend against and defeat. Their weapons had no effect on them and their defenses were as if they didn't even exist.

Jason felt it was odd that it had such a reaction, since this is almost exactly the way they invaded other worlds. The weapons and defenses were useless against the Invaders. Now he was watching his own planet suffering the same fate, and that drove it wild.

Jason was satisfied with the result and shut it all down with orders that no person go near the cage or let the Invader see any other person but him.

"Now, I just have to convince him to get this equipment running. The shuttle. If I can get him to do that, we can figure out everything else. Even if he just fires up some of it. Even turns on a little gadget, we can learn how to do it. See what kind of energy it uses," Jason mused.

"Look. Jason," Gizmo said, "What if you were him? If it were me in that cage, I don't know. First thing I got my hands on that I could kill with, I'd probably use, and for all we know, he might even be able to fight his way out of here, out of the base. Maybe even get back to his ship. We really have to be careful. If he does that and turns his stuff back on, we're in deep shit."

"True. But they sat out there in space a long time and didn't. Died out there, even. I don't think he can right now. But if we can see how he would if he could, then, maybe we can figure out how to get power to it. Maybe we need another one of those shuttles down here."

"You know. What do you think of this?" Gizmo said. "What if I took the shuttle controls apart in modules and hooked up some sort of computer at the other end of it to tell what signals it is getting sent when he tries to turn it on. Then we can get another shuttle down here that can actually work."

"Might work. Might tell us something. But we don't even know what kind of power they use. It's not electrons, so we might not get anything out of it on a computer. I've been thinking of something. I think I have an idea of their power. Let's look at some of their videos again.

"I think that we might be able to get the power they would use, something like it anyway. Then, he just has to show us some moves, what does what, how to turn things on. I can't tell what is a control and what is furniture, to tell you the truth."

"Me neither," Gizmo said.

"One thing seems pretty certain," Jason continued. "They either broke down out there or they ran out of gas. I'm leaning toward them running out of gas, because, why couldn't they fix it?"

"Or, if they ran out of gas, why didn't they drain all those thousands of shuttles and use that?" Eric asked.

"That's what I mean. That's what I'm talking about. Why didn't they do that? That's what gave me the idea. I don't think they use the same thing, not even the same concept of a gas tank," and Jason looked around, "Where is that guy, the scientist?"

"Stanford? He's right over there," and Gizmo called to him.

Stanford came over out of breath, "We were watching the Invader on the screen. You really got some reaction from him."

"Good," Jason said. "I hope to get an even better one later. We need to talk about this transport and the shuttles. You've been through them, right? I mean all through them?"

"One end to the other," he replied. "We even tried reverse engineering. Built one from scratch, every detail. Still can't get a thing to work. What were you thinking?"

"Did you did find anything that would resemble a gas tank?"

"No," he answered.

"And no reactors that you could identify as one, right?"

"No. Nothing like that," Stanford said.

Jason thought for a moment and said, "Would you mind coming to the library with us and going over some of the original footage?"

Up at the library they continued the discussion while Jason doodled on a piece of paper and looked over the raw video of the vessel. Jason paused the machine and said, "If you had a technology that made you far superior to any other species and it allowed you to destroy and conquer world after world…" and he paused again, "and then you broke down in the middle of space. What would you do?"

Thinking for a moment, "Disassemble it!" Gizmo and Stanford both said in unison.

"Me too. I'd disable it. I'd take something crucial off. So what are we looking for? I'm betting it is some piece of something that would look like scrap. If they got boarded or taken over, just like we did to them, we couldn't figure it out."

"Right. Right. It could have been there all along. But Jason, why don't the shuttles work?" Dr. Stanford asked.

"Because, Doctor, they don't need gas or power. The power comes from the main ship. This is what I'm thinking: The power to the shuttles came from the main ship. The main ship didn't have energy storage either, so it came from somewhere else, and I'm guessing it's from their planet."

"What, you think they beamed it or something? That doesn't seem likely," Stanford said.

"No. Not like we think. Not the way we think about it," he said.

"Then how?" Stanford asked.

Gizmo answered, "Quantum Communication. Of course. I get what you're thinking. It makes perfect sense now. There is no energy storage. There is no gas tank or reserve. No batteries. So the energy is somewhere else and is Quantum Communicated straight to the ship."

"Yah," Jason jumped back in. "And think about it. Look at all the questions that it answers. Their travel. How they can jump through space with this monstrosity. It's like a city, it's so big. How we haven't been able to find a single sparkle of power anywhere. It's because there isn't any and there never has been."

"Maybe. Maybe you're right. But then why did they end up adrift?" Stanford asked.

"I have an idea," Jason answered. "A couple, in fact. They were under attack. They were at war. So maybe the thing that communicates got hit. It would knock it out.

"Another is this. You have two particles, or let's say two batches of particles, but, they are together at first, not separated, and you charge them or you create some kind of field on them or something. Then, when you do separate them, you can affect one particle or batch, and it will have a similar effect on the one that is separated.

"We do this ourselves in laboratories now. We did it with photons. That's energy. It's really similar to electrons; almost the same thing, in fact. It's the Scary Entanglement that Einstein talked about. So, if that were the case, they wouldn't need to drag their energy around with them. They just affect the particles at home and, Presto! Their boom boxes or whatever works."

Jason sat and continued to draw while he waited for the response as the others pondered what he had just said. He continued watching the film for something that might look like it would do what he just explained. The trouble is he had no idea what it would look like. He went over the film again and again, paying special attention to the engine room and parts that were scattered around.

"It's actually pretty brilliant," Stanford finally admitted. "It would make total sense. There are no gas tanks or batteries or anything like that. There were no Generators. It makes sense."

"And," Gizmo joined in, "it makes sense for their weapons too. It's too much power to carry around with no generators or energy storage. But here's the thing, Jason. If they can't get the power, how do we? They were out there for decades and couldn't."

"I think we can do it. In fact, I think you already have. In fact, I'm sure of it," he said.

"Me?" Gizmo was shocked. "How do you figure?"

"You did it. I'm sure of it now. You and Cody. Back at the reservation. You did it and I think we can do it again and hook these ships up to it. But we have to go up there first. Up to the moon – to the transport. If I'm right, we can fight these bastards and drop those Walkers at their doorstep too."

"I can't imagine. It would be amazing. I've been here day after day, watching the end come closer and closer almost without hope," Stanford said, nearly in tears.

Jason jarred him out of it by asking how he knew that the Invaders were about to arrive. He'd thought about it, if their communications were dead, how they found out they were coming. But he was always too busy to ask.

"You haven't seen everything yet, have you? Wait until you get up there and you will see it," Stanford told him.

Down at the cage again, Jason was thinking about how he would devise a basic sign language. He was going to try to communicate with the Invader. He played the video of the destruction of his home planet, the transporters coming to the rescue, and them being destroyed as well. The Invader watched every second of it.

Then, the next disk was played. It was a ship like the Star Ship Enterprise, coming in and doing battle around his home planet with the make-believe enemy, blowing many of them out of the ether and giving chase to the rest.

The Invader went wild with excitement. He watched as the stars flew by and the human ship shot phaser after phaser and photon torpedo after photon torpedo, blasting the alien ships into pieces.

They arrived at a planet system where the battle continued. More human ships showed up and were surrounded by the make-believe aliens. Shots were fired from all directions, alien ships were blown up, human ships were blown up, and debris from broken and shattered spacecraft littered the space over the foreign moon. The Invader went wild with excitement.

There was an interior shot of the Enterprise-looking craft showing the crew being flung from side to side and explosions overhead. On the view screen, there was nothing of the humans remaining and very little of the aliens. The remaining humans fired shot after shot and torpedo after torpedo until the final view from the screen showed an energy weapon being fired at the humans, getting larger and larger in the screen as it approached, and then the screen went black.

The Invader squealed and leapt in the air, arms flailing up and down. He turned to the back of his cage and ran toward it, turned and ran back to the front and held his claws to his head and howled in painful anguish.

"Now that's the reaction I wanted to see," Jason said to himself. "Now let him stew while I visit his craft."

Chapter Thirty-One

The ride just past the moon to the Invader's craft was arranged and the time had come to board. Jason was wondering what he would do on the trip. Racking his brain over the Invader power system would take up most of the trip.

If all went the way he wanted, he could soon be conducting war on the Invader planet. He had no idea how long it had been since he had gotten any sleep, and that would have to take up part of the trip. It could be his last chance to sleep for the rest of his life.

The moon was right around 225,000 miles away this time of year, a fourteen hour trip at 16,000 miles an hour. That was more time than he thought he could spare with an invasion imminent, but there was no other choice. He had to go.

Before he left, Jason handed over his drawing and explained to Cody and Dr. Stanford what he would require to get the craft working and that they should have it completed and tested before they did anything else. Again, he made sure that no person went near the Invader.

The Captain of the X-15G stepped aboard and welcomed everybody. He made sure they were all properly seated and strapped in and had their helmets properly secured. Then he put his on and sat next to the co-pilot and belted himself in.

"I didn't know we still flew the X-15s," Jason said to Gizmo, not exactly sure he would hear him.

"This is the space program that you don't hear about, gentlemen," the Captain came in through speakers in the helmets. "The X-15 series was never replaced by NASA, like everyone was lead to believe. The Air Force continued testing, and, well, here it is. This baby is nothing like the Space Shuttles you're used to seeing. I mean no disrespect, if you need a good sized truck; the Shuttle is the way to go. But this baby, it's like a sports car."

The engines fired and they took off, pinning everyone to the backs of their seats. It was on the tarmac for an instant before it lifted off and went at a steep angle toward space. They listened to the chatter over the radio about systems checks and speed and angle. After a moment of break Jason asked how fast it went.

"That is classified, Colonel. But it'll get you there quick enough. We'll be at our destination in about four hours."

"Four hours! That means we're going to be going…what's that, 56,000 miles an hour!" Gizmo exclaimed.

"And then some, Colonel Crozley. We don't go that fast through the atmosphere, and we have to slow down for final approach, but you're not that far off. Just sit back and enjoy the ride, Gentlemen."

As the X-15 powered toward the skies, Jason watched the Earth grow smaller. First, the runway they took off from melted into the countryside, the cities grew more and more miniature until they were indistinguishable.

He was going into space, and what he thought was odd about it was that he wasn't thinking it was odd at all. Just a short time ago he was in a budget meeting, then in his office. He had been led from the Gorge to the Walkers in the cave. Then captured and then released; then brought to a base where he discovered there was about to be an alien invasion, and he was going to do something about it.

All that, when all he had planned, was to go up a canyon, take some samples, go back to his office and quit his job. Why him? He supposed Eric was right. It was because he can, and because he can, he must.

The atmosphere took on a whole new character from how it is seen from below. He could see the layers separated as they passed through. Above the clouds now, they began entering the troposphere, giving way to the stratosphere, the blue, blue mesosphere and then the thermosphere where the International Space Station would be.

Looking down and across the horizon, the troposphere appeared orange, and each layer could have been drawn in pencil across the horizon, orange giving way to white, and then to blue and then the black of space.

It struck him as odd, this atmosphere. How does it happen that the atmosphere is only around twenty percent oxygen, yet that is what we breathe? Why not nitrogen? It being some seventy-eight percent, why wouldn't we breathe that?

In the past, it would have consisted of gasses from the solar nebula, mainly hydrogen. Over time, it transformed into what envelopes the Earth today. But hydrogen was the key. Hydrogen was what he was betting on to defeat the Invaders. Hydrogen, possibly the most abundant element in the universe, was everywhere.

When it had cleared the atmosphere, the X15-G accelerated to its final 'classified' speed. When the engines cut out, all sensation of weight or motion vanished.

As he approached the moon, it appeared bleached white by the sun, but as he got closer and closer, forms and colors and shades became clear. There were things on it, things that did not seem should be there, and he continued past the moon to the alien craft, still strapped with the rockets that had been attached to it years ago to bring it there. He went around the craft and viewed it from every angle. Looking back, he could see the moon and the tiny blue Earth behind it.

He drifted through the bulkhead and saw men, humans, working and studying its parts. He drifted through the bulkhead again, back into space, toward the Earth, down through the brightly colored atmosphere, brighter and more colorful than when he left.

Down toward the ground, down, down toward the cave filled with Walkers, and behind a glass wall was Bradley. He watched him while he seemingly plotted and seethed, deep in his own thoughts, the thoughts of a madman, and drifted out toward the village.

There was Bo and Hellen. Down into the town he went, along the main street toward the Sheriff Office and around his motor home. The colors were brilliant and every sound was clear, the birds, the people, everything could be seen and heard at once with complete clarity.

He moved closer toward Hellen and Bo as they were walking toward the store and noticed the glint of sunlight bouncing off the razor wire surrounding the town. "You have to get them out. Before you leave," a voice from somewhere came to him. "It is time."

"And we are coming up to and about to fly by the Copernicus Crater, folks. Get a quick peek," the voice in the helmet jolted him awake. "We should be at our destination in just a few more minutes."

"Oh, man," Gizmo said. "I needed that. When was the last time we slept?"

"Me too," Jason said as he looked out at the giant crater, "We have to get the village out. Up above the caves."

"God. I was just thinking that," Gizmo said.

"You ever have an out-of-body experience?" Jason asked. "Because I think I just had one."

"I was reading about that happening to astronauts pretty often. They also say they have some sort of ESP when they are out of gravity," Gizmo said.

The moon was growing smaller now as they decelerated, and out the portal he could see the transport approaching. It wasn't as clear as it had been a moment ago, but the rockets were there and everything else looked the same. He watched the wing as the pilot maneuvered the craft into the landing bay. A small jet of compressed gas would be let out now and again for the tiniest of adjustments as they put down.

"Remember to turn your air on, folks. There is a breathable atmosphere inside the craft, but not in the landing bay," the captain informed them. "I understand you have a little business to conduct here and my orders are to wait for you and bring you back when you are ready. Any idea how long?"

"Not too long, I hope," Jason told him. "We just have to look some things over and figure out how to get this thing working."

"Well. If that's all you have to do, they've been working on this for years. Started way before my time. So, that means, what, this is my new retirement station?" the pilot asked sarcastically.

"Hope not, Captain. We can't stay too long. I'd like to get out of here in a few hours," Jason said.

He answered, not sounding very confident, "Well. Hope so. I guess I'll prep for re-entry anyway. Strap on those boot covers. They have magnets to keep you from floating around."

They walked through the rows and rows of alien shuttles to the entrance and closed the door. Air filled the chamber and when the pressure was equalized, the inside door was opened.

"Welcome aboard," the man on the other side said. "I'm Dr. Hilliard. I was told to meet you and get you whatever you need."

After introductions were made, they asked to go straight to the engine room. He explained on his way his idea that parts may have been removed from the stranded ship in case they were boarded. From the scenes of the Invaders, their technology would be a well-guarded secret, leaving any other civilizations unable to defend against it. Obviously, none of the conquered races had it or anything equivalent.

It would be difficult to find something that wasn't there, but they had to try. The best place to start would be the engine room. Not having a point of reference or an idea of any fundamental principles made it even more difficult.

A car motor, when it breaks down, is repaired tracing the fundamentals. It is internal combustion. So, is it combusting? That would be the first question. Is it getting fuel to combust? If it is getting fuel, is it getting the spark to make it combust? Simple.

But you would have to know the basic principles of the internal combustion motor. The first thing to look at is the fuel gage followed by the spark. These two first checks repair the majority of stalled vehicles.

Without this basic understanding, they were going to look for something that wasn't there and they would not know what it would look like if it were. But they had to find it anyway. The future of the human race depended on them finding it, and not just finding it, but fixing it. Something they were sure that the crew of Invaders had tried for years and couldn't do.

"Why did they kill off their people?" Jason asked, thinking back to the video he'd seen.

"They were running out of food," Hilliard answered. "They were running out and the officers locked themselves in a chamber and vented the atmosphere. Near as we can figure, that's what happened. Then, at least, those would live.

"Judging by the remaining stores they had, they could have fed the Invaders for another week maximum. With them dead, their stores could have lasted, who knows, many decades longer."

"Makes sense, and it makes sense that there were two different crews. One was the landing party, and the other, the flight crew. Like the Air force or the Navy transporting the Army. So those beasts down there were probably the pilots or the equivalent of the Navy or something along that line," Jason said. "And they killed their own people."

"I wonder how they feel about that?" Gizmo asked. "Or even if they did feel. Maybe they just look at it differently than we do."

Hours were spent wandering the engine room looking for something broken, but more likely, something missing. Finally they asked to be taken to anything that looked like a spare parts room or a scrap heap. They wandered through that and picked up and viewed parts and put them back down, without ever having an idea of their function.

"I've been doing this for almost six months," Hilliard told them. "I would have left after about six days, if I had my way. The people before me ended the same. They came with no idea and they left with no idea. Smart people too."

"How did you get them out?" Gizmo asked.

"What do mean?"

"The Invaders. The ones that lived. How did you get them out of that sealed chamber?"

"Oh. They starved them out. Took a long time. I guess they didn't think it through. They locked themselves in there to save the food supply, but the food was not in there with them. They would have to come out and get it and bring it back in the chamber. So we, or they, the people that were there at the time, they just took the food away," Hilliard explained.

"Did we look at that room they were in?" Jason asked.

"You've been there three times now. It's on the way to the parts room. We walked through it. They just shut the doors at each end," he said.

So they meandered through the engine room. They couldn't go back to Earth without an answer, and he didn't have decades to figure it out. He had hours. Hours to figure it out and to get it working. He let his mind wander back to the base with the captive Invader and the television shows. He thought of Scottie and his engine room.

There were all those pipes and parts and crystals. Then he recalled a room outside the actual engine room. It was kind of a control room. They had passed through something similar in this craft, but he hadn't noticed anything about the room that jumped out at him.

"You know, those videos of the Invaders, do you have them or are they only back on Earth?" Jason asked.

"We have some here. But whatever you need, they can just send it up by satellite. What do you want to look at?" Hilliard asked.

"Well. I'm sure you did this already, but maybe something got missed, I just wanted to watch what they have on their videos and then see what they have here. You know, take a laptop and walk through like they did when they were filming. Maybe we can see something, see what's missing."

"Holy shit! Never did that! Not me! Maybe someone else did, but not me," Hilliard started getting excited. "Let's do that," he said as he bolted through the doorway.

Jason and Gizmo looked at each other in surprise and ran after him. Hilliard was moving. "Can't believe I didn't think of that!" He would yell now and then while he grabbed a laptop and rifled though some disks. "Can't believe I didn't think of that."

He looked at Jason and Gizmo and screamed this time as if he were in pain, "I can't believe I didn't think of that!" and ran back toward the room they just left. He shoved in a disk of a ship similar to the one they were in. "I think this is some kind of propaganda film they made. Look," he pointed at the screen. "A tour of the ship."

He hit the pause button and lifted up the computer walking toward the engine room until the shot on the screen was the same as what they saw in front of them. Then, he would let the video roll ahead a few feet, and they would all step forward with it and study the shot and compare what was there. "I can't believe I didn't think of this," Hilliard would scold himself as they went.

Suddenly they all stopped. "Look, there!" Gizmo yelled. They turned around to see Jason already sprinting down the corridor toward the parts room. By the time they caught up to him, he had the missing piece in his hand turning it over and looking at it with the care you would give a Faberge egg.

"What is it?" Hilliard asked.

"Not sure," he replied. "But I know what I'm going to call it;   A Quantum Capacitor. Because that's what it does. This is what they power the ship with. But from their planet."

He walked with care, holding the capacitor like it was a newborn child, and placed it on a table to study it. "Can we get some people to go through the rest of the videos?" he asked.

Within a few minutes, there were a dozen scientists with laptops taking baby steps through the rest of the engine room and then through the rest of the ship. News was relayed to Earth and the General was on the radio with Stanford and Cody at his side.

"General. Here's my theory. It all works, if you think about it. They were out here to invade. They were in orbit outside Mercury preparing to come to Earth. Their home planet was attacked and it must have knocked out the relay, the signal or, how do I say, the Quantum connection between the ship and their planet.

"So, how would they get it back in communication? They couldn't do it. Maybe, when they lost power, they got hit by a coronal ejection from our sun. It would wipe the memory clean, reprogram the capacitor. Don't you see? It is probably reprogrammed, but for us, this solar system, our sun, our sun's hydrogen, not theirs.

"I had an idea that this system was Hydrogen based; their weapons, everything. Something we don't know, something, like the electron theory, it works, we just don't know how or why. This is Hydrogen, something is going on with electrons, but it's not based on electron flow, something else. But, if we figure out how to charge it, we might get this alien tub working."

"So what do you need from here?" he asked.

"Well, general. I need some of that plasma I had Cody working on. Is Cody there?"

"Sure, he's right here," he said.

"How you doin', Cody? Umm, when you were younger, did you ever dream of becoming an Astronaut?" Jason asked.

RUBY LAKE

Chapter Thirty-Two

After the arrangements were made to shuttle Cody and the equipment he needed up to the Invader craft, Hilliard sat and watched Jason squint at him in suspicion until he exploded.

"Okay, damn it! Someone's got to answer some questions! None of this shit works. Their communication is dead. There aren't even any aliens up here to answer the bloody radio. So how did we find out the Invaders are coming? How did we find out when they would be coming?" then Jason stood up and yelled, "And where did those dam videos come from?"

"Oh," Hilliard said calmly. "I thought you knew. I can see how that would make things, well, not add up."

"There's an understatement. It makes things really not add up," Gizmo added.

"I think… well here. Let me show you. A picture tells a thousand words." He turned on his laptop, punched a few keys and turned it around so Jason and Gizmo could watch. "These aren't the only aliens we've encountered. Here is an Ambassador I met two months after I was sent here."

Hilliard sat back and smiled as he watched the reaction on their faces when they saw the Grey sitting at the table with Hilliard having a polite conversation about the craft he was sitting in and the beings who once occupied it. They had captured a vessel themselves under almost identical circumstances, but were not able to get it functioning either.

Although the Greys were not able to get the Invaders equipment working, they were able to eavesdrop and duplicated a transmission detailing the invasion of Earth, which was why he was there.

The Grey told the story of his race peacefully colonizing planets, and at times, not so peacefully, as their populations expanded. When the Invaders came destroying planet after planet, killing billions, they had no defenses and were not able to duplicate their science even after they had captured one of the transports.

A coalition of races had banded together to try to counter the Invaders, resulting in a war that lasted many years. The coalition suffered great casualties, and in the end, the war was lost and the Invaders began to aggressively expand once again.

The coalition was now seeking new partners and allies in the effort to contain the Invaders. They were seeking new technology across the

Universe to defend themselves and defeat the Invaders. Now they were here seeking our help as well.

When they had learned that Earth and the humans had one of the Transporters, they had hoped we had defeated the Invaders and had superior weapons. Seeing that we have only nuclear weapons to contribute as the most effective deterrent, they did not see us as a valuable asset in their fight.

There was some discussion of taking human refugees and placing them on some distant planet, but in the end, they would meet the same fate as the Greys, and the Greys were having a difficult enough time of their own without taking refugees.

After the video was over Jason and Gizmo sat for a moment. Finally Jason looked over at Gizmo and numbly said, "What? Do you think this is strange? We saw zombies. We saw aliens. We saw Walkers. We are in space – we're astronauts. Nothing strange going on, right? Remind me to quit my job after this, will you?"

"Zombies?" Hilliard asked. "I haven't seen any zombies yet."

Chapter Thirty-Three

Something was bothering Jason. There is a connection he was missing. There was something that connects the ship to the alien sun or the alien hydrogen or alien plasma. Something that would link it all. There was some other piece he was missing.

Why didn't they just use our hydrogen or reprogram their capacitor themselves? The burning thought made him wonder if he might just be completely wrong about all of it.

This was no time to try to cling onto a wrong idea. There was no place for a bruised ego. Time was running out, so he asked, "Do you think that this ship and how it runs might have been kept so secret that these Invaders didn't know how to reprogram their Quantum Capacitor? Maybe they wouldn't even let their own crew know how it works in case they were captured."

"Possible," Gizmo said. "But maybe the guy that knew died. Maybe the captain got killed, like a mutiny. They vented the atmosphere. Maybe the guy got killed with it."

"Maybe," Hilliard sat for a minute thinking. "I want to show you something."

He brought them down several corridors and into a large room. "We think this is the equivalent of the Captains Quarters. There were these things in here; everybody thought they were furniture for a long time. Footstools, actually. They are listed in an inventory as footstools. But I was in here poking around and turned these things over. See here?" and he pulled one over. "Some kind of circuits."

"What kind of footstool is that? Foot massager?" Gizmo mumbled.

"I think, no. Look at it. It's turned like this on the floor, you can't really see it, but picture a very large helmet," and Hilliard tried to lift it, but couldn't without the help of the others, and continued. "See, the Invader, his head would fit right in there."

"Interesting. A helmet." That's when Jason looked deeper inside and saw it. A logo, a picture or diagram of the gadget they had outside on the table. "What is this? Look you guys. He's right, Gizmo. Look at this. The symbol, they are connected."

He wasn't quite sure when he had lost his mind. He wasn't even quite sure he had lost it. It was a debate Dr. Bradley has had with himself for years. When did he go insane? When did he go mad? Is he mad? Are people just trying to get him to think that?

Those were the questions he asked himself each day when he woke up in the morning, provided he slept at all, and things he debated with himself repeatedly during the day.

The debate raged on, always ending the same. He wasn't mad and he hadn't gone insane. An insane man is the last to know that he is insane. He may never know it.

That's what Bradley had read in a book somewhere. It said that the person is in such a fragile state already, that if he were to view himself as being insane on top of it all, he would truly go mad. Therefore, if he were a mad man, he would never even ask the question.

The argument went on every day and all throughout. It always ended by Bradley stopping it by thinking, "Wait. I am questioning whether I am sane or not. An insane person could never question his own sanity. Therefore, I must be sane by simple scientific reasoning."

This is how he got through his day. That is what the person who wrote the book said. So it is written, so it must be true. It didn't matter that the person who wrote it was mad beyond reason. It worked for Bradley and it kept him going on his important work.

Very important work it was, too. He knew it was, and he was important, very, very important. He must not allow himself to be interrupted or hindered.

"It is important!" He rumbled.

"What, Dr. Bradley?" the lab assistant asked.

"Oh, um yes. Did you get those reports on the neural response tests?" Bradley asked.

"Why yes. I gave them to you yesterday, remember?" she asked.

Bradley walked over to his station and pretended to fumble through some papers, thinking, "I have to watch myself. Can't let myself do that. I don't want her, that hairless chimp who is always in heat, to think I'm crazy or something," and continued to shuffle nervously through the papers.

"Oh, yes. Here they are. It is very important that you tell me when you do these things," and put them down on his desk and added, "Very important."

The assistant looked at him for a moment and shook her head, looked over at the other assistant smirking, and said, "Yes, Dr. Bradley. I'll do that. Okay?"

The book said that the mind rationalizes things that they do. If they do something crazy, then the mind will find a reason for it. That way the crazy person can go on thinking that they are not crazy.

"But what if I have a reason for doing something that is just a reason for doing something?" he would ask himself. Then, that wouldn't be crazy because he already had a reason for doing something.

But if he did something crazy and THEN found a reason for it, then that might be a problem. How would he know the difference? But since a crazy person can't think that they are crazy, he didn't have to worry.

"Problem solved," he said.

"What was that, Dr. Bradley?" the assistant asked again.

"Oh. Um, well. I just solved another problem," he said. "So, problem solved."

"Oh. That's good," and looked at the smirking assistant again.

"You should get back to work. I can't be the only one solving problems here. Pay more attention, you two," he snarled.

That is how Bradley spent his days: debating his sanity with himself, covering up uncontrolled outbursts, and mixed in there, he did research. But today was different. He had gotten word that some outsiders had made an effect on his creations. They had done something nobody but he should be able to do. No. Nobody should be allowed to do.

"Did you contact those people yet, Emily? The ones they brought in from the outside," he asked.

"No, Doctor. They said they were off the base right now and will call me as soon as they are back," Emily said.

"Well, alright," he said. "But we should have been informed first. Make sure they are brought here as soon as they are back. In fact, you get on the phone and make the Army go and get them and bring them here. This is too important for them to be off base at this time."

Emily got on the phone and pretended to make calls and even acted like she was barking out orders to someone. Bradley listened carefully to her and thought to himself, "Good. Finally someone is thinking clearly. Nobody should be doing things like controlling my subjects without consulting me."

His mind wandered to Dr. Gruber. "Gruber tried," he thought. "Gruber tried and look what happened to him. I took care of him. I'll take care of those others too," and continued to think about the operation, killing, murdering one of his pets, his creations, and forcing him to watch while he cut his brain out.

Gruber wanted to find a way to control them. He wanted to find a way to release them upon the Invaders. But he killed it. Then he dissected it like an animal.

"They were too gentle," he thought to himself. "I had to make them protect themselves. Now, nobody can get to them. Nobody can kill them.

I fixed it. Who are these new people now that they are talking about? I should have been consulted. After all, I am the expert. I am the creator."

"Am I crazy? Am I looking at this the right way? Maybe I should let them help. But I am the expert. Catskill put me here. They even know that I killed Gruber. If they didn't think it was the right thing to do, why would I be here? I would be in jail. I may even be the single most important person in the company right now. Hell, even in the world.

"I have made a creature that could save the world. Better than people. Better than the Invaders. I wonder if God is jealous. They want me to find a way to kill them once the invasion is over. Now that is insane. Kill them? Why? It's because they are better than humans, that's why."

"I won't let them!" He said.

"Pardon me, Dr.?" Emily asked again.

"Nothing. Never mind. I was going to…someone was going to do something and I was going to tell you that I won't let them, but now I think maybe it is better that they do. So, never mind."

"Alright then," she said.

He looked back at his research papers and thought, "Hairless monkeys. All of them. Especially that one. A hairless monkey in heat."

Bradley went to his table and rolled out the plans for the base; plans that needed approval from Catskill before anything was built. Of course, his input was needed on all of them. After all, he was the expert in these matters and he'd proven it at the chemical plant.

Of most interest to him was the placement of the neural-inhibitors - tank after tank full of the inhibitor, the same ones that they developed at the plant. Zombies, that's what they called them after they breathed it in. Fools! It was silly name calling, that's all.

He looked over the placement once again, just to make sure. He did his calculations again to make sure. Was there enough for the entire population they would be herding into the facility?

There would be no explosions this time. There would be no need for it. After Catskill finally recognized his genius, they handed over control of the designs to him. A valve installed at each of the tanks without their knowledge was his idea.

"Brilliant" he thought. "They were electronically controlled magnetic valves with him at the switch. There would be millions of people trapped in underground bunkers all over the world. They would be reacting to the controls put on them; the restriction, the schedules, the lack of freedoms, and they would be trapped and held by force deep in these caves.

It was Bradley who came up with the idea to feed the inhibitor through the ventilation system to calm the last remaining population of humans on Earth. It was to keep them calm, relaxed, and easily controlled. But that's not what will happen.

"No," Bradley thought. "They want to kill my creations after the invasion is over. They want to kill them all after they were saved by them. But that won't happen. I won't let it.

"Catskill. What a great company. We developed 8791, no, I did. Now Catskill is the most powerful force on Earth. The Military takes orders from us, from me! Even the President consults us. We rule the world now, and soon, my creations will own it and run free on the surface. They will rule the World without the threat of hairless monkeys."

He checked his calculations again. The cubic air space of the facility and the concentration of inhibitor needed for the right effect and he thought of what a terrific plan it all was. Give them the drug for a while, and for the rest of their lives, they would have to come to Catskill to get more. An entire population of addicts, forced to get their fix from one single company. They would rule the world! Perfect.

Except that won't happen either, because it is Bradley who controls the valves. Catskill executives in their private quarters built in the bunkers will be the first. He will watch them turn rabid first.

"Am I mad?" he asked himself again. "No. Since I am asking myself, I can't be. This isn't madness. It is strategy. We are at war. Catskill will use the Militaries around the world to fight a common enemy to see who will win control of the world. Then I will strike, and it will be me who rules the world. Me. It's strategy, not madness."

The helmets had been carted to the meeting room table before Cody had arrived aboard the alien craft. The discussion now centered on the theory of Quantum Communication, the idea that two or more particles separated by a distance could be influenced by the other or others. This was proving out in laboratories across the world, but the possibility of powering large equipment remotely may never have been considered.

It progressed to Quantum Tunneling, where energy can build up to a point that it would pass through a seemingly impenetrable barrier. Then it evolved to diodes and resonant tunneling diodes, phase space formulation and finally the hydrogen bond.

The concept that one stationary device on a planet surface could be used as a power source across galaxies was now being viewed as the most likely explanation for capabilities of the alien craft. It explained many otherwise unexplainable phenomena. The Quantum Capacitor, as Jason had named it, was the key to receiving the power over a distance.

Sending the power was a whole different thing. Sending the power required something else. That is what Jason had Cody and Dr. Stanford working on down below; the relay - the Quantum Relay.

"So if this is the relay point, this Quantum Capacitor, why didn't they use it?" Cody asked.

"I don't think they could. I think that the war they were having had something to do with it. We don't know for sure and we may never know. It may have knocked out the connection.

"But we do know that this part goes into the control room outside the engine room, and that these helmets were in, we concluded, the Captains Quarters, and it has the same design or logo inside; a picture of the capacitor. So they are connected, maybe it controls it," Gizmo answered.

Several minutes went by as they sat and considered how it might work while rolling the capacitor over and over again and then looking inside the helmet.

"How about this?" Jason said, "Let's think of our sun. We are bathed in all kinds of different things from our sun. Gravity, for example, we are bathed in it. Every atom, every molecule, everything in this solar system is effected by our suns' gravity.

"Then there are photons coming from it. Ions coming from it. It emits radio waves constantly. We are all soaked in energy of different kinds from the sun.

"Now, what if we were to go away? We have been a part of everything in this solar system being influenced by the sun. Now we go away. I think they found a way to influence some remaining element and have that influence be received in this capacitor and that capacitor powers the transporter. Time and space wouldn't even matter. It would be instant. Just like Einstein found out."

They all sat silent again, looking over the items on the table. Finally Hilliard spoke up. "Alright. So whatever is inside this capacitor will be the same thing as they have back on their planet. Like from the same batch of influenced particles, and you're saying that the batch they had might have been destroyed, which is why it is no longer receiving power here."

"Exactly," Jason said. "I'm guessing that there is some plasma inside there, some gas, and I am guessing that it is a very high Hydrogen content."

"Why Hydrogen?" Hilliard asked.

"Because Hydrogen is how everything started, with the exploding nebula, the stars forming, the atmospheres on planets forming. It all started with Hydrogen. So I'm betting that that will be what is in there. But here is the risk. It's a big risk too, so we better talk about this.

"What if we replaced whatever plasma is in here with plasma from this system. We would be using our programming, our sun, our influence, wouldn't we?"

"Yah, maybe," Gizmo said. "But we could also be making sure the thing will never work," and then thought more of it and added, "Then again, it hasn't been working, has it."

"And if these helmets have some kind of programming in it that connects the power, bridges it or something, programs it, then we can program it with our own...our own solar system and power it."

"But we still don't know how to use it, even if we do fill it with our own plasma," Cody said.

"That's true," Jason said, "But we have two of these helmets and we have an Invader down there who, I'm hoping, will show us."

"We can't trust that thing. As soon as he gets hold of one of these, if he is near one of his shuttles or this ship, he's gone, and we're dead," Hilliard warned them.

"That's why we use both helmets. One will be a dud. He'll think he is using it, but it will be dead. We just watch him and copy what he is doing, watch him on camera, but it will be us doing it. If we do it right, he will not even notice anything out of the ordinary. Once this ship is powered up, we figure the rest out, the weapons, the propulsion, that stuff, and I'm sure they have instructional videos somewhere."

"Damn," the General said over the com. "If we can do that, we'll load the Walkers onto that ship and send those bastards a little present. If we can do it before they arrive, it might even stop the invasion. They'll have to turn back and defend their home planet."

"And we can fill those shuttles up too. Hopefully teach our guys how to fly them. We can leave half the Walkers here and take the other half."

"The alternative, so far, has been no alternative but to be invaded and hope for a miracle," the general said. "Just like every other civilization they've conquered. This is the closest thing to a decent defense plan I've heard since Catskill took over. I wish you folks would have shown up a few weeks ago. We are really getting thin on time here."

The details were gone over on how they would dissect one helmet to see if they could find how it worked, and then disable it. How they would test the plasma inside the capacitor and replace it with their own, and how they would get the Invader to spill its secrets. After everyone left the room to get busy, Jason spoke into the com system, "General. Are you alone? Can you speak?"

"Let me clear the office," he said and barked out some orders to whoever was in there. "Just those damn Catskill people wanted to come in. It's just me and a few aides now."

"That's what I wanted to discuss with you, Sir: Catskill," Jason told him.

"Please do," he said.

Chapter Thirty-Four

Jenkins and Eric had been busy back on Earth. Gathering intel was something with which Eric was familiar and he found that Jenkins was easily shown the ropes. As soon as they found it was Catskill and their security firm who had surrounded the village and turned it into a concentration camp, they put all of their attention on Catskill and their influence and control both inside and outside the facility.

Gathering intelligence on them was made easier by the hatred most people in the facility had toward them. From the guards to the officers, they felt they had been treated with such contempt that an opportunity to convey information about them would not be missed. As well, Catskill had become a favorite of the Government and had powers they felt no private industry should have, powers over even the Military.

It was out of fear of The People that they had been endowed with the power and control that was now despised by so many. But more than that, it was their science teams that came up with the DNA sequence they were using to create the walkers. It was never the plan to release them onto the Earth. Not in the beginning, at least. But as time went on, the plans devolved out of desperation to what they are now.

The idea had always been, since the Government had the alien craft, to send the Walkers to the Invader's home planet, along with containers of 8791, the gas that would transform their planet. Catskill showed promise when they discovered a way to replicate alien DNA, so was contracted to discover how to make the Invader craft come alive again. It was a contract that was never fulfilled, and finally, time had run out.

The only thing they accomplished was the production of more 8791 and 8791-1, much more. The invasion was now coming. The great plans became less and less great as the time grew nearer, until it became what it is now. Let the Invaders arrive and destroy whatever they would, then, let them land.

Once they had their ships open and their ground forces unleashed, Humans would deny them entry to their ships and weapons and release our own secret weapon. The Government had committed to the first part of the plan, so it was an easy next step to the next part, and then, after another failure, to the next.

It went this way until they have what they have now, probable extinction. But it was hard to hang the blame on Catskill, they pointed out, when so many other more advanced races had perished under the Invader attacks.

But for the Military, it may be the Invaders that they would fight, it might be the Invaders that would kill them, and after that, it may be the Walkers, but it was Catskill they detested. Catskill, with their own security; Catskill with their monitoring every move they made; Catskill issuing orders; Catskill with their videos in every hallway and every room; Catskill.

Worst of all were their psychs. Catskill psychs. Trying everything they could to determine that one of them was having a mental issue so they could drug it and treat it, even if they had to make it up. Catskill. None had escaped their prying questioning and leading questions designed to convince a person that they needed help. Catskill was the most despised group in the facility.

So when Eric and Jenkins approached the guards for information, it came in torrents. But not without them having to listen to the horrors of being under the care they had given some of their fellow workers; workers who were now far worse off for it.

They were so loathed that a network had already been assembled to gather intelligence, to thwart plans to commandeer the minds and will of their fellows, and to report any activities of its staff. So it didn't take much for Eric and Jenkins to be included.

People were put on cleaning crews so they could move about the base and work in any area they chose with a good reason to be there, and even Eric was seen now and then with a bucket and a mop.

Going over some past orders for equipment, he questioned the new valves that were being installed, why the old valves weren't used and why the new ones were ordered.

It's a failsafe, it was explained to him. If anything goes wrong, like if the power goes off, it throws the switch. If the Invaders hit the base, the first thing that will happen is they will hit the power. It's electromagnetic, so it will automatically open the valves.

A dead man's switch, the valve is held shut with an electromagnet, and as soon as it loses power, it springs back open. They are all wired in series, so if one goes, they all go. The question is who controls the valves when there is power? That was the important question and it became the new main concern and the new mission - to find that controller.

From the General to the Pastor, it became the priority. Find that control. After Eric got the General to watch what happened to the people in the Catskill Chemical plant when this drug was released, and discovering that it was intentional, there was no doubt about it. They had to find that control.

It wasn't long before a network had been set up within the base to spy on every move a Catskill company employee made. Every change they made and every order they placed for material went through the network and was reported to Eric.

The General would come on his inspection of the base and have a meeting alone with Eric and Jenkins until word came that the team on the transport were about to arrive, and that's when Jenkins disappeared.

Lack of privacy on the base began to be an irritation for the men and women stationed there. The prying eyes of Catskill were ever present and without escape until Jenkins mentioned the airshaft they had crawled through, which began a secret search for more. Two were discovered that could be entered without notice. Jenkins took one of them and was now on his way to the village.

Arriving back on Earth, Jason went immediately to the Invader and plugged in the last video. He wanted it to stew while he was gone. He wanted it to consider all his options, and see that there were none. When he showed him this last video, he wanted the monster to think it had a chance.

The video showed another great battle that was being waged. But still, another battle about to be lost. Then it showed Kirk, the human it would know best from previous shows, flying through space to join the fight. The invincible Captain James T. Kirk was coming to the rescue.

The creature stood and watched, hoping beyond hope that there was still a chance, Jason thought, and that's what he wanted him to think. It showed the bridge of the Enterprise and the view screen with the enemy ships about to be engaged, another fleet being destroyed by the Invader's enemies. Then it went blank.

The creature looked at him, the only living thing he had seen since the news of his planet being attacked. Jason walked up to the window and pointed at the creature, thinking that would mean "You". Then he pointed at his own head for "Teach", and pounded his chest for "Me". Then he pointed at the alien shuttle and made a motion upward and outward with his hand for "Fly."

The creature instantly knew what he meant. He responded with pounding his chest for "Me", followed by a similar motion with his hand for "Fly". The response was expected. It was hoped that the Invader would demand that he fly the shuttle himself. Jason closed his fist and held it at an angle across his stomach. That would be "No".

Then he repeated the signs for "You Teach Me Fly", followed by the Invader signaling "No". Jason then walked away.

A short time later, he returned with the helmet carried by three men. The creature stood and watched them lay it in front of him, his eyes darting back and forth between the helmet and Jason.

It was a reaction that was very much wanted. It showed he knew what it was and, hopefully, knew how to use it. Again Jason did his signs, and again the Invader demanded that he fly the shuttle.

Gizmo was set up in the transport with the second helmet on a make-shift stand. If the theory worked, they would be able to see things being powered up with no idea of what they were.

Video feeds were placed all throughout the shuttle to watch the moves the creature would go through on start up. The reach of the Invaders made it so Gizmo had to have three other scientists standing by to mimic the moves he couldn't reach without stepping out from under the helmet.

They all knew and anticipated that at some point, the Invader would see he was in control and would bring the weapons on and blast his way to freedom. They would have to guess when that would be. Predicting that would be the hard part, but one shot would do considerable damage to the base and he could easily escape to the transport.

Again, Jason tried to get the Invader to show him how to fly, and again it refused. He pretended to think for a couple of minutes and then gestured toward the helmet and the shuttle with open palms. The creature tensed up and approached the window and motioned "Me" and "Fly", to which Jason pointed at him, for "you", and motioned with his hand for "fly".

Yes he would fly, and he watched the wheels in its mind turning, the wheels of an animal that butchered entire civilizations and killed millions of their own out in space to save their own hides. "You bet I'm going to give you your own space ship and let you fly it. You bet I'm going to turn over control of all the weapons you need to wipe out the Earth. You bet, you ugly bastard," he said out loud.

Dr. Hilliard caused quite a stir when he gave the Ambassador the news. Their coalition had all but given up on fighting the Invaders, and resigned themselves to failure, spending most of their energy looking for new places to hide their people.

It didn't matter to the Invaders how far away they sent their populations. Quantum communication was instant. But for the Ambassador and the beings that had to hide, it took time, it took tremendous effort, and it took unimaginable resources.

The news was well received and relayed throughout the stars, that this race called Human, on the outskirts of a small distant galaxy, on a tiny blue planet, circling around a tiny sun, could be the ones who put an end to the seemingly unstoppable monsters plaguing them.

They rushed to form a new armada and travel the great distance through space to be there when the Humans arrived. A transport, an Invader transport, with Invader weapons, filled with Humans and some creature they had developed, could be what spares them all from inevitable extinction. They had hope at last.

When the rush of details was done, and the Ambassador expressed his best wishes and thanks to all and in an Ambassador-like manner, he signed off. Dr. Hilliard turned to Cody, "So, what is this device we have to put together for the Walkers?" he asked.

Bradley sat in his lab watching the monitors on the wall as Jason negotiated with the Invader. "Failed," he thought. He watched the men bring the giant helmet up and walk away. When Jason made his motion toward the shuttle and indicated that the Invader could fly it, he recognized his face.

"You're the man in the suit; the one at the chemical plant, you and that other one, Gadget or something. What a ridiculous name. I remember you two," he muttered to himself. "You were there at the apex of my discovery."

He went over those events in his mind, how he was forced into the suit, how he was restrained and beaten while they stood by and watched. He thought about how they humiliated him and breached his laboratory. "Yes. These must be those people they are speaking about. These are the ones who are interfering with the creatures. I will deal with them as well," he seethed.

"FOOLS!" Bradley yelled. "Utter fools! They think they can get that alien transport going? They'll never get it going. Never," he ranted as he paced back and forth in the lab.

"And they will never defeat the Invaders. Only my creatures can do that." He paused to look at the assistant and continued pacing. "And they think I am going to allow them to take half? Half! Outrageous fools! Take half of them off in that craft?"

"Dr. Bradley, we have to have a plan. We can't sit in this cave forever and wait for the Invaders to come in. We have to have a plan," Emily responded.

"But I have a plan! A perfectly good plan!" he bellowed. "I won't let them spoil it."

"Dr. Bradley," she said as she stood up to confront him. "I know you have a plan. Your plan is to release those things against the Invaders. I've heard it a thousand times! But we have nothing to control those things yet. How are you going to destroy them once they are out? You were supposed to find a way to kill them."

He stood there trembling in anger. His hand reached into his lab coat and he rolled the controller over and over in his hand. The controller for the valves he had installed on the gas containers. One punch of a key and it will all be over.

"The Invaders will be outside killing off most of the population, and I will be inside, taking care of the rest. My creatures will destroy the Invaders, and I will rule them. I will be king, no, I will be God. I will be their ruler," he thought.

"I will rule!" He called out loud.

"Pardon?" Emily asked.

"I have made some headway and I will rule…I will rule out some of the chemicals it will take. You know, for the creatures," Bradley said.

"Doctor. You are not right in the head. You know that, right? But we are running out of time here. You understand that, don't you?" Emily said in an attempt to be kind.

Jenkins sat on the rock overlooking the village with Pete Goodwell going over the plan. Pete handed him the Gunnies note with a layout of the compound and security placement and showed the gas canisters that had been placed around the village marked on the map. "Looks like one last little experiment, don't you think?"

Pete came back with, "I think another failed experiment. That's what I think." He was silent for a while, watching the movement of the watch nearest them. "These are not even humans anymore that are doing this. Those are people in there, not test animals."

"I know. We won't let anything happen though, will we?" Jenkins replied.

"I heard on the radio some things," the kid told him.

"Yah? What's that?" he asked.

"People. People in the cities mostly. They are starting to get freaked out. People going missing. Strange troop movements. Things like that." Pete broke off a piece of jerky and offered some to Jenkins. "Some of them are starting to get really angry. Starting to riot. They want answers."

"Well Pete. I have a feeling they aren't going to get answers from the government. They'll get answers alright. Just not from the government. I wish them luck. All those preppers and people like that, they are going to last a while I guess." Jenkins rolled over and put his back against the stone. "But those people in the cities. Doesn't look like that'll be a very good place to be."

"That's why we're going into the mountains, right? Safest place for us?" Pete asked.

"That's right. Get you guys up high above any cave entrances. Up there in the snow and rocks. That's what we'll do," Jenkins said.

"Mr. Jenkins?" Pete began to ask nervously, "How do you think we'll do? I mean this tribe."

"Pete, I'm not gonna lie and tell you everything is going to be alright. Fact is, it isn't gonna be alright. We're going to war and that ain't never alright. Actually, someone is going to war against us. I saw the pictures and movies of what they do, Pete. You don't want to fight them unless you absolutely have to.

"But there are other ways to fight a war besides standing up face to face and shooting at the enemy and getting shot yourself. That's what I want you to do. I want you to get up there and hide. Fight if you have to. Hell yes. But only if you gotta. Get up there and disappear and stay disappeared."

"I think I see the guy that's been working with the gas. See him right there?" and Pete pointed to a man in a blue jumper walking over to a canister near Hellen's store.

Jenkins rolled back around and peered over the boulder again. "So that's the son-of-a dog, is it? Look at him with his pretty Catskill jumper on."

Jenkins rolled back over and rested against the boulder. "So when were they going to release the gas, did you say?"

Pete looked at his watch and said, "About two more minutes."

"Well. I'd like to see them try it without these," Jenkins said, and kicked a pile of gas masks sitting beside them. "Oh boy. Is someone going to get in trouble for this!"

They heard some loud arguing from below and lifted their heads over the top to watch. The man in the jumper was pointing at his watch while two other people were yelling and waving their arms. Catskill employees began darting from station to station searching.

Finally they all stopped fussing and stood by watching a man who was presumably in charge try to make a call on his radio.

"I'd like to see them do that without these, too," Pete said holding up some electronics.

"You have my family covered, right, Pete?" Jenkins asked.

"Mrs. Jenkins was a little upset when we told her she had to go. I guess it's hard for her. Leaving all her things like that. But I told her she could come back when it's all over." Pete looked at Jenkins and laughed. "She looks funny in hiking boots."

Jenkins laughed, picturing what she must look like. "I'm just surprised she agreed to go. Glad though. Thanks, Pete. It's a big load off my mind."

Bradley was riveted to the screen as Jason walked the Invader to the shuttle. "Fool," he thought. "They are all fools." It picked up the helmet and made its way toward it, Jason behind him with a head set on and a weapon in his hand. They got to the shuttle and the Invader stopped before entering and surveyed the large room, looking for advantages, looking for his escape route and any weaknesses.

If he was able to activate the shuttle, it would have weaponry he could use to blast his way to freedom after all these years in captivity. It is what would be expected of him. It was what everyone expected him to try, and mostly, it was what Jason hoped he would do.

He stood feet above Jason's head with massive and powerful arms and a giant body with enormous strength and power as he surveyed the cave for weaknesses; weaknesses Jason was sure to provide.

It saw its escape route. The weakness provided. The loading area, intentionally open with people bringing supplies into the base would be his choice, the choice provided for it. Daylight was what drew his attention to it. It was something he hadn't seen in decades. Daylight meant open spaces for him to fly the craft and to escape.

Bradley watched as it put the helmet on its head, took one last look around, and stepped inside with Jason following. "It's gonna kill him," Bradley thought. "Tear him to pieces as soon as they are in the craft," and they disappeared through the doorway.

"This man. He does things and I have no control, and people do what he says, too. He doesn't consult me. I should be consulted," and waited for screams and people rushing with weapons toward the shuttle as body parts would come flying out the doorway. Then the door closed. "Now he is trapped with the beast. Now he is dead."

He turned away from the screen. "Emily!" He called. "Come and help me with this."

"Yes, Dr. Bradley," she said.

"I want to test this on one of the 8791s," he told her as he held up a large piece of meat. They were working on a way to kill the creatures, his creatures, without poisoning the Earth so much that it would be uninhabitable. That was what she thought, at least.

The various scenarios had been discussed for an invasion which could not be stopped. Using nuclear weapons. The Scorched Earth policy. But they all led to the same conclusion; Remnants of mankind living in bunkers until they were inevitably discovered and dispensed with.

Yes, they would use their nuclear arsenal. They would bomb their own cities and towns, killing as many Invaders as possible. It was the last resort to which all countries had agreed. But it wouldn't stop the invasion and it wouldn't stop the Invaders from sending more. It would just kill as many of them as possible and keep the remaining population cowering in caves, putting off the inevitable.

There was even talk of colonizing Mars as a means to spread the species and hope for some to survive there. But then, reason intervened. The chance of people surviving long-term on Mars was slight. They would have no or few defenses, and the Invaders would be there shortly after they took care of Earth.

Catskill was the answer. The Walkers were created with Catskill science and Catskill scientists. Then, their minds destroyed with Catskill drugs, making them savage and unthinking beasts. They were kept alive with Catskill food, born in Catskill incubators and raised on Catskill farms, the caves they are in now.

But controlling them or killing them, destroying them after they had served their purpose without destroying Earth with chemicals was part of the Catskill promise, and that was Bradley's job. The expert.

He had developed the inhibitor to destroy their brain and turn them into the monsters they have now, but not for the same purpose. They wanted them for a weapon. He wanted them to be able protect themselves.

"They are not cock roaches," he would argue. "You can't just spray repellent around or spread boric acid and expect them to walk through it and die." He was right about that.

They were spawned from a Catskill test tube from a gene sequence taken from the Invaders and then improved upon. Their thick protective covering made it ineffective to spray them. The chemicals needed to gas them were so strong that they would poison the Earth and leave it a lifeless wasteland.

So ingestion was the answer. Something they had to eat, and that was what Bradley was tasked with, he and his team. Time was running out. The Invaders were almost here. Tons of chemicals were standing at the ready to be mixed when the magic combination was devised by Bradley. Teams of chemists and pharmacists were standing ready.

"I believe you may have found the answer, Emily. I want you to come and test it with me so you can see the results yourself. It is exciting, don't you think? You could be an international hero," Bradley said.

He walked her to the containment room designed for this purpose; to test these poisons. Forty feet below them were the test subjects, howling and leaping and scratching at the smooth walls as they looked down through an open ceiling. There was a counter at the side where the food was mixed with the poison.

"Emily. Would you like to do the honors?" he asked, holding up and offering her the chemical filled syringe.

"Oh, yes. I would. Thank you Doctor." She put on a pair of protective gloves and excitedly took it and jabbed it into the side of beef and injected some of the liquid, then picked another spot and did the same. She carefully did this until the syringe was empty.

They looked at each other with excitement and anticipation. It was the moment of truth. What they had spent so long working on. She lifted the piece of meat over to the edge of the wall and dropped it, bending over to watch the Walkers leap and tear at it.

Bradley walked over as well, looked down, and put his hand on her shoulder and said. "This is it, Emily. This is the end."

"Oh! I hope so, Dr. Bradley. I hope so!" She said.

Then he pushed her over the edge and watched as she was first mutilated and then devoured. After a short time reflecting on his genius, he walked back into the control room.

"Another lab accident," he shook his head and said out loud to himself. "Such a dangerous job and such careless people they send me. I will have to call personnel and talk to them about the quality of staff they provide."

Bradley glanced around the room, taking a mental inventory. There was the control for the blast doors, a big red button which he ran his hand over, admiring how smooth and comforting it felt, while picturing his creations finally set free to take their proper place in the world. They would open the cavern and allow his creations out when he and only he chose.

There was the chemical compound Emily stumbled upon, which he took and put in the shredder.

There were the monitors, the endless monitors of everyone and everything in his domain.

Then there was the control for the gas. He reached his hand into the pocket of his smock and rolled it over and over in his hand, feeling and caressing every button and every corner.

"Yes. I am in control," he said to himself, and turned to the view of the shuttle on the screen. "Well. He's dead by now."

Gizmo was under the helmet, tensely watching a screen set up beside him showing the inside of the Shuttle. The cockpit was almost identical in both craft, the only difference being that the transport had a larger station. He didn't know how this worked, the helmet, and nobody did. Perhaps not even the Invader. But now they did know it worked.

Jason had taken a position about five feet from the monster as it sat down at the controls. He held his weapon at ready. When it realized it was being played, it would attack. It would react and attack and it would kill him.

It ran its hand across an object, and Gizmo copied the move and an instrument lit up. It reached across and did it to another one. Gizmo couldn't reach it, so one of the scientists did it, and something else came to life. Then the lights in the cockpit went on. Jason took his eye off the Invader to look at his escape route, the back of the shuttle, where it was still dark.

There is a time that Jason will have to react. He will have to watch for what the Invader does. A person, before he attacks, might dart his eyes back and forth. He might start shuffling his feet as if he is trying to seek traction. He might swing his arms nervously. He could do any number of things, but if the person watching is alert, they all mean the same thing: It is the agitated and nervous acts of a person about to strike.

Now he would have to read this on an Invader. He would have to read a monster who thinks nothing of wiping out an entire species or killing millions of his own people to save his own life by venting the atmosphere of his transport. So, the question running through Jason's mind is this: Will it even show a sign before the attack, since murder and slaughter are so natural to it?

It reached up and pressed something that looked like a completely solid and blank piece of metal, and something started to whir when another scientist in the transport stood on a stool to reach up and do the same. "Never would have caught that. Would never have even seen it," Gizmo spoke into the mike.

All systems seemed now to be on. The lights were on, systems were whirring and buzzing, and the shuttle began to make the slightest motion. It was not moving, but had become weightless.

The monster moved his head quickly to the left and then quickly over his right shoulder to look at Jason and then back to a panel that had just illuminated. It pushed something and Gizmo was reaching for it to copy the motion.

There was the slightest of hesitation that the Invader must have noticed. It was the less than instant response from the panel. The response time that would be required for a weapons system targeting fast-moving objects. The weapons system, the next thing you bring to life after your craft is ready to go and you've done everything else you need to fly the craft. They found it!

Gizmo noticed the reaction and knew what it was and stopped himself from activating the weapons. They were found out. "That's it! Here it comes, Jason!" He yelled.

The monster barely paused when it realized he had just given away the farm. He made a growling noise and spun to attack. Jason had already taken several steps back in anticipation and fired at it.

It stopped and glanced over at the weapons storage. Would they be live too? It took another step toward the rear of the craft where Jason was backing to, weapon raised and yelling at the monster to stop as if it would understand.

The monster took another two steps, quickly this time, and looked back and forth from Jason to the locker. Jason was beside the door to the shuttle now, a door which had been sealed since the Invader was convinced they really were about to fly off. It began to scream and howl.

Jason could see that it had decided against grabbing a weapon. It would do this by hand. It was more enjoyable to these things, more fulfilling. Jason backed further firing several rounds at it.

Further back into the dark he went, firing and stepping back and then firing more. He dropped the magazine and slammed in another one and charged his weapon and kept firing.

Jason was back as far as he could get against the bulkhead and emptied another magazine at the approaching monster. "Just hang on!" Gizmo yelled into the headset. "Any second now."

"I'm outta seconds here, Gizmo!" he screamed back.

The monster came closer. Jason was within its reach now. It looked at him as if it were trying to decide something. Perhaps, should I kill it fast? Should I tear it apart bit by bit? Should I eat it alive? Should I pulverize it?

It put its face right up to Jason's and growled, then stood straight up. It had decided. It looked him in the eye and they seemed to glow. He made a loud raspy noise. His eyes grew brighter and brighter as if light were shining out through them. Then flames shot out of them.

"Oh SHIT!" Jason yelled out as it lunged toward him. Jason dodged to the right and the thing bounced against the bulkhead and fell, light and flames still shooting out through his eyes.

He stood and watched the Invader's head smoldering while smoke rose through the shuttle, when the smell hit him. He darted toward the front of the shuttle, gagging while trying to yell, "Gizmo! Open the damned door," with his hand over his nose and mouth.

The door flew open and Jason rolled out on the ground, straight onto the feet of the General standing in front of a large gathering of men. While he was coughing and gasping for air, he could hear the people up top yelling and laughing from the transport through his earpiece, "Yeah! Lit his head up like a pumpkin! Did you see that? A little thermite bomb in your helmet, pal. How'd you like that?"

Jason gathered himself together, choking in deep breaths, while the Invader was dragged out and onto the ground. He stood up as straight as he could and said, "Okay General. These things hold about two hundred Invaders, how many pilots do we have ready?"

"We're ready. Five hundred here now," and turned around indicating the pilots standing behind him. "We've got two for every one of these things standing by. We're all set, just like we planned," he said.

"Well, I'm ready. Let's see if we can figure out how to fly these things." They began piling in with Eric leading the way. "Gizmo!" He yelled as he entered. "How is it up there? Can you do it?"

"Give me a minute. It looks pretty straight forward. Just give me one more minute," he said as the scientist on the transport buzzed around him while being pushed aside by the pilots on board trying to guess the controls. "Dam, this looks easy. Up. Down. Left and right. Levels. Trim. Jason! An idiot could do this. An Invader could do it."

"General. So far so good," he said.

"So far so good," he answered, "But we're running out of time."

"Let's fill this shuttle up with our men and get up to the transport. We can figure out how to work everything on the way. That'll save us a little time. Then they can take a shuttle back each and get a little experience. Train the rest. I don't think we are going to have time for a training program, are we?" Jason asked.

"No Colonel. Whatever experience they get on the way up there and back may be all the training they'll have. I hope you can get that transport down here."

"Me too, General. Me too," and he piled in with the rest.

It wouldn't be hard navigating to the transport. You just look for the moon and go past it to the black thing floating out there behind it. No star maps needed. No trips through galaxies and around supernovae and gas nebulae.

Just look out the window and drive. Not like the trip to the Invader home planet. But figuring that out would be another problem for another time, a time that will arrive, not in days any longer, but in hours.

The trip up was one of discovery and training. It was new for everybody. The most they could do is watch and see how the craft maneuvered and discuss it on the way. Some of the men weren't fully briefed. Some of them weren't aware of the REAL space program. Some of them did not believe in aliens. Some were overwhelmed by the shift in their reality. Some didn't even know they were about to go into space.

But everyone changed on that trip. When someone asked for an explanation, Eric put it the best. "We are about to be invaded," he said. "We are being invaded by beings that built this equipment and have destroyed and eliminated civilizations much stronger than ours. We have just a matter of hours to learn how to use this equipment and organize our defense and launch an effective counterattack."

He looked around at everyone there and said, "These are the craft you will be flying, and now you know as much about them as we do. This is what you signed up for, and now it's time for you to earn your pay."

There was not much more to be said. They had as much experience by the end of that flight as anyone did – none. But things became clear as Eric would make a turn, accelerate, and slow down. The Invaders had huge hands compared to them. So the movements the Humans made were smaller and slower and more controlled compared to theirs.

That gave them better control and they would be much more capable of maneuvering in small and tight areas, an advantage they all discussed. It was Humans doing what they do best, learning to survive and overcome, how to do things better and improve on and build on what they had.

Eric easily pulled into the landing bay, smooth as silk. Since the power was on, they had gravity and the bays and levels were sealed. Everyone stepped out onto the deck where a man was waiting to muster them.

"Gentlemen. I would like to give you a tour of this transport. I'd like to give you all some flight lessons. I'd like to do a lot of things, but we are out of time. That was your flight training and now, by default, you are the best damned pilots there are on Earth. Congratulations! Next is practice. Here are your assignments and your numbers are painted on the sides of your shuttles. Good luck."

"Make sure you have your Hand Receipt and dispatch!" Someone was screaming. "These are expensive pieces of equipment! Sign your receipts!"

Eric shook his head, watched them grab their papers and climb into their vehicles, turned to Jason and said, "Well. Wish me luck."

Jason shook his hand, "Eric, my friend. Good luck and I'll see you soon, unless we crash this damned thing."

Eric jumped into the shuttle seat and pulled it back out into space.

Jason was running toward the helm. The task now was to get use of the weapons. The scientists and several pilots were darting back and forth around Gizmo, pointing at different controls and arguing over what they thought they were. Some of the pilots were disagreeing and insisting they were something else. Down below on Earth, someone was screaming over the radio something about flight plans. Gizmo was in the middle of it all trying to take it all in.

"Stand aside!" Jason barked as he ran up to them. "Mr. Crozley, let's get this thing moving," he said.

Mr. Crozley, a name Jason rarely used for Gizmo. It was used when introducing him to people to show respect. Jason never did like people calling him Gizmo unless they had earned that right.

"It's disrespectful," he would say, and he didn't use it now. That accomplished three things. First, it put everyone there on notice that the man should be treated properly. Second, it told Gizmo and the rest that something important was coming. Third, it shut everyone up.

Those items out of the way, he continued. "We have to get this thing out of here. This is the first thing they are going to be looking for when they come. Have you tried maneuvering yet?"

"No. Not yet. We were figuring out the weapons," Hilliard answered for him. "I think we know how to target something now."

"Okay. So what say, let's maneuver to something and target it," Jason suggested.

Gizmo brought up the controls in the same way the shuttle controls were brought up. He paused and looked a little bit hesitant about moving the ship, so Jason asked him to let him take over, since he was the only one with experience. Gizmo gladly turned the controls over. "Okay guys," Jason told everyone. "It's really simple, so just watch. The shuttles are the same and you will all be flying them shortly."

He moved the ship toward the moon and stopped it. Then he moved it farther away and did the same. Then he told them to target something on the moon. The targeting system allowed them to point and press on multiple targets on a surface or in space.

The targets were picked and the ship started moving across the horizon of the moon, blasting the targets, sending up plumes of debris for miles into space.

"Wow!" Gizmo exclaimed, "Let's see how far away we can get from a target."

They moved the ship farther out in space and targeted three more. They were blasted, sending out more debris.

"Alright. Well, this is good. But how do you get to a place far away. I mean it maneuvers fine. But we want to get to their planet. How would we do that? How would you go to another star?" Jason asked.

Again, it was an invitation for discussion and debate amongst the scientists and the pilots. It went on for several minutes with no real answers from anyone. Finally Jason started to mumble things with Gizmo. The group took notice and began one by one to pay attention and stop talking.

"So picture yourself sitting there. You're an Invader, and you want to get somewhere far away," Jason was saying.

"Right," Gizmo said, "So, they're sitting here, what would be natural for them to do?" and he reached over to a screen and said, "Look, I would have huge hands," and then he took both his hands and used them as one like you would widen a touch screen.

A new screen appeared a few feet in front of them that now showed clear details of the moon down to small boulders. Then he reversed the motion and it became a view of the entire moon. He did it again and it gave a view from where they were, past the moon and toward the sun.

"That must be Mercury there," Gizmo said. "How do we get there? We can't drive it like a car all the way. How would they do it?"

Hilliard, Jason and Gizmo were now up close to the controls looking at them, looking at the side, looking for a gear shift or accelerator, anything that would make them move there without traversing foot by foot and mile by mile through space.

It had to be a Quantum movement. Try this and try that and try doing some other thing, went on for about thirty seconds when one of the pilots yelled out to look at the screen. They looked, and there was Mercury.

"How did we do that?" Gizmo asked. "Wait. Let's get Earth on the screen and see if we can duplicate it."

They brought Earth onto the screen and repeated the actions they did before getting to Mercury, watching the screen after each action. Finally, there was Earth. Instantly.

"Hah! You just touch on the spot where you want to go. It's bone-head simple. Like I said, even an Invader can do it," Gizmo announced.

"Alright then. That's about all the time we have for today, folks," and Jason turned to the pilots. "You can ride with us, or you can take your shuttles down. I suggest you get as much experience flying those things as you can. But you're welcome to ride."

All of them chose to take their shuttles down by themselves with instructions to teach everyone they could how to use the weapons. After they had all left, Jason said, "What? They don't trust us or something? We are the best dang pilots there are."

It was sad but true and funny but serious all at the same time. They were the best dang pilots there were, for the moment.

"Please tell me you found their home planet on this thing, Dr. Hilliard," Jason said.

"Yes, I did," he answered.

"And did you punch in all the coordinates I gave you on Earth?" Jason asked.

"I did that too," Hilliard replied.

"Good. Then let's land this thing and get to work."

Eric pulled the shuttle just below the boulder that had become the regular meeting spot for the villagers. He stepped out and walked over to the Gunny and the runners waiting there. "Am I late?"

"No," said the Gunny. "You're just in time. In fact, it's show time."

Well placed explosions started going off. The first one, blowing out the backside of the shed Catskill had confined the villagers to, allowing them to move freely up the hill to the shuttle. The next were just to cause confusion.

They drove the Catskill personnel to the center of the camp, personnel that were there for a special occasion. They were executives, flown in on private helicopters to marvel at the results of their new experiment about to take place. Cameras were set up at each corner to witness and record it all.

"Steady," said the Gunny. "Wait. Not yet," as he looked back and forth from the confusion and dust below to the villagers coming up the trail. When they were all clear, one of the guards spotted them and tried to sound the alarm. That's when he calmly and clearly said, "Now!" Pete pressed the device setting off the last blasts.

They all got up and entered the shuttle, Bo bouncing in beside Hellen. Eric powered up the shuttle and they all took one last look at the mayhem out the side door. The explosions had driven the Catskill personnel into two groups, except for the final blast.

The final blast released the gas. But it only exposed one group that was downwind, one half of the total. The exposed group, within seconds became violently mad. They began ripping at anything that moved. The other group tried to escape in vain, trapped behind the razor wire cage they had either ordered built or had built themselves.

The villagers watched them being attacked by the mindless zombies they had created. The door was shut and the Indian Villagers left them to their fate, a fate they had planned for the village.

Eric had had many conversations with the General up to now, and one of them came to mind after witnessing the madness below. It was about man's inhumanity to man. It was about control and who wants it and what kind of people desire it and seek it out.

"It's evolution, I think. Man evolves," he would say, "With it, new methods of controlling him evolve, and now, they have a means of control that is more despicable, more insidious, and more repulsive than ever in history. It is the most inhumane and vile method yet."

It was during a meeting with Jason and Gizmo that he spoke like this. It was when he first asked for help in the real war. Sure, there were Walkers. Sure, there were the Invaders. But the greatest war, the most important war to be won was the war against the minds of Man.

"It's all evolution. It starts out, cavemen, forming a group for mutual protection, and one of them bullies his way into being leader. The group competes for food and women with another group, so they fight and defeat them. Now he is their leader too, and it grows.

"This is now the ruler. A bully. But evolution defeats him. People figure it out. They figure out that this bully has to be put down for their own safety and happiness. So they form a group, a Government. Now it's the bully.

"Various governments form and go to war with each other to see who can be the biggest bully. It's all just for the control of the population. Who will rule the world? Childish.

"New forms of control are made up. Mad religions start playing 'God Monopoly' with the lives of the populations as their monopoly money. One day, someone figures out that blood lines can be used, so they form Monarchies, and they control the population. The biggest bully always wins.

"Somewhere along the line, they decide that it's all anarchy: it's an anarchy of nations; an anarchy of Monarchs; an anarchy of bullies. So, they invent a monetary system to control the people. These people finance the bullies they like. They finance the militaries they pick to win. Now the financiers become the new rulers. They become the new bullies. Now the bullies are hidden.

"But all the way through the history of mankind, the biggest bully, in the end, is always The People. They always figure it out and find a way out. They can take the yoke off their own necks. Always have, and hopefully always will.

"They don't want to be, but they always will be the biggest bully on the block. No matter what kind of control, no matter what kind of slavery and beastly deeds are done by the would-be rulers, The People always manage to get free of it.

"That is, until now. While it has always been the body of man that was enslaved and kept from movement and accomplishment, now, it is the mind that is being captured. Without the mind, man may have no future. It is the free will, the creativity, propelling the race into the future that has been captured by these new rulers, the drug companies.

"They are the new beasts who wish to rule. The new bullies. The pharmaceutical companies. More hidden than the financiers. Why try to keep the population happily working for you and making your pretty things when you can drug them to do it? All through history, Man has been able to cast off his chains from people like this. He has always had one weapon they could not take from him with which he could defeat them, and that is his mind.

"I fear that he won't be able to free himself from this one. He is becoming too drugged to see that he is even under their control. In my opinion, it is the most inhumane act in history. Stealing the minds and enslaving the population with drugs.

"They are the most cruel and inhumane people in history. Any would-be bullies, any wanna-be bullies that might have tried to defeat them are now under the influence of their drugs. Politicians, financiers, religious leaders, and artists, all of them are victims of these rulers, these new and hidden bullies."

That is when the General asked for help. That was when they devised a plan that might free mankind from the cruelest acts in history. Worse than the Invaders and worse than the Walkers. Eternally captured, eternally enslaved, eternally influenced by the drug companies. That is when he told them of the control the drug companies had on the leaders of the country, the leaders from whom he was bound to take orders.

That was the conversation that came to mind upon witnessing the carnage down below. Man always finds a way. He just needs his mind to do it.

During the last two days, the most massive troop movement in the history of man had occurred. They were about to invade another world. The transport had landed and was being supplied and boarded with troops from around the world. The transport ship would keep two thousand of the shuttles and the Earth would keep six-hundred and forty.

Each shuttle could carry four hundred very cramped humans with all their gear. That is eight hundred thousand personnel just in the shuttles that could land anywhere on the Invader Planet surface.

The transport was designed to carry millions of Invaders. They would be carrying about half of that number in Walkers. That left a lot of empty space for tanks, artillery, helicopters, nuclear weapons and launchers, and whatever toys the General and his staff had decided they should bring along, which still left almost one entire level of the craft empty.

"It makes sense," Jason said as he stood watching the ship being supplied.

"What does?" Gizmo asked.

"All the stuff. I see why they send so many Invaders. They are going to go there and they are going to stay there. Look at all this. We are going to conquer an advanced yet very barbaric civilization. We are going to conquer it, but we can't walk away after we kick their asses. We have to stay and occupy it. If we leave, they will follow us back here. It'll be much worse."

Gizmo stood and watched the loading of the troops now. Trainload after trainload had been stacked into the transport and more troops were being hauled in. "So you really think we're gonna kick their asses, eh?"

"Damn right, and we're going to stay there after we do," Jason said firmly.

There was nobody standing still. Every person was running to do something. Jason grabbed someone by the sleeve on his way by, "The controller. Did we find it?"

"No. We haven't found it yet. We've looked everywhere. We're still looking," he yelled back over the commotion.

Eric crackled over the headset that he was coming in. He had deposited the Villagers high on a Ruby Ridge mountain where they would be safe from any ground attacks.

Reports began coming in from around the world. Several major cities had been hit. Two transports had arrived and were following their standard annihilation procedures.

A rumble was felt throughout the base as another city was leveled. Bradley squealed with excitement and ordered everyone out of the control room. He flipped the magnetic locks and ran to the observation deck to watch. "It's happening! It's actually happening!" he yelled to himself, barely able to contain his excitement.

"We need to find the controller!" Jason yelled. "Gizmo, I need you to get up there and sit at the helm and get ready to take off. Don't wait for me!"

Just then, the general came up to him and said, "Jason. It's starting just like we thought it would. We have to load the Walkers and you have to go! It's time to get on board. They're going to need you where they're going. And Colonel, it's been an honor. Good luck to you."

Eric crackled over the com that he was two minutes out. An alarm sounded to clear the platform. The Walkers were about to be released and herded into the transport. Everyone on the floor darted out of their way and disappeared like ants. The second alarm sounded signaling they were about to come out.

Jason scrambled up into the shuttle bay watching them from far above. Nothing. They didn't come. "What's wrong?" he yelled into his headset to anyone listening. "Why aren't they coming?" as another rumble made the entire cave shutter.

"Somebody's disabled the blast doors. We can't get them open," a response came.

"Bradley!" someone screamed. "The button. It's in his lab."

Eric was maneuvering his shuttle though the opening. Explosions could be heard, Earth shattering explosions. Explosions that would shatter entire cities. If the transporter is spotted, all would be lost. It would be an all-out effort for the Invaders to destroy it.

"Eric! Use the shuttle weapons. Blast the doors open," Jason yelled.

He pulled the shuttle around and maneuvered it to the entrance of the cave, powered up the weapons, and fired. The blast took the doors apart.

The pounding of the Invaders grew louder as the invasion came closer. Jason was certain that Las Vegas just went away.

Eric pulled the shuttle around and headed for the bay and was just pulling in when the rushing horde came; The Evil Walkers. They weren't so much corralled or herded into the bottom level. They charged into it.

Eric put the shuttle down and the door flew open. Bo was first out, bounding up to Jason and sitting beside him. Then the runners came out, followed by Eric. They were ready to leave. The explosions were approaching, rumbling the ground and shaking rocks off the cave roof and walls.

Jason looked around the base at what was likely to be the remainder of mankind when his eye was drawn to the observation platform. It was a movement. It was Bradley! He was mad, looking at an object in his hand. "The controller," Jason said to himself.

One of the runners came up to him and said, "Hellen said to give you this," and handed him his rifle.

Jason checked the breach to make sure it was loaded. Then he lifted it to his cheek, put the crosshairs between Bradley's wild eyes and pulled the trigger. The round hurled toward the thick glass.

The shuttle bay door closed, and in a blink, they were gone.

THE END: Ron Howson

251

Look for other books
By
Ron Howson:

Book Two in the Ruby Series
RUBY RIDGE

and

Book Three in the Ruby Series
RUBY RISING